For Daniel

CHAPTERS

CHAPTER 1: WILTON ABBEY, 1093

My feet were numb. As I opened my eyes, I pushed my hair away from my face. Men were shouting in the workroom — something about a false step and New Forest.

I had dozed off while kneeling in prayer. How long had I slept?

Stumbling on the hem of my homespun, I pushed up onto pins-and-needles and hobbled to my door. While my feet burned, I stared at the back of my hand. My palm was cold where it rested on my cell latch.

His bleeding hand clutches mine and he keeps me from falling.

I had dreamt of him again. My dreams were often of him — that boy my aunt had sent away from home, all because of me. He'd had hair like golden threads.

"Sister Edith! Come now!" Brother Godric called.

I watched my hand open my door. Lifting my apron from its splintered hook on the whitewashed wall, I strode into the hospitaller's workroom. Brother Godric glugged ale onto our new patient's bleeding foot — it was hacked in two pieces up to his heel, like a fish's tailfin.

"Another burning," I muttered. How would I ever get the stench out of these rooms?

Two thick coils of rope came first, and I pulled the patient's hands down against the worktable with slip-knots so he couldn't grab us. Then the poppies. Striding to the happy plants under their south-facing windows, I plucked a swollen poppy fruit and punctured it with our sharpest knife.

"Sister Edith," Brother Godric said, "Give him some. Now. Quickly."

I hurried to the head of the workbench and gazed down at the man lying there. Breathing unlabored. Eyes closed. Probably passed out. Good, he wouldn't scream as much.

Pressing my hand to the man's throat, I was ready to push his Adam's apple down so he would drink the poppy milk. I poured the first few drops—

"He is awake, Brother Godric," I said, staring down at the patient's neck as he swallowed without my help. The man's eyes batted open and he stared up at me, upside-down.

"Oh, alright." Brother Godric glanced over to the two huntsmen who had brought our patient here. "One of you hold him down."

One of the two huntsmen stepped forward. I glanced up and down and then up again—I knew this man, though I hadn't seen him since I was a little child. "Henry," I whispered as I stared at him.

As he leaned down onto the injured man on the worktable, Henry looked up at the sound of his name and held my gaze. Did he remember me?

"Sister," he said, barely moving his lips.

With a thin strip of twine, Brother Godric coiled the end of the injured man's leg many times around, clamping the major vessels. Even so, blood still oozed slowly down to the rushes. Brother Godric said, "This is not going to take long. Count to twenty and it will be over."

The patient nodded once and squeezed his eyes closed. Hastily, I dripped more poppy milk into his mouth and held my breath.

Brother Godric laid the iron teeth of his saw below the patient's ankle and heel. Blood coated the knight hospitaller's hands, but he kept a firm hold nevertheless. Heavy, long, downward heaves... The blade seized once. And again. At least, it did not seem he had hit bone.

As I stroked the patient's hair away from his forehead, he groaned low and loud.

I leaned down to his ear and began to whisper a prayer, "God have mercy on His servant—" And with that, the man's head lulled to the side and all his muscles relaxed at once. Pressing my fingers against the valley by his Adam's apple, I felt his blood continue to pulse strongly in his neck.

"Just passed out," I announced. Brother Godric hadn't stopped sawing, nor had Henry eased his hold.

Without the man's moaning, all was quiet except for the flesh tearing away from the man's foot. I closed my eyes and I was listening to Brother Godric gut a very large fish—the sound was nearly the same. Finally, Brother Godric dropped the man's foot in a wooden bowl which we kept specifically for this purpose.

With one hand pressed against his mouth, the huntsman (the one who wasn't Henry) backed up against the wall. I bit my lip. Vomit always seemed to make the biggest messes, larger than even blood spattering.

Oh, it was time for the burning. I strode to the fireplace. While I warmed a clean poker in the hearth, I glanced at the nauseous huntsman. I flinched—Nauseous Man was the bishop of Old Sarum. What was he doing in hunting clothes? He gazed pointedly toward the window.

Through the black smoke, I stared into the flames of the fire. Once the metal gleamed like a star on a clear night, I carried the poker carefully to my teacher's side.

The dead foot lay in the bowl beside its living, breathing owner. It was bluish white like a statue's, if the statue were coated in cherry jam. I always wondered, where did the soul go from that limb? Were there memories left in that foot which were now forgotten forever? And what did Brother Godric do with the foot afterward? I still didn't know, and at this point, I was too afraid to ask.

Cautiously, I held the poker up to Brother Godric. Instead of taking it, however, he gestured toward the amputee. My heart thudded in panic: I would do my first burning today.

Taking a deep breath and swallowing hard, I mimicked the actions I had seen a dozen times before. The stink of charred flesh once again permeated the hospitaller's workroom as I burned the major vessels shut.

In the corner of the room, the bishop yanked the canvas off of the nearest window and vomited onto the shrubbery two stories below.

The patient didn't move—he didn't even flinch. Hurrah for small miracles! Unless he was dead?

I stared at the amputee's chest and watched it rise and fall. No, still alive.

Straightening from his hold on his friend's chest, Henry held the collar of his tunic over his nose and mouth. His thick, heavy eyebrows furrowed together as he stared at me.

Patting my shoulder, Brother Godric said, "I do believe you are ready for Jerusalem, Sister." He removed the tourniquet and applied a liberal amount of ointment made of many different herbs, wine and vinegar. We had made this batch of medicine only last week.

"Thank you, Brother." I bowed my head to his compliment.

Once I set the poker down so its tip was safe on the hearth, I pulled the remaining canvases off of the windows in an attempt to air out the room. The fire fluttered a little, and the room became even smokier. My heart finally began to slow as I doused the fire out with a bucket of ashes.

"You may go and serve the Lord," Brother Godric said without looking up from his work at his patient's wound.

The bishop of Old Sarum was still half-hanging out of the window, breathing heavily. "May God forgive you for what you've done," he said, wiping at his mouth with one hand and crossing himself with the other.

Brother Godric hadn't seemed to have heard him and only gestured to the door. "This unfortunate man will need to spend some time here so I may monitor the wound for festering."

The bishop left immediately but Henry hung back. Was he waiting to speak with his injured friend? Or did he want to see if Brother Godric wanted more help?

When Brother Godric lifted his patient in his arms like a bride, Henry hurried to the unconscious amputee's other side and together, they carried the patient into the adjoining sickroom. Then, with a familiar thud, I knew they had successfully transferred him to bed. As Henry came back into the workroom, there were other soft noises as Brother Godric continued situating his patient.

I took my time cleaning up the mess but when I was nearly done, Henry was still standing there, watching me. Once I finally looked up at him in silent question, he beckoned me toward the door to the stairs.

"What is it?" I asked flatly. "Brother Godric shall surely require my assistance again soon." I was certain Henry was going to scold me for doing what I'd just done. Maybe he wanted to write to my parents about what I was just doing? So tiresome.

"I beg only a moment of your time."

Because I was ready to yell at him, I followed him out to the hallway. He led me down the stone stairs and then outside.

After the stench of burnt flesh in the workroom, the heady fragrance of dog trees was refreshing. All around us, a hazy band of pink and yellow warmed the horizon. Our dusty path crunched softly as Henry led me out of the keep of the abbey and down the hill to the river's edge. From the chorus of babbling water and chirping birds, I picked out a mourning dove's soft song. I loved the sound.

He walked until I no longer could see the abbey up the hill before he turned to face me. "Do you remember me?"

I remembered his last visit to Scotland with his family as though it were yesterday, but I wasn't about to say so. "A bit." I shrugged and wiped my sweaty hands on my apron. By looking over his brawny frame, if I didn't know any better, I would have thought he was Scottish. Not Norman. And yet—did he still look like a boy to everyone else, or was it only my perception? I supposed most others would find his build intimidating, but he was too much like Alexander—my favorite brother—to ever scare me.

I continued, "Your brother—King William Rufus—mentioned you were due to see him. He and my father visited me a few weeks ago." Vividly, I recalled that last meeting with my father, King Malcolm of Scotland. He had taken a blade from his belt, snatched my monastic veil from my head and stabbed it, tearing the material until it hung in strips. Throwing it to the floor, he shouted about how I couldn't wear the "wretched thing" because I needed to marry an "actual man." The nuns had gaped at him. And all the while, Henry's brother, King William, had doubled over and wept from laughter.

"I'd rather you marry *him* than become a nun!" My father had gestured to King William, who then had stopped laughing.

My father had not seemed to care that he'd just insulted the king of England. I hadn't cared much either, except the king's pretty face had been staring at *me* while I was treated like a child. And I wasn't a child anymore.

My father had then dragged me out of the abbey to his horse. I had screamed some sort of hatred toward him then, but he ignored me.

When King William had managed to catch up with us, he had called calmly to my father, "Malcolm, you've made a fool of yourself." From where I was slung over the neck of my father's horse, King William had smiled down at me and laughed. I had stared at his smooth, blushing jaw, his nose like Adonis... and then I noticed how his eyes did not match — he had one brown eye and one blue eye. This small peculiarity made him all the more stunning.

And now, as I gazed at Henry by the River Test on this muggy evening, I found very little resemblance between the brothers. Henry's jaw was muscular, so much so that it created its own odd angles rather than curving gently. It made his face seem squared instead of round. His nose was long like a Roman's and had a distinct bump at the bridge. His eyes hid his thoughts behind a haughty, calculating squint.

"Mm, yes," Henry said. "The king mentioned your father in his last letter... You should have taken that apron off." He gestured to my bloody front.

I crossed my arms over my chest. "Are your brothers with you?"

"We were hunting in New Forest, but my trip has been cut short by Sir Robert Achard's poor footing." He ran a hand over his head, pushing his hair from his eyes. "So, no, my brothers aren't with me. My eldest brother — your dear godfather — remains in Normandy. King William is still hunting with the party." He glanced over to the river. "Is that disappointment I see in your eyes?"

"No—"

"You've gotten — you've become a lovely woman. You were a snotty little girl last I saw you." He smirked without looking away from the river.

Was he trying to make me angry? "Yes I was." I forced a polite smile as he turned his gaze back to me.

"Yes, though I don't like your clothes. The homespun doesn't suit you. You ought to take it off."

"Henry." I jutted out my chin to hide my uneasiness. Clearly, he was trying to shock me. I said calmly, "Break with that talk. I may wear threadbare rags, but do not forget my station."

He grinned. "I could never forget your station. I only meant — King William told me of your father's rage over you wearing a monastic veil. Perhaps he would not want you to wear this either?" He crossed his arms over his chest, mirroring me.

"Well." My mouth moved before I thought about what I wanted to say, "Two can play at this. Here — you stand like a vulture while it picks at a dying rabbit."

He laughed openly. "Mmm. Yes, rabbits do taste sweet as—"

"No—as Satan eyeing Job!"

"Even more apt." He bowed lowly.

"I shall inform the king of your depravity. He'll have you beaten for me, to be sure. Your brother loves me as your mother did—that is, *honorably*—God rest her soul."

"Yes, your godmother did love you dearly. My whole family loves you dearly." He pulled my elbow so I would face him again. "So good and pure, just like Mother. I can't wait to tell them about you burning my teacher's foot shut." He smiled and laughed openly.

"Like you, the king laughs too much for my liking." I bit the inside of my cheek to keep from smiling back at him.

"Don't say such things about our king, *Sister*." As he gazed down at my mouth, the smile faded from his face. "Should I call you that? William told me you didn't take vows."

"No," I conceded. "I'm not a real nun. Not yet, anyway. Only a novice."

"Not yet?"

I shrugged. How was this his business? "Who else is with you, then?"

"Only Sir Robert Achard, the newly amputated, and Bishop Osmund, the one who was vomiting and cowering in the corner. You'd think someone who visits sickbeds so often wouldn't mind the stink of flesh. Though, the burning. It was quite…"

"Right. You shall remember not to cross me, or I'll do your foot too." I smirked.

"I don't doubt it." He laughed again. "Anyway, I had thought of visiting you, and as fate would have it, here I am." Closing the gap between us, he reached out and ran his fingertips down the side of my neck, tickling the stray tendrils loose of my plait. "Our lord king *raved* of your beauty." Was he being sarcastic? Pressing his hand to my cheek, he guided my face slowly to one side, inspecting my features.

I pulled from his grasp and swatted his hand away. "I am not a gypsy mare for barter."

"No, you are far costlier. I don't think I ever heard the king speak so fondly of a woman." He stared back toward the river. "You may not have a swan-neck like poor old Harold's ex-paramour who lives here with you, but you certainly do have your charms. Anyway, I never thought a neck like a swan was very attractive."

"Our lord king is the exemplar of beauty and kindness. You are so unlike him, it's amazing you're related."

"You are virtuous to humble me." He bowed his head again. "So I suppose he doesn't laugh too much after all?"

"I—I just meant..."

"You've grown in other ways, too." Stepping forward, he slid his boot between my sandals. Before I could step back, he curled his arm around me and held my chest against his own.

"Henry." I shook my head once, leaning back against the arm around my hips. I tried to push him away but he held me tighter.

"It's just—" he whispered, "you have um, something in your hair... perhaps a bit of ash from the fire?"

"No I don't." I held my breath.

"Truly, you do. I'll get it for you, shall I?"

I watched as he pulled the tie from the end of one of my plaits with his free hand. "You are clearly exhausted. You should relax..." His breath tickled my ear. Slowly unbraiding my plait, he started near my waistline and worked his way slowly up my chest. "They work you too hard here. It's not right. You belong in palaces, not abbeys."

"You shouldn't be so familiar."

His eyes were dark green and flecked with yellow and brown. Like oak leaves in autumn. "We are practically family, love." He grazed his hand back down my hair rested it on my hips. He smelled good. Like the woods and leather.

"Um, you must…" Must what? What did I want to say? Coming away this far from the abbey had clearly been a mistake. "Family? You mean to say you do this with your sisters, then?"

"You don't have to fight it. No one can see us."

"Henry—" But he cut me off with his mouth on mine. He tasted like wine.

He let me shove him away finally. Surprised, I stumbled backward and nearly fell but he caught me with a hand on my arm. "Do not touch me, you dirty scullion!" Without a thought, I smacked him hard across the face. The clap shook its way down the riverbed. "Touching a nun that way!" I shook my head gravely. What was even happening right now? Obviously he was teasing me.

"I thought you weren't a nun?" He took a pronounced step back from me and bowed his head. Was he actually surprised that I hit him? "You don't wear the veil, after all."

I was shocked to see my handprint on his cheek. "I shall soon travel to the Holy Land to tend to the pilgrims there. Brother Godric and Abbess Mother Christina expect it." I lifted my chin. "What is *wrong* with you?"

"Nothing's wrong with me. Nothing that won't be fixed in a little more time with you." He smirked and winked.

"You must think I'm a child who cannot understand you—"

"I'd never say such a thing to a child! You are certainly no child. And you are certainly no nun. I'd sooner believe you were defending your promise to your betrothed, or even some nonsense mockery of love for my brother, before I ever believed you were meant for Jerusalem."

"I have never been so offended upon meeting a man."

"But you're not just meeting me. You forget how well I know you, even if I don't see you often."

"Goodness, you don't know me."

"Well, not yet in that sense."

"Not yet in what sense?" I knew exactly what he was saying.

"I only meant—my brothers and sisters always mention you to me if they hear of you. That's all." He pressed his lips together. "I beg you forgive my familiarity. I forget myself, Edith."

I despised the way he said my name. "Hm." Should I have apologized for hitting him? I couldn't make myself do it. He absolutely deserved it. "Did you know my father promised me to be betrothed? Even my sister isn't supposed to know about that yet." Though, I honestly never shared secrets with my sister, Mary. She hated me. I supposed people often called her ugly compared to me, but how could I do anything about that? She was far sweeter than me, in any case.

"Alan Rufus? I know your betrothed personally, actually. You should have heard him bragging about you." He clenched his jaw as he spoke through his teeth. "Could have run him through then and there, the chitty-face."

"Well… I never intended to marry him. We haven't been formally betrothed in the Church. Everyone knows it, even the abbess here." Alan Rufus. I had nearly forgotten about the promise my father had made to him. I sighed. "It is only my father's scheming. Nothing more. No one shall force my hand."

"Good." Henry bit his lip and glanced down to my bloody apron again. "Perhaps you shall give your hand to someone else, then."

"Yes. Perhaps I shall. In any case, the decision certainly has nothing to do with you. Think no more of it." I had wanted to sound forceful but my voice cracked when I'd said "decision" and so he was smirking at me again.

Turning, I stomped back up the bank of the river toward the abbey. I assumed Henry was following, but when I checked over my shoulder, he wasn't behind me. "Good," I spat.

It had been a long evening already. However, I was ashamed to realize it, but I was a disappointed he had given up so easily. Did I crave a fight so much?

No one had ever kissed me before. I'd never imagined it would be that... intoxicating. Was kissing always like that? Had I actually enjoyed his kiss? Or did I only enjoy the rush of doing something I wasn't allowed to? My mind was too clouded to think.

A little wave of nausea clenched my stomach. How dare he touch my clothes?! Granted, I wasn't actually a nun. But still.

Crossing my arms over my chest, I strode back to the abbey.

CHAPTER 2: LAMMAS DAY

As dawn approached on Lammas Day, I knelt at my bedside to pray instead of attending Lauds. I hated Lauds. It used up the best part of the day.

Sunshine beamed into my small chamber as I pulled my homespun down over my chemise and tied my rope belt loosely around my waist. After I quickly re-plaited my hair into my usual twisting cords, I poured some water mixed with ale into a wooden cup, swished it around my mouth, and spat into a basin. Picking a few mint leaves from Brother Godric's plant by the workroom window, I pressed them with my tongue so they stuck to the roof of my mouth. I was ready to start my day.

Veering off down the long halls, outside down an ambulatory, and down the path to the kitchen house, I retrieved the amputee's breakfast. The sick and infirmed were allowed to eat a real meal in the morning.

Spying the fruit bowl in the corner of the kitchen, I grabbed two pears from the top. And from the larder, I scooped up a cup of beans left after last night's supper, along with a cup of watered ale, of course.

Balancing the tray precariously on one hand, I lightly knocked at the sickroom door. As expected, there was no answer. Easing the door open and, seeing that my patient was asleep still, I rested the tray on the bedside table.

He was still dressed in most of his hunting attire: a gray-black tunic, a thin cambric underneath, and gray leggings. A bloody leather boot stood solitary on the floor. The man—Sir Robert Achard, I reminded myself—looked older in the harsh light of day, perhaps as old as forty. As I turned to leave, I noticed a sheen of sweat on his forehead mixing with the dried blood at his temples.

He chose this moment to wake up. He gazed down to where his amputated toes should have been and then up to me. "I'm at an abbey?" he asked. "Which one? Where are Lord Henry and Bishop Osmund? Gone home?"

I tried to smile reassuringly. "This is Wilton Abbey. Brother Godric and I tended to you last evening. And I pray you forgive me, I am not certain of Lord Henry and Bishop Osmund's whereabouts, but I do know that they were here as of last evening. I will ask if they are still here, if you'd like."

He didn't seem to be listening. "Is this for me?" He eyed the breakfast tray.

"Yes, sir."

"Thank you. Are you my nursemaid? You don't look old enough to be. How old are you?"

"Yes, sir. I'm Brother Godric's apprentice. I am fourteen years of age."

He squinted as though he were trying to look into the sun. "Is that so? I thought perhaps you were no less than seventeen or eighteen."

"Um, thank you, I suppose."

"Does Edith of Scotland still live here?"

"Yes, sir. I—"

"I know where Henry is then."

"What do you mean?"

He laughed. "Oh, only that he wastes no time when it comes to pretty faces."

"Hm. I shall be sure to warn her." I gave a dry laugh. "Shall I pull the canvas from your window?"

He nodded. "Thank you." As he watched me uncover his window, a sweet, warm breeze blew into the small room. "So a novice nun is a brother's apprentice? That's interesting."

"Well. You should be thankful he spared your heel. You will be able to walk again." Yet another person who suspected my teacher of something weird. Poor Brother Godric... "Brother Godric is part of the group called the Knights Hospitaller, who tend to the pilgrims in Jerusalem. A most honorable and noble group on the rise."

"That explains his somewhat unorthodox methods. Isn't he needed in the Holy Land any longer?"

"He has been back from his journey there for two years, though he spent all of last year studying in Amalfi. He shall journey back to Jerusalem again in a year or so. He has humbly inquired with the king to see if the group may be formally recognized in England soon."

Sir Robert tried to sit up. I moved to help him but he shook his head and raised his hand to stop me, so I stayed where I was.

"He needs to find people to join him," I continued. "He's chosen me to join the nuns in Jerusalem who tend to the women. He continues to look for other possible monks and nuns to join his cause."

"Ah, I see. God bless your good works, Sister."

"Thank you. I have dispensation from attending daily services so I might tend to you." I smiled politely again. "If I don't come right away when you call for me, it might be because I'm getting water from the river. A bit of blood got into our tub last night, so I need to clean it. Even so, do not stand on your own yet, alright? If I don't come immediately, wait a moment and call again, if you will. I shall check on you if I don't hear from you for a while as well."

"No need to worry about me. I shall endeavor to be no trouble to you."

"You are no trouble at all." I smiled genuinely then. This man had lost half his foot and was actually worried about bothering me? "You're getting me out of Lauds every morning, after all," I laughed.

He laughed too. "Well, thank you. And thank you for the poppy milk last night. It helped."

"Certainly, sir. Brother Godric shall be back tonight to check on you. God bless your recovery." And turning, I closed the door behind myself.

My empty bucket hung from one hand and a plum was raised to my lips in the other. Scuffing my feet along in the pebbled dirt path, I thought of how Brother Godric said it was good for my heart to pump this hard sometimes. I had to teach my body to work hard so when a patient was in need of my help, I would be ready.

I was thankful the abbess allowed dispensation of fruit for morning manual labor. With this heat, I might have passed out without it, like I used to at Romsey. I certainly did not miss my aunt, the abbess there.

At the riverside, I stopped under the blazing sun in a wispy-white sky. As I finished eating my plum, I gazed out at the white light twinkling on the rippling water. Sweat formed a small trickle down my spine. I wished I could walk around bare-chested like some of the men I'd seen in Old Sarum before.

As I reached down to scoop river water into my bucket, I glanced up. On the other side of the water stood a huge willow tree. I loved sitting under its boughs. It reminded me of my first morning at Romsey Abbey and that boy — Tristan — I'd met there. Was he having an easier time as a monk at Hayling Priory than I was with becoming a nun?

And that's when Henry stepped out of the shade of the willow boughs. His dark hair was wet and shining in the bright sun. He was also naked.

As he was at least forty yards away, I was relieved I couldn't make out the details of his body. Despite this, I could tell he was far more muscular than he appeared when wearing clothes.

As he waded into the river water, he waved to me. I couldn't help it when a gasp escaped from my lips. He caught me staring at him. As he slowly swam across to me, I stared pointedly down at my bucket. I had the feeling he had been sitting there for a while. Perhaps he had watched me for all eight trips to and from the river? It took me entirely too long to realize I could just walk back to the abbey. There was nothing holding me here to wait for him. I turned away from the river.

Unbidden, one of my few memories of him — my first memory of my life, perhaps — floated into my mind. I remembered Henry as a boy. He had lifted me high into the air and then had pretended to drop me, only to catch me again before I hit the ground. I had been terrified, but then I had laughed along with him each time.

Pushing the memory from my mind, I started up the hill from the river before Henry could catch up. But my bucket was too heavy to allow me to rush, especially after carrying my previous loads.

"Do you want some help?" Henry called after me. He was dripping wet and still completely naked.

"No." I continued trudging away. A long moment later, he hurried up to my side and matched my pace. When I glanced over at him, he smiled cheerfully down at me. I looked sharply away again, embarrassed by the look in his eyes. He was bare-chested still, but he'd pulled on his leggings and was hopping along as he pulled his boots on.

"Do my leggings dissatisfy you?" he laughed.

"Shut it."

"Shut what?"

As we walked, he pulled his cambric on. And then, with his tunic and belt slung onto his shoulder, he pulled my arm, stopping me. The smile had fallen from his face, and his thick eyebrows were low and furrowed. Was he angry somehow? It was hard to be sure.

The heat won and I simply shrugged a shoulder. "Fine. Take it."

"Take it?" he repeated, raising an eyebrow.

"The bucket, you filthy man."

"Filthy?" As he took the bucket from me, his fingers lightly grazed the back of my hand. I had to wonder if he touched me on purpose. I thought probably he had. "I'm clean now from the river. You're covered in sweat. Perhaps you should have joined me?"

I hastily wiped my forehead with my sleeve.

As we walked, he leaned closer to me and whispered, "It's alright. I like the rose in your cheeks."

His body moved in a way that was smooth and purposeful as he matched my pace. It irked me that he was able to carry my bucket with only one hand and wasn't even winded. Obviously he wasn't trying to say anything by the way he was carrying the bucket. At least, I didn't think he was.

"I'm quite taken with you, you know," he said as we continued to walk up the hill. His voice sounded more controlled than a moment ago.

"Oh." My throat was dry so it came out in a hoarse squeak. Was he sincere or was this only a new way to tease me?

It was silent for a moment before he spoke again. "Alan Rufus is a dimwit," he murmured. I wondered if I was even supposed to be able to hear him. I frowned as I glanced up at him. Our eyes met for only a moment before I looked away. I decided to pretend I hadn't heard him as we continued in silence.

Finally, we reached the door to this side of the abbey. Why was he making me nervous? Was it only that I was afraid he'd try to kiss me again and maybe a nun would see? I grimaced to myself before I was able to wipe my face clean again. Why was it so confusing to even stand next to this man?

For a moment, we stood in silence before the door, neither of us saying goodbye.

"Forgive me, I was watching you just now. And for teasing you."

So he'd only kissed me to tease me? I was an idiot. I wished I were part of the wind so I could float silently away and not have to exist anymore. "I forgive you as God forgives," I murmured, staring down at my hands.

"Thank you. And thank you for taking my mind off of my worries. When we spoke by the river yesterday, I had been overjoyed that a dear friend should survive that which would kill most men. And he survived by your hand, no less." He bowed lowly to me.

In turn, I bowed my head to him. "It was, err, my pleasure." Pleasure? I took pleasure in burning flesh? "An honor, I mean."

He handed the bucket back to me and our hands grazed one another's once more. He did it on purpose, I knew, because I purposefully tried to swing my hand out of the way. Was he only teasing me again?

His confusing facial expression lulled me into staring at him for too long. Was he sad? Frustrated? This time, he was the first to look away.

"See you, love," he said and awkwardly patted my shoulder before turning to leave. As he walked away, my gaze dropped from his thick dark hair to his muscled, hunched shoulders. The light, gauzy linen of his cambric was sticking to him.

"I'm not your love!" I called after him. Without looking back, he waved his hand as he continued back toward the river.

As I trudged up the stone steps to the workroom, I stared down at my hand. It felt warmer where he'd touched me.

So he knew about my betrothal to Alan? Alan had promised me his discretion. Of course, my father *had* shouted about it last time he'd been here, so perhaps word was out now. Yes, King William would have told his brother, of course. Especially if the king remotely considered me as a possible bride.

I dumped the bucket of water into the tub slowly. The tub of water in the workroom had gotten bloody last night. After emptying it, bucket by bucket, I had scrubbed it out with ashes from the fireplace. Now, I had finally finished re-filling it again.

The contrast between Alan's coldness and Henry's… opposite of coldness… toward me had never been, nor would ever be, more striking than in that moment. No matter what happened, I needed to stay away from Henry. That much was certain. I was far too easy to tease. My brothers had always told me so when I was little.

I still had a lot of gardening to do, and the patient to tend to, so there was no more time think about such trivial things. None of it mattered, anyway. I was going to be a nun.

CHAPTER 3: FROM OLD SARUM IN THE RAIN

I had set up a basin of water along with a crushed handful of lavender for Sir Robert. After I set out a fresh spare tunic from the big bag of clothes the nuns kept for the poor, I laid out a linen cloth for him to dry himself. Then I hurried to the kitchen house to get his supper for him.

After I delivered his meal, I hurried down to the kitchen again and had a quick supper alone — the other nuns were on their way to Vespers.

As I sat there in the silent kitchen, I watched the sky through the uncovered window. Storm clouds darkened the sky a few hours too early. I stood and covered the windows with their canvases.

Suddenly, I had a terrible sense that something had gone wrong.

Though I would be scolded for it, I left my meager meal unfinished at the kitchen table and hurried back to Sir Robert in the hospitaller's workroom. Perhaps there was a second patient waiting for me? Perhaps I had missed something about Sir Robert and he had died in the short time while I was gone?

Back in the hospitaller's rooms, I found Sir Robert as I had left him, though he was now noticeably cleaner, and he'd finished his food. There was no one else waiting for me.

And yet, Brother Godric wasn't here. What if Brother Godric was to be my patient? He'd stepped in an odd hole in the road and couldn't walk. His heart had suddenly stopped beating in his chest. A robber had stabbed him. The spirits in the vapors had invaded his brain and now he was lost in the woods. All these possibilities were real inside my mind for a moment before passing to the next. I was full of fear for my much-loved teacher and also full of fear that I would have to use his lessons on him.

"What time is the knight hospitaller due back?" my patient asked, looking over his shoulder at me. I lifted the corner of a canvas and gazed out to the field below.

"Around now, actually," I said, relieved he had mentioned it first. I walked to the doorway and looked down the hallway. No sign of Brother Godric.

"Can you see him?" Sir Robert asked.

"No. He's never late."

"Hmm." My patient looked down at his leg again. I listened to the rain as it pattered against the stretched canvases. "I'm sure everything's fine," he tried.

"I'm going to go out to look around. Just for a moment."

"Alright." He picked at his nails.

I swung my cloak around my shoulders and pulled up the hood. Outside, the rain immediately soaked my sandaled feet.

It took a short while of running down the edge of the abbey's farmland before I reached the fence gate. Just as I thought I might have to run all six miles of muddy road to Old Sarum, I spied a man walking toward me through the heavy rain.

It was Brother Godric. He walked in a hunched form, as though the rain were going to push him over. When he finally met me at the fence, he pushed the gate open and faced me. He didn't seem surprised to see me there.

The rain was loud so I was forced to shout. "Are you alright?!"

"Yes, I'm fine! I've heard news—the best sort!"

"Thank God! I had the worst feeling that something had happened to you! What is it?" I matched Brother Godric's quick pace. We were both already completely drenched. The path had turned to a stream of mud.

"The archbishop of York was in Old Sarum." He pushed his salt-and-pepper hair from his face where it stuck in fat cords.

"Of York?"

"Yes, he has given me commission to travel back to the Holy Land!" He squinted through the rain at me as we hurried toward the side yard entrance. "We are to travel out with a few monks he has chosen to come with us!"

"What? When?"

He swung open the side door, stepped aside until I went inside to the landing, and then he shut the heavy wooden door behind us. The rain wasn't nearly as loud inside the stairway.

He glanced up the stairs before continuing. "One week from today. You will need to take your vows this week with the abbess's blessing."

"Oh." This week? I had thought we wouldn't be allowed to travel out for at least another year.

"It's more than we could have hoped!" Brother Godric pulled me into a hug and released me quickly again.

I tried to smile. "Yes." I nodded.

"Don't worry, Sister. You're ready. You'll do wonderfully."

"Yes, um, I pray…"

He waited a moment for me to finish my sentence. When I said nothing, he continued, "I will stay here tonight and tell the abbess in the morning. Oh yes, someone will have to tend to our patient here once we leave. Well, no matter. Perhaps Sister Mary would fill in for you? You both inherited your mother's goodness, after all."

What would people say about a nun travelling with monks? Wasn't that against some sort of rule? Wasn't there some way to delay for a while longer?

I would be a nun within the week.

I wasn't ready. I didn't want this. But if I didn't become a nun, I'd have to marry Alan after all, as my father demanded.

Henry's laughing face suddenly came to mind.

"Aren't you happy?" Brother Godric asked me.

It was jarring to hear his voice again. I glanced up. "Thank you, Brother Godric," I muttered, hugging him around his waist and pressing my cheek to his wet homespun.

He laughed uneasily as he patted my back. Gently, he pulled away from my embrace before he turned and started up the stairs.

I stayed where I was for a moment, my thoughts skittering back to me like mice towards crumbs in the dark.

Brother Godric thought I would take vows that week and become a Bride of Christ. Aunt Christina would be thrilled to announce that her niece was following in her footsteps and would someday take over as abbess.

But I would not. I could not.

I had hugged Brother Godric not because I was happy, but because my heart was saying goodbye. I knew I could not go with him. I desperately wanted to thank him for his kindness toward me, and I wanted to keep helping the sick. But I couldn't. Not when my heart so desperately did not want to live a life as a monastic.

Everyone here at Wilton thought I was a good woman. Pure. Strong. Perfect. I was fulfilling my calling from God at the age of fourteen, after all. How wrong they all were. And how wrong I had been to lie to them.

I took the stairs two at a time and went straight to my cell. I heard Brother Godric's voice a moment later, speaking low to our patient, who then spoke softly back. Still soaking wet, I knelt at my bedside to pray, but I couldn't concentrate.

What was I going to do?

Father didn't want me to be a nun. I thought I'd have another year to convince him of my calling… and yet, I had not written one letter to even try to persuade him.

Perhaps marrying Alan wouldn't be so terrible? Perhaps I could marry him and then visit Mammy for large parts of the year? Richmond and Alan Rufus weren't far at all from my family in Dunfermline.

I clenched my hands tightly together. There were two choices: I could leave with Brother Godric in a week as a nun, or I could make my father happy and marry Alan.

Or, there was a third choice.

I could run away. Only an idiot would run away. I wasn't suicidal, after all. Obviously running away wasn't a real option. But, if I did…

I knew if I ran away from Wilton Abbey, I could not go home and I could not go to Jerusalem. My father would not accept me without a renewed promise to marry Alan Rufus.

Unless I married someone with just as much money and political advantage? I could become queen, as was my birthright. I would have to marry Henry's brother, King

William of England. He was handsome, and kind to me. It was far more than I could say for Alan Rufus. Yes, King William had laughed at my father and me, but was that so bad? It was annoying, but it hadn't physically hurt me.

Had Henry been telling the truth when he'd said King William raved of my beauty? Perhaps he'd only been teasing me? But, why would he lie about that?

My parents would be so overjoyed to have their daughter as queen that, perhaps, Mammy would forget I wore the veil and my father would forget the betrothal he'd set for me.

In any case, all could be right again, just as long as I did not take vows in the coming days. I had to run away.

CHAPTER 4: REBORN FROM THE RIVER NADDER

The River Nadder flowed to the south of Wilton Abbey, curved around its eastern side, and broke down into shallow riverlets to the north. There was one rickety bridge over the southern side.

With my basket held high over my head, I splashed through the shallowest part of the eastern curve, startling birds into flight from nearby trees.

Once I reached the other side of the stream, I tore my sodden clothes from my body with trembling hands. And from my basket, I pulled a white chemise down over my head, soaking it immediately. I followed this with a cheap blue dress and then a pair of heavily-worn leather boots on my cold, pruned feet.

Glancing around, I shoved my wet monastic clothes under the base of a large rock. My lungs pulled in three gasps of morning air without remembering to breathe out again. Now was not the time to cry. Without looking back, I sprinted into the wheat fields. My basket jostled where it hung on my arm.

In the middle of the night last night, I had attended Matins because I couldn't sleep. Then, when the other nuns went back to their cells for a few hours, I had found the dress in the huge sack of clothes for the needy. I had stolen some food — perhaps a week's worth if careful.

When I left before dawn fully broke, Sir Robert Achard had still been sleeping. The whole time, I had amazed myself with my composure.

But after sprinting through the gardens, wading through the cool river water, stripping naked, pulling on stolen clothes, and then sprinting again, a fire had started inside of me.

Now that the urge to cry had passed, I was fighting the urge to laugh. Even though I was not happy, hysteria tightened my throat and clenched my teeth into a grin. Abbess Mother would no longer decide what I did and when I did it. From now on, no matter what happened, I would no longer be "Sister." And unless King William decided to marry me after all of this, I would be a stranger to my parents forever.

After running a little over a mile through the wheat, my tired legs forced me to slow. Glancing over my shoulder, I couldn't see the abbey anymore. I could only see muddy road, golden wheat, a blue sky with delicate white clouds, and a thick green forest far off ahead of me.

Saliva coated my mouth as my stomach prepared to vomit. What was I doing right now? Was I truly leaving everyone and everything that I knew? Where would I go? King William couldn't marry me. I'd have to show up in what I was wearing — unless I stole again. And even if I found the best possible clothes, I couldn't very well go and offer my own hand to him. Betrothals weren't made that way, especially with the king.

The wind whipped over me, as though an invisible hand were trying to push me further from the abbey. My stolen blue skirt billowed forward with the wind, cooling my legs.

I watched my skirt flick and swim in the wind as my heart lulled to a calm.

As the wind died, my skirt dropped down around my legs again. Without much thought as to what I was doing, I forced my legs to trudge forward another step, and then another. With my gaze still down, I stumbled forward and then I ran, faster and faster, willing myself to drive more distance between the abbey and myself. My threadbare blue linen flicked like a ship's sail in the wind again.

I startled a sleeping fox who fled deeper into the wheat field next to me. A split-rail fence rose up from the ground to guard the wheat fields from the road. I ran until my legs collapsed under me.

Leaning against the rail fence, I pressed my hand to a stitch in my side and pulled quick, hungry gasps of air. I wished I had thought to bring a skin of watered ale.

I was thankful that the air was thinner now. It was easier to breathe now than before the storm yesterday.

"When one speaks of the wolf," said a low voice, "one sees its tail."

I flinched. "Henry! What are you doing here?"

As he ambled closer to me, he let his fingertips brush against the tops of the golden buds of wheat. "I suppose you're not looking for me then?" Only the fence stood between us.

In vain, I tried to slow my ragged breaths. I pressed my mouth closed as I continued to breathe deeply through my nose. "Of course not," I gasped, dropping my hand from the stitch in my side. I wiped my forehead with the back of my hand. "I was just taking a walk —"

" — you mean 'run' — "

" — and thinking."

"I was just doing the same." He glanced over his shoulder. His brown palfrey waited on the other side of the field. Her reins were tied to the limb of a tree.

I squinted up at him. "I interrupted you. Pray, forgive me." Even though my knees were made of pudding, I turned and strode further down the road. He easily matched my pace on the other side of the fence.

"I was just thinking about you," he said.

I did not have time for this. "Oh."

"Where's that girl who was pretending to be a nun? I kind of liked her."

Halting, I closed my eyes in exasperation and raised my face to the sky. "I beg your forgiveness," I muttered.

"Yes, you should be so repentant. I do not endure disappointments with a glad heart." I could hear the irritating little smirk in his voice.

"Right. Yes, might the Lord deign to um…" I glanced at him from the corner of my eye. "I forgot what I was going to say. Oh yes!" I pointed my toe and turned my face down toward the mud. "I pray a man of your lofty grace may one day grant the forgiveness of God's lowly servant—"

"You're still as snotty as you were as a child. You aren't even trying to hide it."

I looked up at him again. "I will not speak honeyed words to make men feel better about themselves. Especially to you—a man without the honor to treat a woman with dignity. It is wasted breath."

He lifted his foot to the lower of the split rails between us. "Aren't you afraid of me?" For a moment, I thought he was going to hoist himself over the fence.

"Oh, yes! I am deathly afraid!" I spat. A quiet voice in my head, which sounded similar to my Aunt Christina, warned me to brace for his palm to strike my face. The problem was, I didn't care if he caused me pain. I welcomed it.

"I've never known a woman to speak to me as you do. Only my brothers speak to me so casually."

"Of course women speak a certain way to you. You seem the sort of man who might enjoy hurting someone who can't hurt you back."

"I do?" His eyes widened.

I smiled. "Strike me dead if you like. I can't stop you. But I won't try to make you happy for my sake."

He let his foot fall from the fence. "My father's favorite thing to do was pull my mother's hair. And you know what? I think she liked it when he did. She was good like you. Always in church. And yet, my parents had so many children, my father couldn't remember all of our names." Reaching toward me, he lightly tugged one of my plaits. "Do you want me to hurt you?"

Before he let go of my hair, I grabbed his wrist with both of my hands and dug my nails into his skin. "Just because a person is always in church, it does not mean they are good. However, as all good queens should be, your mother was the example of gentleness and goodness. Do not speak ill of my godmother, even if she was your mother."

"Mother was short like you. She was smaller in her curves, though." He gazed down at my fingernails in his wrist but he didn't try to pull away. "You do have a lovely figure."

"Is that why you want to hit me? I remind you of your mother?"

"What a strange thing to say," he laughed.

"*You* are the one saying strange things. I was only trying to understand you."

"I only meant that these blue rags suit you better than the brown homespun." With his hand I still clutched before my face, he caressed my cheek.

Despite my sweat, I felt goosebumps rise down my arms. Reflexively, I dropped my hold on him. He needed to go away. I had said and done appalling things already. I didn't need to add to the list. "Henry —"

"You are so familiar with me that you have yet to address me by anything other than my first name. Never 'my lord' — not once. Have you noticed?"

My mouth fell open. Was he right? I tried to think back. "But you never called me 'mistress'… Well, I — I didn't mean to act —"

"It is proof enough for me." As he pulled my chin toward himself over the split-rail fence, I shut my eyes. But he didn't kiss me. Instead, he grazed his nose against mine as he asked, "Aren't you going to fight me?"

I sighed and whispered back, "I don't have time for any more inane —" But he cut my words off with a gentle peck to my lips. Instead of hitting him or yelling, I simply pulled my chin away from his hand.

He laughed and smiled easily. Taking my hand in his, he pressed a kiss to my knuckle. "I do love to tease you. I like to watch the color rise in your cheeks."

"But what if I teased you back? I feel sure you would become violent."

"Never. I beg you, tease me to your heart's desire. I will do nothing to stop you."

"Right. How about this?" He watched me closely as I pretended to think over what I would do. Slowly, I ran my fingertips over the stubble of his jaw, over his cheek, and then quickly pinched his nose as hard as I could. "Got your nose!" I tucked my thumb between my first and second finger knuckles. "Ha!"

He snatched at my wrist as he laughed at me. "Give me my nose back, Edith."

I swung my wrist hard, breaking his hold on me. In doing so, I accidentally punched him squarely in his nose. He held his face in his hands as he stumbled a step back from me.

"Zounds!" he yelled, blinking tears out of his eyes.

"I was only teasing you, *my lord*," I mocked in a sing-song, falsely-low voice. Secretly, I was shocked that I'd hit him. I hadn't meant to do it.

After wiping his nose with the back of his hand, he muttered, "Ah, not even bleeding." Suddenly, he grabbed my wrist again and yanked me toward the fence and himself. "Now it's my turn to steal something of yours. Mmmm... what ever shall I take?" He pinched the side of my waist first.

"Stop that!" I shrieked.

"Oh? You need that soft bit there?" When I slapped his hand away, he took a handful of my skirt and lifted it to my knees. "Is there anything I may have under here?"

"I said stop!"

Immediately, he dropped my skirts. "I beg your forgiveness." And he bowed his head. "I forget we are not as well-acquainted as that."

I hissed through my teeth, "I hate you, you midden barmpot! You do the king's court a disservice with your continued existence!"

His eyes widened. "That's probably the most insulting thing anyone has ever said to me." He glanced up the road toward the forest. Was he trying to hide his shock? "Are you ready to admit that you are running away?"

"No, I'm not. Not running away. I'm *allowed* to wear normal clothes." I started further down the road. He slowly followed me. It was quiet except for the occasional birds chirping and the mushing sounds of mud under my feet. I was tempted to turn and apologize to him but I couldn't do it. "It's just… Aunt Christina never approved of regular clothes at Romsey, and so I grew accustomed to the homespun."

"Yes, I suppose Aunt Christina wanted to keep dirty *barmpot* hands like mine off your fair skin. But, you know, the homespun didn't stop me before." Reaching over the fence, he grabbed my wrist again and yanked me hard. I stumbled toward him and ran into the rails.

"Don't bite me," he whispered, "or I'll bite you back."

I counted the flecks in his hazel eyes. "What?"

Though he held me tightly, I was surprised by how soft his lips were as he kissed me. Like kissing rose petals.

I shoved him away too late. I whispered in a shaky voice, "Stay away from me and do not touch me again." Turning to the forest once more, I ran further up the road, stumbling on my already-tired legs. He didn't call after me or make any move to follow. Glancing back, I saw he was walking into the wheat field again and toward the copse of trees where his horse waited.

Surely he'd understood. He was going to leave me alone. Finally. I didn't need to run anymore. No one else would follow me. Probably, no one had even noticed my absence yet.

But soon, I heard the sound of horse's hooves galloping up the road behind me. I ducked between the split rails so the fence was between us again, this time with me nearer to the wheat and him on the muddy road.

He slowed his horse so he was parallel with me.

"I beg you. Leave me alone," I muttered.

"Not likely," he said. "I'm not going to let you die. I swear by the blood of Christ. You go off on your own, I doubt you'd last three days."

"I've studied botany quite extensively. I won't starve."

"It's not botany which will force himself on you when he finds you alone in the woods." Henry ran his hand down his horse's mane to try to calm her.

"See? It is *you* from whom I must distance myself, Sir Rakefire."

Halting his horse, he swung himself down from his saddle. "No, it's not me you need to keep away from."

"Oh really?"

"I don't force myself on women. They come to me willingly." He caught up with me and walked next to me again as he led his horse by the reins. "No, it's just most of the other men in England… and everywhere else."

"You *just* kissed me. I—I'm not going to… Just leave me *alone*."

"I know, I know," he said. "There is Alan to deal with yet, but he will be easily managed."

"Actually, I'm sure he'll forget me once he knows I've run away, as long as I'm not found. There was never any love between us."

"Well good. No love lost then," Henry said, nodding once. "Though, you should send a letter to him explaining that you're alright. He has the means to send men to look for you."

"I will send no such letter. Don't presume to command me."

"Yes, *mistress*," he said, bowing lowly.

I ignored him. I needed to get him away from me but there was no way I'd outrun his horse and I certainly couldn't get away from him by force. What would it take for him to leave me alone? Perhaps I'd let him travel with me until nightfall and once he was asleep, I'd make a go of it into the night? Though, of course, it would be dangerous to travel alone by night, especially on foot. And I was already tired from running so much.

Belatedly, I realized Henry was watching me as he walked next to me. His horse clomped along behind us.

"Where were you going to go?" he finally asked me, breaking my reverie. "Since you are running away."

"I don't know," I said as I thought, *to your brother.* "Somewhere I cannot be easily found."

He frowned. "There aren't many places which fit that description."

"Perhaps I'll go home to Scotland." There was no way I'd go back to my father.

"Mm, but of course you aren't going home. If you were, you would not need to run away. And anyway, you wouldn't get there on foot very quickly by travelling in this direction. But we're likely to pass Old Sarum soon."

"I know."

"May I accompany you?"

"You're going to go all the way to Scotland with me on a whim?"

"Certainly, if only to ensure your safety. Were you going to take a ship perhaps?"

"What about your friends?"

"You know I have to leave my dear teacher, Sir Robert Achard, at Wilton Abbey perhaps for a month or more. He will take a while to heal, surely. And Bishop Osmund left before dawn to go home to Old Sarum. He's surely already back. My brothers will leave me alone. I'm free to go where I wish at the moment, though eventually I'll need to return to Normandy."

"Oh yes, that's right. You are Count of Cotentin."

"No… not anymore—"

"Why not?"

"My brothers. It's a long story."

"Oh, or perhaps only an embarrassing story?"

"I am Lord of Domfront now, at least."

"By the way, aren't you a bit old for instruction? Why do you still have a teacher?"

"I have a duty to my title to not be an idiot. If a royal is ill-educated, no matter how popular they are, they are really worth nothing more than an ass wearing a crown."

"Well then, why aren't you staying with Sir Robert Achard or Bishop Osmund? Surely you don't want to be an ass with a crown on its head?" I glanced over at him.

"I had already planned to stay at Wilton for a while in order to convince you not to marry Alan Rufus. However, as you are leaving, I shall leave with you."

The fence was at its end and no longer stood between us. I stopped and turned to him. Halting his horse, he turned and looked down at me expectantly. Hiking my hands to my hips, I looked up at him. "I don't know what your intentions might have been with me, but I will be honest with you for your sake, as you and I might see more of each other in the coming years."

His eyes brightened. "Yes, dear Edith?" He leaned closer, as though he were going to kiss me again, but instead he only waited, listening.

"I am going to London. It is the Will of God that I become a queen, as my mother is in the north."

Henry smirked at me. "You intend to offer you hand to my brother? With no one to speak to him on your behalf?" He ran his free hand through his hair.

"Yes," I said, gritting my teeth together. "I've heard I am the only woman to have ever turned his head. Why shouldn't I go to him?"

"Well, it is true you are not a stranger to him." Henry studied my face, seeming to evaluate me. "I was going to pass through London anyway to visit our lord king before crossing the South Sea again. I will accompany you for your safety and I will speak to him on your behalf."

I thought about this for a moment. "Why?"

"I like you. I wish to see you succeed."

"No," I said, shaking my head. "No, there is clearly something else to it. You're hiding something from me."

He gazed into my eyes. I couldn't help but gaze back. "Can you truly read me so well? You would make an excellent queen. Anyway, what say you to my offer?"

"I give in. You're wasting far too much of my time. Follow me if you wish. I cannot stop you." I turned from him and continued walking down the road. Henry and his horse quietly followed behind me.

It wasn't long before we reached the edge of the forest. The trees were sparse where the road continued through. "Instead of walking, let us ride for a bit—just so we are beyond the sight of the wall of Old Sarum. Uncomfortable questions if we run into Bishop Osmund, you know." Henry gracefully mounted his mare.

"Right." As I had lived at Romsey Abbey since I was very young and then moved to Wilton Abbey only a couple of years ago, I hadn't had the opportunity to ride horses much. I *had* learned. However, it had been years ago when I was a small child at home in Scotland.

"Come on, ride with me." He held his hand down to me without looking at me, as though the words made him uncomfortable. Or perhaps he was hiding something?

Would he ride off somewhere else once he had me on his horse? Surely it was possible he wished to kidnap me? Or, perhaps he must have guessed I'd rather walk than ride in a saddle with him?

"Is that entirely necessary?" I finally asked. "I doubt your mare can handle the load."

"She can and has before."

I raised an eyebrow. "You often ride with women in your saddle with you?"

"Not daily, but yes, I have before. We should ride so we may conserve our strength. Anyway, not many women are as short as you. Lilt will be fine."

Lilt? Oh, his horse. "But," I said, searching the forest edge for another reason to keep my feet on the ground, "I — I need to…"

"Don't be so prudish. You know I'm only trying to help you."

"I don't want your help if you're going to be uncourtly toward me."

"I have done nothing other than show you courtly love."

"You should treat me as a mistress of my station."

He dismounted his horse and grabbed my wrist. "And *you* should treat me as a man of my station," he said in a hard voice.

"You're wicked!"

Pulling me closer, he leaned down until we were nose to nose. "Yes, you know me well already."

I considered him for a moment. Was Henry truly as forceful as he seemed? The fact was, I still didn't really know him. Yes, his mother and eldest brother were my godparents, and his other brother was king. His sisters had always been kind to me when they visited my family when I was little. But Henry…

I only had memory of him because of how strange he had been compared to the other boys. He had always sat off on his own and read for hours while the other boys jousted or shot arrows at targets. And then, when he did stand to fence or the like, he would best all the other boys in a moment.

What else could I remember? My mind strained to recall. At the end of Sunday Mass once, he had poked me awake after I had fallen asleep against his arm. When he would walk in front of me, I always was sure to kick the back of his knee to make him kneel. At dinner, he would eat my peas when I pushed them to the side of my plate. He and Alexander had tickled me dozens of times until I cried from laughter.

In any case, I wasn't afraid of him. Not at all.

I stopped trying to pull away as tears stung my eyes. "Henry."

"Yes, Edith?"

I bit my lip. "Don't be rough."

Glancing down at my lips, he shook his head slightly. "Forgive me, mistress. We should make haste before they drag you back to that abbey."

Shoving the reins into my hand, he lifted me to his horse's back so I was sidesaddle. As he mounted the horse so he was behind me, I felt dazed.

Gently, he slid his arm around me. Pulling my right thigh over the saddle, he forced me to ride like a man would, hiking my dress up a bit as he did.

"Take me back to the abbey." I bent my knee up and half-heartedly tried to get off the horse. The part of my mind which sounded like Aunt Christina was completely indignant.

As I knew he would, Henry pushed my thigh and held it down. "I'll never take you back there. Upon my head, you shall be gone forever from that place now."

"Henry," I said, pushing his hand from my leg.

"I love it when you say my name." Releasing my thigh, he pushed my hair away from my shoulder. Light as a feather, he kissed my neck.

"My father would run you through if he saw you touching me this way."

"Mm. This is just so I may be sure you won't fall off." Without warning, he snapped the reins and the horse took off like an arrow. I cursed to myself under my breath as my hands flattened on the horse's mane. I had forgotten the basket on my arm until it jostled violently as we rode.

I tried to keep my eyes open as trees rushed by, but this was the fastest I had ever moved in my life. I felt sure I would have fallen if it weren't for Henry holding me tightly against his chest.

CHAPTER 5: THROUGH THE FOREST AT NIGHT

We didn't ride at full speed for long. "That was fun," Henry said, still gripping my waist as he slowed the horse to a trot. Gently nuzzling his nose into the crook of my neck, he pecked a kiss behind my ear, sending chills down my back again.

"I hate you," I said, shutting my eyes.

"You're a terrible liar."

"May I walk now?"

Henry pulled his horse's reins and we stopped. After he dismounted, he helped me down without looking at my face. We ventured from the road and into the forest.

A squirrel ran up a tree with an acorn in its mouth. The path down the thin deer trail was steep. My old leather boots pinched my toes as I tried to keep from stumbling. The horse's hooves were the loudest sound around us.

I tried to sort out my thoughts but my mind was a mess. Foremost, I knew I needed to get away from Henry as soon as possible. But how? Perhaps it was unwise to leave him if I did want to marry into his family. But why was he even helping me? Would he really speak to King William on my behalf?

"We'll follow the River Bourne if we're going to walk," Henry said, "in case anyone is looking for you."

"Fine."

Henry's horse seemed to be enjoying herself. She bobbed her head every once in a while, as though she wanted to run again.

Finally, we reached the bottom of the hill and walked along the river. "I beg you forgive me for, well, forcing my company on you," Henry said conversationally. "I don't usually do this sort of thing."

What sort of thing was he doing? "You mean kidnapping me? You are not forgiven."

"You see why though, don't you? You can't travel alone."

"I shall always do as I wish. Do not forget it."

"I never forget anything," he said, and smiled at me. "But pray tell, if you always do as you wish, how is it you found yourself in your current quandary?"

"Hmph." I pushed away my nagging concerns about impropriety. Travelling alone with a man wasn't *that* terrible. Also, no one would make assumptions about us if they never knew we travelled together in the first place. It would simply need to remain a secret.

I didn't actually care about impropriety, anyway. That was just Aunt Christina wedging herself into my mind, as always.

I took a deep breath of damp, woody air.

Wasn't it more sensible to use Henry's help? I had run away from home without any solid plan for what I would do. I did not honestly believe I would marry the king of England. If King William had wanted me, he surely would have said so by now.

Why did my bright ideas before sleep always seem so ridiculous in the light of day?

"I suppose you'll accompany me all the way to wherever I go?" I gazed down at the moss and leaves underfoot. "No matter whether I want you with me?"

"Yes," he said, gently clasping my hand in his. "Pray, do not — truly, I have the most honorable of intentions. I would never intend to harm you or do anything to disgrace our families."

"You already *did*."

His heavy eyebrows furrowed. "No. I would never kiss or touch you if you didn't wish for me to do so."

"But I didn't —"

He looked over at me with patient curiosity and said nothing.

I felt my cheeks warm. "The word 'no' will never mean 'yes' when it comes from my lips. I'm not an imprudent woman."

"Hm." A grin threatened at the corners of his mouth. "Running away from home without a plan. Yes, surely you are always prudent, dear Edith."

"Tsk. Stop talking." I pulled my hand away from his.

For most of the day, we walked in silence. The sun slowly began to set. Only the warmest rays of light bounced off the stream's surface now. The stream sparkled and danced like a thousand little stars. Red, orange, pink. The beauty of it made me think of my mother. Queen Margaret's jewelry was the finest that Scotland had ever seen. In fact, I could not remember Mammy's face without remembering the glittering jewels which always surrounded it.

Henry spoke for the first time in hours. "Let's rest for a bit." He led Lilt to the water's edge. Then he knelt, scooped up some water for himself, and drank from his hands.

"Alright." Hesitating at first, I knelt and drank too. The cool, sweet water made me realize how overheated I was. I wished I could take my heavy dress off and dip in the stream.

Henry said, "You shall ride Lilt as we travel by the river tonight. This way, you can sleep tonight and during the day tomorrow, once you have more distance from the abbey, I'll make camp and sleep while you keep watch, alright?"

My gaze darted to his face. "Alright." Had I already earned his trust just by walking calmly with him for the day? Of course he couldn't actually read my mind, try as he might. Didn't he guess that I still wanted to run from him? Well, my plan wasn't smart, all things considered. Perhaps he assumed I had seen reason and now welcomed his companionship?

After securing Lilt's reins to a low-hanging bough of a tree, Henry took out some bread and cheese from my basket. He handed me my share and we sat down and began eating. Though I hadn't noticed that I was hungry, I ate everything Henry had given me in hardly any time. Lilt languidly grazed the weeds nearby.

Once he was finished, Henry strode to Lilt's side and held out his hand, ready to help me up. Hesitantly placing my hand in his, I slid my foot into the stirrup and swung my leg over the saddle as quickly as I could. I expected Henry to mount the saddle behind me, but he didn't. Instead, he led Lilt by her reins as he walked alongside the river.

After a long moment, I said softly, "Henry?"

"Hm?"

"Aren't you… why aren't you riding with me?"

"I can stay awake more easily if I walk. Also, Lilt will have less burden. And if we're attacked, I will be injured first while you shall remain safe enough to ride away."

"Oh." They were good reasons. "My lord, are you quite sure—"

"My lord?" He laughed and glanced up at me. "I'm sure. You are welcome to it."

"Welcome to what? Your life?" I laughed uneasily.

It was quiet except for Lilt's clomping for a moment. "Yes, Edith. My life. I would lay it down for you." He glanced up at me again. Though I couldn't see his face very clearly in the dark, I knew he wasn't smiling. "I swear by the blood of Christ."

It was quiet again. As he guided Lilt's reins, we continued at a strolling pace along the stream. The light was dying early in this thick forest. A torch would only alert others to our presence, which would not help if anyone had followed us this far. I couldn't help but feel vulnerable on Lilt's back. And, though I hated to admit it, I was worried for Henry's safety.

"Henry?"

"Yes, Edith?"

"I want you to ride with me."

"I thought I wasn't allowed to touch you again?"

"It's just, I don't know how to sleep on a horse's back. Perhaps we could make camp now, instead of the morning?"

"No. If we make camp now, you'll run away as I sleep."

I pretended to laugh. "I beseech you, my lord. Ride with me."

He slowed Lilt to a stop and grabbed my ankle. "I was right, then? You planned to run off?"

"Perhaps."

"I don't suffer fools." He swung himself up behind me again. "Don't be foolish," he whispered in my ear.

"Alright," I whispered back. His hand warmed my waist.

It fell silent between us. I tried not to lean back on him but it was difficult.

Henry had been born as the fourth son of his parents, not the third. Richard, the second son born, had been shot by a hunter in New Forest and had died while on horseback. As we rode together in the dark, I thought Henry was most likely thinking of him. I was thinking of him, after all.

"Are you thinking about wolves?" I asked him, mostly to try to distract him.

"No," he said. His answer hung in the air for a moment.

"Serpents?"

"I'd rather not tell you my current thoughts," he said after a moment of silence, "though serpentine thoughts are never far from my mind." When I glanced over my shoulder, he gave a small smile.

He was too close, so I turned my back to him again. "Why would you rather not tell me what you were thinking?"

"I'm surprised the nuns didn't teach you about the sin of idle talk."

Aunt Christina had taught me about that sin daily as a child. "You and I haven't spoken all day. Even the nuns speak more than we have been."

"Hm."

"Perhaps you don't like it when I speak? I'll have to talk more."

"I like your voice —"

"You're taller than I always thought of you being."

"That happens sometimes when kids grow up," he said. "You probably still think of me the same as when I was... how old were we when we met?"

"We met when I was a baby."

"Yes, and I would have been about ten years old then. But I saw you last when you were about six or seven, I think?"

"Why didn't you ever visit me after I left Scotland? Your sisters always visited Mary and me at Romsey whenever they were nearby."

"I didn't want to. And I'm glad I didn't."

"And pray tell, what is your reason?"

"Because you're beautiful and I enjoy the company of beautiful women. It would have been a shame if I'd developed a brotherly sort of love for you."

"If I didn't know better, I might take your words to mean you have some other love for me instead."

"But you know better?"

"Yes. Truly, you are only a bored flirt."

"Forgive me if my reputation precedes me," Henry said slowly. "I shall endeavor to be more serious with you from now on."

We were both quiet again. With Henry's body heat warming my back, I felt safe even though I knew I probably wasn't. Gazing up between the tree branches, I watched the thin wisps of clouds, backlit by moonlight, as they passed over my head. In the dark, the branches of the trees were skeletal arms, reaching for me to stay there in the woods with them forever.

After a while, Henry wrapped his arm tighter around me. Gently, he guided my leg so I would ride sidesaddle. Under his guidance, I slid in the front of the saddle until my thighs were together again. Immediately, my whole body relaxed a little.

"Lean against me."

His hand guided my cheek to lay against his chest.

I tried to relax but I felt too guilty. What would Aunt Christina have said if she could have seen me? However, I needed to sleep if I were going to make the most of my getaway in the morning when he planned to sleep. Hesitantly, I wrapped my arms around his waist.

All around us, the leaves on the oak trees rustled with the wind. It was the first soft chant of Matins in the dead of night. As the wind strengthened, the leaves hummed stronger with it. I closed my eyes as the full choir sang. And just as gradually, silence surrounded us again.

I took a deep breath. "Henry," I whispered. I lifted my cheek from his chest and looked up at him.

"Yes?" he whispered back.

"I—" In the little bit of moonlight which reached us between the canopy, I saw his face as he gazed down at me. Something I saw there made me stop talking for a moment. There was no smile playing at his lips now.

"What is it?"

"I can't sleep."

"Try." He kissed my forehead and then looked back up at the forest around us. I laid my head against him again.

I did try again to sleep, but it was too quiet, even with the river babbling nearby.

Softly, Henry began to sing. It was so soft, I wouldn't have heard him if I wasn't so close to him. Low and sweet, he sang one of the many lullabies my mother used to sing to me when I was a little child. I had sung it to myself dozens of times while mopping. The novice nuns had even tried to sing it in rounds but it had never quite worked. His voice comforted me, as though he knew it would.

As I finally drifted off to sleep, I was not sure if it was the wind or his lips which brushed my hair.

When I awoke, the sun was only peeking above the edge of the earth, not yet above the trees. It cast bright orange and yellow hues on the tree leaves and the forest floor. Henry's arms were still holding fast to me, keeping me steady on Lilt's back.

"Good morning," I said quietly. From sleeping on Lilt's back and not moving the whole night, I was beyond the point of soreness and desperately wanted to get down. Lilt probably didn't want to carry us anymore either. The horse's eagerness for travel had clearly ebbed.

Henry's eyes had purple crescents under them. "Good morning," he said, smiling widely. His eyes crinkled in the corners.

"You'll have crow's feet if you grow old," I said without thinking.

"I hope I get crow's feet, then."

"Will you help me down?" My back audibly cracked as I sat up from my curled position against his chest.

"Of course." He halted the horse and she obliged immediately. Henry slid down first and then held both hands up, so I slid down into his arms. Despite his sleepiness, he easily lowered me to the ground. My skirt followed me as it dropped off of Lilt's back.

"Are you ready to sleep?" I asked.

"Well, let's eat a bit of your meager stores first."

The river had widened overnight as we followed it. Henry took down my basket from a strap on the saddle and he pulled out some bread and plums. After splitting the food evenly, he handed me half and we sat down on the riverbank.

"This will hopefully be enough until we reach Basingstoke. We may eat a proper meal there," he said through a mouthful of plum.

"Are we close to there?"

"Yes, though further away than I'd hoped. While you slept, we travelled east along the road toward London. I kept us just off the beaten path, under the cover of the forest. We are near the River Test now."

"Ah." I tried not to grimace.

"I regret we didn't make better time," he said. "There wasn't much moonlight to go by. I didn't want to risk injuring Lilt."

"Of course." I'd had no idea whether we had made good time or not. I hated the River Test only because of its association in my mind with Romsey Abbey. "No. It's fine. Thank you for, well, for getting me this far."

He bowed his head to me slightly. "It was my honor, mistress."

I felt my face warm. Why was he being so formal? Was it because he was tired? Belatedly, I bowed my head slightly to him in return. "My lord."

Once he finished with his breakfast, he pulled his tunic off, leaving him dressed in a cambric and leggings and boots. Lying down on the stony riverbank, he balled up his tunic to use as a pillow and closed his eyes.

I shoved the rest of my bread in my mouth and chewed as I tried not to watch him fall asleep. His cambric was thin and I could see the outline of the muscles of his arms and chest.

I knew I should run as soon as possible if I were going to leave him. But which way? I felt as though God had picked me up and dropped me in a foreign land. By the sun, I thought north was upstream, but I wasn't quite sure. How many times had I sat by this river while at Romsey Abbey? Which way did it flow? It flowed south. Of course it flowed south, right? The sun was at my right, so yes, the river flowed south.

Why was I so afraid to leave Henry?

Again I wondered if I should stay with him. I could allow him to accompany me to London. Certainly I was safer with him than travelling alone. At least, I *probably* was safer.

Did I truly want to marry King William and be queen?

Even though he was lying at least ten feet away and sleeping, I could still feel Henry's touch around my waist and on my cheek.

Perhaps my best option was to go home to Scotland and beg my parents to call off my wedding to Alan Rufus? Or else, I could follow this river and go to Aunt Christina at Romsey Abbey… Or perhaps I should simply go back to Wilton Abbey and pretend I… Not that I was kidnapped. Perhaps I got lost in the woods?

I began to whisper the Lord's Prayer, but I stopped after the first few words. It didn't calm me as it normally did. Instead, it became harder to take a deep breath. By leaving Wilton Abbey and Brother Godric, I had turned my back to God.

I tiptoed to Henry's sleeping form. I needed to leave. It wasn't right to stay with Henry. It was time to go…

And just as I began to tiptoe past him, I slipped. Falling to the stony riverbank, I cracked my head hard.

My vision went black before I lost consciousness.

CHAPTER 6: THE AUGUST SUN

Henry is warm and the sea waves are cold. I forget how to swim in deep water like this but it doesn't matter because Henry's arms are strong and he holds me up above the threat of the waves. Slowly, he kisses me and he drags a flower crown made of forget-me-nots from his hair. The crown is on my head now and it is heavy. I am struggling against Henry's hold as I fight to keep my head above the waves but I can't break free.

He kisses my forehead and it feels like fire. He whispers in my ear, "Arise, Good Queen." But is dark now and I want to sleep.

Coughing hard, I fought to wake up. Squinting through my eyelashes, all I could see was Henry's face as he stared down at me.

"You nearly drowned in the river. I thought you were surely dead," he said softly. I could feel his warm breath on my cold, wet cheek as he spoke. "Are you alright?" His heavy eyebrows furrowed together.

"I've had a—a dream." I was shivering even though the August air was warm.

"Oh?"

I took a deep pull of warm air and breathed out again slowly. "We swam together in the sea. You took a crown from your head and placed it on my head."

Henry glanced over my face — to my lips, my cheeks, my chin, my nose, and back into my eyes. What was he looking for? I was content to keep looking into his eyes, which shone like glass. I didn't want to tell him any more of my dream. I wished I had not said anything about it at all, but it was too late.

He opened his mouth and shut it again. "Edith…" He flexed his hand next to my face, as though he wanted to cup my cheek or maybe pet my hair. Had he really thought I was dead? Suddenly, he began inspecting my head, gently moving his fingers through my long, dark plaits of hair. "Well, no lumps or bleeding at least…"

"Oh. That's good," I whispered. Henry's face was still the only thing I could see. He was outlined in sunlight. His black eyelashes, the dark stubble trailing over his worrying jaw… "You look so serious," I giggled. "Oh, you can't fool me." I closed my eyes again because my head hurt.

"Edith," he said again. "I think we should — take my hand. Let me help you. Can you stand?"

He lifted me to my feet with one arm around my waist. "Rest a while in the warmth of the sun."

"I'm fine, really. My head just aches a bit is all."

"I only woke because of the cracking noise of your head on the stone by me. Finding you sinking into the river was a terrible way to wake."

"I'll try not to wake you in that manner again."

"What happened? Did you slip?"

"Oh, mmhm… I was trying to fish."

He sat me down on a large rock on a drier part of the stream bed. "Well, the River Test *is* excellent fishing. Let's have a better breakfast and travel on. I am no longer tired."

While I waited for my dress to dry in the summer heat, I ignored my dizziness as I watched Henry wade into the river. He stood very still as he gazed down into the rippling water. My head thudded in pain and so I closed my eyes to shut the sun out of them. I couldn't be sure how long it took him — perhaps I'd dozed off — but I opened my eyes again when Henry was at my side.

"A trout," he said as he built up wood for a fire.

"You caught it with just your hands?" I asked lazily.

He raised a cool, damp hand to my forehead in the same way Brother Godric would. "Stay awake, alright?"

"Henry do you see that willow tree down the river a bit?" I pointed.

He gazed to where I pointed. "I do, Edith."

"Go and scrape some of its bark from the trunk and bring it to me."

He looked at me like I was crazy. But without a word, he did as I asked. A moment later, I took the bark from his hands, and I shoved a bit of it in my mouth and chewed.

"Are you... are you sure you — "

"I've not gone soft in the head," I said too sharply. I didn't want to talk.

He stared for a moment longer before he said, "Mm. I need to find striking stones." He pressed a quick kiss to my forehead. And with that, he walked along the riverbank, his gaze downcast. As I chewed my willow bark, I watched as he eventually found two stones that would work to strike together. He made quick work with the stones on a bit of gathered tinder and the fire was lit.

With a thin rock, he cleaned a lamprey that had been stuck to the trout. Once he gutted and scaled the fish, he roasted the trout and lamprey until it looked like the fish was going to fall apart.

He brought the fish to me. We both started breaking pieces of it off its spit, and we soon did the same with the lamprey. The food immediately lightened my spirits. I wasn't used to being hungry.

"I never had a lamprey this way," he said. "It isn't bad."

As the sun peered down between the clouds, the stream's ripples were thrown into blinding, glittering brilliance. Suddenly, the whole river bed—the outcropping rocks behind us, the stones and pebbles underfoot, the trees across the stream—shimmered with the webbed shadows of the moving water. A sweet, warm breeze swept down the valley over the stream and brushed my newly-dry, curly tendrils back. Closing my eyes, I lifted my chin to the wind until it died.

I felt Henry watching me. It was welcome. Comforting, even. Opening my eyes again, I met Henry's gaze. Belatedly, he smiled at me.

"We're wasting time," I said softly. I took his hand and stood carefully.

Scooping up his tunic, he pulled it on and fixed his belt. "Are you alright to ride?"

"Yes," I said, though I didn't know.

He hastily kicked the remnants of the fire into the stream and wrapped his arm around my shoulders. As we walked slowly toward Lilt, she stamped when she saw us coming closer. Apparently she was ready to go, too.

He gently lifted me onto Lilt's saddle, sidesaddle again.

"Your dress seems to be dry again."

"Mm."

"Is it still your wish to ride east to my brother, the king?" He stepped up with the stirrup and settled behind me.

I didn't want to turn my head because my head throbbed. "Yes, it is still my wish to go to King William."

He didn't say anything to this. Lightly snapping the reins, he coaxed Lilt into a trot. We travelled north up the stony riverbank.

Though we travelled slowly, I felt as though the earth was trying to tilt sideways. But Henry held his arm tightly around my torso as he had before, hugging me to his chest.

His touch was good, and soothing. "I am happy to ride sidesaddle again," I said, wrapping my arms around Henry and nuzzling my face against his chest.

He kissed my hair in response. Soon, I fell asleep again.

After a long stretch of dozing against Henry's chest, he woke me with a kiss to my forehead. We passed a cottage, and then another. The pathway widened and the trees were replaced with two-story buildings and quaint wooden houses.

"Where are we?" I asked quietly. My head still throbbed.

"Just outside of Basingstoke."

"Oh good. That fish did not satisfy me. We shall stop here and eat a real meal, as you mentioned." I realized that I was being demanding but my headache made me reticent to speak.

"I'd hoped we'd make it to Windsor today but perhaps I was too optimistic." I could tell by his voice that he was smiling. "We shall stay here and rest for the night. Anyway, Lilt is to her limit, I'd say. We'll risk someone recognizing you if we stay here, of course. Though, it's a small village. Well, it'll be fine. I will keep you safe, no matter what."

Henry's hold slipped away from my waistline and I shivered. Jumping down from Lilt, he easily lifted me from the saddle and set me on my feet.

"Thank you," I said softly. He offered his arm and I held onto his elbow gratefully. I felt as though I'd been at sea for a week. If it weren't for him steadying me, I would have fallen down.

There was a pub on the edge of the town that was private enough, according to Henry. However, when we came in through the heavy wooden door, noise assaulted my already-aching head. Men spoke effusively over top one another, generating a roar of conversation. A fair number of women sat alongside the men, or else in their laps, and they punctuated the roar with high-pitched, unrestrained laughter. Sing-song children wove their way between the merry adults like fish around rocks in a stream. The air was warm and heavy with the stench of acrid beer, slopped over and over into the tamped-down rushes.

I longed for a cool, quiet bed.

When the barman looked up at Henry and me expectantly, Henry hesitated for only a short moment, and then he grabbed my hand.

"We'll need a room tonight, if one is available," Henry said to the plump, scruffy man behind the bar. The man met his eyes for a moment and did not speak. Henry just held a polite smile on his face until the man finally spoke.

"Are you married? Can't have that sort of business," he said in a matter-of-fact voice, wiping his sweaty palms on his stained apron.

"In which sort of business do you imagine I partake?" I asked sharply, crossing my arms.

"Of course we're married." Henry laughed easily as he met my surprised glance with a steady gaze. "We're newlyweds, in fact," he said, looking straight into my eyes. Henry dropped my hand and ran his hand down my hair like I were some exotic pet of his. "Want to spend as much time with my wife as I might before I'm off to serve King William and his campaign in the north."

"But what then of your wife?"

Henry looked back to the barman and I looked up at the man too. I thought this perhaps was a chance to get away from Henry. I was about to explain that Henry was lying, but something about the beady look in the stranger's eyes, and Henry's warm touch, made me reluctant to speak the whole truth for once.

"She'll come with me. Can't bear to part with her."

"Oh, yes. I will pray you have a safe journey. But perhaps she could stay on here as a maid while you're gone? It wouldn't do to have her abroad with your fellows, you reckon?"

"I reckon we only need a room until we travel north, and you leave well enough alone what you reckon, man," Henry laughed. "I don't blame you for trying though. Isn't she a beauty?" And then bending slightly, he smacked my bottom.

"Henry!" I squealed, smacking his arm as hard as I could. He didn't even flinch.

"My apologies, dear wife. I know—I promised to wait until we were alone, but..." and then he leaned down to my ear and whispered, "I've wanted to do that since I saw you climb up onto Lilt's back last night." I closed my eyes as he pressed a kiss to my neck. "I pray you forgive me, my love."

I could barely make myself speak. "Mm." I opened my eyes and remembered that the barman was watching us. Oh right, Henry was just pretending with me again. I was an absolute fool.

The barman simply grunted and shrugged. After they set up for Lilt to be fed, watered and sheltered for the night, the man offered us pottage and we gladly accepted.

At a sticky table in the corner that had more than its fair share of crumbs, Henry and I sat down to eat. I didn't mind the crud really, but I couldn't help but imagine what Brother Godric would say about such filth. It made me smile.

"What's funny?" Henry asked, looking up from his bean stew.

I shook my head. There was so much noise and music around us, it would have been difficult to have a conversation without shouting. But I was still smiling, and he smiled back at me.

As we ate supper, the sun set outside. I caught the barman looking at us a few times. I grinned politely at him, and he nodded back. It was strange, but I was relieved to have Henry with me now. If I had been here alone, surely the man behind the bar would have accosted me, at least. That is, if I even would have made it this far from Wilton Abbey.

Henry finished his trencher and cleaned his bowl. As my throbbing headache was making me nauseous, I pushed my bowl toward him and gestured for him to take it. He didn't hesitate before he finished off my stew. Once we both finished our ale, he took my hand in his and led me toward the stairs.

CHAPTER 7: THE PUB IN BASTINGSTOKE

The strangers lining the rickety stairway were calmer than the ones downstairs.

Quickly opening our door and peeking inside—no one appeared to be in the room already—Henry pulled me in behind himself. Once he slammed the door shut, he drop my hand. As he made his way around the small room, he drew the curtains shut and lit the candles.

"Oh Henry, it's already so hot in here. Can't we leave them open?"

"Not if we're hiding you from inquisitive eyes," he said, "or sharing a bed." He winked.

I bit my lip. I supposed he had a point about hiding. Though, who even noticed we were here? No one other than the barman seemed to have even noticed us. But, sharing a bed? For a moment, I was afraid. If I tried to leave now, what would happen? Would he run after me? What would the bar patrons do? Wouldn't they only laugh? He *did* just announce we were married.

He stopped fussing with the candles long enough to look over at me. I realized I must look frightened—my fingers flipped over each other as though they wanted to dance. I tried my best to clasp my hands together and hold still.

"Forgive my poor joke, Edith. I'm not going to touch you. I gave you my word."

I didn't know what to say, so I just stared at him for a moment. Then, I finally managed to speak. "Did you notice the way the barman looked at me?"

"Yes, I did. He was quite barefaced, wasn't he?" He seemed relieved I had changed the subject, or maybe just that I was talking.

"Yes," I said, trying to smile, though I wasn't quite sure what Henry meant. It was quiet again.

Henry sat down on the edge of the bed and pulled one of his boots off. "May I ask... if my brother refuses you, what is your plan?" He pulled his other boot off.

"I do not have any other plan."

"Perhaps I could convince you there is a better man for you."

"A better suitor than the king? It's practically treasonous to say."

"Is it only the crown that appeals to you?"

"It seems that it may be God's Will that I be queen." I said it to try to convince myself as much as to convince him. "My mother is a good queen. She is practically a living saint. She helps the poor... washes their feet... I would endeavor to do as she taught me. Otherwise, I doubt I would willingly consider marriage at all. What do I need a husband for?"

He laughed. "I see."

"Do *you* want to get married?"

"Well, my brothers want me to become a bishop but I don't care about what they want." He smiled proudly. "Yes," he said, nodding, "I wish to marry. But it must be to a woman who is my equal. She should know three languages—the same three that I know—so we might converse in any language I speak."

I was distracted for a moment: I knew three languages.

He continued, "She should have a pleasant voice, so she won't grate on my nerves. She should have a strong belief in God and know the Scriptures well, so as to honor the memory of my mother, as well as to deal with bishops and priests for me—most of whom I despise." This shocked me but I tried to hide it. "She should perhaps be of an Anglo-Saxon descent—also like my mother—so as to satisfy the people of the country if I am ever to be king. She needs to be the legitimate daughter of a king, of course. And, no doubt, she should also be beautiful."

I was still wondering why he hated bishops and priests but didn't want to ask. "You don't want much. There probably aren't many women who fit that description."

"Certainly not," he said, smirking. "I believe I know of only one."

"Oh." I hated the sound of my own voice, and he certainly didn't think I was beautiful. But who could he possibly mean? Was there another woman who was of Anglo-Saxon descent who was also the daughter of a king? I could think of only my sister, Mary, who was still only a child and living at Wilton Abbey, but she couldn't speak Latin.

"Why don't you want to marry?" he asked.

"Why?" I repeated, stalling. He nodded. "There is so much more to do in life than stay silent and simply be some man's wife and nothing more. And…"

"And what?" He watched me closely.

"And," I said, "I helped a lot with Brother Godric's patients. He'd have me help in Old Sarum, especially with the women… It's hard for me to separate having babies from marriage. And there are so many women—they can't afford to feed the children they have and they give birth to another. So many of them die, no matter what we do. You don't know how many women have come to our door at the abbey, all hours of the night, begging Brother Godric for some answer for what could be done. How many leave their baby with the nuns..."

"That wouldn't happen to you, Edith," he said, standing up from the bed.

"You say so, Henry. But you don't know. There are some decent men out there that, well, they can't leave their wives alone. They end up with nine, ten children. You know. You've seen them, the families. Those women—"

"My mother had that many children. None of us starved."

"Your father was King William the Bast—Conqueror. Of course you didn't starve."

"But you'll be fine," he said dismissively. "Your own mother has had how many? Eight? Anyway, your brothers are honorable. They would assure the safety of your children if no one else did."

"I would never ask any such thing of my brothers." I didn't want to keep talking about this, but words fell out of my mouth of their own accord. "Or what of those poor women who can't have children? They could go years without pregnancy only to begin to show—then they bleed and lose the child after a few moments of happiness." Tears sprang to my eyes but I fought them back. "How many barren women beg Brother Godric to magically make them fertile? Those poor women, treated as less than dogs once their secret is found out—after years of marriage with nothing to show for it."

"If you were my wife, and you were barren, I wouldn't let them find out. I'd just tell them we weren't lucky enough yet—or rather, we weren't *blessed*, as you would prefer me to say... Or, I don't know, we'd steal some of those starving children you mentioned and raise them as our own."

"Don't tease me. Not about this."

"Edith…" He closed the gap between us and gently hugged me. I had to stop myself from hugging him back. I wanted him to let go of me, but I couldn't bring myself to push him away. It was too pleasant to be comforted by him. "I beg your forgiveness," he whispered into my hair.

"You regret you asked, to be sure." Laying my head on his chest, I found myself holding him close, hugging him back.

He began to run his hand down my hair, not unlike the way he had by the wheat field with the split-rail fence between us. But this felt different. It was gentle, and kind. "You are unlike any other woman I've ever met," he said softly.

"You must think I'm pathetic, crying like this. Really, I do not cry often."

"No, I think you're brave to tell me any of this," he said. "I've seen a woman give birth before. Any woman who faces childbirth without fear is a fool. Your fear only shows you are wise."

There was a knock at the door and he was gone, leaving me cold in his absence.

What was wrong with me? Did I crave a loving touch so much that I would take it from *him*? A man who thought of me as a silly little woman to be smacked and teased and pinched? I grimaced and shut my eyes. It wasn't that I craved a loving touch. I wanted *his* touch. I still wanted to hold him at this moment, even though I knew he only did it condescendingly.

"M'lord, the barman was wondering if yea'd like me to help yeh with anythin'?" said a ragged, hungry-looking boy.

"No. Tell your barman I thank him, and I thank you as well." Henry pulled a few coins from his coin purse, which hung from his belt. After handing them to the boy, he shut the door.

"Huh. So he does recognize me," he said. "I've been here before. I remember him."

"Should we leave?"

"No, I think we can trust him." Henry pushed his hair back from his face. "We'll just leave in the morning anyway. If that barman meant us harm, he probably would have done something already. Unless you *want* to leave now — "

"No, let's stay."

He nodded. "Good, because I'm honestly quite tired. I didn't sleep long by the river this morning."

"It's my fault you are so exhausted. I should thank you."

He laughed at me and shook his head. "Your company is thanks enough for me." Then, I watched as he pulled his belt off before I realized what he was doing. I turned my face away.

When I looked back, he was pulling the bedclothes back. I was thankful he still wore his leggings.

I nodded once to myself. Of course he'd get the bed — he'd paid for the room and my supper after all. I grabbed a pillow from the side of the bed and moved back toward the door where there was more room to lay down.

"You're going to sleep on the floor?"

I looked up at him. "It wouldn't be proper to sleep in the same bed together. You've had far less sleep than me. It's only fitting that you should have some comfort. I have no issue with sleeping on the floor."

"But... well, of course." He shook his head. "You are too good, Edith. Of course *I* shall sleep on the floor." He stepped toward me and tried to take the pillow from my hands but I held onto it. His eyebrows furrowed as he let go and met my gaze. He said slowly, "Did you notice that there is no way to bar the door?"

I hadn't considered this. I glanced toward the door. "It'll be fine. They have no reason to come in." I crouched down with my pillow and knelt on the floor. "Unless they're peeping toms." I felt heat radiate from my face and immediately regretted my joke.

He grinned at this. "Or they're after the king's brother," Henry said lightly. "Or there's already a summons from the archbishop to bring you back to Wilton and this pub has a do-gooder amongst the heathens."

"Yes, well…"

"Just come to the bed with me. I won't touch you. I want you close to me in case we need to leave quickly, alright? So I might protect you."

I glanced up at him. "It's not right."

"No one will know." His face remained blank as he gazed back at me.

"If no one will know, then it's unnecessary."

"No one will know unless it *is* necessary."

I looked at the door once more. "Fine. If you touch me though, God forgive you."

He rolled his eyes. "Thank you, Sister Edith."

"Right," I murmured to myself. Slowly, I stood and placed the pillow back on the bed. I turned my back to Henry. As I loosened the knot in the ties at the collar of my dress, I took a few deep breaths, trying to calm myself. I decided I would sleep in my dress with just the neck undone like it was already. Even though I was overwarm in this little room, I didn't think I could fall asleep in only my chemise with Henry in the same bed.

I blew out the candles on my side of the room.

When I turned to face him again, he was already tucked in, sitting up against the headboard, looking pointedly away from me. The warm glow of the few candles next to him made his dark hair glow a little too, as though it were streaked with fire embers. I couldn't help it when I glanced at his bare chest. He had the frame of a man who was compact and strong. Like a Scotsman. I looked away.

Pulling the covers back, I stepped up into bed. Sliding down, I turned onto my side with my back to him. He blew out the last candles and we were in total darkness.

He said in Latin, "Goodnight, my darling, my beautiful one." The bedclothes ruffled a little as he slid down further.

I said back in Latin, "Thank you for watching over me."

He laughed quietly and said in the usual Anglo-Norman English, "You're welcome." Light as a feather, his hand trailed down my arm. I knew I stiffened under his touch. He'd said he wasn't going to touch me. He was a liar.

I pretended to already be falling asleep. I was sure he knew I could not have yet, but he let me pretend anyway. He pulled his hand away from my arm.

Soon after, I heard Henry's breathing change to the unmistakable rhythm of sleep.

My headache was gone.

Rose-hued light peeked between the heavy drapes. It was too weak to be called morning yet.

My headrest, I realized, was Henry's arm. And my right leg was resting on something warm—his left leg. My right palm rested on a small tuft of chest hair over his heart. In my mind's eye, I saw myself roll over in my sleep and find him in the dark. A source of comfort.

Henry lay flat on his back, snoring slightly as he slept. His thick black hair fell over his forehead and ears, making him look young and easy while he slept. It was a shame he became so different when he was awake.

Gently, I tried to roll away. However, his arm under my neck reflexively curved around me, stopping my progress. My cheek pressed up against his chest as he held me. Immediately, I wondered if he was teasing me again and that he had actually woken too. But his breathing was still even and light and there was no hint of a smile on his lips. My stomach flipped — what if he woke with me here like this?

Gently, I unwound his arm from around my shoulders and slid sideways out of the bed. It was stiflingly hot in the room, so I tiptoed toward the window. Pushing the drapes apart a bit, I yanked the dusty canvas from the window frame. Dawn was only a strip of light over the rooftops of Basingstoke. The relief from the cooler early morning air was instantaneous. Kneeling, I closed my eyes as the morning breeze cooled my face.

Had I woken Henry? A quick glance over my shoulder — he was still asleep.

A wink of metal glinted at the foot of the bed. With only a slight rustle of the rushes, I crawled toward the glinting metal — it was a knife on a tray of food. It sat on a small table near the foot of the bed: as we slept, someone had come into our room. My hot skin went cold and clammy. I knew it was probably only the servant boy from last night who'd come in here. Even so, someone had seen me in the same bed as Henry.

Belatedly, I bent over the breakfast tray — the food was still warm. My hand moved to the knife on the tray and picked it up. As I turned it over in my hand, I watched the thin rosy beams of sunlight glint on the blade with each turn.

If I wanted, I could have left then without anyone trying to follow… at least until Henry woke. I glanced back at him. He was still sleeping peacefully.

But no. I couldn't make myself get up and leave. Not now. He'd saved my life over and over. He slept and let me sleep last night. He was kind to me. And, honestly, all I really wanted to do was crawl back into bed and stay as close to him as I could. How could I be so cruel to myself as to run from him?

And yet… what if he still wanted something from me that I wasn't willing to give? I slid the knife up my sleeve.

With sluggish hands, I tied the strings at my collar together, closing the neck of my dress. As I took a deep, calming breath, I came to Henry's side and sat down on the edge of the bed. Gently, I pushed his hair from his eyes with the tips of my fingers.

"Mmm…" Henry peered up at me through squinting eyes. I took a deep breath, ready to confess what I'd just been thinking. But I was distracted. Henry was beautiful, even if he was not the definition of handsome like King William. He took my wrist in his hand and pressed a kiss to it.

Pulling away, I turned my back to him. "Better get up. It's morning." I stood and pulled the curtain back the rest of the way. "We should be off."

He said softly, "How long have you been up?"

"Not long. There were some muffins and whey left here. Someone was in here while we slept. You were right." My gaze darted down to the breakfast tray and back to Henry.

"Yes," he said, "they did come in, but they didn't mean us any harm." He barked a short laugh. "The tray wasn't here when I woke in the middle of the night."

"You woke?"

"I always do. It was hard to fall back asleep. Usually…" When he sat up, his chest was left uncovered. I forced myself to look away. "Well, anyway, shall we have breakfast?"

"Oh. I usually wake in the middle of the night before it's time for Matins but I slept through last night." I couldn't stop myself from speaking too quickly. "Maybe because I'd bumped my head." I brought the tray to Henry and sat down with it between us on the bed. "I never eat breakfast. You should have this."

"We shouldn't waste it. Otherwise we shall make sinners of ourselves," he said lightly, raising his eyebrows as he lifted a cup of whey to me. "I want you to eat with me. Then we may travel for longer without needing to rest."

I took the cup from him. Together, we had a quiet little picnic there on the bed. Every bite I took seemed incredibly loud somehow. My eyes wouldn't stop glancing at his chest. I didn't eat much.

After breakfast, he dressed while I forced myself to look out the window and re-plait my hair. As we left the bedroom, he reached back and grabbed my hand. Squeezing it a little at first, it seemed as though he wanted to make sure I was actually there. My heart betrayed me by fluttering in hopeful surprise. I squeezed his hand back.

We made our way downstairs to find a few tired men nursing their pints. After we settled our tab in the ledger with the barmaid, Henry took my hand in his again and led me through the heavy wooden door.

CHAPTER 8: A DEATH IN THE CLEARING

The pub door swung shut behind us. In the forest clearing, four armed men stood waiting.

"Lord Henry," said one, straightening up from his lean against a tree. He held a loaded crossbow. "You are far from home, Count of Cotentin." The other three men held swords ready. By the look of the four men's clothes and lack of shoes, they were clearly poor.

Henry held my hand tighter. "You are behind the times," he said quickly. "I haven't been Count of Cotentin for about three years now."

"Fine. Doesn't matter."

"Truly," Henry said, bowing without looking down.

They glanced at each other. "Yes, well, your brother is still the wretched ruddy king," said one.

Henry laughed easily. "He is quite ruddy, isn't he?" Dropping my hand, he sidestepped so he stood in front of me. I could no longer see two of the swordsmen. "You know my full name, and yet I don't know one of yours."

"Not likely to find out, neither," said the crossbowman.

"Shall we be brief? You either want to kill me or extort money from me, correct? But the problem with the extortion part is I haven't much money on me, nor does the girl."

"So I suppose we'll just kill you," said the crossbowman, raising up his weapon and pointing it at Henry's chest.

"No. That will not do. My brother, the *king*, will kill all four of you and your families when he finds out what happened to me. And no one shall ever ask any further questions after you die." It was silent for too long. I pressed my palm to Henry's back. He said, "My brother is why you want to kill me in the first place, right?"

"No. Your father murdered my —"

"I pray you find some sort of peace but I cannot give it to you. I will never repay the sins of my father. It is not possible for any one man."

"Shut your mouth, you bastard's —"

"King William and I are on good terms at the moment. Guilty until proven otherwise is his way of going about things, just like my father before him. This cannot end well for you. The girl knows the king quite well. In fact, you are interrupting her journey to hold a private audience with our lord king. When she is queen, she shall remember your faces. If you still are not convinced you ought to leave me and the girl alone, note I am unarmed. It would be most dishonorable to kill a man who did not have the chance to defend himself."

The one with the crossbow laughed. "You want us to give you a weapon?" Then he lifted his chin to the two swordsmen who I couldn't see. "Tie them up. We'll take them to the Tower and have ransom."

"That is a grave mistake." Henry shook his head.

Slowly, a swordsman strolled closer, sheathed his sword at his hip, and began to slide a coiled rope down from his shoulder.

A weak gleam of steel in the morning sun was all the warning anyone had. I stumbled back as Henry suddenly lunged, swung his arm, and sliced the rope-man's chest — where did Henry get a sword? The rope-man's chest opened wide like a gutted animal, and a crescent of blood and organs dripped toward us as the man fell to the ground.

And Henry leaned close to me — was he going to attack me too? — no, he wanted to tell me something. But no sound escaped his lips. With blatant fear, he glanced past me. I crouched. A deafening church bell clanged in my ear. And another glint — like a fire poker pressed to my arm, I was cut — I bled fast, soaking my sleeve and dripping crimson onto my cheap blue dress. Had it been Henry or his opponent who had cut me?

A quick rustle of dead leaves on the forest floor. The other swordsman ran toward Henry's back. All I could see were white stars in a black night as I pushed myself up from the soil and moss. Wrenching my stolen knife from the sleeve of my uninjured arm, I readied myself to fight. An arrow pinged into the air and the swordsman fell at Henry's feet. The arrow pointed up from the back of the swordsman's neck.

It was strange to meet the crossbowman's gaze then. I laughed at him for accidentally killing his friend as I doubled over, holding my bleeding arm against my chest. Tears streamed from my eyes and I fell to my knees. As my vision went starry again, I drew long, shaky breaths.

Soon, I calmed. It was too quiet. Henry was still standing. With his sword still at the ready, he shifted his weight from foot to foot, clearly still ready to fight. But the swordsman who had been fighting Henry had already dropped his sword. The man stared at his gutted friend, and then at me. And turning his back to us, he ran away into the forest. The crossbowman already had run away, apparently.

As rain began to trickle down in the clearing in the front of the pub, Henry hurried toward me. I watched his face shift from one passion to another as he dropped his sword. Falling to his knees before me, he threaded his hands into my hair and pressed his lips hard against mine.

It was strange and soothing to be kissed like this. Anyway, I didn't have the strength to fight him. My arm was still bleeding fast, though I was trying to hold my wound closed as I pressed it as hard as I could against my middle.

"Henry," I said finally as he moved to kiss my neck, "I'm hurt."

"What?" He leaned back onto his heels. I watched his eyes go wide as he gazed down at the blood on my dress.

"Just a cut on my arm."

"I'll take you back to Brother Godric." He pulled the knife from my grip and absently dropped it to the ground.

"No, you can't." Though it was morning, I was exhausted. I whispered, "I beg you. I don't want to go back." I started falling forward where I knelt. But Henry caught me and held me steady. The sprinkling rain fell a little faster. Once he scooped me up into his arms, he stood and cradled me against his chest.

"But just to see Brother Godric?" He carried me quickly back toward the pub.

"No. Not to Brother Godric."

"Well, perhaps Wilton is too far away now, in any case."

"Is she dead?" came a woman's voice. The barmaid hurried to Henry as he carried me through the door.

"She's been wounded," he explained unnecessarily. He lay me down on a table, much to my embarrassment.

"I'll live. I just need some clean linen to bind it," I said quietly, gazing around and seeing the few bar patrons gawking at me. The barmaid took a dirty-looking threadbare blanket and tore a strip off of the end. I was trying to shake my head but I was so tired…

Gently, the barmaid wrapped the strip of blanket around my arm. "That'll do her. She'll be fine."

"For your kindness, maid." Henry pulled his coin bag from his belt and handed it to her.

"T-thank you."

"Henry…" I needed to tell him something but I forgot what it was.

"Everything will be fine." He kissed my forehead. My vision faded away before I lost consciousness.

In a daze, I woke some time later. The rain had slowed to a trickle—just enough to keep us soaked. It felt like a lot of time had passed but I had no way of knowing.

How far could we be from London now? I forced my eyes open, but then they drifted closed on their own again.

How long could Lilt run with such a burden? Or, was this a different horse?

"Henry," I managed to whisper. My arms and legs were heavy. These strong arms around me were Henry's, weren't they? I could smell leather and woods and plums. He held me as though my head belonged against his chest and no other place. Yes, I was still with Henry.

I wanted to tell him that perhaps he had been wrong. Perhaps everything would not be alright. But what use was it to tell him? He would know when I was dead. Eventually, anyway.

"Just a little while longer," he said in my ear. "Stay with me."

"I'm alright…"

Later, the drizzling stopped and Lilt managed to pick up speed. As we were traveling mostly uphill, Henry nuzzled me into his chest, trying in vain to warm me by rubbing his hand up and down my back.

Through my lashes, I saw we were in a misty twilit fog and trees canopied overhead. Henry whispered, "Thank God. Finally it's Reading."

A while later, I heard a babbling river. Lilt slowed as Henry coaxed her uphill. And then, finally, we stopped.

"Constantine!" Even though I could still feel his body against mine, Henry's loud voice sounded far away. Lilt stomped and I heard birds take flight. It was quiet again. Henry slid down from the horse's back and pulled me down with him. Though he stumbled, he didn't drop me.

"Henry…" I wanted to tell him I would walk but I was too tired to say anything else. I couldn't force my eyes to open.

With Lilt's reins in the hand under my legs, Henry tried the latch at the gate. He sighed and then the gate loudly creaked open. As he walked through, he tucked my head against the base of his neck. I tried to wrap my arms around him but it was as though I had ragdoll's arms.

I shivered violently. Where was I? Rain rapped against glass. I lay in a soft, cool bed.

A fire crackled. I was warm and comfortable.

"It wasn't planned," came Henry's voice, as though in a dream. "She was badly cut and I didn't know where else to go."

"You aren't travelling with any men? Not even Sir Robert Achard?" a second voice said, his voice growling and low.

"No. She and I… sort of ran off together, you might say —
I needed to assure her safety as she travelled — she is going
to be my wife now."

"She's your wife? But our lord king? Doesn't he —"

"Upon her name and character, she is my wife," Henry
said in a hard voice. "Our lord king will understand. He will
give his blessing, surely. "

CHAPTER 9: THE COTTAGE IN READING

I woke to the smell of pork stewing. It was dusk — or maybe dawn? — outside the window over the head of the bed. I watched tiny streams of rain outside snake their way down the windowpanes. My mind strained to remember what had happened. I was stomping away from the abbey through soft mud in old boots again…

Henry had fought some strangers. Lying on the pub table… he lifted me… Lilt had brought me here up a steep hill… I had dreamt that Henry called me his wife and gave me watered wine to drink.

As I pushed myself upright, the covers fell down from my chest and I felt a chill — I was naked. Henry — or someone else? — had taken my boots, dress, and chemise off of me. Glancing over at the wooden chairs before the hearth, I spied my clothes laid out before the fireplace. I shuddered when I realized Henry, in all likelihood, saw me completely naked for any extended period of time. Clutching the blankets over my chest, I cringed as the feeling of invasion consumed me. I was reluctant to get up even to dress myself.

I remembered shivering. We had ridden in rain. He wouldn't have left me in wet clothing. He had only been trying to help me again.

"Ouch!" As I clutched my blankets, pain shot up my right arm like fire in my veins, all the way up to my shoulder. I sucked air in through my teeth and cradled my arm against my chest. Thin gauzy linen was wrapped around my right forearm. I unwrapped it. The stitches were so uneven that my flesh gaped as though my forearm was growing a few extra mouths. What a wretch this would be to fix.

I wrapped the linen back around my arm, frustrated. Well, at least I hadn't bled to death.

My other arm had a long, shallow cut. I was confused by this, but then remembered my stolen knife. I must have cut myself when I pulled it out of my sleeve.

I looked around. To my left, a pot hung from a rod over a crackling fire. Facing this fireplace, a couple of high-backed cushioned chairs held my drying clothes. In the center of the room, a scrubbed wooden dining table had a few wooden stools tucked around it. Across the room, two doors stood at a right angle. One was clearly a door to outside, as it was barred. There was another doorframe to the right of my bed, but I couldn't see into that room from here. From within, two men spoke quietly. Though I couldn't make out what they said, I recognized one as Henry's voice.

I forced myself out of bed, hurried over to the fireplace, and slipped my chemise on. It was cozily warm and dry, thankfully. At least I was covered now. My dress though… grabbing a fistful of dirty, blue skirt, I knew it was still sodden.

From within the other room, Henry sounded like he was trying not to laugh. But the responding gravelly voice had a concerned twinge to it.

"Right, Lord Henry, good to see you again. I'll see you again tomorrow," said the stranger. And the man came through the doorway into the larger room which I had found myself in. There was no time to cover up with more clothes, so I ducked behind one of the chairs and hid. "Ah, I think she's escaped," the man growled, but then he chuckled. I heard Henry's quick steps into the room. He stopped and laughed a little too.

"A modest wife. Well, that's good then," said the stranger.

Wife? Had I gotten married while I was asleep?

I peeked up over the top of the high-backed chair and saw a short, portly man. I forced myself to smile at him. Stepping out from behind the chair, I stood up straight.

When he smiled back, I was greeted with a large space between his two front teeth. He averted his gaze from me. I knew my chemise was somewhat see-through, which was why I had hidden in the first place. However, I wouldn't allow any man to laugh at me as though I were some silly little girl.

Drawing a cloak around himself, the man covered his shiny head with a physician's cap. "Beautiful to boot," he rasped to Henry.

"You stitched my arm," I accused.

"Thank you again, sir," Henry said quickly, glancing to me. "If there's any way I might repay you, only say the word."

"Well, that won't be necessary, my lord," the old man said. "You just be good. Don't do anything I wouldn't do. Or maybe I should say, don't do anything your dear mother, God rest her, wouldn't have done." He pinched Henry's cheek, forcing Henry to bend over a little. His wheezy laugh died away as Henry barred the door behind him.

"How long have I been asleep?" I asked.

Slowly, Henry walked toward me. "All day, all night, and most of today. It's impressive. I tried to make you drink, and managed to get some watered wine down, but not much.

You were quite tired... Are you hungry?" His gaze flitted quickly over my chemise.

He was not wearing much either: only a threadbare cambric and a pair of long braies.

"Yes, very." I crossed my arms over my chest. "And thirsty." In the back of my mind, as I had bled so much, I knew it was a bad sign that I did not need to use a chamber pot right now. But there was no point in telling him this. I simply would be sure to drink as much as I could.

Pulling his gaze from me, he strode to the chest under the window nearby and drew a blanket out. As he wrapped the blanket around me as though it were a shawl, he smiled. "That's better." Hastily, he took a step back. Then, taking my hand in his, he led me to the room he'd been talking to the physician in.

On the southern and western sides of this room, the walls each had multiple glass-paned windows. This room must have cost a fortune.

By our low candlelight in here, I could see dark forest outside and tiny rivers of rain trailing down the panes of glass. Herbs and vegetables grew in raised gardens along each of these glass-windowed walls. Brother Godric would have been impressed.

There was some bread on the workbench sliced into thick wedges. I reached out and touched it. "Did you bake this?" I asked, glancing up at Henry. Henry's bread was different than the sort I was used to having at the abbey.

"Yes."

"Right." I recalled how he had been travelling without anyone to serve him—he'd only had his teachers. I wanted to keep holding the lovely, warm, golden fluffiness but I forced myself to pull my hand away.

"I've made pottage."

The scent of pork was unmistakable though I had hardly ever smelled it. The nuns never ate anything with four feet and only rarely ate poultry or other fowl. I tried to hide my excitement as he led the way back into the larger room.

He brought the board of bread to the table. After he ladled two bowls of stew from the pot over the fire, he brought them to the wooden table too. As I sat down, he poured a goblet of wine for himself and a goblet of water mixed with a little wine for me.

"I'm not allowed wine?"

"Oh, forgive me," he said, raising his eyebrows. "I assumed —"

I immediately felt bad for trying to tease him while he was being serious for once. "No, you're right," I said. "I should drink water first. Thank you."

He picked up his spoon and started eating. I had figured he wouldn't pray in the pub before we ate there, but I was surprised he didn't pray now. Didn't everyone pray before they ate?

"Everything alright?" Henry asked when I had stared for too long.

"Yes," I said, half-smiling. I picked up my spoon.

"Oh, right," Henry said, standing. I did too and Henry recited a prayer aloud.

"Thanks. Routine, I suppose."

We both sat down again. "It's alright. I always had to pray when I ate with my mother. I just… got *out* of the routine, I suppose." He half-smiled at me and I tried to smile back.

The broth of the stew was so good, I picked up the bowl and drank. When I set it down again, Henry was watching me.

"Forgive me." I felt my cheeks warm.

He smiled at me. "Would you like more?"

I nodded. Henry stood and ladled more into my bowl.

"Who was that man?" I asked. I was nearly finished with my goblet of watered wine already.

"The retired physician, Sir Constantine. An old friend of my father's. He lives on this land in a cabin not far from this one as groundskeeper. William — lord king — technically owns this land now, though it truly ought to be mine."

I was surprised. Did he mean that the king ought to give him lands purely because he was the king's brother?

"Anyway," said Henry, "if you follow the river down, you'll soon find an unfinished castle."

"He seems like a kindly sort of fellow — Sir Constantine."

"Mm. That he is." It was quiet while Henry took a bite of his bread which he'd soaked in his stew. Once his mouth was empty again, he said, "When I was just a boy, my father would go on hunting trips here. I was the only one of his children he'd invite to join him." He paused to take a long drink of wine. "This land, and some other bits of land, were actually my mother's, left to her by her parents. When my father died, I suppose he remembered he and I would go hunt together here because he left me all her lands."

"So King William took your land from you?" was all I could think to say.

"Yes. I do love it here. Reading has always felt like my home away from home."

"I wish I had a place like that," I said. "Nowhere has ever felt like home to me except for Dunfermline."

"I wish you had a place like that too." It was quiet for a moment until he said, "I let Sir Constantine believe that you and I are married."

"Oh."

"And I told him your name is 'Matilda.' I didn't want to tell him your name was 'Edith' in case he'd heard from anyone who might be looking for you."

"Matilda? Like your mother?"

"It was the first name that came to my mind. He didn't seem to think it was odd that it was my mother's name."

"Did you know 'Matilda' is my second name, actually? After your mother. So you didn't completely lie."

"Ah. Well, good. I think 'Matilda' suits you better than 'Edith.' May I call you that from now on?"

"I suppose so. Just don't let my father hear you." I shrugged and smiled.

Henry laughed. "I didn't have the heart to tell Sir Constantine everything of what really happened or why I'm with you. And I had no idea how to stitch up your arm. When you said you didn't want to go back to Brother Godric, I decided to take you here as this was the closer option anyway. Sir Constantine is a trustworthy second choice."

I stared down at my trencher. It was fluffier than any bread I'd ever had. I wondered if this was the way people in Normandy baked or if it was just Henry. "You saved my life, Henry," I said. "I am forever indebted to you."

He smiled kindly. "I would gladly save you again tomorrow, and any day after, if ever you needed me."

I poured myself a glass of wine.

CHAPTER 10: BY THE FIRESIDE

As my third helping of undiluted wine warmed my belly, I hummed a lullaby as I strolled over to the dying fire. Embers floated up in little waves as I stoked it.

"If you were a commoner, no one would want to kill you," I said. "And if I were a commoner, no one would care if I were a nun or not. We could live here, a man and his little wife," I giggled. "We wouldn't even need a blessing from a priest. No one would care." Stumbling a little, I poured myself a fourth goblet of wine. "And then I'd stay here and live in your house while you go fight battles for a king who you don't know." After a long moment of silence, I prodded the fire once more.

"Not quite. If I were a commoner, I would work the land for the knight who owned the land and *he* would go to battle. You need to know these things if you are to be queen, love."

I giggled. "Oh, right. Even better."

"Have you come up with a plan yet in case the king refuses you? You *could* stay here," Henry said it evenly, as though this must be what bothered me.

"Oh, who cares?! Aunt Christina…. Alan… William… one of them will surely have me back." I waved the poker in front of me like it was my sword.

"You're on a first name basis with my brother?"

"No, William de Warenne. Though honestly, I doubt our lord king would care if I called him only by 'William.' He does like me, you know."

"William de Warenne? As in—do you mean the Earl of Surrey?" Henry asked, scrunching his nose. "That's quite random."

"He proposed marriage to me but I turned the churl down. Forgive me, the, err, *Earl*…" I made a snooty face and twirled my poker as I bowed.

Henry laughed. "You should keep away from wine once you are queen, for your own sake."

"*Queen. Quueeeeen.* Such a silly word." I met Henry's eyes. "What does that face mean?"

"You are drunk as an ape off of three glasses of wine."

I gulped down the rest of the wine in my goblet. "Four," I said, holding up the empty goblet. "Perhaps I bled too much. Anyway, we don't all grow up with bottles of wine surrounding us. Wine isn't wise for a hospitaller's apprentice. The abbey never closes, after all. Watered ale? All the time. Expensive *wine*, though—"

"But surely you've had more than three or four helpings at a time before? What else is there to drink?"

"Cow's milk. Goat's milk," I said, my voice dipping and rising.

"I haven't had milk since I was a little boy."

"Well, it's delicious. Maybe you'd fatten up a little if you did."

"I think I'm quite large enough."

"You may be brawny, but you have hardly enough fat to pinch. You forget I saw you naked before." I laughed loudly though part of my mind wished I would shut up.

"Hm, *you're* one to speak of fatness." He stood up and stepped toward me.

"What do you mean?"

"Right." He picked me up with one arm and hugged me against his chest. I held my breath as he swung me like a pendulum a couple of times. Looking up at the corners of his eyes, as though deep in thought, he said, "Yes. You're far thinner than I am. You ought to know, hospitaller's apprentice, wine makes you far fatter than milk. Just look at my dear father, God rest his soul."

"What do you mean?" We were nose to nose.

"He invented the wine diet." He set me down on my feet again, and I held his hand as I dropped myself down onto the rug. Henry sat down next to me.

As he gazed at the fire, I watched him. I must have stared too long because he eventually glanced over at me but I looked away. That's when I happened to see my wound dressing. Without making a decision to do so, I started to unwrap the linen.

"What?" I asked, because I knew he was still looking at me—I could feel it. Glancing up again, I watched as Henry opened his mouth to speak, but I decided I didn't want to hear what he had to say. "That bag there. It looks like a physician's bag. I want to fix this," I said, nodding to my arm.

"I don't think that's such a good idea in your condition."

"Would you rather me be completely sober when I re-stitch it?"

"I... I don't know..."

"Well, I don't have any poppy milk." I was alarmed to find, when I tugged gently on one of the stitches, it just fell out of my arm. I could feel my wound literally pulling apart at the seam. The wine churned in my stomach.

Seeing this, Henry stood and brought Sir Constantine's bag to me.

"Thanks," I said. I started laying everything out that I would need. "Do you have any ale?"

"Perhaps?" Henry went into the gardened room and soon came back with a jug of ale and set it next to me.

"Good," I said. Once I heated the needle in the fire — Brother Godric was adamant about this step — I pulled the rest of my stitches out.

Upon closer inspection of my now-open wound, I saw a hardened glob of congealed blood in the wound bed. I had expected to see this. However, I hadn't expected to see angry tissue and gloppy yellow pus along the edges. Brother Godric would have been furious.

"You might want to look away," I whispered.

"I'll be fine."

"I don't want you vomiting into my wound. Look away, Henry." He did as I told him. Quickly, I scraped out the clot in my wound bed. It was like my arm had been sliced open by a blunt knife all over again.

"Huh," I said, re-swallowing my wine that had bubbled into my throat. "That wasn't as bad as I thought it would be. You may look again." He met my gaze before I looked down at my gushing wound. "Hold my arm steady for me."

Henry gently held my arm, streaking his hands in the wound's fresh ooze of blood.

Holding my breath, I doused my arm with ale. "God Almighty!" It burned as hot as the fire crackling next to us. In a way, I enjoyed the feeling because this would get rid of the festering "vapours," as Brother Godric called them.

"Edith," Henry said quietly, "pray, tell me what to do."

I hadn't realized I was making a face. "I thought my name was 'Matilda' now?" When Henry didn't laugh for once, I took a deep breath. "I'm fine." Once the burning subsided a bit, I dabbed some ointment into the wound bed. It smelled like an ointment Brother Godric had taught me to make—of calendula and honey—so I felt it would be safe.

I was ready to begin re-stitching my arm. Wordlessly, I guided Henry's hand to work as a second hand for myself. I was satisfied—he caught on without any explanation.

"We should play a game," I said after we sewed the first stitch. It was strange to stitch my own arm and, even with four goblets of wine, it was excruciating. I needed something to take my mind off of the pain.

"Alright," he said, his eyebrows furrowing. "What game do you want to play?"

"Let's play 'Two True, One False.'" I'd played it with Mary and Sister Agnes many times before. Two stitches in.

"That's the one where you say three things…"

"And only one of them is false, and the other person has to guess which it is."

"Alright."

"Okay, you go first," I said. Three stitches.

"Hmm. I have never been knighted. I am named after my uncle. And my brother Robert once threw me in jail."

"Well… when I was a little girl before I left Scotland, I remember your sisters visiting and telling us your father had knighted you. It was big news for us girls."

"Truly?"

"Mm. Of course. I remember imagining you in heavy armor and fighting in battle."

"So you thought me handsome even when you were a small girl?" Henry laughed.

I smirked. "And I knew you were named for your uncle, too. So, should I ask why my dear godfather threw you in jail?"

"Well, really my greedy uncle, Bishop Odo, did it," he said, shaking his head. "I gave Robert over half of my inheritance because he wanted to fight King William and try to win England from him. In exchange for the money I gave Robert, he gave me some land and the title of Count of Cotentin in western Normandy. After we made our deal, I went to England to try to get my mother's lands back which King William had stolen from me, but he wouldn't give them back, of course. When I came back to Normandy, Robert was convinced that King William and I were conspiring against him. So Robert kept my money and took the land and title back and threw me in jail."

"That's just base thievery."

"Can you see why I hate my brothers?" He laughed. "Luckily everyone in Normandy likes me more than Robert — other than Odo, the ass — so my men persuaded Robert to let me out."

He just admitted that he hated King William? He must have had too much wine too. I decided to pretend to forget he said it. "I am appalled on your behalf."

"Yes, well, I'm still rich even with less than half of my inheritance left. And I'll get my mother's lands back. Just give me a bit more time."

I wondered how much money he'd had, but even as drunk as I was, I knew it wasn't polite to ask. "Well," I said, "now it's my turn. My favorite food is venison. I enjoy singing even though I sound bad when I do. I don't know how to be friends with girls."

"Easy, your favorite food isn't venison. It's lampreys, just like me." Five stitches.

"Ha. That trout we had by the stream, at least, was pretty good. I don't know about the lamprey though."

"I like the sound of your voice when you sing."

"When have you heard me sing?" He was close enough I could smell the wine on his breath and the woodsy smell of him. I breathed deeply in.

"You were humming while you were attempting to stoke the fire." Six stitches.

"Attempting? I stoked it. I am an excellent fire stoker."

"So what's your real favorite food?"

"Hmm... honeyed roasted almonds. What about you? Surely your favorite can't really be lampreys?"

"Well besides lampreys, it'd have to be goose liver pâté. We have it on Christmas every year. It's delicious."

"I've never had it." We finished the seventh and final stitch. "Your turn again," I said quietly.

"Right. I once threw a man from the top of a building in a fit of rage to the cheers of a crowd." His hands tremored a little as he wrapped my arm up with a fresh strip of linen. "I once dumped a chamber pot on my brother's head. And my first thought this morning concerned my desire to better serve God and country."

"You wouldn't push a man from a building." As I said this though, I thought of how he'd fought the men outside the pub. He'd definitely killed one of the men. But it had been to defend himself, and me. Not rage.

His touch was as soft as butterfly wings as he finished wrapping my arm. "That one is true." He tucked the end into the edge of the dressing.

"Oh." I met his gaze accidentally before looking back down to my arm.

"Though maybe I shouldn't have mentioned that. I'm not proud of it."

"Um."

"Guess again."

"Your first thought wasn't about serving God and country."

"Right—"

"Who did you kill?" I glanced at him from the corner of my eye.

"This poor man who just got too big for his braies. In Normandy, of course. I think about him often… Truly, he was only a boy."

"That's terrible."

"I shouldn't have said anything about it. Must have been the wine."

"I will pray for his soul."

He squinted at me before looking away. "Mm. Alright."

We were quiet, neither looking at the other. Standing up, I threw the old bandage into the fire and poked the logs again. Henry stood too and gently took the poker from me. He stoked the fire too, but the fire became larger somehow when he did it. I was annoyed by this. I was perfectly capable of stoking a fire, it just took me a moment.

"How did you know the chamber pot one was true?" he asked. "Pretty gross, don't you think?"

"You like to laugh." I shrugged. "Which brother was it? That got the chamber pot on his head?"

"Robert."

"Was there a reason?"

"No. William and I thought it'd be funny to dump a chamber pot on Robert one day. Apparently dropping such a thing not only makes a mess, but it also hurts when you drop it from a balcony to the floor below."

"Oh, no!"

"Yes. And Robert came up to us covered in, well…" He smiled as though he were recalling a fair summer day. "William tells everyone he is weak because of his arm injury he sustained in battle. The truth is, our lord king has been a weakling from his infancy. So Robert went after me instead. Naturally, I hit him back. Neither of us were willing to stop... Eventually, Father had to break us up. It was pretty embarrassing for everyone involved, all said. Father came to my aid because I was a child. Robert was a young man already by then."

I grimaced and looked up at him. "To think the future king of England once dumped a chamber pot on the future duke of Normandy's head."

"Right," Henry said, laughing with me. "And Robert started a war against my father as a result."

"Wait, what?"

"Yes. Your godfather is a complete idiot, I am regretful to say. It is a blessing he did not inherit the crown. William may be heartless, but he's not stupid."

"King William is kind. He's quite a gentle man, I think."

Henry shook his head. "I know him better."

"I've gotten some blood on me." I held my hands up to show him. "Might I wash it off?"

"Yes." Henry led me to the wash basin in the closet by the front door. "Do you think less of me after that story?" he asked. He stood in the doorway as I poured water from a pitcher into in a basin.

"No," I said, "but I am unhappy you don't get along with your brothers."

He frowned. "So am I."

"Well, anyway, what about the false thing?" I wanted to change the subject in hope he would smile again. "What was your real first thought this morning?"

"My first thought was worry over you. In truth, you have been in my every thought since first seeing you in the hospitaller's chambers."

"Oh." I set the pitcher down next to the basin. I forced a smile to my face. "Forgive me for troubling your thoughts. I am grateful for your help." I bowed my head to him.

He smiled. "I enjoy thinking about you."

"But perhaps you should save your thoughts for a more worthy subject?" I laughed as I stared at my basin of water.

"More worthy than the future queen of England?"

"Ah, what if our lord king heard you say that?" I grimaced as I glanced at him. "I fear I have been presumptuous."

"You no longer believe you are called to be William's queen?"

Slowly, I pushed my fingertips under the surface of the basin's water and moved my hands around, blooming flowers of blood. "If there was one thing I learned from Brother Godric, one may work so hard, but we all die." I turned my hands over. "Young children die, eyes wide, and the tiny babies, after living in this world for only a moment, leave it again." I looked up at him and saw he was staring steadily back at me. "There is no such thing as a calling from God. Or, perhaps it is only God's Will that we all shall die, and nothing more." I looked back down at my hands because he was staring so intently at me. "If I'm blasphemous, so be it. No one is destined for anything other than the grave."

Henry took a quick breath. "No. You are destined by God to be queen. Of that I am certain. Your dream when I saved you from drowning — that was a sign."

"Perhaps dreams are nothing more than dreams."

Stepping toward me, Henry grazed his fingertips over the backs of my hands. Blood lifted from his hands too. "I hold no claim over you," he said, gazing down. He curled his fingers lightly around my palms. Our hands floated and danced together. "I'll take you to my brother if that is still your intention. Or Scotland, or even Jerusalem."

Bravely, I turned my hands over so my palms pressed against his. His thumbs grazed down the insides of my wrists.

"But a woman can't live alone safely," he continued softly as he kept his gaze down on our hands. "I'd like to... I'd like to—if William won't marry you..."

Finally he looked over at my face. All I could see were his eyes looking back into mine.

The water in the basin swished and spilled a bit as he pulled his hands from mine. Turning from me, he strode back into the larger room.

My heart had been in my throat and now it was in my stomach. Why did he walk away? I immediately followed him. When I faced him again, his gaze raked over me.

I asked, "Why shouldn't King William marry me?"

"I won't deny it—I do not wish for you to marry William. However, I confess I know of no other bride he has seriously considered other than you."

My drunkenness felt like it had worn off already, but I knew it could not have. I crossed my arms over my chest, pulling the blanket tighter around my shoulders as I did. "You believe I should not be queen."

"No. I think you would be an excellent queen. An equal to my own mother." He turned and stoked the fire again, seemingly just for something to do. "You must be smart to have helped Brother Godric so much. From the stories I've heard about you tending to those in need of the hospitaller's help, you are really quite kind. And, I think you know this already, but you are beautiful." I watched him turn the poker over in his hand.

He thought I was beautiful? "I think you had too much wine, like me." I tried to smile.

He ignored my joke. "Most of all though, the vision you had by the river. I had the same sort of vision not long ago — an angel in a dream told me to go to England and there I would find my bride with raven hair and eyes like sapphire jewels. She would be my queen and my wife."

Was he serious? Did he mean he thought it was God's Will that he, *Henry*, would become king and I would become his queen? If Henry were to become king, where did that leave King William?

"Have I frightened you?"

"Not frightened. Never. You could never frighten me."

His shoulders tensed. "But you hate me for the way I treated you."

"No. I... I did not appreciate your uncourtly behavior. I feared you teased me with your every word. I still do."

"I see." He swallowed hard and shook his head. "Well. You should rest. I'll sleep here by the fire again tonight. Can't quite get the whole hovel-in-the-woods experience without sleeping on the rushes, after all." He was looking past me.

I nodded. For once, I was sure he wasn't mocking me, and yet I still felt bothered by him. Pacing to the closer side of the bed, I pulled the covers back. After I slid down under the bedclothes, I turned away from the fire and shut my eyes.

"Goodnight, Matilda."

"Goodnight, Henry." I had already forgotten he was going to call me by my second name from now on. It felt dishonest.

I heard him pace across the room and then the door creaked open. The pattering rain outside was loud in the small cabin before the door creaked shut again. Suddenly, the air was too still around me in the ensuing silence. Where was he going?

No matter what I learned about him, I felt I would never learn quite enough. As though there was something so elusive that, once I found it out, I would finally understand him.

CHAPTER 11: UNDER THE YEW TREE

"Did you have a bad dream?" Henry sat in a chair before the fireplace, which no longer had a fire.

"How — ?" The sun beamed through the window over my bed, forcing me to squint as I sat up.

"You were moaning 'no' in your sleep."

"I dreamt of an apricot tarte on a warm spring morning under a blooming willow tree."

"I see." He laughed as he finished pulling his second boot on. "Have I not been feeding you enough?"

"Yes, pork with wine for supper? Undeniably paltry."

"Forgive me. I shall have a word with the cook."

He watched as I pushed myself from the bed and walked closer to him. "I should tell you, that wasn't the whole dream. After I ate the tarte, I knelt down in a homespun and my Aunt Christina tonsured me as a nun." I watched as the smile faded from his face as I came closer. "I was supposed to become a nun and leave for Jerusalem this week. That's what I was running from." Once I reached the arm of his chair, it struck me as strange how he had to look up at me for once.

But then he stood and I was looking up at him like usual. "Were you tonsured? Had you made any vows?"

"Not yet."

"Oh." Henry said, crossing his arms as his gaze flittered over my chemise. "You know, not even the king could marry you if you'd done anything to promise yourself."

I crossed my arms too. "But even with no promise, I have an uneasiness in my heart. Have I gone against the Will of God? What if God needed me to go to Jerusalem? And now—"

"That's all nonsense. You said so yourself only last night. You can't guess what God wants. It's impossible." He pulled me into his arms—did he know I was about to cry?

"If you think that, then why did you say you believed I was destined to be queen?"

"Well," he said, "God chose to have you be born of a king and queen. It's an excellent presumption."

"I beg you…" I shook my head. "Let me leave you." I tried to keep my voice steady as I pulled away from him. "I must go. Today. I should travel to the Holy Land. It is my duty. Perhaps I am not too late to save myself."

"Calm down," he said. "I will take you to London. You may write to your father and wait there for your answer in comfort. You must answer to your parents first before you travel to Jerusalem. That is what a good daughter would do." Henry glanced back over his shoulder and then to me again. "I'll go and tell Constantine, alright? We'll leave now if you feel up to it." He kissed my forehead.

"But my father will be infuriated that I have jilted Alan."

"So be it." Henry pushed the hair from my face. "It is one of the Commandments that you must honor your mother and father. If it is not your father's wish for you to go to Jerusalem, how could it be God's?"

I shook my head. I hadn't thought of it this way. Henry gave me a smile and then he left the cottage.

As we rode, my legs immediately felt sore again. I pressed myself against Henry and he didn't hesitate to hold me tighter.

"Are you tired?" he asked in my ear as we rode. "You lost a lot of blood."

I nodded.

"It shouldn't take long for us to reach Windsor. We'll stop there for the night."

A deep red line traced the horizon over the tree tops around us. On the top of the hill in the distance, we could see a tall rounded structure amidst many other shorter squared buildings. "Windsor Castle," Henry whispered in my ear. "One of the many things my father never finished."

As Lilt trotted toward a thin, trickling stream, Henry hoisted himself off of the horse's back. "Let's eat here and then we'll head up to the castle for a bed later tonight. It'll be easier to hide you if less people awake."

"Alright." I was nauseous and achy from riding, and my injured arm tingled strangely, so I didn't argue against the likelihood of being thought his mistress.

Henry led Lilt to a nearby tree and secured her reins to a low-hanging branch before helping me down. Then, he sat down next to me in the grass and we had a supper of nuts, cheese and wine. Another gift from Constantine.

As Lilt continued grazing the weeds, I packed up the things left from eating. Soon, Henry stopped me by pulling me onto his lap. Sliding his palm against mine, he pressed a kiss to my knuckles.

"Henry," I said quietly.

"Hm?" He pecked a kiss to my neck.

"You shouldn't do this."

"Forgive me," Henry said, straightening and letting my hand go.

I shook my head as I let my hand fall to his chest. "I meant only that you don't have to pretend with me. With courtliness and all that fadoodling. I don't want your affection out of pity. Truly, I think I would rather you were honest." I watched his brow furrow.

He said nothing for a moment as he stared back at me. He lifted one of my plaits and pushed it behind my shoulder. "What if I *am* being honest?"

"Well…" Was this man falling in love with me? It didn't seem possible. "You decided you would play with the girl that your brother found pretty. Perhaps you kept me alive only because your brother and my father would have had your head if you had let me die." I forced myself to keep looking back at him. I didn't mean to count the flecks in his eyes, but there were eleven. "I didn't want your pretending when you were a stranger, but now that I know you, I want it even less."

"I have never been more honest in my life. I have not pretended with you." He gently cupped his hand over mine where it rested on his chest. And lifting it, he kissed my knuckles again. "My only pretending was with Constantine when I told him you were my wife, and it was only for the protection of your character—a lie that truly brought me selfish contentment. It would give me pure happiness if that lie had been true. And as for your father or my brother—I hope they assume we are in love and I have had you already just so I might keep you."

"Keep me?" I laughed as I imagined I was small enough to fit in his hand.

He grazed his nose against mine. "I have never seen a more beautiful sight than the rare vision of your smiling face."

"Don't say that." I tried to rest my head on his chest but gently, he lifted my chin again. His other hand pressed confidently into the small of my back as though he wanted me to melt into his own body, and he kissed me.

As he trailed kisses down my jaw to my neck, I shivered despite the warm summer evening. Without thinking of what I was doing, I ran my hands over the knots of muscle in his back and found his lips with my own. My heart hammered hard in my chest. When he pushed my skirts up my legs, his hand against my thigh made my breath catch in my throat.

Suddenly, I felt as though I was being watched. I glanced around. But no. Instead, I saw only a tree where I'd thought a person had been standing. It was a fat old yew, with huge wild branches fanning out in every direction.

"Wait," I whispered. I wasn't ready for this.

"What is it? Are you alright?"

"God hasn't blessed us," I pushed his hand from my thigh.

"God can't see us from here. The trees are in the way." Henry smiled at me and kissed my cheek.

"But Henry," I said, unsure what I wanted to say. I pushed my skirts down as I moved from his lap. "You're not my husband. You'll never be my husband."

He ran his hand over his hair. "I'm glad you stopped me. You're a good woman. Forgive me."

I glanced up at the yew tree once more, which towered over us. I shivered again. "I beg you forgive me," I said softly.

"Are you cold?" Henry asked. Glancing away from the tree and back to him, I thought he looked angry at first. But when he met my gaze again, I knew he was only unhappy.

"I'm fine. I'm just…" I stared out at the river as my eyes unfocused slightly. I wished I could go hide in a warm bed somewhere and sleep for a hundred years. I was tired of trying to figure out what to do with my life. It seemed like whatever I did today, tomorrow, and the day after, would affect the whole world forever. I knew this wasn't the case, but it definitely felt this way.

Henry said, "I have fallen in love with you." He didn't say anything else, and he tried to smile as the silence stretched between us. I frowned as I gazed from his eyes to his sunken cheeks under his cheekbones, and to the stubble covering them and his jaw. "I have never felt this way about anyone," he said. "I have known enough women. God knows. There will never be a woman for me who is more perfect than you are. I want you to be mine. Forever."

"Henry…" I shook my head. Whatever I did, I logically knew I couldn't marry Henry. I was made for greater things, or so I had always been told. Mammy, Father, Sister Agnes, Brother Godric, even Aunt Christina. They had always set me apart. Aunt Christina wanted me to be an abbess. Mammy wanted me to be a queen. Father wanted me to marry for as much money and political advantage as physically possible.

So why did my heart want nothing other than this man who sat next to me by the river? "Yes, Henry." I ran my fingers down his jaw as it worried. "Shall I be your wife? Your paramour? Your servant? I am yours. Forever."

"What?" Though he still didn't smile, his eyes brightened as he looked at me.

"I will not go to the king. I don't want to be queen if it means I can't stay with you." I looked to the river again. I couldn't look at Henry. If he said no, that I had to be queen, or a nun, or go back to my parents, I would do as he said. "I give myself up to you. I don't want to go anywhere except where I already am—at your side. You have saved me from drowning, bleeding, the forest, my parents and aunt and Alan, from a life wherein I am dead in my heart. You have saved me from God Himself." Finally, I forced myself to look at him again. "If I cannot trust you, whom may I trust in the world?"

He looked as though I had slapped him. "No, don't say such things," he said. "You don't mean it. You have not been saved *from* God, you have been saved *by* God. Why else would you be born as you were? You shall be queen one day, I am sure of it."

I shook my head. "You contradict yourself." I knew it. He would tell me to do something else other than love him.

We were both quiet as Henry took my hand in his again. Mustering my courage, I took his hand in both of mine and I kissed it. And cupping my jaw, he pulled me into another kiss. Though I was angry at him for being confusing, I let him kiss me.

Touching his forehead to mine, he said, "I do not contradict myself because I know I shall be king one day. You shall be queen as my wife."

"It is treasonous to say," I breathed. "Do you pray for your brother's death? I cannot hear it."

"I cannot change the Will of God just as I cannot change the fact I was born as William's brother."

"I can barely think. I thought you didn't believe in the Will of God?"

"Be my wife," he whispered against my lips. "I beg you, my love." He held both of my hands in his. I watched as he kissed the backs of my hands. "Will you marry me?"

"I still wonder if you are doing all of this only for my sake and not at all for your own."

"I could never be so selfless."

I laughed and pecked a kiss to his lips. And then another...

"Yes?" he asked, pulling away slightly.

"Yes," I whispered. "Let us get our blessing from the Church."

He pushed my hair away from my face and kissed me. Was I sure? Yes, I had to be sure now. I'd already given my word. Why did I have this twinge of uncertainty in my heart, despite my happiness?

I thought aloud, "I doubt my father will give us his blessing to marry."

"Not right away. I will need to prove my worthiness to him. I have far more to offer than Alan Rufus, in any case, so it should not be that difficult. We will go at once to London. I will surely have King William's blessing as he already holds you in such high regard. He should have a bishop there who may marry us — once you hear from your father and mother, of course. Then you shall travel back to Domfront with me."

"Domfront?"

"Yes, in Normandy. That's the town where I live," he said, as though this was obvious.

"Oh, of course. Yes." I forced a smile as I fought the tears that inexplicably came to my eyes again. "Yes."

As night was already beginning to fall, and as I was exhausted, we didn't travel to Windsor Castle to sleep.

Instead, we lay down in the grass, and holding each other, we eventually fell asleep under the yew tree.

When dappled sunlight shone between the yew branches, we woke. After we ate the rest of our cheese, and watered the rest of our wine and drank it, we rode for London.

The twilit hills were covered with golden knee-high wheat. Henry and I had travelled east all day and now left the cover of trees. I felt naked without them around me. Though the shadows of the forest were unsettling, the trees had meant we hadn't made it to London yet.

Swinging my left foot out to the side a bit, I let my boot graze over the tops of the wheat. It was calming. In the distance, I could see men still working, swinging their sickles. It was hard to believe that Lammas Day — the first day of the harvest — had been only a few days ago. That day felt as though it had been months ago, if not years, or perhaps another lifetime.

The fields gave way to small cottages with thatched roofs and then the thatched houses grew into stony buildings as Lilt ambled through Bishopsgate. The guard was friends with Henry, and so we were allowed through without payment.

We travelled slowly past a priory which I had heard of before, called St. Helen's. The storefronts of London looked like crooked teeth in a small mouth, as though they were all jammed in, fighting for space on the street. The sky was clear and bright blue above us. For the first time in my life, I could see neither trees nor horizon in any direction, only people and buildings.

Though I knew it made me look like a foreigner, I couldn't help but look up at the buildings around us. I had never been to London. I had never seen so many people in one place before, except perhaps as a small child in my father's court.

As we passed, some merchants shouted at us to buy whatever great thing they were selling. The smell of freshly baked bread wafted toward me overtop the heavy, putrid stench of the roads, which reeked like an overused privy.

Though it was quickly becoming night, the city showed no signs of tiring. A pair of women shouted happily to each other from their windows overhead, and a small group of men were annoyed at having to part for Lilt. A blacksmith clanged away as we passed him, his fire ablaze in its hearth.

And just as I thought we were going to continue right into the river, Henry halted Lilt and jumped down from her back. As he helped me down, I looked up. Before us stood the most imposing, square, stony castle that I could have barely ever imagined. It had been an arresting sight from the gate of the city, but here, it was magnificent and terrifying at once.

This closer view of the Tower of London did nothing to calm my nerves. I was going to get married to Henry. It could be as early as tonight if my father happened to be here, which was not an impossibility. I wished I had something nicer to wear than this bloody, torn dress.

"Let's go see dear King William, shall we?" Henry smiled reassuringly as he took my hand in his.

"My hands are cold," I warned him quietly.

Two men came hurrying out of the front gate toward Henry. One took Lilt's reins and led her away.

"I wish to meet with my brother. Notify him at once," Henry said to the other man.

"The king gave orders that you were to be brought to him as soon as you arrived, my lord. Alone, I do believe," he said, eyeing my dress.

"We must part for a while," Henry said, kissing my cheek. "I'll see you later. I promise."

I nodded and swallowed as he turned and left me where I stood.

I was shut up in a little sitting room. A table was set with a goblet of wine and a plate of bread and cheese. A glass-paned window looked down on the river below. Standing in the corner, a graying, buxom woman smiled pleasantly when I looked at her but she didn't speak and so I didn't speak.

Every moment which passed made me more nervous. What could Henry and King William be talking about for so long? Did it only feel like a long time? It felt like hours, but really, by the light coming in from the window, hardly any time could have passed. Twilight was lasting for days.

I forced myself to drink some of the wine, if only to calm my nerves. But while the bread looked fluffy like the stuff Henry had made, I couldn't force myself to eat.

After an eternity, the door opened again. I was only mildly disappointed when a man—a lord or baron, by the look of his dress—silently led me out of the room as though I were a prisoner. I assumed this man was leading me to Henry but I was afraid to ask.

We soon arrived at a heavy wooden door which appeared the same as tens of others before it. My escort knocked and waited.

"Enter," said a familiar voice softly from behind the door. "Just the girl. You may leave us, Fitzhamon."

The man named Fitzhamon opened the door for me and stepped aside. As soon as I stepped over the threshold, the door closed behind me.

Crimson drapes were pushed open by the windows along the wall. To the left, a huge stone fireplace had wood prepared for a fire. A handsomely carved cherry desk sat nearby. Ahead of me, a crimson canopy was suspended over a huge, high bed.

To my right, there was a seating area. Even though the benches were wooden, they looked comfortable as there were tens of plush pillows scattered over them.

A man stood by a glass-paned window straight ahead of me. For a moment, I had convinced myself it was Henry and I nearly approached him. But this man was taller and he had ashy-blonde hair. In an instant, I knew he was King William.

He turned around. Though he was older than Henry by at least a decade, he was objectively more handsome than his younger brother, though he was far less attractive to me now.

What was it that made him seem so feminine? Was it only because I compared him to Henry now, whereas I hadn't before? Or was it his ruddy complexion which made him seem to be profusely blushing? It didn't help that he seemed to match his plush surroundings.

"Lovely to see you again, Mistress Edith. You have had quite the journey. Come and sit down with me." He gestured to the wooden benches. As gracefully as was possible while this nervous, I walked to the nearest bench. The king followed me and we both sat down.

Before I had the chance to say anything, the king spoke. "You missed seeing your father by only a couple of days. He was completely insufferable about some land or whatnot, so I had to boot him out. He was not happy to leave." He laughed loudly.

"My father's temper does not take humor lightly. Perhaps the king of England does not care for his allies to the north?"

I smirked. "Do you plan to boot me back to Scotland as well?"

"I would never boot such a pretty face, Scot or not."

"It is unfortunate my father is not more handsome, then." I smiled when King William laughed. "I confess I am unhappy that I missed my father. I dearly want his blessing to marry your brother. It is no matter, though. Waiting a few weeks for his letter won't injure me."

"I believe it is against the Church to marry your godfather, though I could be wrong. I don't care much for such rules."

"Henry and I are in love," I said, forcing a smile to my face. "Pray, I beseech you. Will you give us your blessing, King William?"

"Henry needs to keep a clear head on his shoulders. If you fully understood what a dangerous thing it would be to become Henry's wife, I think you would agree. Things are too… tenuous… right now to allow Henry to marry just yet. And to such a lovely girl."

I stared at William, unable to speak. So he wouldn't allow Henry to marry me? Injustice bubbled up in my heart. I literally bit my tongue to keep from speaking my mind.

"Obviously, Henry is first in line for our throne after my dear brother Robert," he continued. "The reason why Henry is here in England at all is to come begging for money so he may have a chance to defeat our brother Robert, in fact. And I wholly support him of course. But obviously, *now* is hardly the time for the young one to take a wife."

I shook my head. "Why should you be the one to decide when Henry marries?"

He laughed loudly. "Don't be silly. Need I remind you I am king?" The corners of his mouth curled up. "I see why Henry likes you. He likes to fight."

My head began to pound with the sort of headache normally reserved for all-nighters with one of Brother Godric's dying patients. I supposed the warmth of the room was making me sleepy.

"So what *do* you know?" He pursed his lips as he was obviously trying not to grin.

"About what?"

"My dear brother."

I shrugged. "I really only know he is handsome and chivalrous and that I love him. And I am well acquainted with his family, as our lord king will remember."

"*Handsome* and *chivalrous*?" King William guffawed, "Quite."

"He has earned my trust. I know he loves me."

"How would that be?"

"I see it. The same as the sun rising and setting."

"It's a shame Queen Mother isn't still alive to see this. She would have been thrilled you have fallen in love with one of her sons. Henry and I both heard the story so many times — how, when she held you as you were baptized, you pulled at her veil. It was a portent you would one day wear that veil and be queen."

"Oh," I said, unsure what else to say to this.

"Well, Sister Edith, or shall I say *Mistress Matilda*," he said, winking as he stood. "It was lovely to see you again. I believe you will enjoy it here. I'm glad to see you no longer wear that monastic veil, though I suppose you can't, since it was shredded to bits."

"Thank you, King William." What did he mean 'I believe you will enjoy it here'? Was he going to try to keep me here? "My lord king, may I attempt to appeal to your mercy? You were merciful to me before, when my father attempted to take me from the abbey. I had hoped to be so blessed twice by your hand. I beg only a moment of time to speak to your dear younger brother. No more than that. "

His smirk was oddly familiar. "Good try, Mistress Maude."

I followed him to the door and he opened it for me. "Goodnight," he said.

"Goodnight." I tried to smile at him, but I thought I probably only grimaced. I still had so many questions and now I was dismissed.

I found myself following the man named Fitzhamon down endless hallways again. I knew I probably should try to remember the passageways, but they all looked so much the same and I still had so many questions.

Even though it was still summer, the corridors of the Tower of London were drafty. I felt a shiver down my spine.

Surely Henry wouldn't allow his brother to keep me here. He promised he would see me again. How soon would we leave? Perhaps Henry would come and steal me away to Normandy tonight and we could marry there instead. Why did we need King William's blessing, anyway?

CHAPTER 12: THE TOWER OF LONDON

I found myself in a large, round room, having little recollection as to how I had arrived there. I was alone — Fitzhamon had shut the door behind me.

In the middle of the room, a heavy red canopy hung overtop a large bed which stood as high as my waist. There was also a chamber pot hidden behind a screen, a handsomely carved chest of expensive dresses, a couple of chairs, a bench, and a chiseled stone fireplace.

On the curving wall behind the bed, black-lined diamond panes of glass covered every window. Slowly, I approached the closest window and laid my palms on the cool glass. I gasped. I could see for miles and miles to the north and to the east: the city was laid out below me to the north. The golden wheat-covered hills rolled peacefully beyond the gate.

Heavy red drapes were pushed open at each window. Turning to the nearest drape, I crushed the heavy, soft material between my fingers.

I flinched when I saw her. I was not alone after all. A woman — the same woman who'd been in the waiting room with me before — stood near the stone wall by the fireplace. She had her hands folded over her apron.

"Well—hello," I said as I stared at the woman.

"I beg you forgive me for startling you, mistress," the woman said, bowing her head slightly.

"It's alright," I said. "Were you here the whole time?"

"Only a moment, mistress. I came in when you were looking out the window."

"What do you need?"

"Nothing, mistress." I wished she'd stop with the 'mistress' stuff, but I thought it'd probably be rude to ask her. "I was sent by King William."

"Oh. Do you have a message for me?"

"No, mistress." The woman glanced to the door, obviously uncomfortable.

"Why did he send you here then?"

"I'm to be your chambermaid, mistress." She sounded nervous.

"Oh, of course." I vaguely remembered having servants as a small child but I had forgotten how they flitted silently in and out of rooms like this. I felt guilty that I'd made this woman nervous. The servant grinned politely back at me.

"Where is Henry?"

"I'm not sure, mistress. But I've been told I'm not allowed to take you to him."

"I see."

"Yes, mistress."

"Well, are you permitted to offer anything to eat and drink?" I asked, smirking. Now that I was no longer waiting to see the king, I wished I'd eaten the cheese and bread in the waiting room.

The woman laughed. "Yes, mistress. Would you like me to bring food up or would you like to dine in the hall?"

"Is Henry in the hall?" I had no idea what the normal custom was, nor did I actually care.

"Likely not," said the chambermaid.

"I think I'd like to eat here, if that's not too odd."

"Not odd at all, mistress. Is there anything you particularly fancy?"

"Just whatever is most convenient."

"Yes, mistress." The chambermaid bowed her head and left.

I felt guilty I hadn't even asked the woman's name, but I supposed I could ask her when she came back. I sat down at the little seating area close by the fireplace. Above me, huge wooden beams bridged the conical walls of the vaulted ceiling.

Tired, I moved to the bed and half-hopped, half-climbed up onto it. It was so plush, I sunk at least a quarter of a foot into it.

As I lay there, I thought only of how to find Henry without the king finding out. I hoped Henry would suddenly burst through the door because I had no idea how to start searching without getting lost or into trouble.

Eventually, the servant woman came back carrying a tray of food on one arm and a pitcher in her other hand.

When I heard her enter, I stood before I fully pushed away my sleepy doze, and yet I was already on my guard. The servant woman set the tray on the bed and the pitcher down on the bedside table.

"Forgive me, I don't know your name," I said.

"My name is Rosamund, mistress."

"Nice to meet you. My name's Ed —" I cleared my throat, "Matilda. My name is Matilda."

Rosamund bowed her head once.

"Have you eaten supper?" I felt rude not offering her some food since she was just standing there, watching me.

"Oh, I'll eat later on, mistress," Rosamund said, smiling a little.

I realized she must have been waiting for her next order. "Well, how about this? I want you to go eat supper and relax for a while."

"Yes, mistress." She looked like she was trying to see a catch.

I explained, "I have a lot to think about, and it might be better for me to be alone while I eat. Truly, I couldn't possibly have you stand here and watch me eat while you are hungry too. You may tell King William I've promised not to leave my chamber if need-be."

"Yes, mistress." Rosamund bowed her head and shut the door quietly behind herself.

The tray was completely laden with food. A duck leg with a thick white sauce; warm bread not unlike the bread Henry had made at the cottage; a bowl of creamy soup that tasted like some fresh herb that I knew I'd never eaten before; stewed plums stuffed with a salty, crumbly cheese that made my salivary glands want to jump right out of my mouth from overwork; and, there was a small peach tarte with sugar glazed on top. I rarely ate any one of these things in my life. This tray was like a Christmas feast I would have had as a child back home.

I carried the tray over to the bench by the fireplace and brought the pitcher of watered wine over too. Once I prayed, I tucked my leg under me, turned toward the tray, and began eating.

After I'd eaten about half of the food and drank half of the watered wine, I wiped my mouth on the linen napkin and stood, feeling a little guilty I wasn't able to finish everything.

At least I was now well-fed. I was ready to steal away to Normandy with Henry.

Peeking out the door to my room, I found the hall deserted. I guessed Rosamund would not come back for quite a while still, as I knew I'd eaten quickly due to nervousness and lack of conversation.

From the bedside table, I grabbed a lit candelabra. Tiptoeing back to the door, I made my way out to a short hallway, and down a twisting, spiral set of stairs. Randomly choosing to turn right once I reached the bottom, I started down a long hall. The sun was fully set now, and even with the couple of candles, it was difficult to see further than a few feet in front of me. It was a little creepy too, with the candlelight bouncing off the gray stone walls and casting overlong shadows.

Soon, I stood in the nave of a chapel, having little remembrance of how I'd gotten there. A candle remained lit on the altar. I made the Sign of the Cross over myself and turned to continue trying to find my way to Henry.

When I turned around though, I ran full-on with someone else. My first reaction was to protect the candles, so my back took the brunt of my fall.

"Who's there?" called a familiar voice. I looked up, holding up my candelabra with a trembling arm.

"Matilda?" he asked. And I knew who it was without even fully seeing his face.

"Henry!" I gasped. Leaving the candelabra on the stone floor, I stood and threw my arms around him, ignoring the pain in my stitches. Gently, he hugged me back. Then, he picked up my candelabra.

"Are you alright?"

"I'm fine—"

"Did he give you the queen's chamber?"

I shook my head. "I don't know whose room it is."

"I will assume he did." He simply grabbed my hand and led me out of the chapel.

I whispered, "Let us leave now before anyone sees us together."

"No, not tonight, my love," he whispered back.

Soon, he'd led me back to my chamber. "Is this it?"

I nodded. The room was the way I'd left it, and yet it felt as though so much had changed here in just a moment. The room felt much smaller with Henry in it. He shut the door behind himself.

"Matilda." He failed to smile at me as he closed the small gap between us. "I shouldn't stay long. William doesn't want me to see you."

"I know," I said, though I didn't understand why Henry cared. Didn't he hate William? "I spoke with the king."

"Yes? What did he say?"

"He had a lot to say. I don't know. He was confusing." I shook my head. "He said you're fighting Robert and you needed money from him—"

"Yes, that doesn't matter." Tugging my hand, he led me to the bed. We sat on the edge and faced each other.

"I need to know." I tucked one of my legs under me so I could face him on the soft bed. "Do your brother's wishes mean enough to you…?"

"My feelings haven't changed. I still intend to have you as my wife."

"Yes," I said quietly, "that is what I needed to know."

He studied my face. "No matter how long it is until we see each other again, I will come back to you. I will love you in five days or five years. Someday things may be better and then we may live as we wish…"

"Henry…" What was he talking about? He was going to leave me here and go fight my godfather? Over what?

"Forgive me, my love." He kissed my cheek, and then his lips found mine.

"Henry," I said, breaking away from his kiss. "Why don't we just leave now? How could your brother possibly stop you?"

"He has an army of men behind him." He pushed a twirling plait from where it fell in front of my face.

I let out the breath I was holding. "You were so brave with me and now you cower before your brother."

"I won't let my pride make me stupid. Not after Cotentin. Never again," Henry said immediately. "Leaving tonight would be foolhardy. I am playing the long game with William and I need him to trust me again. He didn't trust me for a long time because of what I did with Robert, but then Robert betrayed me in turn—"

"And King William isn't betraying you with his denial of his blessing for us to marry?"

Henry leaned closer to me. "I fear William is right. If I love you at all, Normandy is not the place to take you. I have friends there, but I also have enemies. You would be under constant threat. It's not like here. Do you remember those four outside of the pub who attacked me? Imagine hundreds of those men possibly trying to target me through you. I can't allow it. I won't bring you there until it's safe for you."

"You're just trying a different tactic on me. I'm not that simple. I don't care if it isn't safe. If it is God's Will that I die, then I shall die."

He made a frustrated groan. "Alright listen," he whispered, leaning so close that his lips brushed my ear. "I cannot fight both of them at once. Don't you see? I need to get the easy fight out of the way before I fight the hard one.

I am not leaving you, I'm..." Leaning back slightly, he glanced from one of my eyes to the other and back again. "I'm just keeping you at *home*, my love. I cannot help but come back to you." He looked down at my lips.

"Promise me." Pulling myself up onto my knees on the bed, I wrapped my arms tightly around him, pressing my cheek against his rough stubble.

"I promise you." Leaning back slightly, he kissed me.

I wished he would smile. I wasn't used to seeing him frown. He looked angry when he was unhappy.

His hand trailed up under my skirts as light as a feather. I didn't stop him when he lay me down now. So much was different now than yesterday by the river. I was desperate — the only person I trusted in the world now was going to be taken from me. I was to be trapped in this tower for eternity.

He gazed up at my face in silent question and I tried to smile. Though my hands tremored, I pulled his belt from his waist.

New starlight came through the windows. Around the room, candles fluttered in the drafty, turreted chamber.

It was strange I had seen his bare chest before this but was unable to see it now. I laughed at this thought as I pulled up at his tunic. He helped me pull it up over his head, and he finally smiled again.

Once his tunic was off, his eyes darted to a dozen different points on my face. His dark hair glowed with dying embers in the low light, and his green and brown-flecked eyes were shining.

Afterward, Henry held me to his chest. He ran his hand down my back, over my pale, freckled skin.

I was happy.

"I love you," he whispered, and kissed my forehead.

"I love you, too. Completely," I whispered back, and pecked a kiss to his lips in return.

Pulling himself from my arms, he sat up on the edge of the bed and pulled his cambric and tunic back on. "I really do have to go," he said softly. "If I'm found here, we won't be on good terms with the king. Especially you."

"No," I said, sitting up. I laid my hand on his shoulder.

"I must." He turned to face me, and, almost reluctantly, he took my hand in his and kissed it. "You will know soon enough, my love. William intends to marry you. He actually thanked me for bringing you to him." Henry's eyebrows furrowed, and he looked angry. "I am to go back to Normandy and fight Robert for control of the land. William gave me the necessary funds in order to find victory."

I watched as he pulled his leather boots back on. "I won't marry William. I can't. I'm already married to you now in God's eyes."

Henry finished dressing without saying anything. Finally he said, "You don't need to be afraid of William. He won't want to bed you."

"What do you mean?"

"William..." Henry clenched his teeth. He glanced at me through the corner of his eyes and looked back down to his boots. "How do I say this? He prefers the company of er... of men. I don't know how else to say it. He knows you're pretty but it won't have an effect on him."

"I—"

"You must not repeat this to anyone. Though honestly I think a lot of people already figured it out a long time ago."

I was confused. "Then why would he marry me? He should just let me go."

"Why does anyone get married? For the political reasons. He needs an heir." He ran his hand over his hair. "Well, most people marry for that reason, anyway — you and I obviously wouldn't benefit politically. Not yet anyway."

I tried to smile but couldn't quite manage it. Tears were blurring my vision and my mind was racing: was Henry only interested in me because of the possible political benefits I provided?

I immediately felt terrible for doubting him. What more did he need to do to prove his love?

Henry continued, "The bishops have been pressuring him for years to marry and produce an heir. He wants you for the connections to Scotland, as well as the English side your mother provides. You're Malcolm's daughter. And you're Margaret's daughter — you're one of the people. My father threw this whole country into upheaval when he came here from Normandy. And William doesn't have my father's golden tongue to keep the king's peace and smooth things over."

Henry certainly had a golden tongue…

"Keep in mind though," he said, "William is truly his father's son, nevertheless. He may laugh and joke with you one moment only to stab you in the back in the next." It was one of the few times I ever heard Henry's voice waver.

"How could you ask me to do this?" I knew I needed to try to control the volume of my voice, but it was impossible.

"He doesn't like the idea of me *ever* marrying you. Our union would potentially become too powerful if the people were to learn who my wife is. Especially with all the dissonance already all over the countryside between the Scots and the Welsh hating him and the English hating the Normans. And the bishops also don't like him because he's so, well, against the Church as a general rule. If the people were to decide that the new royal family was still alright, and just that they don't like *him*, well you and I could easily take his place and rule the country."

I barely listened. I'd fallen in love with this man. I had just shared my bed with him though our union wasn't blessed by the Church. It couldn't be undone. He did this knowing he would allow me to marry his brother if the king so desired. And now he was leaving.

I couldn't find the courage to say any of this though. Instead, I could only slowly shake my head and fight my tears. I couldn't make sense of it.

"The last time he saw you at Wilton, he was no longer interested in marrying you because of all that business with the monastic veil. However, my desire for you seems to have reawakened his interest, unfortunately." He stood and faced me. "He wanted me to seem indifferent to you so when I left so suddenly, you would forget me. He told me he wouldn't mind if either of his brothers died fighting the other. But he also said he didn't want you to mourn my death. After all, he knows we ran away together." He watched me while I found my chemise and pulled it on over my head. "We were as good as betrothed and we were... we were as good as married, really, any way you look at it, from the devotion evident in such an act." He took my hand in both of his and kissed my knuckles. "I risked a lot for you — travelling unaccompanied as we did. You easily could have turned on me and said I'd kidnapped you or the like. And so, you obviously trust me. He knows it."

"I see."

"He may marry you before I have the chance to come back for you. It won't be so bad. It'll only be for a little while maybe. A few years. I just need to get Robert out of the way first."

"Years?! No, no, no," I said, shaking my head. "Think of it, Henry. I can't be your brother's wife!" I grimaced as tears fell from my eyes. "This just doesn't make sense. How could we be together again if I marry him?"

"Let us pray his reluctance toward women works in our favor." As I laid my hand on his cheek, he kissed the inside of my wrist. "I don't expect — I don't expect you to be faithful to me. You will have to act the part if you are to endure this."

"Henry… what a horrible thing to ask of me." I lay my head on his chest.

He pressed a kiss to my forehead. "I beg you try to keep a level head. I just need to know you're safe. Hopefully I'll be back before you have to actually marry him. Just — don't run away. I beg you listen to me. He could take your leaving as a reason to harm you."

Despite my anger, or perhaps because of it, I pulled him down and kissed him. My anger and confusion ebbed away as he wrapped his arms around me. When he lifted me up, I wrapped my legs around him.

The door opened.

"Rosamund!" I yelled, pulling myself from Henry's hold as he set me down on my feet again.

"Mistress." The servant's gaze darted all over the room except to Henry and me. "Pray, forgive," she said, turning. She hurried away.

Before I even had a chance to react, Henry ran to the door, swung it open and grabbed Rosamund by the arm. As he dragged her back into the room, he shut the door with his heel.

"Edith — Matilda — begs your forgiveness for shouting at you," Henry muttered loud enough that I could hear him. His voice was so changed that, if I couldn't see Henry speaking, I wouldn't have believed it was his voice.

"Yes," I whispered.

"Now, Rosamund. If you tell anyone about this, your mistress may be in trouble with our lord king. He wishes to marry Mistress Matilda, and I am to go away to fight my other brother, Robert, for control of Normandy. However, Matilda and I are in love. What do you think of this?"

"I," She glanced to me and then glanced fearfully to Henry again. "My lord, I—well, it's not for me to say," she whispered.

"Your mistress and I wish to have the blessing of the Church, but we have been stopped by King William. I must leave her in his custody for the time being or risk ruining my tenuous relationship with him. You will be smart about this and help your mistress, won't you? I will come back to her soon."

"Yes, I will do my best, my lord," she said.

"Thank you, Rosamund." He looked back at me. "I commend you to God, Matilda," he said. "We will survive this. You'll see."

"I commend you to God, Henry," I said. "Come back to me."

"I will. You have my word." He came toward me but I couldn't find the strength to lift my face to him. He bent down and kissed the corner of my mouth.

And with that, he left.

Rosamund stood there for a moment, obviously unsure what to do. She said, grinning kindly at me, "In the morning, it might not all seem as bad. Maybe things will sort themselves out."

"Yes, I hope you are right."

Walking forward, she took one of my hands in hers and guided me to sit on the bed. I felt like a child when Rosamund did this, but I didn't mind it. "Anyway, you've been through quite a lot. Just clear your mind now." Rosamund tapped my cheek lightly. Reaching down, she guided my feet into bed and tucked me in under the covers. Slowly, she made her way around the room, blowing out candles.

"Goodnight, Rosamund," I said quietly.

"Goodnight, mistress. And do not worry. Our secret is safe." The door quietly clicked shut behind her.

Though it was nearly impossible, I tried to sleep. The bedclothes still smelled like Henry.

CHAPTER 13: THE LIBRARY OF WESTMINSTER ABBEY

I sat down on the cold stone window ledge and looked out at a blue strip of horizon under a black sky. How many times had I been up before dawn? Thousands, probably. But I'd never watched the sun rise up over the horizon before. The sky was slowly becoming the deepest shade of orange, the stars twinkled their last and died away. One by one, they faded to blue haze. The whole room was cast in a glow of weak golden light.

There would be enough light now to try to find my way through the castle. I still had not fully healed from my journey here, and I knew I should probably sleep more. Nevertheless, my need to find Henry was greater.

After I pulled my bloody, torn dress and my boots back on, I wandered out the door and down the hall. Though I was afraid to try most of the doors at first, I finally did try one. It wouldn't open. The next one wouldn't open either. Soon though, a woman walked quickly up the corridor. It was my maid.

"You rise early, mistress."

"I do," I agreed. "One of the many advantages of an upbringing in abbeys."

Rosamund pulled a comb from her apron. "Allow me to assist you, mistress."

I was annoyed with this. "No—"

"It will only take a moment. Were you trying to find me?"

"No," I said again as the older woman combed my hair there in the hallway. "Will you tell me where I might find Henry?"

"I cannot." She yanked some of my hair out with her comb.

"Why not?"

"Well, I think I might help you. But only on the condition that you forgive me for it afterward."

"Of course—"

"Alright, I say this in charity," she said and I nodded impatiently, half-smiling. She gave me a long, detailed set of directions to a door with an ornate latch on it.

"Right, end of hall, left, end of hall, up a flight, left, second on left," I recited.

"Well done, mistress."

"Thank you." I left my chambermaid with her comb in hand. Following her directions, I walked as fast as possible without breaking into a run. When I approached the door, I nearly flung it open in my impatience, but I stopped myself. Taking a deep breath, I knocked.

The knight who had led me through the halls the night before answered the door. And I realized why the hallway seemed familiar. The knight disappeared from the doorway immediately. King William was there instead.

"What may we do for Mistress Matilda?" he asked, taking a bite out of a peach.

"I... my lord king..." The shock of being led astray hadn't worn off quickly enough. He opened the door wider as I made a mental note to never trust my chambermaid again.

With an obnoxious flourish of his hand, he gestured for me to enter the room. He took another bite out of his peach and then chewed with his mouth open.

"I beg you, let me see Henry," I said calmly.

"Why would you want to see that halfwit?" he asked without looking at me. "And who told you that you were allowed to come to my chamber without being called to them?" He sat down at a desk by the fireplace and intently read a scroll of parchment, still with his fruit in hand.

"I..." I crossed my arms over my chest. "I need to see him."

"Matilda, come over here." Still, he did not look up. Slowly, I made my way across the room and stopped about two feet away from him. After a long moment where he finished reading the scroll, he finally looked up at me and grinned. "Never speak of him again. You must promise this because if you are to live here, I can't have you whining about him."

"I don't whine."

"You are whining now," he said, raising his eyebrows. "And you need to call me 'my lord king' or 'King William.' I'm more patient than my father was, but that's not saying much at all."

"I do not care to talk any more about you." I jutted my chin out to cover up the fact I had shocked myself with my own words. "I beseech you to allow me to leave here with my love."

"Well, well, what-what-what a cheeky little-little-little wench you are," he said, standing. He was no longer smiling. As he raised his hand to hit me, I shut my eyes, bracing for the blow. But he only gently tapped my cheek a few times, as gently as Rosamund had tapped my cheek the night before.

"You stutter when you're angry? How regal." I forced a laugh. "You're an old man, picking on such a young woman."

"How-how…" He swallowed hard. "How many times have you been struck? Youuu-you are of noble birth and you expect a hand to-to strike your face?"

I shook my head. "I beseech you, allow me to see my love before he leaves me."

"Ugh, Henry. H-h-how he woos women with that face, I will never understand. It-it-it doesn't matter. It was just a juvenile infatuation. I can't have the people thinking you're in love with him. It just wouldn't do." He scratched at an invisible fleck of dirt on his desk. "Anyway, as dear Henry so kindly informed me, he never so much as laid a finger on you. He said you seemed appalled by him at times, in fact, and you are quite a prudish girl. Lucky for you, I am not bothered by prudishness."

"I thought you weren't *bothered* by women at all?"

And with that, he backhanded me hard across the face. The strike stung bitterly, of course, but Aunt Christina had hit me harder many times before this. Being struck had oddly made me feel a little better.

He seemed shocked that he had hit me, far more shocked than I was. "Are… are… are you so b-bold as to continue to attempt to defy and insult your king?" He took a deep breath. "You must have thought I am a saint with unlimited patience. You know now I am truly a devil."

"I am making no attempt to insult or defy you. It is only by your good grace I do not scourge myself by speaking. But you are surely no devil. A devil would have injured me far worse than that by now. Perhaps you truly are a saint. You are all goodness, my lord king, except you won't tell me where you hide my love," and I bowed lowly to him, pointing my toe as I did.

"Y-y-you are mocking me now?"

"Never," I said too quickly, dropping my gaze.

"Aren't you feisty?" He sat down at his desk again. "It makes sense—you and Henry are one in the same. Single-minded and headstrong."

"We are one in the same. You're right."

William narrowed his eyes. "I don't see how you could love Henry. You were only with him for what? A week? No, less than that."

"What length of time is required to fall in love? I will remain with Henry for the rest of my life if I must convince you."

"Do not believe for a moment he would ever be faithful to you. Not when he will be gone for perhaps months or years. Forgive me if I seem unkind, but it's the truth." He didn't sound the least bit remorseful. He was just trying to shock me more than I'd shocked him.

"I know. I realize you're being quite kind. Things could always be worse." I forced a smile to my face.

"Your home is with me now, Matilda." He laughed. "We will leave in the morning for Thorney Island."

"You don't live here?" I asked, glancing around the opulent room.

"No. Not permanently anyway. It's not finished yet. I was only here to meet with my brother and check on the finishing process of some of the rooms. Don't worry, you'll feel right at home at Westminster Palace." His gaze raked over me. Quickly, he gave directions to the servant boy standing near the door to have my maids prepare a bath. The servant boy left immediately. Then, he turned his attention back to me. "Go wash and change into some of your godmother's old clothes. You need to look and act like a queen now. Not a Saxon dog."

"My lord king." I bowed my head before leaving.

After roaming the hallways for hours in a futile search for Henry, I reluctantly arrived back at my room. My maid, Rosamund, stood waiting by an empty wooden tub like the one in the hospitaller's quarters at Wilton Abbey. Another younger maid stood with her.

"This is Emmaline," Rosamund said quickly, and nudged the girl forward. Emmaline couldn't have been any older than me.

"A pleasure to meet you," I said automatically.

"Ah," she said, looking down at her apron.

Despite the warm day, a hot pot of water hung over the crackling fire in the hearth. Next to the tub, some large pitchers of water were waiting. "I see your face is quite ruddy, Emmaline. I do beg you forgive me this warm work. It's unfortunately by orders of the king, and not myself, or I'd call the whole business off."

"Ah," she said again.

"It's no trouble, Mistress Matilda. None a'tall," Rosamund said loudly, eyeing the younger girl.

Before either maid attempted to help me, I pulled my torn, bloody dress from my shoulders and let it fall to the floor. And lifting my chemise over my head, I dropped it onto the nearby table. "Throw the dress away, Rosamund. It's ruined."

"Yes, Mistress Matilda," she said without looking at me.

What did I care if these maids saw me naked? I was a hospitaller's apprentice—a naked body was only a naked body as long as it was treated that way. Emmaline clearly thought otherwise, but oh well. It seemed she would be embarrassed no matter what I said or did.

I unwrapped the linen from my wound. Emmaline gasped at the sight but I was satisfied — the wound was healing well. No gaping and no redness or festering.

Rosamund handed me into the tub. Then, she ladled some hot water into one of the cool pitchers of water nearby and stirred it. Meanwhile, Emmaline gently unraveled my plaited hair.

Kneeling in the tub, I tilted my head back as Rosamund poured a bit of water on the top of my head. "Is the temperature alright, mistress?"

"Yes, it's fine." It was pure luxury, actually. I didn't want to say so in case I embarrassed Emmaline again, but I was used to ice cold water in winter and tepid in summer at the abbeys, when I was allowed to bathe at all.

Rosamund poured more water, soaking my hair. Then, she massaged fragrant herbs into my scalp, crushing them into my skin. As she did, Emmaline combed the herbs down my hair.

"Emmaline was it?" I asked, though I remembered her name perfectly well.

"Yes, mistress," she said quietly. Her voice was higher pitched than I would have thought it would be.

"Your hair is quite lovely. Did you plait it yourself?" It was something to talk about.

"Yes, mistress," she said, brightening.

"Mm. I shall want your assistance with my hair every day, if you would be so kind. It wouldn't do to have Rosamund do all the work, wouldn't you agree?"

"Oh," Emmaline glanced at the older woman.

"Mistress," Rosamund started. "My daughter's work is usually to tend to the fires."

"Daughter?" I had hoped Emmaline would become my friend, but obviously this wasn't possible if she was

Rosamund's daughter. I persisted anyway. "Then this is better work for your daughter, wouldn't you agree? Someone else will fill her old job."

"Yes, mistress."

"My lord king's goal is that I should not look like a Saxon dog. It could prove to be more difficult work than the fires." As I shrugged, Emmaline glanced down at my breasts. I couldn't help it when, after glancing at her chest in turn, I swallowed a laugh. "Perhaps in good time, lass." Emmaline blushed profusely and hurried to stir the hot pot of water. "Forgive me," I said, biting my lip as I tried to stop laughing. "You remind me of my sister, Mary."

"Thank you, mistress," Emmaline said, bowing her head without turning to face me again.

As though washing me was very hard work, Rosamund pressed her lips together as she scrubbed herbs down my arms. "Oh, mind my stitches," I said and sucked air in through my teeth. I looked back up to Emmaline who looked quickly away. "I was cut down with a sword in a pub brawl," I laughed.

Rosamund obviously hated me. Why else would she have sent me to the king's bedchamber without having been called there? Nevertheless, I knew Rosamund would have the answer if anyone would. Freezing the smile still playing at my lips, I asked, "Henry left, didn't he?"

"He left before dawn, mistress." She wouldn't meet my eyes. "Rode south on a black stallion belonging to the king." Emmaline gently rinsed my wound while Rosamund started with the herbs on my back. Then, Emmaline rewrapped my arm in fresh, clean linen.

"Is it alright, mistress?" Emmaline asked softly.

"Yes. Thank you." I nodded. Why hadn't he ridden away on Lilt? Had he left her as something to remember him by? Or was he only letting her rest?

"Mm, mistress." Emmaline gave a shy grin.

I made myself smile back at her. "Be ready. You both shall travel with me in the morning."

Westminster Abbey was far larger than either Romsey Abbey or Wilton Abbey. I was free to roam Thorney Island as I wished, as long as I did not leave the gates. However, as there was so little for me to do other than walk and sit prettily, I felt as though time were at a stand-still.

The Great Hall, which was only just being finished, was massive. The only place to rival its hugeness was perhaps the Tower of London itself. It had clerestory lancet windows spaced all along both sides which seemed twice as tall as I was. Centered on the far wall from nearly the floor all the way up to the ceiling, panes of glass allowed in so much sunlight, it made me wonder how the wall even remained standing. There were no fat pillars despite the largess of the room. How did the ceiling not collapse?

The monks walked about the grounds in unobtrusive discussions with each other, or else in prayerful meditation. It was a familiar sort of sight to me, though they were men instead of women. Unfortunately, King William didn't like for me to go to services without him, and never on feast days, so I was limited even in this small bit of normalcy I found.

"Lost?" King William asked me one day. He'd found me alone in the infirmary garden. The sky above us was covered with bright white clouds. Footpaths etched and curled their way between rows of all types of flowers, vegetables and herbs growing here. Where William and I stood, there were blooming white and red rosebushes as tall as my shoulders.

Beyond the roses, there were other flowers, like little white bells and other fragile-looking shapes. Far off on the other side of the garden nearest the stream, a monk seemed to be pruning a bush. Watching him work gave me the feeling of utter calm.

I shook my head. "I fully intended to come here."

"Do you like it here? I would have thought you'd prefer the abbey garden."

I nodded. "I thought I might find some peace here, as so many monks walk the abbey garden. But all the gardens are beautiful. Not just the gardens—but also my chamber, and the Great Hall—"

"The hall is not big enough by half, and is but a bedchamber in comparison to that which I mean to make."

"It is already truly magnificent as it is, my lord king," I said honestly. "Surely it will bring almsgivers to the abbey here, too. You do good works by having such plans." I tried to smile.

"But you do not seem as happy as your words sound," he said, squinting in the sunlight as he surveyed the garden.

Rather than respond, I stepped toward him. A look of shock passed over the king's face as he looked down at me. I grinned, trying not to laugh at him. I thought of taking his hand or touching his cheek just to tease him, but I couldn't make myself do it. Instead, I knelt before a rosebush. As my fingers trailed lightly over the crimson petals of the nearest rose, my thoughts jumped to Henry's soft touch. I closed my eyes and it was that night in the Tower of London again. I felt Henry's lips on mine…

The king knelt next to me and I was suddenly kneeling by a rosebush again. Pulling a knife from his belt, he slowly pruned the rose I had been caressing. After trimming the thorns off, he tucked the rose behind my ear.

"You are lovely." He met my eyes for a moment and, taking my hand, he pulled me up to my feet. "I fear you may forever look like a child to me. I am old enough to be your father."

I grinned as I pulled my hand from his. "This is the dilemma when stealing the lover of a much-younger brother."

"You were mine first," King William said, grinning back. "When I first came to Wilton Abbey, it was weeks prior to visiting with your father. I'd heard of your betrothal to Alan Rufus and wanted to see you for myself, as the bishops are ever pressuring me to find a bride."

"I didn't know." I crossed my arms, hugging myself.

"I came secretly, dressed as a servant. As the abbess walked with me in the garden, I pretended to admire the roses there. That's when I saw you. You were beautiful, but you wore the veil. At once, I sent word to your father and insinuated he needed to go see you as you were being rebellious, though I did not say in what manner. He met with me soon afterward."

"That explains why he came without any sort of warning."

"Yes. In truth, I had hoped your father would do exactly what he did, which was prevent you from wearing the veil. From the moment I saw you, I knew you weren't made for those homespun rags you wore. You were made for finer things. Your face and manner are that of a queen."

"Thank you, my lord king."

He nodded and turning away, he strolled back toward the palace.

For the next four days in a row, the king appeared in the infirmary garden while I was there. He was always the first to greet me and we would talk about the weather before he would leave again.

Soon after, the king left "to travel about the kingdom." I was not allowed to come with him.

Two months to the day after Henry had left me at the Tower of London, I sat down on a stone bench under an open window. I was down the hall from King William's chamber. Gazing out toward the sprawling city of London, my eyes trained on the distant yellow and brown leaves on the sparse trees dotted about the city.

From a small purse on my belt, I took out a few olives from midday dinner. The cool air of early October brushed my tendrils back, tickling my ears and neck, as I spit an olive pit out the window.

"Mistress Matilda," said King William from behind my shoulder.

"Oh!" I stood quickly and faced him.

"Forgive me, did I startle you?" He stole an olive from my hand and popped it into his mouth.

"A bit. I didn't know you were back from Normandy yet. I thought you weren't to be back until at least tomorrow."

"Raw food is unfitting for a queen."

"Yes, my lord king, but I am not a queen."

"Yes, well, sit down again. There's something I want to tell you." He chewed with his mouth open as he sat down next to me.

"Yes, my lord king?"

He spit his pit out the window. "Feel free to rummage through the monks' library at the abbey. You'll be the first woman allowed in there."

"Thank you, my lord king."

He smiled widely, as though he were only a little boy who was overly proud he'd done something right. "Yes, I know you read," he said smugly, "and I'm glad you do. I know that not only do you read English, but also read and write in Latin and French."

"Yes, I do."

"I'd like you to give yourself an education. A queen should know things of the country she is to help rule."

I raised my eyebrow. Certainly he had gotten this idea directly from Henry's mouth. "Yes, my lord king."

"Good, it's settled. We shall meet again tomorrow evening. How about in the abbey garden, if the weather holds? I want to see you once more before I am forced away from here again."

"Fine."

"Do you know where the library is?"

"Um… no." I stood again as he did.

"Come, I'll show you." He offered me his arm and I took it hesitantly. We strolled quietly downstairs, out of the palace, and across the courtyard to the abbey. From there, we walked down an ambulatory and in through a door that I felt sure was reserved for priests and bishops. I felt like we were doing something illicit.

There, we entered a hallway. To one side, the door to the Pyx Chamber was open and a bishop stood within, reading something. The chamber was full of the priests' vestments and all the shiny, important things that they needed for services. I was always curious about the sacristy rooms. They were like treasure vaults.

But we weren't going in there. William walked just past this and turning right, he led me down a short hallway and stopped before a set of double doors.

"There are plans to build a prettier library separate from the cathedral soon, so it's only here until then, as the old building has been torn down before its replacement,"

William warned. Then, he swung the double doors wide. I was ready to see another beautiful cathedral ceiling in the style of the nave of the abbey. Instead, the sight before me was even more striking and unusual. A shallow foyer area was flanked by two hard wooden benches. Beyond this, there were rows and rows of narrowly-set bookshelves. The ceiling was probably two stories high, but as the shelves were so close together, I felt two stories was not nearly high enough. On each stack, rickety stepladders made painful scraping noises over the gray stone floor when they were moved.

How could one person ever have enough time in this place? "Thank you, my lord king," I said earnestly, turning toward him again.

"My pleasure. I beg you forgive the library's ugly appearance. I think this area would be better served as a meeting hall of sorts—"

I shook my head. "I think it is lovely just as it is."

"Well." He grinned. "Enjoy yourself, and I will see you tomorrow." He turned on his heel and left.

I read well into the night and fell asleep at one of the tables in the back of the library. I woke in my bed in the palace, having no recollection of walking to it the night before. On my bedside table laid the same manuscript I'd been reading. A gold embroidered bookmark held my place.

I didn't ruminate over my mysterious travel. Instead, I sat up in bed and forgot to say my morning prayers. By the light of dawn, I finished reading the manuscript.

CHAPTER 14: THE KING'S FORTRESS

October turned into November and November into December. I had yet to receive a letter from Henry, though I sent letters to him often. I had started to worry that he had forgotten me.

By candlelight, I searched the titles in the library and found a manuscript titled *The Canon of Medicine*. My heart leapt as I pulled it from its dusty shelf. Sitting down with it at a table nearby, I drank in every word that I read.

"Didn't you know candles aren't allowed in the library?" said a familiar voice from behind me.

I shuttered in surprise. I had thought I was alone. "Henry," I breathed as I glanced over my shoulder at him. As I stood, he wrapped his arms around me and kissed my forehead. I hugged him tightly in return. Looking up at him, I explained, "Henry, I am so happy to see you — King William granted me permission to look in here, and — " But he cut off my words by pressing his lips to mine. The still-unfamiliar pull of desire awoke deep inside me as I returned his kiss.

All too soon, he pulled slightly away. "I didn't mean to disturb you. I needed to see you before I left again," he whispered against my lips.

"Oh — " He kissed me again. I hadn't even known he'd been here in the first place. I felt strange, like I was kissing a corporeal ghost, or living inside a dream. Lacing my hands into the back of his hair, I tugged.

"Ouch." Laughing, he kissed my nose.

"I wanted to make sure you're real."

"Ah…"

"What—"

"I'm here on errand—" He kissed me again. "William forbade me to see you."

"Take me with you back to Normandy," I said quickly, my lips brushing his as I spoke. "I beg you."

Henry smiled into my kiss but he shook his head. "Soon. I promise. Why don't you answer my letters? I understand if you are too miserable to be troubled… but, selfishly, I began to fear you had forgotten me already."

I shook my head back. "I sent you perhaps more than a dozen, but I never received one from you."

"Well, of course. They are surely being intercepted by my brother."

A lick of hatred renewed in my heart for William. Henry continued, "It's no matter. In any case, I am happy you aren't overcome with melancholy."

"How can I be unhappy when you are in my arms? All is now right in the world."

"I…" He kissed me once more, just a peck this time. "I fear you wouldn't say such a thing… Could it be that you do not know?"

"Know what?" I laughed, "You haven't married someone else have you?"

I'd expected him to laugh, but instead he frowned. My heart plummeted into my belly. Had he truly married someone else? How could he? Numbly, I let him lead me back to my chair. He knelt before me and took both of my hands in his.

"Edith." He looked down rubbed the backs of my hands with his thumbs.

"My heart is breaking just from your reticence," I said coldly. "Say it. I beg you."

He met my eyes. The guilty look on his face made me want to pull my hands from his but I was too busy holding my breath, waiting for him to speak. "It is my unfortunate duty to tell you that your brother, Edward, the heir to the Scottish throne, and your father, Malcolm the Third, King of the Scots, have fallen asleep in the Lord."

"What?!" I immediately assumed it was somehow King William's fault, though I didn't logically see how.

"It was in Northumberland," Henry said, and paused, waiting for me to respond.

"I... I don't..."

"Your father coveted the English lands there and was in the midst of laying siege back in mid-November. I feel certain it's why he wanted you to marry Alan Rufus."

"Did you kill them?"

"I had nothing to do with this," Henry said quickly, holding my hands tighter, "I've been in Normandy this whole time, fighting your godfather."

"King William. He did this."

"Well, Alan, perhaps. Alan Rufus, your estranged betrothed, is also dead... But your father and brother? William says he is not stupid enough to cross the Scots, but the fact is, *his men* killed both your brother and father at what was supposed to be a peaceable meeting. His men, as all men, may be fools. I suppose they probably just wanted the siege to be over."

"You're—you're covering for him—"

"No. No, of course not! Though I have no proof, it is certainly possible that William gave orders to kill Edward and King Malcolm. It is just his nature to have planned to pretend it was an accident when it was not."

I couldn't look at Henry anymore. "William *murdered*... My father and my... dear Edward, my big brother — you and he were friends once, weren't you?" I suddenly remembered watching Edward and Henry playing at fencing when they were boys. Henry had won.

"I pray you find some peace from this pain, my love." His eyes shone like glass in the candlelight. There was something else. Henry's shoulders were too tense.

"What aren't you telling me?" I asked sharply. "Say it. I can feel your restraint as though a stone wall stands between us." I held my breath again.

Henry whispered slowly, "Margaret, Queen of the Scots — your mother — I beg you forgive me for being the one to tell you, my love. She had been taken ill for a while, apparently. When she heard of her husband and her first born son's demise, she fell asleep in the Lord only a few days after your father and brother."

I was infuriated to see unshed tears shining in Henry's eyes. I wanted to scream. My lips and fingers tingled like fire and ice at once. When I stood, my vision faded to black and so I was forced heavily down on the chair again.

Henry grimaced as he said, "I commend the king, queen, and heir-apparent of the Scots to God."

I pushed back the overwhelming urge to vomit as I bent and stared down at my own feet. Without any thought as to why, I pulled as hard as I could at my hair. All I could see was black. 'Perhaps I should breathe?' was the only coherent thought I had. Pulling racking, stabbing breaths into my lungs was easy enough, but I couldn't remember how to breathe out.

I heard, as though from far away, "What can I do?" Henry took my hands firmly in his own again and I was no longer able to pull my hair, though I still looked at my feet for a moment until he pulled me from my chair.

"Nothing," I whispered. And dragging as much air into my lungs as was possible, I said softly, "There's nothing you can do, is there?" I meant to punch his chest but instead I only smacked it a few times without any force behind it. "You did nothing to stop him... And William—how you want me to—to *whore myself to the murdering devil* as you stand by and do nothing, just as you have done nothing." My tears were hot on my face in the cool air of the library.

"Edith, I beg you, quiet yourself," Henry said steadily. As he pulled me closer to himself, I lay my head against his chest and began to cry.

"Henry..." My voice tremored as I finally remembered how to breathe out. I couldn't finish what I wanted to say. As I wept, I clutched his tunic and buried my face into his unyielding chest. He held me just as tightly as I held him. Though I was angry, I also longed for comfort. I struck my fist against his chest and I wished his body was softer.

"Your chest is too hard," I whispered into his tunic. When I smacked his chest again, I felt myself silently giggle. And my giggle grew into laughter. In another moment, I was laughing hysterically, tears falling fast down my cheeks. I forgot how to breathe again. "Oh God, I think I might die now too!" I cried out. I could see that I had frightened Henry, but it was as though my body had been possessed by Satan and I could only watch myself. "God is just!" I howled, "God is merciful, is he not?! I long for comfort and He grants me your unyielding chest!"

Somewhere in the back of my mind, I was surprised that Henry looked so miserable. As I hid my face in the crook of his neck, he wrapped his arms around me. Cradling my cheek, he wiped my tears with his thumb. "Edith... shh..."

After a long time, I was able to calm down. I was embarrassed but I didn't know how to explain why I had laughed and cried at once.

Resting my head on Henry's shoulder, I was overcome with exhaustion. I asked, "Who of my brothers is now king?" I fully expected him to say simply "Edmund" and for that to be the end of the conversation.

Henry shook his head. "Your father's brother, Donald, has claimed the throne."

"He doesn't even have a child to name successor." I lifted my heavy head from his shoulder so I could see his face. "This shall ruin every one of my brothers' futures."

"Your uncle has satisfied no one perhaps in the entire world, let alone Scotland, with his taking the throne. Well, except himself. I have been in close contact with your mother's brother, your Uncle Edgar. With the help of a few of my friends, he has successfully sent your little brother, David, south to Romsey Abbey for a time to stay. Your Aunt Christina is there with him. Mary remains at Wilton Abbey."

"Finally, a boon. What of the rest of my brothers?"

"Your eldest brother attempts to rally against your uncle. He intends to take the throne—"

"You mean eldest surviving? Edmund?"

"Edmund has sided with your uncle, unfortunately. It is Duncan, your truly eldest brother, whom Edgar and Alexander now rally behind."

"Oh." I had forgotten my half-brothers from my father's first wife. I didn't like this idea, but if my brothers want Duncan as their king, what else is there to say?

"Yes… I have convinced King William to assist Duncan where he might, but until the fight in Normandy is over — "

"May I send a letter to Alexander with your help? If my letters to you were not delivered, I suspect none of the others were. Alexander and I were almost like twins as babies, you know."

Henry gave a weak laugh. "I do know. In his latest letter, after I assured him of your safety, he confided that he hoped I would marry you one day. He wrote he would hand you over to no one who loved you less than he does."

"Truly?" I was genuinely surprised, but tried to hide it. "I haven't received a letter from him in so long. I know he must worry about me. I just want to be assured of his safety, and I would like to assure him of mine as well." It was quiet for a long moment while Henry stared down at my hands as they clasped one of his.

"No, my love," he said too gently. "I agree with King William. No one may know you are here. It is safest for you. I pray you understand."

Though I felt guilty for it, I turned all my anger toward Henry. "How can you side with William?"

"I would never do such a thing," Henry said softly. "It is because I love you that I say so."

But no. The deaths of my parents and Edward, and now my uncle's claim and the chaos between my surviving brothers — this was clearly, somehow, all King William's doing. "I once thought you were a serpent in the grass," I whispered, leaning closer to Henry's face.

"Perhaps you were right," he said, pecking a kiss to my lips.

"No. I was wrong. So completely wrong. Your brother. Our beautiful lord king. He is a true antichrist. This is his doing. He put down my father's fight in the worst possible way."

Henry shook his head in a sympathetic sort of way and it made me feel terrible.

My seething anger ebbed as I rested my head on Henry's shoulder again. Closing my eyes, I breathed his deeply of scent. "My father died because he was covetous," I whispered.

Henry pressed a kiss to my forehead. "Don't speak ill of the dead."

"And William had him put down like a lame dog. I shall never forgive it."

"I beg you, do nothing against him. You must keep acting your part. It's the only way. I know I seem a coward, but I beg you trust me, my love."

"Then, *my love*, if I must continue to bear William's company, you must do something for me in turn."

Henry pushed my hair from my face and ran his hand down my plaits. "I will do anything for you."

I turned my chin up and met Henry's gaze. "You must kill your brother for me. I cannot not abide him any other way." I took a deep breath. "You must kill your brother. God forgive me."

Glancing around us as though expecting for us to have been overheard, Henry pulled me to my feet. "My love, let me see you to your chamber. You need to rest, I think."

After he blew out my candle, he offered his arm. I took hold of him with both of my hands as though I were elderly. Together, we quietly made our way out of the library and he stole back to my chamber with me.

Rosamund was sewing. She popped up from her chair as we entered and Henry guided me over to the bed.

"Stay, maid," Henry called to Rosamund as he slid my boots from my feet. Standing again, he untied my collar. As he pulled my dress from my shoulders and down my arms, I held onto his upper arms as I stepped out of my dress.

He kissed me slowly, and then let his lips lingered over mine. "I love you with all my heart," he whispered. "Hold fast. I will be back for you as soon as I can be. In time, I will give you everything. You have my word." Then, pulling the bedclothes back, he lay me down and tucked me in. I watched as Henry kissed my hand, and with one more glance back to me, he left.

Though I was exhausted, I barely slept. In the morning, I sat down in the abbey garden with *The Canon of Medicine*. The sky was low and gray and there was a definite winter chill to the air. As I pulled my shawl tighter around my shoulders, I stared down at the open manuscript in my hands.

But all I could see was my mother's beautiful face, pale and waxen as she lay in a dark room.

Mammy.

Queen Margaret hadn't had her daughters at her deathbed. How could she have found peace? How would it have been possible without her husband, her daughters, her first born son — the beloved heir to the throne? She must have died with her eyes wide, holding onto life for as long as she could.

It wasn't fair. I had seen deaths without peace many times. It wasn't a death meant for my mother. It wasn't a death meant for even the worst criminals.

At every opportunity of her rule, she gave the poor and hungry peace. And yet she was robbed of one of the most important moments in life. Was it possible — could she have found peace without me there? And without her first born son and without her husband? She was such a good, Godly woman. Could I dare to hope as much?

I should have been there. I could have been there if I hadn't been such a coward. If I had ran back to my parents from the abbey, like a good daughter would, instead of coming to London with Henry...

This was my fault. It was my comeuppance for my reckless, shameful cowardice.

I saw my brother gasping for breath, lying on cold, hard earth, crying for help. I saw the king's men bite their lips and do nothing while my father lay dead at their feet.

Why was I still here, hiding? Why wasn't I helping them? Wouldn't it be better to die than hide?

The thought of my mother not breathing—her skin unmoving when I clutched her hand in my own—the thought of her concealed in the earth forever...

I forgot how to breathe again.

"What are you reading?" came King William's voice from behind me.

I flinched and wiped my face with my sleeve. "On the four humours." A few cold drops of rain pattered onto the manuscript. I snapped it shut and looked up to the sky. The rain fell faster and faster onto my face and rolled down my neck.

"Come!" King William tugged my wrist, pulling me to my feet. I let him drag me, though I didn't mind the stinging cold drops. I would have sat in the rain for hours.

As he pulled me along, I looked down at the wrist he held in his hand. Then, looking to my other hand, I saw that I was still carrying *The Canon of Medicine.* It seemed to have survived the rain.

At a jog, he led me down the hall to his chamber and I stumbled after. "Come in with me," he said, turning on his heel at his door as he caught his breath.

"No." I dropped the manuscript to the king's feet and bent, resting my hands on my knees as I pulled in deep breaths of cool air. I watched as water dripped from the hem of my dress, forming tiny puddles on the stone floor.

He laughed as he gazed down at me. "Are you trying to tempt me with your heaving bosom?"

I straightened up and twisted my hair, ringing the water out. "I thought women's figures didn't appeal to you?"

"Yours does."

"You are a liar."

"Silence. Come in with me for a moment and dry by the fire. You don't have time for your long-suffering, noble king?" He grinned. His teeth were straight and white, which was distracting.

I stared at him. "You are not suffering. But I suppose I might make time for you anyway."

"Good. I'll have the servant get you some dry clothes and a warm drink." He bent and picked up the manuscript lying at his feet. "I wanted to hear what you have to say about the four humours." When I didn't answer, he opened the door for me and grabbing my elbow, he pulled me into the room.

His chamber here was much like the one in the Tower of London, but far, far larger. I thought perhaps the entire cottage in Reading would have fit in this room. The ceiling was as tall as the nave in Romsey Abbey. A canopied bed was centered on the far wall and a magnificent stone fireplace was positioned between lofty many-paned glass windows. Before the fireplace, three long benches sat in a fat curve, all covered with pillows. A screen hid a chamber pot.

To the boy waiting in the corner, the king gave orders for dry clothes and blankets to be brought up for me. "Oh and two flagons of hot mulled mead," he added as he set *The Canon of Medicine* down on his writing desk. The servant boy nodded and shut the door behind himself.

"Well, I've been told I am quite sanguineous because my face is always so ruddy," he said. Without warning, he stripped off his wet tunic and cambric and threw them into the corner of the room. They made a wet slapping sound when they hit the stone floor. "What can you tell me about the humours?"

"There are four." I looked away from the king's bare chest.

"What are they?" There was another wet slap. I thought he must have taken his leggings off but I did not dare to look at him to find out for sure.

"Um, the sanguineous, the serous, the bilious and the atrabilious," I said from behind my hand. I hadn't realized he was so close to me until his warm hand was on my cold one, pulling it down from my face. I relented and let my hand fall. Our eyes met for a moment. As I glanced from his brown eye to his blue eye and back to his brown, his passive gaze turned softly into a grin. He was not completely naked, I noticed from my peripheral vision. Only nearly so.

"You *are* a prude," he laughed. "Henry was right." My throat constricted at the mention of Henry, and so I didn't explain that I was hiding my eyes out of hatred of him and nothing more.

The king pulled on dry clothing. A servant appeared from seemingly nowhere (though really he'd been waiting by the wall) and helped the king dress. "I would think a nursemaid would be used to seeing naked men," he said, breaking the silence again.

I shivered and crossed my arms tightly over my chest. "I wasn't a nursemaid. I was an apprentice to a knight hospitaller. Anyway, there is a difference between brazenness and the brief necessities of the infirm."

The servant boy came back with a flagon in each hand. Emmaline followed him in with a fresh dress and chemise for me, as well as some folded blankets.

The king turned to me and asked, "Would you like to build a pillow fortress?"

"Do I want to build a what?"

"Pillow fortress. It's the best place to drink hot mulled mead. Change your clothes. I won't look. I'll be too busy building the pillow fortress. Don't take too long, though. Your mead will get cold."

I wracked my brain, trying to think of what a pillow fortress could be. "Yes, my lord king." He walked to the other side of the room to the benches and the many pillows. As the two other servants seemed to melt back into the wall, I turned my back to the king and quickly changed with Emmaline's help.

When I turned around again, what I saw was almost an exact replica of what I'd imagined. King William had begun to build a sort of cave out of the pillows and benches.

"Come." He peered out of the makeshift cave as I made my way forward cautiously. "Try your hot mulled mead. Have you had it before?"

"I do not believe so, my lord king." I knelt down at the mouth of the pillow cave.

"Careful." He pushed one of tankards into my hand. "Don't scald your mouth."

I took a sip. After a moment of him staring at me, I forced a grin on my face and then took another sip. Just because he was staring so intently, I wiped my mouth with the back of my hand.

"Thought you'd like it," he said, smiling back at me. "Come in. It needs a woman's touch."

"It's already bigger than my cell was at Wilton Abbey," I said.

"Truly?" he asked, raising an eyebrow.

Guilt panged my gut, but I ignored it. Why was he making me feel guilty? I should be the one making him feel guilty. "No, not really."

I could not help but listen to the rain driving against the glass-paned windows. I felt ridiculous sitting there in the dark little cave of blankets and pillows. Was I really sitting with the man who, whether directly or indirectly, was responsible for the deaths of both of my parents as well as my eldest brother?

I saw myself dropping my hot wine in his lap and reaching my hands around his neck. I wanted to choke the ruddy color from his cheeks. I imagined his face turning blue, and then purple, and his eyes turning from white to blood-red, and then he would breathe no more.

King William spoke again before I had time to imagine it any further. "I used to make these fortresses with Henry on rainy days when he was little. I was nearly a man already, but it didn't make it any less fun."

"By this, should I assume you no longer consider yourself to be a child?"

"I am not a child any longer, even if I do still make pillow fortresses. Would you say *you* are a child any longer?"

"Definitely not. I may say with full certainty my childhood ended somewhere between running away from the abbey and the deaths of my parents."

William set his flagon down on the floor between us. "I — when did you find out?"

In the awkward silence that followed, I slid out from the cave of pillows and stood up. William did the same. "I overheard in court." I handed him my tankard. "My lord king."

William bowed his head slightly. I quickly left his chamber.

CHAPTER 15: CHRISTMAS AT WESTMINSTER

Rosamund dressed me in a blue gown which she said had been my godmother's favorite. Emmaline spent hours gently plaiting my hair on the top of my head into an intricate crown. Then she combed the rest so it fell in waves down my back.

At Christmas supper, King William sat at the center of a long table. There were so many guests that two more tables had been added to the ends of the king's table. King William had insisted I sit at his right. As I ate, I listened to the king's constant jokes and stories and I forced myself to smile when everyone else laughed.

There was posset to drink, which I found strange. I had thought people only drank it medicinally. And there was mulled mead, fruit wine, and ale for the servants.

I had never seen this much food served at once, not even in my father's court when I was a little child. I was disgusted by the end. There was chicken-stuffed duck with white sauce, parsley-encrusted sturgeon, fruit pastry-pie, roasted loin of veal with sugared plums, saffron-dusted boiled eggs alongside wafers and a mint jelly, and clotted cream with pomegranate seeds and caramelized sugar. And, I finally tried Henry's favorites: a small bowl of stewed lampreys at the start of the meal, and toward the end, some goose liver pâté.

As I finished eating, I wondered if any of the guests here would deliver a message to him for me, but I already knew it was useless to ask. Only those who were absolutely loyal to King William had been invited today. Otherwise, I knew I would have been shut up in my tower.

It was strange that no one was formally introduced to me. And so, most of the men seemed to have assumed I was King William's lover. Two different men had tried to grab my bottom before supper but only one succeeded. King William actually had stopped the second one from touching me. He had been delighted to announce that I was his and his alone. More than a few men thought this was hilarious. Or else, like Fitzhamon, they looked downright sullen at this news.

Other than servants and me, only one other woman was present. Every time I looked at her, she scowled openly at me. I had no idea who she was.

As supper finished, many of the guests stood and milled around, talking loudly over the musicians' cheerful music.

I walked slowly away from the musicians and stood apart from the rest. As I paced toward the fire, the heat warmed my nose and fingertips and still I walked closer. I stared down at the huge, burning logs. Cinders danced toward me, and I thought of that night with Henry in Reading when I had re-stitched my own arm. He had been my other hand for me as I stitched, and he had held me steady.

Had he thought of me today? Where was he right now? Perhaps he was dead? Perhaps he'd lost his fight against my godfather? I knew King William would fail to mention his brother's death for as long as it suited him. For all I knew, my lover had been killed a week or two ago.

I was acquainted with my maids, Rosamund and Emmaline, but they served my enemy in greater measure. Truly, I was alone.

I held my hands up to warm them before the fire. For a moment, I imagined touching the flames. How badly would it hurt? Would anyone even notice if I burned myself right now?

Suddenly, someone grabbed my arm and pulled me violently out of the fire's trance. I stared down at a jeweled hand and then up at his ruddy, handsome face. "When one speaks of the wolf…"

"You were thinking of me? Only good things, I hope?" King William asked, dropping his hold on me. "You looked like you were about to step directly into the fire."

"I was simply warming myself."

"I'm going to send a man for you later. I want you to come to my bedchamber tonight."

My heart stopped. "No," I said blankly. "Absolutely not. I beg you—"

"Just to talk," he said, waving a hand as though to wipe away my thoughts.

"Fine," I said quietly.

A few hours later, there was a knock at my chamber door. "I suppose I must go now," I said in small voice.

"Yes, mistress," Rosamund said as she moved to open the door. "Have hope."

"Thank you, my dear friend." Stepping forward, I pulled her into a hug. She hesitated but patted me a few times on the back.

"Have my bed warmed with coals. I hope to be back soon," I said quietly. "And do drink the wine over there in the jug. I wish for you to share it with Emmaline."

"Oh, she will be delighted. Thank you, mistress."

"Good tidings," I said softly.

"Come with me," the man said from the doorway. He was Bishop Ranulf Flambard, I reminded myself. Somehow, I felt that this particular bishop would be nearly impossible to befriend.

I followed him down the dark, winding hallways and stairways to the king's chamber. He knocked at the king's chamber door. King William answered it himself.

"Thank you, Ranulf," said King William.

The bishop bowed lowly. I smirked at the flourish of his hand. "My pleasure, my lord king."

The king's gaze shifted to me. "Welcome, Mistress Matilda."

"Thank you, my lord king." I bowed slightly to him.

"Would you like to sit down near the fire with me? Though, that dress is a little tight on you. Perhaps you'd rather stand?"

I looked down at myself and cleared my throat. Oh, how I wished I could go to bed. How much longer would I have to stay here with this man? I pressed my lips together to keep from saying anything.

"No, no, it's nice. You should always wear that shade of blue." He raised and eyebrow as he glanced down at my chest. "Rosamund is a wicked old bird, isn't she?"

"Yes, my lord king." I crossed my arms.

King William grabbed my elbow and led me to the benches near the fireplace. Orange hues from the fire flickered over everything in the room.

"That dress was my mother's," said King William, "though she wore it differently. She was shorter than even you, if you could believe it. But you do look like she did. She had lovely long, dark hair like you." He sat down and so I did too.

"She was quite petite, though she was grand in presence."

"Yes! Ha! You are like her in that way as well."

"You are kind to compare me to such a magnificent queen. It makes me think you want something from me."

"Would you like some wine?"

"Thank you, my lord king."

King William poured two goblets of wine from a jug on the table nearby. With a jolt, I realized there wasn't a single servant in the room with us. Handing me a goblet of wine, he held up his own. "To hope, truth, and love."

"To hope, truth, and love," I repeated. I sipped my wine as he drank deeply from his. "May I take the liberty of thanking you, my lord king," I said, "for your excellent Christmas feast tonight and the —"

"No," he said, "and stop calling me 'my lord king' when we're alone. Act like yourself."

My heart fluttered with delight at annoying him. "Only a few months ago, you struck my face for doing what you've just asked."

"That's not why I struck you."

"What would you like me to call you instead?"

"When we're in private? Just 'William.' You are privileged. Only my siblings may ever call me that."

"I could never agree to do such a thing. What if the servants heard me? They would think we were lovers."

"I would be overjoyed to have such rumors circulate. However, my intention is truly only to nurture friendship between us."

I took a long pull of wine while I tried to think. Being mistaken as his lover would have been so welcome only a short time ago, and now even the idea of it broke my heart.

My fingers turned white from clenching my goblet. "William..." I said, looking away. My gaze landed on the fire crackling in the fireplace.

"And now we have that settled, there is something I wish to ask you."

"What is it?" I asked flatly.

"How do you like the wine?" He leaned back and crossed his legs.

"Oh." I glanced down at the goblet clenched in my hand. "It's very good. Thank you. Why? Is it poisoned?"

"I hope not," he laughed. "Now, I beg you hear my whole proposal before you decline, as a Christmas boon to me, if you will."

It was silent except for the crackling of the fire as he waited for me to speak. I had nothing to say.

After a long moment, he continued. "Once you and I are better friends and I have won Normandy from Robert, I wish for us to marry. I know you do not love me. I do not love you either. Nor could I ever love you, I believe. At least, not as a husband should love his wife. Like you, I also love another."

"Not long ago, I had prayed I might marry you one day." A sad laugh escaped my lips.

"Is that so? Before you ran from the abbey, I suppose?"

"Yes," I whispered. "It's strange to think of that now." Suddenly, I was violently angry with Henry. Tears blurred my vision. I took another gulp of wine. How could he abandon me when I needed him the most? He should have just let me bleed to death in Bastingstoke or drown in the River Test, as God had intended.

William studied me before speaking. "Don't you see how your love for him is all that stands in your way? You force me to ask what I know may be impossible: you must forget him."

"How could you —"

"I'm not as heartless as I might seem. I will not ask you to live a life without love. Instead of Henry, you could find a, shall we say, a stallion? A man who is politically invisible to keep you... happy."

I looked down at my hands in an attempt to hide my face. My foot wanted to take the first step forward on a long journey away from here. But instead of dry earth under my foot, there was nothing there. I was nowhere and I had nothing.

Even so, I shook my head.

He continued, "I am nearly forty years of age and have-have-have yet to produce an heir. This is a major problem for me, as I-I am sure you understand already."

Had I made him angry? "I refuse to understand you." I let my tears fall as I held my face up again. I didn't care if he saw me cry. What did it matter? "Why won't you simply allow me to marry Henry? He and I will produce an heir for you, perhaps. Naming your nephew as your heir wouldn't seem strange."

"But Henry is not the king. I-I-I am. *I* need an heir." He huffed out. "And, honestly, I am as interested in keeping you from him as I-I am in marrying you."

"But I do not understand why. You said you are in love with someone else, too. Do you have so much to gain with this plan?"

He gave a polite laugh. "Marriage and love have nothing to do with each other, my dear Matilda. Where ever did you find an idea to the contrary?"

"But..." What a terrible thing to say! Why not marry a man I loved? It was lying to God to marry for any other reason. I thought quickly. "If I have a... a man... as you suggested, my child would not be your heir anyway, even if

I were your wife. He'd just be a bastard. Surely someone would find out if you weren't the father of my child."

"Well, yes, that dirty work. Perhaps I shall have to bed you until you produce an heir for me and we can be done with any such business. I'll keep my hair unwashed so you can pretend I'm Henry." He gave a smirk.

"I have absolutely no interest in any such arrangement. I beg you forgive me if I led you to believe otherwise. Now, you have wholly offended me and cannot possibly have anything further to say." I set my wine down on the table nearby. As I stood, I wiped the tears from my face.

King William stood as well. "It is perfectly fine that you give this response for now. Honestly, the thought of being forced into a marriage bed together is as repugnant to me as it is to you. This is why it is vital that we become friends. It is for your sake as well as my own. Sooner or later you will come to realize Henry is not the man for you. I am saving you from a terrible fate."

"I certainly will not change my mind on this matter, come whatever may. Even if Henry were to perish, God forbid it."

"If Henry perished? Now there's a thought."

I took a sharp breath. "I despise you."

"Hush, child. Time will tell." He shrugged. "You shall change as you grow older."

I shook my head. "My response is that of anyone who views marriage seriously. You propose to make a farce of it." I stepped past him and strode toward the door.

"*I* propose to make a farce? Look at your beloved Henry!"

I turned to face him again. "What do you mean?" I asked quietly.

"Forgive me," he said loudly, "Oh, only that he keeps a whore in every major city. He's already fathered five known bastards that he refuses to legitimize. The first was when he was only nineteen years old. That we *know* of, anyway. There probably are scores yet to be discovered. Perhaps he's making another as we speak?"

"You are a liar," I whispered. "I would be a fool to believe you."

William gazed at me and I watched as his face changed. He was no longer amused at all, which did more to convince me of the truth than his words.

"Surely you *know* Henry? He lied about keeping himself from you, didn't he? You *must* know he was not saving himself for his marriage bed? It's Henry, after all."

I only shook my head, turned, and left.

"Good tidings," he called after me.

CHAPTER 16: ON ROMSEY ABBEY

The horses' stables stood off by the River Thames, not far from the Great Hall.

When I had first travelled from the Tower of London to Westminster, King William had allowed me to ride Lilt for the journey across London. I had already grown to love the horse and to view her as my own. A sort of pet. After all, we'd both been left behind for these past months by Henry. And so, soon after Christmas, I began visiting Lilt every morning.

The first time I wandered into the stables, the stableman stared openly at me.

"Hello." I was only trying to be polite.

"It's you." Though he spoke quietly, I heard him clearly. His voice resonated wherever he was, like a psalm read in the crossing of a cathedral.

"Yes, I am Matilda of Scotland." I assumed he knew who I was because he'd probably heard rumors of my supposed affair with the king. "Forgive me for intruding on your morning work. I am only here to visit my horse."

"Of course, Mistress Matilda," he said slowly. "But you used to be Edie. Edith of Scotland."

"Rich Normans like my second name better, I suppose," I said. "Anyway, I didn't think anyone here knew my

Christened name, other than the king. I think he'd like my first name to stay a secret for now."

"Do you…?" It seemed he was about to say something else, but he shook his head. He said under his breath, "I pray you forgive me," and continued working.

"You haven't offended me."

He looked familiar, like the blonde boy I had met at Romsey Abbey years ago. Except that boy had been short, and narrow, and awkward. This stableman was none of those things. He was clearly a man. I thought he was probably closer to Henry's age than my own. And the way he moved had a distinctly Norman way about it. He was confident and graceful in every move he made.

After that first day, I visited Lilt every morning. And every day, the same stableman was there, caring for a half a dozen horses, sometimes more. For weeks I would say a polite "hello" to the stableman—usually when I caught him watching me. He would simply bow his head back to me.

After a few weeks of only nodding, he said, "Good morning, mistress."

After another few weeks this grew to, "A pleasant day to you, mistress."

One day, despite the falling flakes of late-winter snow, he was working just as he always was. He had already mucked out all of the stalls. Now, he was changing the water for the horses and had slowly made his way down to Lilt. I asked him, "How old are you?" I was brushing Lilt's mane.

"I'm sixteen years old, mistress," he answered, glancing up from his work toward me.

Younger than I thought. His accent was a familiar one— Hampshire, like the sisters at Romsey Abbey. I wished he would talk more. "Forgive me," I said, "I couldn't be sure of your age by looking at you. I felt sure you must be nearly ten years older than you are."

"Oh. I'll be seventeen, mistress, in only a few weeks."

"I'll be fifteen soon. On the first of June."

"Ah. And I always thought we were the same age. I suppose we nearly are."

I took this as a compliment and thought nothing else of it. When he came nearer to me as he worked, I asked, "Do you sleep here?"

"No, mistress. I sleep in the servants' quarters." Tilting his head slightly, he stared at me for a moment before he continued working. Most girls probably would have found his staring strange, but I didn't mind it. It made me happy how he openly gazed at me without embarrassment. It was innocent, as though he were staring at the stars in the night sky.

"I didn't know there were servants' quarters. Well, that's good. It's been so cold. I couldn't sleep last night because every time the wind howled, I worried you were freezing."

"I thank you for your kind feelings, mistress."

Wrapping my shawl tighter around me, I watched him for another moment. "What's your name?"

"Tristan."

"I knew a boy once by that name. He's a monk now. You have the same color hair as him."

"Are you sure he's a monk?"

"Yes."

"Hm."

"I do like your name."

"I have that name because my mother died giving birth to me, and so sadness shall follow me all my days."

"It can't be so sad here, tending horses, can it? You're free."

"I suppose it's not so sad, mistress." He shrugged. "It's good work, to be sure. I have a roof over my head, and food every night. And good company."

Until I thought over our conversation again days later, I hadn't notice the compliment he'd paid me. "Who named you if she died? Your father?"

"No. I never knew my father. The nuns at Romsey Abbey named me."

"Oh!" I dropped Lilt's brush. When I bent and picked it up, I tripped on my skirt and stumbled. By the time I righted myself, my face was radiating heat despite the cold air.

"Are you alright?"

"It's you!"

"That I am." He smiled openly at me.

"You are—you aren't a monk." I smiled just as happily back at him. I remembered him as he was when we first met. His eyes and his mouth were still the same. "Did you run away? From Hayling Priory?"

"No. I never went in the first place."

It had been my first day at Romsey Abbey. It had been Tristan's last. "Do you remember that day as clearly as I do?" I asked.

"I believe so. As though it were yesterday."

***

I made my way to the other end of the garden and ran downhill toward the river. As the balmy breeze blew my long, dark plaits back behind my shoulders, I glanced back. I felt my throat tighten as it readied itself to laugh—the nun wasn't even trying to run after me.

Snatching my leather sandals from my feet and throwing them down into the tall grass, I skipped to a stop. The scent of baking bread halted my thoughts. I hadn't eaten all morning. I inhaled deeply, hunting the scent as I gazed slowly over the abbey ground. Though the weather was fair, a squat stone building's chimney had smoke billowing from it. Clearly this was where bread would be baking. I left my sandals where they were and ran barefoot through the grass.

It was shadowy in the kitchen house even though it was morning outside. And so, it took a moment for my eyes to adjust. In the corner, there was an old nun snoring in her chair, her head tilted back against the wall and her mouth hanging open.

Directly across from me, a boy worked at the ovens. He looked to be about my age. As my eyes adjusted, I watched as the boy picked up fresh loaves of bread and placed them into a large basket. I could take a loaf…? But no. Something even more tempting waited for me: a small fruit-pastry tarte.

The boy stopped what he was doing and looked at me expectantly. "Hello, Sister," he whispered.

"I am not your sister." I walked closer to the work table and leaned forward, staring back at him. I enjoyed looking at his face now that I could see him properly. He had a gentleness in his eyes, as though they were older than the rest of his body.

"We're all brothers and sisters in the eyes of God," he said. He was well-suited to his homespun. Not like me — wearing a costume.

Picking up the tender little tarte, I began to back away. The boy wore a surprised look on his face. But why? Clearly he didn't know who I was.

"Hey," he hissed, and glanced at the sleeping nun.

I stopped walking backward. "Don't wake the old brown bat."

Glancing at the nun again, the boy strode around his worktable and reached for the tarte but I leapt backward out of his reach. He whispered quickly, "It's for an important person who's coming to visit the abbey. A bishop or someone."

"Oh. Then it must be for me."

"Why would it be for you?" He reached for the tarte and laughed quietly again.

I evaded him again and half-stumbled backward out of the doorway of the kitchen. "Today is my first day here—"

"I know that. You're one of the abbess's nieces."

"Yes. And so this is clearly for me."

I turned and, with the tarte held aloft like it was the Holy Scripture, I ran away. To my astonishment, the boy ran after me. I ran to the back of the kitchen house and ducked between the boughs of a white-blooming willow tree. There, I turned and waited for the boy to catch up.

What a relief that I found someone to play with! I'd had to leave all my brothers behind when I was forced to come here, and my baby sister would never play anything other than dolls.

When he ducked between the white-and-brown boughs, he stopped a hand's breadth shy of the tarte. But he didn't try to grab it again.

"Your name, boy?" I held up my chin the way Mammy always did.

"Tristan."

"Well I am Edie, daughter of King Malcolm the Third and Queen Margaret of Scotland. And I do proclaim this peach tarte as mine."

He smirked. "Oh really?"

I didn't let my smile show on my face. "Yes," I swung a plait over my shoulder.

"Well, it's apricot." He nodded once and placing his hand over his heart, he half-bowed. "I didn't know you were of noble birth. I pray you forgive me."

I sat down on the grass and broke the tarte in half. Glancing back over his shoulder toward the kitchen house, he sat down too.

"Here, for your, uh, fortitude." I offered him the bigger half of the tarte.

He took his half and held it with his fingertips as though it would burn him. "What is fortitude?"

"Fortitude?" I repeated, stalling. I didn't know. I took a dainty bite of my tarte and nibbled like a noble girl should even though I really wanted to shove the whole thing in my mouth. Once I swallowed, I said, "Of course, it is what you did by running after me."

"Oh. I hope there's enough sugar left to make another one of these."

"Why wouldn't there be enough sugar?"

"There is never much sugar." He shook his head.

I shook mine too. "Perhaps there is more sugar in Scotland than here?"

As we made quick work of our stolen dessert (he must have been hungry too), I heard someone calling my name.

"It's Sister Agnes," whispered Tristan, glancing over his shoulder. "We should tell her you're here so she isn't worried."

"No. Wait a while longer," I whispered back. "Let us stay here and pretend this willow tree is our fortress. We are the king and queen and those nuns are the evil trespassers on our lands who wish to usurp your throne."

Tristan raised his eyebrows at me like I was possessed by a demon before he turned his gaze down to the grass. "Fie, we'll be in such trouble."

I nodded gravely. "I hope we are well-enough appointed with the necessary swords and arrows for this."

It was quiet between us while Sister Agnes trudged down to the kitchen, then to the river, and back up toward the abbey. Meanwhile, I started pulling blue forget-me-nots from the grass and began making a flower crown.

When I finished it, I placed it on Tristan's head. He laughed. "Flower crowns are for girls." But he didn't try to take the crown off of his golden blonde hair. I thought he looked too pretty with the crown on his head so I grabbed it and flopped it on my own head instead. "That's better," he said, matter-of-factly. "It's the same color as your eyes."

Looking down, I pulled at the long blades of grass around me because I'd already picked all the forget-me-nots nearby. "Why do you stare at me like that? Did I get apricots on my face?"

"No." He looked down at the grass instead. "You sound strange when you talk."

"I sound normal. It is everyone else here who sounds strange."

Tristan glanced back over his shoulder but he didn't get up. "I should get back to work."

I said in a smart tone, the way Mammy often talked, "My lord king, look upon the ramparts and pray, have the men at the ready. Pierce their savage breasts with poison-dipped arrows."

"Ah, now you sound like you're from here." Tristan gazed at me for a moment and then peeked out between the boughs of the tree. "My — queen — many of the, err, savage breasts are out looking for you now. Perhaps you should, um write a peace treaty, and forgive them their trespasses as we forgive those who trespass against us?"

"I shall never barter peace with those who wish my most beloved husband dead!"

"Oh no," Tristan whispered, "I think the savages heard you." He pushed himself to his feet and then gave me a hand so I wouldn't trip on my homespun as I stood.

Sister Agnes ducked between the willow branches. "Sister Edith! Brother Tristan! Our new abbess is absolutely furious! What are you two doing?" She tore my hand from his hold. "Why are these flowers on your head?" She pulled the flower crown from my head, pinching out a few hairs along with it, and tossed it aside. "Never mind, come back with me this instant."

But Aunt Christina parted the swaying willow branches with the backs of her hands, and marched to Sister Agnes's side.

After she broke the end of a thin bough from the willow tree, she pulled Tristan by his ear around to the front of the kitchen house. I trudged behind Sister Agnes and joined the small crowd of waiting nuns.

"Hold out your palms," Aunt Christina said coldly. Tristan did as he was told.

Lifting the switch high over her head, the abbess mother swung down with all of her might and hit Tristan's hands. Though he scrunched his face as though he were going to cry, he didn't make a sound.

I knew that pain well. At home, Mammy had expected excellent behavior from all of her children. If I said something now, we'd both get switches to our hands, but I needed to speak up because that was what would be right. I couldn't get the air to leave my chest in order to make sound.

"You took it! Confess!" Aunt Christina shouted, raising the switch again. This time, he visibly tensed: he was ready to be struck.

"Yes, Abbess Mother, I took it," Tristan whispered.

After he was hit a third time, Sister Agnes said quietly, "Abbess Mother, I beg you. Have mercy upon the child."

I knew from experience that Aunt Christina would not usually stop until she'd whipped once for every year of age. She was only just starting. Nevertheless, she stopped.

Glancing around, I realized the other nuns were appalled by their new abbess. More than a few had tears in their eyes. My heart leapt hopefully as I looked from face to face.

"It is not proper to have a boy of your age at a nunnery," she said, tugging at the part of her veil which touched her chin as she glanced at me. "You must leave here. Today I will write to the monks of Hayling Priory. At dawn tomorrow, you shall leave this place with my letter and walk there on your own. You will be given toll for the ferry and the clothes you are wearing now, except your shoes. May God save you."

It wasn't fair! I needed to try to change her mind. "Aunt Christina—I—I mean, Abbess Mother Chris—" With a swift smack across my face, she silenced me. As I stumbled sideways from the blow, I heard Sister Agnes gasp next to me, and a wet hand clutched mine, keeping me from falling. Staring down at the tall grass underfoot, I blinked hard a few times, forcing the tears from my eyes. Though his hand was bleeding, Tristan's hand held fast to mine. Hastily, I pulled my hand free of his without looking at him.

When I looked back up, Aunt Christina had fabric shears in her hands instead of her willow switch. Before I had a moment to wonder where the shears had come from or why she had them, she snatched a plait of my hair and cut it roughly. I felt the sting of my skin breaking open from the shears' graze on my scalp. A few of the nuns gasped.

"Aunt Christina!" I screamed, my hand flying to the top of my head. Short, uneven hairs bristled under my fingertips. She might as well have torn my clothes from my body and left me naked. I would have felt just as cold.

"You there, Sister, hold her still." I heard Aunt Christina's voice as though from far away. Suddenly, my arms were held behind my back by strong, thin fingers. I didn't try to fight against the nun's hold. Instead, I squeezed my eyes shut and whispered to my aunt, begging her to stop. But I knew she wasn't listening to me.

Methodically, she pulled each of my plaits taught from my head and then with a grinding *shick*, the pull on my hair was gone. From the light feeling after she was done, I knew I was left as bald as a field peasant. Then, a tight, dark veil was shoved over my head and securely tucked under my neck just as though I were monastic.

"You shall wear that veil until your hair grows down your back again, or I shall shear another bolt from you, Sister Edith. This is your punishment for thieving and then not confessing your sins."

I stared down at my plaits in the grass, which looked like dead snakes, and said nothing. The strong, thin fingers released my arms and I fell to my knees.

My aunt cleared her throat. "Perhaps the previous abbess of Romsey Abbey allowed common thievery?" She gestured with her shears toward the kitchen. "But that which you robbed was meant for the bishop of Old Sarum on his meeting of the new abbess here! I will not stand for it!"

A few of the nuns glanced at each other, but no one said a word. At that, my aunt handed the shears to the nearest nun, turned, and trudged back toward the abbey proper.

The nuns slowly dispersed, wearing guilt-stricken faces. A few of them gently tapped Tristan's cheek or shoulder as they passed him, but no one said anything. Sister Agnes walked away with a few of the other nuns. She seemed to have forgotten about me as she whispered with them. When all the nuns had made their way back to their morning work, I was left alone with Tristan again. He offered his hand, though it was still bleeding, but I stood up without help.

I stared at the tears shining in his eyes. The tarte in my stomach churned. I whispered, "I saw some yarrow over by the river. Come here." I wanted to hug him but I knew my brothers hated my hugs. Tristan probably would, too. Instead, I took his wrist and led him to the river bank. In the grass where I'd left my sandals, there was yarrow growing. It hadn't bloomed yet.

"Hold out your hands." I picked the yarrow weeds and, once I'd crushed it a bit between my fingers, I rubbed it over the wounds on his palms. My heart thudded when I touched his hand—he had seen my aunt cut my hair. "My brothers use yarrow when they play at fencing and hurt each other."

Tristan nodded. "Thank you."

"Yes. You'll live, I think."

"I didn't think I was about to die." Though there was wit in his voice, a few tears trailed through the dirt on his face. I fought the urge to hug him again.

Sister Agnes was marching back down the hill toward us.

"What are you doing now? Why didn't you follow me?" Sister Agnes grabbed my arm in one hand and Tristan's in the other. Her voice was shaky. "Come on—you don't need more punishments, either of you. Thank merciful Heaven you will go live on that little island tomorrow, boy. Go, Brother Tristan, back to work! Quickly! And Sister Edith, my goodness, child! God forgive you!"

"Do not speak to me that way, nun!" I pulled my arm from her grip and hiked my hands to my hips. "And I've had enough of this 'Sister' business! I shall not be a nun!"

Tristan laughed softly and shook his head. "I commend you to God, Edie." With handfuls of crushed up yarrow, he ran up the hill from the river.

***

I frowned and shivered. "I pray you forgive me for the pain I caused you. You lost your home because of me. Aunt Christina wouldn't let me write to you. Of course, I know now that you weren't there, but, I'm glad to know you are alright. And I am thankful I have the chance to beg your forgiveness."

He shook his head. "I never harbored any bad feelings for what we did. You didn't mean me any harm. Truly, I thought of you as a dear friend for years after that."

I let out a nervous laugh. "What a gift it is to see you again!" How could I not have known that this boy was standing here with me all this time?

"And it is a gift to see you, mistress." He smiled back at me as we gazed at each other. Suddenly, he flinched and hurried to continue his work again.

"How is it that you never went to Hayling Priory?" I watched him walk off to the far side of the stable house.

"When I left Romsey Abbey," he said, glancing up at me again as he dunked his pail into a barrel of the steaming-warm water he'd lugged in earlier, "I took a wrong turn while walking south. I ended up miles and miles away from where the ferry was, though I didn't know it at the time." He carried the pail of water toward the furthest watering trough. "From the Hampshire docks, I joined a crew looking for lads to do the scrubbing. It was a rough go of it for a while. After a time, I stayed ashore in Normandy and found work at a vineyard."

"What freedom you've had! And now you have come back across the South Sea."

"Yes." His smile faded from his eyes. "We are all free as long as we do not fear death. Isn't that what the nuns taught us?"

I watched my hand brush the same spot on Lilt's back over and over again as I thought about what he said. I couldn't recall any of the nuns ever saying that to me.

Did I fear death? Who didn't fear death?

Tristan finished watering the horses and now was pitching hay into each stall from a small cart. He said, "I suppose you escaped the vows, same as me."

"Mm." I stopped brushing Lilt again as I gazed at him. Despite the silent, fat snowflakes falling outside, I watched a drop of sweat weave its way down his temple, over his jaw and down his neck.

"And, you're the king's lover, now. Aren't you, mistress?" He glanced up again and met my gaze. "Forgive me, it's not my—"

"I'm not the king's lover," I said quickly. I kept watching his beads of sweat as they snaked down his skin. When was the last time I had worked that hard? I envied him. "He and I have an understanding. Actually, he wouldn't mind at all if I took a liking to someone else, if only I would forget my love, who had to leave me here in safety while he battles in Normandy."

"Ah, I see." He gave a polite nod.

CHAPTER 17: THE STABLES

As February of 1094 passed away, the first spring flowers of March blossomed and Tristan and I became fast friends. As I rarely spoke to courtiers, I would have had no updates at all of Henry, or any other news, without Tristan.

Just as we did every day before talking about other things, Tristan and I spoke of the weather. We both agreed it was a pleasantly sunny day, especially for this early in spring. Tristan mentioned he'd heard that King William (and therefore, Henry) had secured a strong standing across the South Sea. The people there no longer stood behind Robert, though he remained the duke of Normandy for now.

Though I shrugged in response, honestly I was elated to learn this. "I hope this doesn't mean I'll be seeing the king more often."

Tristan laughed. "I dare say, 'tis a real danger now."

As the sun shone in through the stable doors, I secretly enjoyed how his blonde hair glowed like golden threads of silk. "What would you do if you didn't tend to horses here? If you could do anything?" We'd had similar conversations many times over the past weeks. Every time I asked, he came up with a different variation of the same answer.

Today he said, "I suppose I'd keep some of my own horses and keep a bit of a farm." He glanced at me. "I would build a home somewhere. Your land in Scotland from when you were a small girl sounds like it'd be my sort of place to live. They're more my kind there, I would think."

"Ah, me too," I said, nodding. "I do miss Scotland, though I barely remember it."

"From what you told me, you seem to remember it quite well."

I shrugged. "So you would keep a farm and a cottage?"

"And perhaps I would keep bees and make my own mead. Maybe even sell some of the honey. Of course, I learned how to make fruit wine in Normandy —"

"Yes, you told me." I smiled encouragingly for him to keep on the conversation. If I didn't stop him from talking about winemaking, I knew he would go into long, specific details. The whole morning would be gone before he was finished re-explaining the tedium of cutting back canes, or else how the Greeks and Romans aged wine before they drank it.

"Right, and the man there — Alphonse — he taught me the basics of keeping bees. It's quite tricky, but I think I'd be up for it. You just have to have a calm hand, and I believe I do."

"Yes, I can see that in you." He was certainly patient and steady with the horses.

We were quiet for a moment before he spoke again. "What about you?" he asked, giving me a small, reassuring smile. As he pitched hay into the feed troughs, I watched his biceps flex against his thin tunic and relax again.

The first time he had asked me this, I had said, "All I want is to love, and be loved, live by the grace of God, and be happy."

"Ah. But can the four of those happen at once?" had been his response.

I'd had no idea what to say to that so I never gave my completely honest response a second time. Rather, I often said, "to do good works by the grace of God," or some other vague, safe answer. Today though, I said, "I would tend to the sick. I was trained in such things at Wilton Abbey."

He straightened up. "I didn't know."

"Didn't I ever tell you?" I knew I hadn't.

"So you were a sort of nursemaid? Or what is it called?"

"I was an apprentice of sorts with a knight hospitaller. Though, obviously I could never be knighted. I was supposed to travel to Jerusalem with him to tend to the sick. As a nun."

"That's quite good then, isn't it? You're downright skilled."

"Well, I wouldn't call it a skill. I was just lucky enough to be taught. I am honestly quite ashamed that I am squandering all I learned. You, though. You have skill. Between horses and wine and bees and sailing."

"No," he said, shaking his head. By the way he kept his face downcast to hide his smile, I could tell he'd appreciated my compliment. It was quiet between us while we both continued grooming our horses. Tristan said, "If you don't mind me asking..."

"Yes? You may ask me anything."

He raised his eyebrows a fraction at this and looked down at my hands, which were busy brushing Lilt's back. "What sort of arrangement do you have with the king?" He met my gaze again. "I mean, other than your talks in the garden. I've heard stories of his raucous parties and men doing things that God didn't intend—"

"Well, if such parties take place, he's never invited me to any of them," I said. "He asked me to marry him. I told him I don't want to marry him. He said he's going to wait until I marry him. I am letting him wait forever. That's about all there is to it."

"Aye? But you said before—you said it months and months ago, though I remember it clear as day. You said your heart belonged to someone else. It isn't the king, I understand, but then...?"

"I did say that, didn't I?"

"That you did."

"Well, he was kind to me." A pang of anxiety grabbed at my chest. Why was I so reticent to talk about Henry with Tristan? Perhaps, I thought, I should change topics. But why? Tristan was my friend. I trusted him. "My heart belongs to the king's brother, in fact. Lord Henry of Domfront. Perhaps you've heard of him?"

"Oh." Tristan's eyes widened in a rare look of surprise before his gaze snapped down to the straw-strewn floor.

"Honestly though, I barely know him. How much can you learn about someone in less than a week's time?" I forced a smile to my face and shook my head. I wanted to explain to him how well I truly did know Henry, but I could not make myself say the words.

"Well, I remembered you from Romsey Abbey and I had only spent the afternoon with you one day."

"I remembered you too," I said. "I know it didn't seem like it at first, but you just look so different now." I laughed quietly. The air had been sweet with baking bread and spring that day, just like today. "But we both went through a lot that day. Of course we remember it."

"Aye. And every day is an eternity when you're a child."

Summer mornings were endless with pleasant, quiet conversations with Tristan in the stables each morning.

Most evenings, I continued writing letters to Henry even though I knew they would not be delivered. I also wrote to my siblings and other relatives and friends from the abbeys—even to Aunt Christina, on occasion—but just as with Henry, I never received one letter back. Still, I never stopped. What if one happened to get through one day, even once? I couldn't give up hope. My letters allowed me to pretend that this life at Westminster was normal and I was not the captive that I was.

One morning at the end of August, rain started to pitter-patter on the river nearby. Then it fell faster and faster outside the stable doors. In a moment, it thrummed on the stable roof and tittered at the surface of the river, creating a sort of humid cocoon around us.

Tristan had just finished telling me the only news of my brothers that I was to have during this summer: my half-brother, Duncan, had succeeded in ousting my uncle from the throne. I knew this meant that my other brothers were allowed to return safely home to Scotland again. As I smiled at Tristan, I listened to the rain and I was happy.

Briefly, I remembered the rain Henry and I had ridden through from Bastingstoke to Reading. I had tried to open my eyes and speak but I couldn't. All the while, he'd held me close to his chest and kept me warm. And then I realized—I had lived an entire year in Henry's absence. As I glanced out at the rain misting in through the open stable doors, I felt the smile fall from my face.

I tried to remember what else had happened with Henry during those few days we had spent together. I remembered re-stitching my wound with his strong hands steadying my arm. I remembered eating fish off of a stick over a fire. I remembered the new, strange pull of desire in my belly when he had kissed me. I remembered feeling anxious, and desperate, and hopeful. "I can't remember what he looks like anymore."

Tristan glanced up at me from the saddle he was cleaning. "What was that?"

"I—" I took a small step closer to Tristan as thunder groaned far away. "I can't recall Henry's face in my mind." I took a few more steps closer so we stood next to each other.

"Oh." Tristan's brow furrowed before he looked back down at the saddle.

I closed my eyes and listened to the rain as it fell loudly all around us. I remembered Henry's low eyebrows, the stubble along his jaw, and the curve of his shoulders…

As a test, I successfully recalled my father's face, my mother, my sister, all of my brothers. I recalled Sister Agnes. I recalled Aunt Christina. Still, I could not see Henry's face in my mind. "I remember my parents as though they are still alive and well. My eldest brother too. But not Henry."

"Oh." Tristan's hand moved a little slower as he scrubbed the saddle. "I sometimes think I can remember my mother's face, though I know it isn't possible."

"Perhaps you've seen her in dreams?"

"Perhaps."

The rain started to slow and thankfully, it wasn't as loud on the thatch roof as it had been, though it was still quite loud on the river.

He shrugged as his hand froze, mid-scrubbing, on the saddle. "I think I must look like at least one of my parents. Most people do. If I see my reflection in water, I sometimes wonder if it's my mother looking back at me, catching a glimpse of her son." He gave a short laugh. "You must think I'm strange."

"It's not strange at all." I held his gaze. "Do you ever…?" I wasn't sure how to say what I wanted to say. But then the words fell from my lips, "I feel guilty every time I think of my mother because I am not thinking of my father or brother. It feels sinful to mourn her more than them."

"I see," he said, nodding. "No point in feeling guilty. How could it be a sin? Missing one doesn't mean you loved the other any less, or that you curse the dead, or some such thing. I miss Alphonse the Winemaker more than my own parents. And yet, I still wish more than anything that I could have spent my childhood with my parents instead of the nuns and Alphonse."

"Yes, you're right. I didn't think of it that way." I fought the sudden urge to hug him. I whispered, "Sometimes I forget Edward is dead. I don't know if I will ever believe it. I sat down to write letters last evening and I almost wrote him one."

"Write a letter to him anyway." And when I said nothing, Tristan said, "Write that you pray for his soul and tell him that you love him. I would write such a letter to my mother and to Alphonse if I could. And my father too, though I don't even know if he's dead or not."

"Oh." Though tears came to my eyes, I wasn't embarrassed. I kept looking up at Tristan.

"Don't worry." He smiled kindly as he watched my tears slip down my cheeks. "Truly, they know what's in your heart."

I couldn't make myself smile back. "I'm, I'm so..." I wanted to say "thankful for you" but the words wouldn't come out of my mouth. My tears blurred my vision and tightened my throat. I bit my lip to keep it from trembling.

"It's alright," he said quietly again, the kind smile fading from his face.

I wiped my tears away with the heels of my hands. It was quiet except for the thunder rolling loudly around us. Finally, I smiled back at him. "Thank you, dear friend."

It was quiet again. I watched tears fall from his eyes too, but he didn't wipe his away. Finally, he turned back to the saddle and hoisted it into his arms. I watched his back as he carried it away and laid it on its plank. When he walked back to me, I forgot to look away. He stopped closer than he normally did and said quietly, "What you said before—"

"Yes?" I didn't mind that he stood so close. It was cozy to be close to him, and the rain was still loud enough that it was hard to hear him.

"Are you sure I could never offend you?"

"I am certain. You could never offend me."

Glancing toward the stable doors, he asked quietly, "Is your love for him true or does it fade now?"

My heart beat hard enough for me to be distracted by it. I lay a hand over my heart, willing myself to calm down. I glanced down at Tristan's hands, slack at his sides. How was he always so calm? "I want to believe my love for Henry was true." I couldn't make myself look at him as I confessed. "Sometimes, when I'm trying to fall asleep at night, I think about how I didn't have anyone else except for him. I needed help in order to survive. And every day we spent together, he saved me from death. I have never been brave, not like you were when you left Romsey and crossed to Normandy." He shook his head but I continued quickly, "My father promised me to Alan Rufus even though I barely knew the man. At the same time my dear friend, Brother Godric the Knight Hospitaller, expected me to leave for the Holy Land and take my monastic vows—I did not feel called to any of the paths set before me, so I carved a new one for myself."

"You are braver than me. You're the bravest person I know."

I shook my head and swallowed my tears. "If it weren't for Henry, when I ran, I would have died. I know it."

"He helped you when you were your most vulnerable," Tristan said, as though this explained everything. "If only I had been the one who helped you leave instead."

"Thank you." I was afraid to breathe out the whole way. I knew I shouldn't read into what he was saying. And anyway, what was he saying? "You would help anyone, even a leper, if you could."

He gave a quiet laugh and tilted his head like he always did. Like I was an exceptionally detailed high relief stone carving. "Well, a leper would probably need *more* help than you did, so I believe you may be right. Tell me you wouldn't help a leper who stood before you in need."

I smiled. "I hope I would, but I've never had the occasion."

"Ah, well." His cheeks were pink in a pleasant way.

It was quiet for too long between us. I forced myself to look back down and my gaze landed on his lax right hand again. "It's strange to think about it now," I said softly, "but when I left the abbey, I told Henry I was going to become queen because it was God's Will. And as he led me to his brother, the king, I grew to trust Henry so quickly and fully, I could see no other possible happiness without him. He saved my life and he hid me here despite everything that was happening with my family up north and with him fighting down in Normandy… I'm grateful to him. Even if he did not love me, I truly loved him."

"Do you love him still?"

"I—" I wanted to say that I did love Henry. What sort of woman was I if I didn't love him still? "I gave my word to him that I would be his wife." Tristan kept staring at me as though I hadn't spoken. Without thinking, I said, "Though I don't know whether to believe it, I have heard that Henry has relationships with multiple women and has fathered perhaps a half a dozen children."

Tristan's mouth fell open a fraction. "Forgive me." He gave a pitying sort squint which caused me to cross my arms over my chest. "I've heard the same, mistress. Truthfully, I saw one of his lovers and their children. It was years ago, though, when I was near Domfront once on some business for Alphonse. I remember her. Her dress looked expensive… she was well-fed—I mean, suppose she's taken care of, one way or another. I beg you forgive me. I didn't know whether I should tell you, or how. Anyway, this had to have been before you journeyed with him, so perhaps it is truly of little consequence in the scheme of things."

"I see." I suddenly couldn't swallow. "I am a fool, aren't I?" I tried to laugh but I couldn't manage it.

"No."

"If I'm honest, I hardly know him. To say I love him now? How can I still think I love him?" I felt dizzy, so I pressed a hand to my forehead to try to cool myself. It didn't help.

Neither of us pretended we wanted to move away from the other. I wanted to lay my ear to Tristan's chest and listen to his heartbeat. I wanted him to wrap his arms around me and comfort me.

But what if he thought I was trying to take advantage of him somehow? I could not ruin my only friendship in the world. I wouldn't risk it.

"Did he love you?"

"Yes," I said quietly. "I believe he did—he told me he loved me."

"Aye?" His voice cracked in its whisper.

"And he took my virginity with him when he left." I stared ahead at Tristan's shoulder. "A woman doesn't forget such a thing easily."

I could feel his gaze on my face. "Well, if I had been given such a gift from you, there could be nothing to keep me from your side. Truly, even if you *hadn't* given yourself to me, I would never leave your side. Not once I knew you needed me there."

I gasped as I looked up at him. He looked steadily back at me. I couldn't speak.

"Not even to rule Normandy," he said. "Not for all of England."

I took an unsteady step backward. "You don't know what you're saying," I whispered. I hated myself for wanting to run away from him. Would there ever come a day where I wouldn't want to physically run away when I was afraid?

"I beg you…" Tristan grabbed my wrist, but I pulled away and hurried out of the stables and into the rain.

CHAPTER 18: BY THE RIVER THAMES

I skipped my morning talks with Tristan for the next few days. Still, I couldn't stop thinking about what he'd said.

He wouldn't have left me.

How strong could Henry's love be for me if he was willing to place Normandy ahead of marrying me? He hadn't bothered to visit me again in the past *year*, except that one horrible evening where he told me my parents and brother had perished. When I thought about this small fact, I felt foolish for still hanging onto the idea of loving him. And yet, I told myself that I still wanted him to come back to me.

After those three days had passed, I couldn't make myself stay away any longer.

When I first entered the stable, my heart stopped for a beat. Tristan wasn't there. But then, with his back to me, he straightened up. He stood in Lilt's stall.

I smiled, relieved. "Tristan," I said, striding down to the front of the stall he was in.

"Mistress." He glanced at me as though he didn't know me. He didn't pause in his work.

"I was afraid you were gone."

"Where would I have gone?" He stabbed at a bale of hay with his pitchfork.

I shook my head. "Will you sit down with me?" I glanced around even though I knew no one but the two of us ever came in here.

He left the pitchfork in the hay bale and sat down next to me on a small pile of straw. I stared at him as he stared down at the floor, and we both waited for the other to speak. "What's wrong?" he asked finally, glancing over at my fidgeting fingers and then over to my face.

I wanted to tell him how, while he was a beloved friend to me, I had already promised myself to Henry. But what if I had misread what he had said before? It had seemed Tristan wanted to take Henry's place in my heart, but what if he meant *hypothetically* he wouldn't have parted from me because he would never bed a woman — any woman — and leave the next day? Surely that much was obvious. He was a good man.

I didn't know how to form the words on my lips to say this. I didn't want to ruin my friendship with my only confidant by confusing kindness with affection. "Nothing's wrong. I wanted to tell you something, but it seems to have slipped my mind."

It was silent for a long, painful moment. "I shouldn't sit for long," he said. "I have a lot of work to do. I don't want to lose my place here."

"You won't lose your place here if I have any say."

"I would hope our friendship wouldn't influence such a decision," he said gently. "Anyway, what happens when the king's man sees you sitting here with me?" He raised his eyebrows. "You said it before, the king wants to marry you."

"What man? Someone follows me here?"

"You didn't know?" He stood up and helped me up. I felt my face flush with heat from touching his hand, but he seemed to have not cared about touching me. In fact, he dropped my hand as quickly as possible. "There he is." He gestured by tilting his head forward once, staring through the open stable door.

Bishop Ranulf Flambard leaned casually against the high, stony outer wall of the Great Hall as though he were trying to hold it up with his back.

"And have you seen this man every day I've come here?" As I stared, the man looked over at us and straightened up from his lean.

"Every day for the last few months, perhaps longer. Not in foul weather, though." I knew by his tone that Bishop Ranulf had been absent three days ago when it had rained.

We watched as the bishop slowly walked away. I hurried out of the stables and Tristan followed slowly after until I stopped at the wide doorway.

"Is it always the same man?" I asked without taking my gaze from the man's back. We watched as Bishop Ranulf opened a heavy door to the Great Hall and disappeared inside.

"It's often him."

"His name's Bishop Ranulf Flambard. He's quite close with the king."

"There was another man while the king was away last time, when he went to Normandy last—Fitzhamon?"

I turned to face Tristan again. "Why didn't you ever tell me?"

"I thought he was guarding you on your behalf. Why would I tell you something I thought you already knew, mistress?" He grimaced slightly, looking down at me.

"Forgive me. I'm not angry with you. I'm angry with King William."

"Oh." He nodded politely. "I should get back to work now. Tell me what you did these past days. Have you been ill?"

"Yes, I suppose I was."

The next day, I couldn't wait to see Tristan. I was utterly thankful I hadn't ruined our friendship. As I walked through the double-doored entrance and down the stairs out of the Great Hall, I heard muffled footsteps behind me. Continuing as though I hadn't noticed, I walked across the yard and to the little road which led to the stables. I waited near the stony outer wall of the Great Hall. Soon enough, Bishop Ranulf found me waiting for him.

"Why do you follow me every day?" I asked him.

"It's the king's orders, of course." He raised his eyebrows and looked down his nose at me.

"Why?"

"I doubt he wishes for me to divulge —"

"You report my goings-on to him, correct?"

"Obviously."

"And he knows I saw you?"

"Clearly he gave orders to keep following you despite you noticing me yesterday."

"Tell him, tell him he may foil *his* plans if he doesn't stop sending you after me. Alright?" I didn't mean what I insinuated, that I was finding a man to keep me "happy" while wed to the king. But I also wouldn't allow the king to watch my every move. "If you say so, you will be done with what I'm sure is an incredibly boring task."

"I understand," Bishop Ranulf said, bowing slightly to me. Turning, he went back through the door.

I continued down to the stables as though nothing had happened, though my teeth clenched so hard that my jaw ached. I had done wrong to my friend. I shouldn't have lied. But it was too late now.

Upon seeing Tristan already working in the stables, I swallowed my surge of guilt. What if the king confronted him eventually about what I'd said? He'd probably think I was disgusting. After all, *I* thought I was disgusting.

Tristan smiled at me and I gave a nod back.

By the time 1095 turned into 1096, Henry's eldest brother and my godfather—Robert Curthose—had decided to join the Crusade against the Saracens in the Holy Land. He sold Normandy to King William for the high price of ten thousand marks. William was forced to pay for it with tax money.

Because many of the servants' relatives tenanted farms nearby, all the talk in the servants' quarters was about the ridiculously high taxes on the whole of England. The king was given all the blame, of course, though truly it was all Henry's fault. He was the one who ultimately talked Robert and William into the deal.

Fat flakes of snow began to fall. Tilting my head back, I closed my eyes as snowflakes came to rest on my hair and melted on my cheeks. The crisp smell of winter mixed with the fallow infirmary gardens. It reminded me of home—of Dunfermline. For a moment, I let myself pretend that I were back there.

"Mistress Matilda," came King William's voice from nearby. "Have you been here all this time? Even the stableman didn't know where you were."

I opened my eyes and gazed up at the king. "What is it?"

"Henry shall stay in Normandy indefinitely. He shall lead the people there on my behalf as duke of Normandy." Sitting down next to me on the stone bench, the king took my hand in his.

"You're going to get your lovely furs wet."

"Listen to me, Mistress Matilda."

"Yes, my lord king," I said softly. "Henry shall never come back to me. I heard you quite clearly."

As he lowered his chin and closed his eyes, I knew it would be more bad news before he said another word. "Also, your uncle, the usurper Donald, killed King Duncan and took the Scottish throne back. I thought I should tell you before you hear it elsewhere."

Lifting my chin to the falling snow, I closed my eyes again. I hadn't known Duncan well. He was one of the sons from my father's first marriage, after all. Even so, another of my father's sons had been killed. When would it end?

King William continued, "Most of your brothers once again must flee their homes."

"Of course."

He looked out at the snowy gardens and said woodenly, "Forgive me for bearing the news."

"You're forgiven," I said, staring up at the heavy, gray clouds. "Though I am parted from my love for these long years, I am grateful to be hidden here in safety and that I am not caught in the fray at home."

"Speaking of your so-called love, I will soon journey to Normandy to help Henry secure things a bit more. As usual, I won't have you travel there with me, so do not to ask. I'll be back as soon as I am able, perhaps as early as Lammas Day, at which time you and I will have another little talk. In the meantime, I will leave Fitzhamon to watch over you. So don't try anything such as leaving here."

"Yes, my lord king."

My days passed pleasantly in the king's absence.

As the weather became warmer, and I spent more of my time each day with Tristan, I quickly developed the habit of skipping meals. And so, Rosamund began bringing me a basket of food every morning which I'd take as a picnic for my midday dinner. After she helped me dress in one of my godmother's old dresses every morning, I hardly ever saw her or the other maids for the rest of the day.

After Tristan finished with his morning work, he skipped his meal with the gatekeeper and the other groundsmen. Instead, he and I would hide behind the stable on the bank of the Thames, or in an empty stall in the stable on rainy days. Together, we would share whatever Rosamund packed for me.

The first day of June that year, the Thames shimmered in the midday sun next to us as Tristan took a large step back. "Right, toss it. I'm ready."

"Are you quite sure? You fed the last one to the fish in the river."

"No, *you* threw it in the river. I did nothing of the sort!"

I plucked a grape from the bunch, aimed carefully, and tossed it in a high arc. "Ah, too far!"

He stumbled back on the scree by the river, caught the grape in his mouth, and then fell down. "Got it anyway!" he yelled. He pushed himself up as he chewed. "Right, your turn!" He jogged back toward me.

As he grabbed a grape from the bunch in the basket, I saw that his hand was hurt. "You're bleeding." I took his hand in mine and examined his palm.

"Oh." He shrugged. "It doesn't hurt."

I pulled him by his wrist so he sat down with me. "Come here."

"Truly, it's fine. I didn't even notice. It'll mend on its own."

"I wouldn't want it to fester. It'd be my fault."

"I suppose I must save you from worry then."

"Of course you must." I pulled the jug of ale out of the basket, uncorked it, and poured it over Tristan's hand.

"Fie, that stings." He bit his lip. "Where's the yarrow when you need it?"

I laughed. "You have made me feel doubly guilty now. I beg your forgiveness."

"You need not beg me for anything. You're so serious." He touched the tip of my nose with his free hand.

"Don't get blood on my face." Lifting my skirts a little, I reached down and tore a strip of fabric from the hem of my chemise.

"What are you doing?"

I pulled his hand back to me again. "Are you surprised because I've ruined my undergarment or because you just saw my knees?"

"Eh, yes," he laughed.

I wrapped the scrap of fabric tightly around his hand. "That'll do you."

"You're too kind to me." He examined his hand and belatedly bowed his head to me, though we still sat in the grass together.

"I'm not half as kind to you as I pray to be." I felt my face warm. "I didn't mean anything by that—I just meant—"

He laughed. "Bless you on the day of your birth, dear friend." Taking my hand, he kissed my knuckles. "May God grant you many, many years."

"Thank you." I smiled back at him as I pulled my hand from his. Standing again, I took a few steps back from him. "Now, where's my grape?"

It had now been three whole years since I had spent those few days with Henry. Though I claimed I still loved him, I could only barely recall our days we spent together. My mind became murky and clouded when I tried to recall his voice, his face, his laugh, or why I had so desperately wanted to stay with him.

I had begun to dream of Tristan most nights. It was a variation of the same dream every night: he and I share an apricot tarte on a warm spring morning under a blooming willow tree. And then, in every dream, he kissed me.

Most mornings during this summer, I could barely greet him without feeling I might combust from shame. Why didn't I dream of Henry? I desperately wished I would, though I never did.

The day after he arrived back from Normandy, King William summoned me to the abbey gardens. He offered his arm to me as we strolled by the Thames. "Do you still visit the stables every morning?" he asked.

"Yes, I suppose so," I said, shrugging. I hoped the king couldn't tell how nervous I'd just become. Tristan was my most beloved friend. King William already had taken too much from me. If he took Tristan from me too, there was little chance I would find the strength to continue playing his game.

"Now that the insurrections in Normandy have been put down, I will turn my attention to the north."

"What do you mean?" I asked quickly. Was he saying he was going to fight my brothers and try to take Scotland?

"The treasury simply would not allow it before now. However, I am now in the position to give my full support to your brother Edgar so he may secure the throne back from your uncle. I'll do everything in my power to get the usurper

Donald out for good. It's time your brothers went home again."

"Truly?" I raised an eyebrow. "Don't kill my uncle, though."

"If that is your wish. I'll just have him maimed and imprisoned, then. It's no matter."

I found it hard to swallow. Somehow, if he could give such an order so flippantly, it seemed this was proof he'd killed my father and brother. "What's in it for you?"

"Foremost, your happiness," he said plainly. "If I do something to make you happy, I believe you are more likely to enjoy my company. Also, I'd rather have your brothers rule Scotland if you are to be my queen. They all clearly love you dearly, from what they write to me. Though, have no worry, they still do not know you're here."

"They write to you?" I asked softly.

"Yes, of course they do. They know Henry hid you away. But obviously, I haven't written where you are, nor has Henry. They're grateful to us that we have ensured your continued safety and they're smart enough to know that continuing your father's fight with me would be a losing battle."

"So you admit it," I whispered as I let go of his arm and turned to face him.

"Admit what?" He turned and faced me.

"You fought my father and had him killed."

"Your-your father fought with *me*. His death was an accident."

"Why won't you just say the truth?" I pulled his arm so he would have to bend down toward me.

He shrugged me off. "It-it-it… it is amazing how… e-*excellent* you are at pretending to be an adult… *most* of the time, little girl."

"At least I am honest!"

"Now who is the liar?"

"I have no idea what you mean." I turned away and crossed my arms. As a monk walked by, he quickly looked away when I met his gaze.

He took a deep breath and then spoke distinctly slower. "L-lilt hasn't been exercised well since arriving here," said King William, "though she is the best-groomed horse in the kingdom. You ought to take her out for a run."

"You'd let me leave Thorney Island? And on horseback?" I turned to face him again.

"You may go every day, as long as it is fair weather."

"You are only trying to distract me."

"Perhaps I am."

"What is the catch?"

"You may only go if you take the stableman with you. I wouldn't want you getting lost. And God forbid, if the horse bucks you off or some other tragedy." He shook his head gravely but then he grinned. "Just make sure you're back by dusk or I'll have to send men to look for you and that's far too tiresome."

"Yes, my lord king."

"And if you decided to leave permanently and not accidentally get lost, well, I'd still find you. And, of course, no sending any letters to anyone. Any wrongdoing would mean unfortunate things for your friend."

"Yes, my lord king," I said again, this time quicker. I took a step back from him.

"Right. Have fun, Mistress Matilda. See you tomorrow."

Without saying goodbye, I turned and ran through the gardens, through the palace courtyard and into the stables.

But Tristan wasn't there. I realized he was probably eating supper or perhaps resting for once. After all, he never would have expected I'd come to see him this late in the day. An outright fear flitted through my mind that he was gone forever, but I pushed it away.

Just as I was about to leave, Tristan walked in through the door at the opposite end with a large, heavy-looking bale of hay on top of his shoulder. "Mistress," he said happily when he saw me. "To what do I owe the pleasure so late in the afternoon?" He hoisted the bale off of his shoulder and into one of the stalls.

I walked quickly toward him. "I was afraid you weren't here." I smiled widely to cover up my embarrassment.

"Why would you be afraid? Of course I'm here," he said, smiling. "Where else would I be?" It was quiet between us for a moment. "What's wrong?"

"The king just granted me the permission to take Lilt for a run," I said quickly, "and he wants me to take you with me so he knows I am safe."

"Truly?" He looked back to me, his eyes wide.

"Yes, I just have to be back by dusk."

"That's alright then," he said, nodding. I followed him to the other end of the stable. Once he was finished saddling Lilt, he turned to me. "Shall I help you up?"

I nodded. "If you would."

He stepped closer to me. "Forgive me," he whispered. Gently, he picked me up by my waist and set me sidesaddle on Lilt.

"I don't know how to ride very well," I warned.

"Shall I ride with you then? It wouldn't be good if you fell off."

"Would you?" I asked, surprised.

As an answer, he hoisted himself lithely to Lilt's back so he sat in front of me. "Hold on," he said over his shoulder.

I hastily rubbed my sweaty palms on my skirt before I wrapped my arms around his torso. "Thank you."

"'Tis no trouble." He directed Lilt out of her stall. As we came nearer, the gatekeeper opened the gate for us and bowed his head to me.

For the first time since arriving there, I left Thorney Island.

CHAPTER 19: THE MOORFIELDS

As we rode north along the outskirts of the city of London, Tristan coaxed Lilt to a canter. A little while later, he slowed her when we'd reached the sprawling, gently rolling green of a puddled marshland. The sky was overcast and there was a chill to the air despite it only being early September.

"Have you ever been up here?" he asked over his shoulder.

I shivered. "I haven't. Where are we?"

"The Moorfields. During my first winter here since coming back across the South Sea, I came up here to skate with some of the others who were given a day off. Since then, I sometimes exercise the horses here, though not often."

"Skate? What do you mean?"

"We all strap cow bones to our feet and we sort of glide around on the ice. It's good fun. Perhaps the king will let you come up with me when the water freezes and I'll show you."

"I'd love to." I adjusted my grip on him so he was closer. I hoped I wasn't making him uncomfortable, but I was thankful to have a reason to hug him. "This place is quite beautiful."

"I never thought so before now, but you're right," he said, glancing around. "Let's go up that small hill over there." He raised his chin toward the horizon. "There's a willow tree."

"Are you trying to tease me? I do love willow trees."

"I would never tease you." Absently, he rubbed his hand over my hands where they were clasped just above his belt. "I just thought we might sit there for a while before we have to go back."

"Alright," I said quietly. The touch of his hand on mine had warmed me down to my toes.

As he coaxed Lilt, she splashed through the shallow marshes. Soon, we rode up the hill to a singular willow tree. After hopping off Lilt's back, Tristan helped me down and led me between the boughs. He took a curled up length of rope from the saddle and tied Lilt's reins to a thick bough.

The willow was overgrown like the one at Romsey Abbey had been. It felt as though we were inside a small room when we stood under it. Leaning back against the tree trunk, Tristan rested his forearms on his upward-bent knees. Immediately, I thought of the day I'd met him and how we had sat under a willow tree then too. He'd been beautiful and kind, even back then.

And then I thought of my recurring dream and I had to look away.

"Alright there?" he asked, smiling up at me.

I sat down in the grass between his knees. He didn't seem surprised that I was so close to him. "I have my most beloved friend with me. Of course I am fine. Do you forgive me for adding work to your day?"

"Work? This is boon." He laughed and shook his head. "Do I seem put out? I'd go riding with you every day if I could."

"The king said, as long as the weather was fair, we *could* ride every day."

"Perhaps I should teach you to ride, in that case?"

"Would you?"

"Yes, but I don't think I should."

I couldn't hide my look of surprise before glancing away. "Forgive me. Of course it would be even more daily work for you." I shook my head as I met his gaze with mine again.

"No it's not that," he said softly, "It's just, I think I prefer to have a reason for your arms to be around me."

My face was overwarm despite the breeze over the marshes. "Oh?" I didn't know what to say because despite my surprise, I was also happy. "I enjoyed that too," I mumbled back.

"The color rose up in your cheeks before my eyes just now." He smiled at me. "Forgive me, mistress, but I love when that happens."

Holding my breath, I reached forward and took his hand in mine, pulling his arm down from where it rested on his knee. He gazed down at my hand in his. His knee that no longer had an arm resting on it then relaxed and straightened into the grass.

"Your hand is rough from work," I said.

"Forgive me." He started to pull his hand away but I wouldn't let him.

"No, I like it. I like holding your hand," I whispered. "What do you think of my hand?"

"Your skin is soft." His brow furrowed as he kept staring down at my hand. "It's lovely, mistress."

"Will you call me 'Edie' as you did when we met at Romsey? At least when we're alone? I wouldn't want you to get into any trouble, of course—but, if you would rather not be so familiar…"

It was quiet except for the sound of the wind rushing over the Moorfields. He still stared down at our hands, and I was terrified I'd crossed an invisible line between us. Finally, he nodded once. "Yes, mi—Edie." I watched as his cheeks blotched with pink.

"I like the sound of that. 'My Edie.'" I swallowed hard.

"I do believe my ears deceive me." He finally met my gaze with his own. "I hardly believe you."

"I only mean—we are the best sort of friends. I am your Edie, to whom you tell all your stories and secrets." I tried to keep smiling. "May I call you 'my Tristan'?"

"You may do whatever you like," he smiled back at me. "I cannot possibly stop you."

"No, don't say that. When we are under this tree, we shall be as we were on that day when I stole that tarte," I said brightly, staring down at his hand in mine. "Therefore, you may stop me if we are under this tree. I am not 'Mistress Matilda' here, and you are not a stableman here."

"Mm." He nodded. With the hand that wasn't holding mine, he pushed a plait back from my face and then rested his hand against my cheek. "My Edie."

I tried to suppress my laugh as I wrapped my arms around his torso and hugged him. Though I wanted to kiss him like I always did in my dreams, I only rested my head against his chest. His heartbeat was loud in my ear. "I am thankful for you," I said into his chest.

He wrapped one arm around my waist and ran his other hand down my back. "And I you."

I closed my eyes. "How are your hands so warm?"

"Well, it is a warm day," he said slowly, "though it always seems a bit cooler here... I think I am always a bit warmer than others, though. Sister Agnes used to say it was the Holy Ghost moving in me." His hand rubbed down my back again. "Are you bored? Is that why you're saying I may call you mine? I'm afraid you're going to forget this conversation tomorrow."

"How could you ask me that?" I asked without any anger. "I could never forget saying this to you. You are my much-loved friend. You're my *only* friend."

He stopped rubbing my back. "Right. We are the best sort of friends. And your heart still belongs with Lord Henry."

"No." I dropped my hold on him and sat up. "I must be true to myself: I cannot love someone I cannot remember. I cannot remember him, try as I might."

"But if you could remember him, you would love him still." He said it so gently that it was annoying.

"I never forgot you," I said loudly, as though I were announcing it.

"I never forgot you either." We listened to the wind on the Moorfields for a while, and neither of us moved. We simply stared at each other's eyes and for a moment, I was lost. In the dappled light under our tree, his eyes were so softly blue that they were almost grey.

Finally, I rested my head on his chest again. After a long moment of me hugging him and him not touching me, he wrapped his arms tightly around me again.

"Your heart just started beating faster," I said.

"It's because of what I am thinking of saying to you."

Sitting up again, I looked into his eyes, trying to guess what he meant. "What is it?" Here it was. He couldn't love me because of the king, or Henry, or because I was a noble woman and he was a common man. Worst of all, our friendship was ruined now.

"My Edie, I love you."

"What?"

"I love you."

"Truly?" I started giggling.

"I'm afraid so."

I burst out laughing and hid my face in my hands.

"Alright now," he said, pulling my elbows so I had to look at him again.

"Oh, forgive me…" I couldn't stop laughing.

He smirked at me. "I had no idea I was so funny."

"I beg you forgive me," I said as I kept howling with laughter. He dropped hold of my elbows as I slowly stopped laughing. That was when I noticed the tears in his eyes. Had I hurt his feelings by laughing or was it just from the wind? "I love you, Tristan."

He wouldn't look at me.

"I have fallen in love with you," I said, pushing his hair from his eyes. "I don't even know when I started loving you." I was relieved when turned his face to look at me again. "You are the first person I think of when I wake and the last person I think of before I sleep. I thank God every day in my prayers for leading me to you and letting me spend each day with you. You are in my every thought, my every feeling. Would you believe — when you were ill this past spring, I could feel it inside my own chest when I woke that morning? Before I even saw you. Without you, I wouldn't — I wouldn't — "

"By Christ, don't lay it on so thick. You're frightening me a bit." But he smiled.

"Forgive me," I said and smiled too.

"May I kiss you?"

As a response, I moved one of my hands to his jaw, and I pressed my lips to his.

As a response, as he kissed me, he ran his hand over my shoulder, down my hair, and then it rested on my waist. His touch was strange and gentle at once. "Lord God, I love you," he whispered, grazing my nose with his as he pulled away.

I laughed again but he cut my laugh off with another kiss. Weaving his hands into my hair, he cradled my head.

"You're so gentle," I whispered. "Your lips are much softer than your hands."

"Edie," he whispered back. "Your hair is so heavy. How do you lift your head each day?"

I laughed. "I'm stronger than I look."

"Clearly."

I ran my hands down his arms and then over his chest. "I have gazed at you for so long." I ran my fingertips over the cords of his neck. "It feels like a dream to be able to touch you this way."

He looked down at my wandering hands on his chest. "Perhaps you shouldn't touch me that way or I might be tempted to do the same to you."

As an answer, I guided his hand to my chest, and I kissed him again.

When I tried to pull him down to lie on the cool, dry grass, he pulled away. "Fie... For a girl brought up under the care of nuns, you do make it difficult." As he leaned back against the trunk again, he closed his eyes and took a deep breath.

"Forgive me. I wasn't thinking."

"It's alright." He reached out and pulled me onto his lap. As he wrapped his arms around me, I tucked my head against his shoulder and neck and so he rested his chin on the top of my head.

"Let's take Lilt and go north," I whispered. "We will get the blessing from the Church." I reached up and ran my hand against his cheek. "I never want another day to go by where I don't see you first thing in the morning."

"Edie," he breathed.

"Once we're married, not even the king can do anything about it. It'll be done."

He peered down at me through his eyelashes as he said, "He would hang me." He touched his forehead to mine as he closed his eyes again. "Perhaps he'd say I kidnapped you."

"I would deny it to anyone who would listen. I would tell everyone *I* kidnapped *you*."

He laughed as he leaned back against the trunk again and opened his eyes. It was quiet while he absently played with the material of my skirt. "At least," he whispered, "he'd probably banish me. Where would that leave you?"

"I would follow you wherever you went. I left Scotland when I was a little child… it is likely I shall never go back there again." I gently pressed my lips to his cheek. "I want my home to be wherever you are."

"Hearing that makes me so selfishly happy, I'd almost let you." He stared up at the boughs of the willow tree. "Lord God, I still can't believe what you're saying." He wrapped his arms tighter around me. "You would give up too much if you married me. I could never ask you to do that."

I lay my hand on his cheek and gently guided him to look at me. "I don't care about any of it anymore. My life is nothing without you in it each day. Truly, you are my every happiness."

"And you are my happiness, my Edie."

"Come away with me." I pressed a quick kiss to the corner of his mouth. "I beg you, be brave with me."

"Is it brave to run away? Wouldn't it be braver to stand where you are and do what is right by God?"

"And which choice is right by God? Have you ever heard God's voice?" I rubbed my hand against his beard. "It is brave to take what you are yearning, even though you fear the taking."

"I know what it feels like to worry where your next meal will come from. If Alphonse hadn't found me, I would have starved to death… I can't risk doing that to you. I don't care about being brave if it means harming you. Call me a coward if you want."

"But you were a child then. We're not children anymore. We'd be fine. Have faith, Tristan," I said quietly. "We could go north and cross into Scotland. My brothers would help us. I am sure of it."

"And what? Add fuel to the fire between England and Scotland when King William orders you be kidnapped back here? Anyway, most of your brothers aren't even in Scotland right now. Or else—I couldn't live with myself if King William turned against you because of me. He could hang you just the same as me."

"But truly, we *could* go…" I sat up straighter and dropped my hold on him. "I understand completely. Men are all alike. You enjoy my kisses, but that's all the affection you have for me."

"I'm in love you with you, Edie," Tristan said. "I love you without end. I beg you, never doubt it."

Did he truly love me so completely? Could I dare believe it? "Then why won't you marry me?"

"I told you. Let's not talk of this anymore. Tell me more about your favorite book, the one about the humours and medicines. I like hearing you talk about that."

"No. I'm too angry to—" But he kissed me again.

CHAPTER 20: BLOOD IN THE GARDEN

For the next two years, Tristan and I would ride Lilt up to the Moorfields almost every day after his daily work was done. We would sit under our willow tree together until dusk and then ride back again. Every day was blissful and frustrating, just like that first day.

During these years, I rarely had to see King William. He was too busy with some problems in France, or else the revolt in Northumbria, which was apparently helped along by my usurping uncle. But fortunately, King William took this opportunity to help my brothers finally throw my uncle in prison. He then led my brothers back into Scotland once again to reclaim their birthrights.

In May of 1099, Westminster Hall was finally blessed to be in use (though King William had already been using it for informal gatherings). There was a large gathering for the event, so of course King William told me to stay in my chamber.

Was he afraid Henry's men would steal me away? Or perhaps the wrong bishop would see me and notify my Aunt Christina? I doubted anyone cared where I was any longer, but I didn't see a reason to fight him. I disliked large crowds, anyway.

However, when Rosamund was called away to help in the kitchens, I snuck down to the corridor outside the king's chamber. From the window and bench nearby the king's chamber door, I was able to watch the people coming and going in the gardens. It was more amusing to watch people than the open fields outside my chamber windows.

I didn't notice until it was too late that I had been caught breaking the rules. King William gave me a disgruntled face as he led a few men down the corridor toward his chamber. I immediately recognized my nose and mouth in the king of Scotland as he spoke with the king of England, and I hurried to him and hugged him before he realized who I was.

My brother Edgar looked utterly taken aback at first. "Oh! Dear sister!" he said, and he pulled me back into his arms for a second hug. I'd caught him with King William, Bishop Ranulf, Fitzhamon, and a couple of other men. "How wonderful to see you! I didn't know you'd be here."

"I've been hidden here these past years for my safety," I said quickly, smiling and glancing to King William. "May I steal my brother for a moment?"

"Certainly," King William said, bowing his head slightly.

"Thank you, my lord king," I said quickly. Before King William could change his mind, I took my brother's hand and led him to the nearby stone bench. "Let us talk. Tell me everything." We sat down.

"King William is truly a great man," Edgar said, glancing back toward the king and group of men as they entered the king's chamber.

"Yes. What high aspirations the king of England holds and achieves," I said, shaking my head. "I was happy to hear of your enthronement."

"Thank you. King William is, well, he would make a most excellent match for my sister. He's a strong ruler, to be sure. Has he asked you to marry him yet?"

"What?"

"He mentioned your beauty in the letter of invitation he sent for this occasion. But it was confusing. I was forced to wonder how he knew where you were. I had thought you were hidden by his brother, Lord Henry of Domfront. In fact, Alexander said that you would be soon be married to that man. Honestly, King William's strange mention of you along with Alexander's strange mention of you is why I came so far south from the Scottish court. And now my suspicions have been made clear. I suppose they both sincerely want to marry you."

"It makes me happy to know you care so much for your little sister," I said, and I pulled him into a hug again.

"Pray, why do you never answer my letters?" he asked, pulling away from my hug.

I smiled and shook my head again. "It was King William's doing. He wished for me to be safe from Aunt Christina, as well as safe from Uncle Donald before you were enthroned. There is still a bishop's summons out for me to be brought back to Wilton, after all."

"I see. So long as you are here of your own volition?"

"I am. Don't worry, big brother. I'm very fortunate to be here."

"I had hoped that is what you would say." He smiled as he gazed out the open window. "I would happily give my blessing for your marriage to either the king of England or the duke of Normandy. You need only to send word that one or the other has won your heart."

"Ah, perhaps it is I who cannot win the king's heart," I joked.

"That's not possible. You're too smart and pretty for that to be the trouble."

Soon after that, as a distraction from each other under our willow tree, Tristan asked that I begin bringing manuscripts to read to him. Often, he would pull me onto his lap while I read. As he played with my hair, he watched the words pass under my finger as I pointed to what I read to him. After a few months of this, he took over reading to me, and he did just as well as I did to him. And so Tristan learned to read.

After his hands inevitably wandered so much that neither of us could pay attention to what he read any longer, his lips would find mine. It was an unspoken fight between us. We both wanted what we would not allow ourselves to have. However, neither of us were unhappy in our fight.

Tristan and I, two children who were forever adrift in the world, had found a home in each other. There was never a day I didn't want to run away with him.

On my twenty-first birthday in June 1100, I still looked the same as I had when I was fourteen, though my face had perhaps become a bit thinner. Tristan had a full beard by then.

The morning was gray and drizzling with rain, so I was a little late waking up. Hurrying to the stables, I was surprised to see Fitzhamon there with Tristan. I was ready to tell off the king's man when Tristan waved to me. Striding forward, he said loudly, in a voice that was totally unlike him, "God bless you on the anniversary of your birth, dear friend," and when he came up toe to toe with me, he said softly, "I'll be right back." Tristan strode out of the stables without another word and Fitzhamon followed him.

Out of boredom, I completed his morning work for him. I was sweating because of the humidity hanging in the air after the drizzling stopped. It was well after midday when he came back again.

Without preamble, Tristan jogged into the stables. With a glance, I saw that he was alone. He came as close as he could to me without pulling me into his arms. "Fitzhamon led me to the king's private chamber. The king and I talked."

"What about?"

Tristan glanced from my left eye to my right and back again and then he swallowed. "Nothing." He shook his head. "Don't ask me. I shouldn't have said anything. It's not right. I just feel… it was strange. The king is very persuasive. But as I look at you now, I know I could never…"

I bit my lip. I couldn't say why, but I was terrified. I raised my hand to his chest to try to comfort him, though I didn't know why he needed comforted. "The morning chores are done." Though it was risky here, I pecked a kiss to his cheek.

Without a moment of hesitation, he pressed a short kiss to my lips in return. The third kiss lingered overlong, and I tasted wine on his lips. And then, grabbing my waist, he pushed me up against a post of the nearest horse's stall and kissed me again. He'd never kissed me this way when we sat alone under the willow—he was ravenous, and unyielding. Soon, he grabbed fistfuls of my dress, and pressing his chest against mine, he began to hike my skirts up my legs.

"Tristan," I managed to whisper. "Wait, my love."

Immediately, he pulled away and, turning so he hid his face from me, he caught his breath. He coughed a few times. Was he crying?

"Tristan?" Hesitantly, I rubbed the back of his shoulder. "I love you, you know. No matter what he said. It'll be alright."

Tristan shook his head and didn't say anything for a long moment. "I beg you forgive me. I didn't intend to frighten you," he said finally. "The king is waiting for you."

"I was not afraid." Shakily, I took his arm. We started out of the stables and then through the courtyard on the way to the abbey garden. When we caught sight of the king where he waited on a stone bench on the far side of the garden, Tristan stopped.

Was I about to find out what he and the king talked about? "Tell me?"

"The garden," he whispered. I looked around at the grass and flowers and bushes. Then I noticed the puddles. In the hazy, overcast afternoon, it was unmistakable.

Thick, crimson blood bubbled up from the earth.

"It's an omen," Tristan said. My hand slid from his arm as he crossed himself.

"No," I said, glancing around, trying to think of some explanation for there to be blood bubbling up from the ground. "Perhaps some birds died in the storm this morning? Or perhaps it is only some part of the earth mixing with the water? Perhaps there were dead buried here, long ago?"

"Your dress, Edie," Tristan said, looking down at me.

Around the hem, my rose-colored dress was soaked in deep crimson.

Suddenly, King William grabbed my arm. I hadn't noticed that he was nearby. "Come, Mistress Matilda, let us come in from this strange weather," he said. Without another word to Tristan, the king led me away to the closest door of the palace.

Ever since the strange blood in the gardens bubbled up and then disappeared, Tristan hadn't returned my kisses the way he had before. In fact, it seemed like he didn't want to kiss me at all anymore. For weeks, I fell but never hit the ground.

It wasn't long before the king proposed to me again. This time, during a walk in the abbey garden, he explained how I was now old enough to marry without question, despite how much older he was than me. He said, "You can have the stableman. I would never touch you, save for all that wedding night nonsense." King William glanced back at Fitzhamon, who waited by the edge of the rose bushes. And leaning closer to me, he whispered, "Of course, we would have to give the appearance we've consummated our marriage. I only ask that you call your children mine. Tristan's son would be king one day. Perhaps this could convince him. No one would ever need to know the lie except us. And Fitzhamon would know too, whom I trust with my life."

And God would know, I thought sadly, though I knew King William would only laugh at me if I'd voiced this thought aloud. "Tristan would never do something so dishonorable," I said instead. I was comforted by the look the king gave me in return, despite my hatred for him. "He wants me as his wife, not his paramour." The truth was, I wanted Tristan as my husband. It hurt my chest to even think of treating Tristan this way. "I beg you, let me leave you, my lord king."

"Henry would go after you if I didn't," he said, shaking his head. "I couldn't possibly. Do not ask again."

July of 1100 was at its end. Tristan had finished the morning's work quickly and efficiently and without much conversation. Then he told me he had something to say to me, and I should leave the manuscript behind today.

Under our willow tree in the Moorfields, Tristan gently took my hands in his. It was the first time he met my gaze all morning. "I love you."

"And I love you," I breathed. I tried to smile at him but he didn't smile back.

"I pray every night you would be my wife," he said quietly. He'd said this once before, over a year ago while ice skating out here with me.

A smile played at my lips but it did not reach my eyes. Both of the other times he'd mentioned marriage, we had fought. Marriage was the only thing we ever fought about. "And I pray you would be my husband," I said softly. Tears clouded my eyes as I looked down at our intertwined hands. I was trembling as I held in my tears. Though I wasn't quite sure what reason he would give for leaving me, I knew that, in some way, he was already gone from me. It wasn't necessary for him to say anything more.

"I know," he said. I could hear in his voice how he was trying to sound strong. After spending nearly seven years together, he couldn't fool me.

"I'm married to you in my heart," I said, lifting my chin, "and I will be, for all of my days. No one can change that." He kissed me as I knew he would. He always kissed me when I lifted my chin this way to him.

He pulled away almost immediately. "That's not enough for me."

"Let's go. Right now. Forgive me, but I beg you, my love—"

"No." He shook his head. "I won't let you."

I stood up and looked down at him. "Why not?" I crossed my arms over my chest.

"You know why not." He stood up too. "I won't stand by and have you be some other man's wife, even if that man is the king. If it is not God's Will for us to marry, then we must—"

"You told me once that you'd never leave my side if you knew I needed you there. You lied to me."

"I—I meant what I said, but—my Edie, you don't need me."

"How can you say that? What did the king say to you in his chamber last month? Whatever he said on that day, I need to know. At least give me this much."

Tristan pushed his hair back from his face in exasperation and shook his head. "The king showed me a large, well-appointed chamber meant for a member of the royal family. It would be mine. It had a secret passageway which led to your chamber. The queen's chamber. Did you know of it?"

"I didn't." I wondered if Tristan had seen my bedchamber. Oddly, I hoped he had.

"The king told me that, on nights when he wanted to give the appearance he bedded you, you would use the passage and sleep with me while he would sleep in your chamber alone. He told me my son would be king one day."

"Yes," I whispered. I shook my head as I read the pain on his face.

He took a deep breath. "Your maid, Emmaline—I'm going to marry her."

I gasped. "What did you say?"

He grimaced at my hand which he clutched in his. "Over the past few weeks, I have confided in her about my feelings for you, and she… Emmaline and I spoke a few times by the hearth in the servants' quarters, just quietly. I don't believe we were overheard by anyone, as it was always late at night. She is a trustworthy girl, as you know." He glanced at my face and back down again. "And well, I thought perhaps— as she is healthy, and a hard worker, and so… I asked her and she has accepted. I will marry her soon after Lammas Day."

"What?" I didn't care that I was crying anymore. "Do you love her?"

"No. I barely know her. You know I love *you*."

"How could you do this?"

"My love isn't good enough for you, Edie. You need to forget me."

"I can't stand the thought of it." I fought to control how loud I was but I knew I was failing. "You have torn the very fibers of my heart…"

"You…" He glanced around us, as though he hoped someone would help him. "Forgive me, but you'll forget me just as you've forgotten—"

"Don't say it! Don't even think it! I never forgot you. Isn't that what you said to me? I know you love me still. You know I mean every word that I say to you. Why do you doubt me if I may not doubt you?"

"I beg you, don't make it any harder than it already is, mistress." He grimaced as his eyes shone like glass.

"Mistress?" I breathed. Stepping forward, I threaded my hands into his hair as I pulled him down to kiss me. He didn't push me away, but he also wasn't truly kissing me either.

"Edie," he warned, gently pushing me away.

I grimaced as I wrapped my arms around him and lay my head on his chest. His shoulders were as unyielding as knots in a tree trunk. "Tristan, don't do this. Stay with me. What is the point of living if you do this?"

I thought he would push me away again. But instead, I felt his shoulders relax. "Fie. Don't say that." With a hand to my cheek, he kissed me. Wrapping an arm around my waist, he held me against himself and tucked his face into the curve of my neck. "Edie…"

When he kissed me again, we led each other back down to sit in the grass. I stopped crying and instead only tried to slow my breathing. Did this mean we were going to run away together and get married? Could I dare to hope as much?

As I pulled him to lay down with me, he trailed kisses down my neck. Soon, he unfastened the collar of my dress as I unfastened his belt and slid it from his waist. With tears falling down his cheeks and into my hair, he leaned back enough to look into my eyes. I looked up at him, searching his face.

"No, don't think about it," I whispered.

Gently, he wiped the tears on my cheeks away. Just as slowly as he had before, he kissed me again, cupping the side of my face with his hand.

"This is just what *he* did to you," he said without fully pulling away from my kiss. Tears fell from his eyes and into my hair. "It is because I love you that this must be our parting kiss. I beg you, find it in your heart to forgive me one day. The worst thing I ever did to you was love you." He started to get up but I stopped him with my hands on both his arms.

"I'd rather die with you than live another day without you." I ran my hand down the muscles of his back as he lay over me, supporting some of his weight on his elbows. "We could go to my brothers in Scotland. Oh—let's go to Jerusalem. I will tend to the sick while you tend to their horses. I could sell this dress I'm wearing and we could have enough money to feed ourselves for a season while we find work. We will save money and buy land—"

"You can't leave the king. He won't let you." He gently pushed my hair back from my face.

"Then..." There was no getting past that. King William's hand was as far reaching as half-way across the world. We couldn't even go to Jerusalem to be away from him. "Then..." I said again. I nodded once to myself as Tristan wiped the tears from my cheeks again. "I commend you to God, my love." I took his face in my hands so he would have to look into my eyes. "I wish you the greatest happiness. When Emmaline loves you, give her the love I have given you. Leave me and be happy."

"Fie, I can't hear these words. You don't mean that."

"Can't you let me pretend? Tristan, the jealousy is already festering in my heart for my maid."

"Edie—"

"Why was I not born as she was? Truly, *what* would I give up if I married you?" I asked angrily. "A sceptre and a ring. A loveless marriage to the man who killed my parents and my beloved brother. A load of thankless responsibility to a country, half of whom despises my very birth. The blame for an extravagant, flamboyant man who flouts the Church at every turn." Tristan tried to look away to my shoulder but I pulled his chin so he'd have to keep looking at me. "If you may happily leave me to our shameful, murderous king and to a life where I may never be home again," I dragged in a shaky breath as I lay my hand on his chest, "then it is better that I never see you again. I have no use for a happy farewell from you." I knew I was only saying all these things in anger and probably, I wouldn't even remember my exact words tomorrow. But Tristan, who would never do such a thing, never raise his voice to me—I knew I was injuring him forever.

When I half-heartedly tried to let go of him and stand up, he pressed a kiss to my lips and then he checked my reaction. When I didn't move, he kissed me again.

"I can't. I won't leave you," he whispered.

"Tristan," I whispered back. "You'll marry me?"

"God, yes. My heart is already bound to you forever. I shall bound my soul as well." He shook his head and more tears fell as he kissed me again. "Tomorrow at dawn," he whispered. "We'll ride north. Bring only what you must. Don't take any jewelry or things that would be missed. Only essentials. I'll meet you in the stables. We'll ride as though we're coming here to the Moorfields and simply keep going."

"You don't know what joy I feel at hearing your words."

Soon, I couldn't think any more about how he'd hurt me, or about planning to run away. His chest pressed against mine as he kissed me again.

CHAPTER 21: DAWN

"Wake up, Mistress Matilda. Quickly, now." Rosamund shook me awake. Dawn had not yet broken and so it was dark except for my chambermaid's rushlight.

"What is it?" As my dream ebbed away from my mind, yesterday came flooding back to me.

Tristan. I had to see him as soon as possible. We were going to leave today. I had a bag packed full of coins, a blanket, a knife, and some food. It was stashed behind my headboard. Is that why Rosamund looked worried? Had she found my bag? Maybe she guessed I was taking Tristan away from Emmaline?

"Abbess Mother Christina is here with Lord Henry. They have an audience with the king." She threw my bedclothes back.

"What?" I crawled out of bed. "Henry's here?"

"Yes, the king wrote to him. King William apparently claimed a date had been set for your coming betrothal and wedding. Lord Henry is not happy about it." Rosamund dragged a blue gown down over my chemise. It was the one I had worn on Christmas years ago when King William had proposed to me.

"This dress? I hate this one."

"The king likes it." Rosamund shook her head as she helped me pull my boots on.

"But it's too tight." I was panicky at the thought of seeing Henry again. "Why is Henry here with Aunt Christina?" And more importantly, how would I sneak away if he was here now? Did Tristan know Henry was here?

"Oh, what they talk of! The king says you're to stay here. Abbess Mother wants to take you back to her abbey. Says it isn't moral for a girl who's intended to become a nun to live as you do. She's only just found you. It was all Bishop Ranulf Flambard's secret deeds. Well, that's what Lord Henry says."

"Henry let her find me?" A bitter twinge of hatred panged my chest. I supposed I shouldn't be surprised, though. Henry had abandoned me, after all. "He clearly doesn't care a fig about me. It's just as well that he has forgotten me because I had already forgotten him long ago."

"Well, no, mistress. It seems Bishop Ranulf Flambard told your aunt your whereabouts against Lord Henry's wishes."

"Oh." I closed my eyes and took a slow, shaky breath. "So this is just some bishop meddling in the king's affairs, as usual. Perhaps Henry will leave without seeing me. You shall tell them I don't feel well and I'll just slip back into bed, shall I?"

"Mistress Matilda, you cannot ask a lowly maid to lie to the king for you." She yanked a comb through my hair.

"Why not?"

"Lord Henry quarrels outright with our lord king over your hand in marriage. He says he wants to take you back to Normandy with him today against Bishop Ranulf's advice and the king's demands." Rosamund yanked my hair again with her comb. "Bishop Ranulf wrote a letter on Abbess Mother Christina's behalf and lent her his horse, but he didn't accompany her here."

"Huh. Coward."

"If you want a say in the course of your own life, you best go and speak your mind now."

"Are you quite sure Henry still wants to marry me?" I could hardly believe it. I was sure he'd forgotten me just as completely as I had forgotten him. "Anyway, do they care at all what I have to say in the matter? I have no intention of leaving here with Henry." My plan was to go *north*, with Tristan.

"Yes, mistress. They sent me for you at once. It seems you may be able to sway the decision at least somewhat."

"It sounds as though Henry, King William, and Aunt Christina are passing me around like a baby to be nursed and coddled."

Rosamund let out a dry laugh as she continued yanking the comb through my hair. As dawn broke over the horizon, yellow rays of light beamed into the room and accented the dust motes in the air.

Pure dread weighed heavy in my throat at the thought of seeing Henry. What if he lusted after me as he had seven years ago? The thought of kissing him repulsed me now. He had wanted me to wait for him and I had said I would, but I hadn't.

My chambermaid turned me around to face her again. "Now go to the king's chamber. He expects you. God be with you, mistress."

I shook my head. I didn't want her blessing and I didn't want to go. "God be with you," I repeated mechanically as I turned toward the door. Perhaps if I got this over with quickly, they'd leave me alone again?

Before I had the chance to take a step forward, the door burst open. Aunt Christina, who was as pale as the whitewashed walls, hurried into the room. She met my gaze with an angry stare as she rushed toward me. "My dear niece!" She pulled me into a rough hug. "Thank God you're alive! When I heard you were missing from Wilton Abbey, and *right* before hearing the terrible news of my sister, and her husband and son, I was devastated! I pray daily to the Mother of God for her Intercessions so you may be guided to the right way! And yet, in my fallen state, I felt sure you were dead these long years!" She started crying louder than she'd been talking.

I patted her back, though I felt no pity. I knew her too well for her dramatics to have any effect on me. "I pray you forgive me," I muttered.

"My lord king," Aunt Christina said, turning to King William as he followed her belatedly into the room. Her nails dug into me as she held my hand in hers. "I beseech you, allow me to take my niece back to Romsey Abbey. It is her *home*."

"I feel it necessary to mention," King William said delicately, "I do believe it is no longer Mistress Matilda's wish to become a nun, Abbess Mother. Perhaps she should not live in an abbey?"

As he entered the bedchamber, Henry pressed his lips together, as though he were trying not to laugh.

"Henry." I stared at him. "I mean, Lord Henry." Did he want a more familiar greeting than this? I would not make myself go to him. He looked the same as he had seven years ago, perhaps a bit thinner. Now that I saw him, it was strange that I had forgotten his face. He felt familiar to me and like a stranger to me at once.

"Mistress Matilda," Henry said, bowing to me. "Come with us, my lord king. You may see Mistress Matilda safely to Normandy and you shall see what I've been doing there on your behalf."

"You don't have to take your vows until you're ready," Aunt Christina said, sniffing and turning back to me. "You may live a celibate life there like the sisters, but without taking your vows. It'll be as though you are simply new to the faith. I'm sure it'll be fine. Or if you like, you may go back to Wilton Abbey. Brother Godric the Hospitaller would love to have his apprentice back, to be sure, as he has just recently journeyed back from the Holy Land after all these years. He is once again in search of more sisters and brothers to join his cause." She pulled me into a hug once more. Barely making a sound, she whispered into my ear, "I am your only chance of leaving these wretched men."

As I glanced over my aunt's shoulder, Henry and William both stared back at me.

"No, Abbess Mother, forgive me, but I won't come with you. It is my wish to remain living here at Westminster with our beloved lord king. This is where I shall stay." I glanced to Henry and back to William.

Henry looked confused and, unexpectedly, hurt. William looked delighted.

"Well, brother," William said to Henry, "Mistress Matilda has chosen." And looking to Aunt Christina, he bowed with a sarcastic flourish and lay his manicured hand on his chest. "Now, dear Abbess Mother. Little brother. Depart in peace and go and serve God."

"Abbess Mother," Henry said, speaking with a decidedly more serious tone than his brother. "With regards to your niece, you may resign yourself to the knowledge that our lord king and I will act as honorable men do."

"Henry," I said quietly. Everyone was quiet as they watched me. "I beg you, leave me in peace."

"I certainly shall not leave you," he said at once. "What has he done to you? Surely he has addled your brain.

Perhaps he's threatened you in some way? Whatever it is, I shall undo it. I promise you. You don't need to be afraid anymore."

I hadn't noticed my tears until they began to roll down my face. They were hot on my cold skin. "He hasn't done anything other than patiently wait for me to forget you."

"We both know that isn't true," Henry said between his teeth, turning his attention to the king.

"Little brother." King William crossed his arms. "I suppose I am overdue for a visit to my lands across the South Sea." He raised an eyebrow to Henry. "Mistress Matilda and I will accompany you to Normandy, but she will return here whenever I do. We will need to plan our wedding. Isn't that right, Mistress Matilda?"

I looked sharply to Henry, who looked downright angry. Was the king only trying to show how much power he had over Henry and me? Surely he hadn't guessed at my plan to run away? "Yes, my lord king."

"Alright. It's time to go." Henry started toward the door.

"No! I don't... I need to say goodbye to—to Emmaline yet," glancing to Rosamund. "And I must pack for the journey," I whispered through my tightened throat. What would Tristan think when he saw me leave with them? He knew me better than to believe I was choosing them over him, didn't he?

Or, would he see Henry's sudden appearance as some sort of divine intervention?

I could barely breathe. He had thought that strange blood-like stuff in the garden had been an omen. I knew Tristan too well.

Henry answered patiently, "Is Emmaline a maid? There will be new maids to befriend in Domfront." He stared at me as though my thoughts were written on my face. "Are you afraid of sailing? What is it?"

It was quiet while the king, my aunt, Rosamund and Henry all stared at me. "No. It's nothing," I whispered, thinking fast. "It's, it's just, it's my women's time. I need to lie down."

"Oh, no! Oh! Surely! Romsey Abbey should be enough travel and then you may rest," Aunt Christina said while at the same time, Henry said, "Your rosiness suggests otherwise."

Rosamund stared blankly at me but did not betray me by revealing my lie.

King William, however, said simply, "No, you just had that last week, almost two weeks ago. Are you sure it's not the flux? I have heard women may be easily confused by their bodies."

"My lord king!" Aunt Christina spat indignantly.

I stared at the king and said nothing.

"You haven't actually taken William as your lover, have you?" Henry made a disgusted face as he glanced between us. "I know what I said before, but I honestly did not think it was possible."

"Edith?!" Aunt Christina wailed, grasping at my arm. "Have you taken a man as a lover?!"

I pulled away from her nails. "Gah…"

"Well, with that confusion out of the way, let us depart in peace," King William said meeting my angry stare with a grin. "Our servant friends shall have to survive without us."

Without a moment of hesitation, Henry led the way out of my bedchamber and down the stony gray hall. The king grabbed my arm and pulled me through the doorway while Aunt Christina followed behind, covering her mouth with both of her hands.

"God be with you, mistress!" Rosamund called to me. I didn't respond.

What would I say to Tristan? Wasn't there any way I could stay behind? Perhaps if I spoke to the king again. I could ask for a quick private audience with him.

"My lord king, may I speak privately with you for a moment?" I asked as he continued to half-drag me down the corridor.

"There will be plenty of time for your love-talk later," Henry said over his shoulder.

"Is there a problem?" the king asked sweetly, ignoring his brother.

"Yes. Truly, I don't feel well. I'm not well enough to travel across the South Sea."

"Would you like me to carry you, Matilda?" Henry slowed so the king and I would walk alongside him.

King William gave a look of mild annoyance. "It's clearly Henry's stench which is causing you unrest. You'll get used to it. Or else, just pinch your nose."

Henry smirked. "She has gotten too used to your perfumes over the years, to be sure."

I clenched my teeth. "Do not speak that way to our lord king, you fopdoodle."

Henry raised his eyebrows. "What have I done to deserve your wrath?"

"I believe it's what you *haven't* done in the course of these past seven years which irks her," the king explained. "But, no matter. I have taken care of her in your stead."

"Oh my!" Aunt Christina shrieked from behind us. "What slanderous, wretched talk this is over my dear niece!"

"Now, be nice and play along," the king said to me, ignoring my aunt. "I promise you shall safely return with me soon enough. Your lord king will protect you from the crooked-nosed fopdoodle. Oh! Forgive me, brother! I mean the crooked-nosed duke."

"Let us have peace, shall we? My head aches," I said softly. I was just trying to think. However, the harder I tried, the more my mind swirled in foggy panic. If I pretended to faint, I knew Henry *would* carry me then. It wouldn't help anything. What if I stole the blade from Henry's belt and stabbed myself? That was no good. I might actually die. Maybe I could actually go with Aunt Christina to Romsey Abbey? The king would probably not allow it, but it would certainly keep me closer to Tristan rather than crossing the South Sea. Then I could steal away, perhaps in the night, and return...

As we walked down the steps of the Great Hall, I wondered if Tristan would even be in the stables yet. Dawn was only just breaking over the skin of the Thames.

I felt Henry's gaze on me as we walked down to the stables. Leaning toward me, he said softly, "My dear Matilda, you look the picture of health and beauty in my mother's dress. I regret your feelings of ill health."

I ignored him. When he tried to take my hand, I slapped him away. "Do not dare to touch me."

He only laughed. "You haven't changed at all."

When we reached the stable, Tristan was already there. He saw the king first and then met my eyes. He was anxious. Certainly, the appearance of the king at this moment was an absurd coincidence. When he finally glanced back to me in silent question, I shook my head a fraction.

Thankfully, just from this, he understood. Belatedly, he fell to his knee. "My lord king, my lord duke."

"Rise, boy," King William said, glancing to me.

It was absurd to see Tristan stand before Henry. Tristan was taller than him, and far more handsome. And yet, he clearly envied Henry. Henry, on the other hand, seemed to notice nothing of Tristan.

Why hadn't we travelled north yesterday? How foolish we were to have not realized it had been our last chance to steal our freedom!

I imagined we had ran away already. We might have had a whole day of travel done before anyone noticed our absence. Though, as Henry happened to come now, he would have tried to find me. It would have been easy for him to guess I would travel north…

Suddenly, I was relieved Tristan and I hadn't ran yesterday. I knew Henry was more than capable of killing another man.

In my mind, I begged Tristan to understand. Was there any way to explain without giving us away? Any show of familiarity on my part would surely harm him somehow.

"We are taking a quick trip across the South Sea, boy," the king explained to Tristan, glancing to me again. "The duke of Normandy wishes for us to take a gander with him through the lands he watches over for me. We'll be back soon, to be sure. The quickest possible trip to a place as far away as Domfront. Ready the horses. Mistress Matilda and I are hasty to leave so we may return and plan our wedding. Isn't that right, my dearest love?" The king smiled at me.

"Ah, yes, my lord king," I whispered.

Henry looked sideways at his brother but said nothing about this bit of over-explanation. Fitzhamon, who had just joined our group at the stables, looked almost as jealous as Tristan at the king's words.

Tristan saddled a large, black stallion and then a dappled grey stallion and led them forward. Fitzhamon took the two sets of reins from Tristan.

"My lord king," Fitzhamon said, smiling as the king took the reins of the larger horse. The two men then continued a little ways away and they mounted their horses.

Henry asked Tristan, "Did the abbess bring a horse?"

"Yes, m'lord," Tristan said in a hard voice.

"Then ready the horse for her, boy."

Aunt Christina crossed her arms. I was bitterly amused by her silent anger.

In hardly any time, Tristan offered his hand to Aunt Christina so she could step up to her saddle.

Ignoring him, she instead turned to me. As she dug her nails into my palms, she whispered in my ear, "How you disgrace your mother's memory! She did not raise you to act this way, nor did I. The duke of Normandy is all lies! The philanderer that he is, so presumptuous! God sees every deed you do, Edith. He said he would treat you as good men do and then did *that* — touching you as we walked here. And the insinuations of our king — the godlessness you must have endured in his company — "

I said in a falsely bright voice, "Thank you, Abbess Mother," and yanked my hands from her grasp. Yes, there was no way I could pretend to go with her, even if her abbey was closer than crossing the South Sea. She would prove to be far more difficult than Henry or William to sneak away from, no doubt. "Go and serve God."

Making a "tsk" sound, she climbed up into her saddle without Tristan's help. I was happy to see the back of her as she slowly rode away. The gatekeeper was clearly perturbed at having to actually be awake enough to open the gate.

Once Aunt Christina was gone, a man rode a brown horse through the already-opened gateway. "It is Lord Henry!" the stranger shouted. "How wonderful to see you again! Ah, and our handsome lord king! You are ready for New Forest, I see!" While the shouting man rode closer to the king and then swung down from his saddle, Bishop Ranulf Flambard led the rest of the group of riders in through the gate.

"Roger de Clare, hello sir." Henry strode forward and the two shook hands.

King William and Fitzhamon stayed mounted on their horses and rode slowly toward the gate. "Oh, yes, I'd forgotten about the hunting trip," I heard King William call to Roger de Clare. "Perhaps we may pass through New Forest on our way to Normandy."

The men spoke too loudly for this early. I couldn't help but listen as they planned the forgotten hunting trip around the journey to Normandy.

Turning, I realized Tristan and I had been left alone in the doorway of the stables. He had the same look he always gave me before he would kiss me. I wondered what would happen if he did kiss me right now. But then the look was gone and his gaze was downcast.

Henry called over from where he spoke with the other men, "Come, Mistress Matilda! Tell the boy to hurry up!"

"I heard him," Tristan whispered.

My chest ached as I forced myself to keep looking at Tristan. "Wait," I whispered back. I took two steps and stood before him, toe to toe. He met my gaze warily. With a glance, I saw that the King William was telling some sort of animated story as Henry and the others listened and laughed. Fitzhamon was watching Tristan and me, but I didn't care.

Looking up into Tristan's glassy stare, I whispered quickly, "I see the doubt in your eyes. I beg you believe me, I shall come back to you as soon as I can and together we will quit Westminster forever. I promise you—I promise with everything, every fiber of my heart. Let me be damned if I am wrong. I will *never* stop loving you. If you know this, it will be the only thing to give me solace in parting from you. I beg you, do not marry Emmaline."

Tristan gazed down at my mouth instead of into my eyes. He whispered slowly, "I will feel your kiss when the morning sun warms my face each morning." He gazed overlong at my chin, my hair, my tear-stained cheeks, and then his gaze melted into mine. "I will see your eyes in each star as they wake in the night sky. Forever. In everything, I love you. I commend you to God, my Edie." Dropping to his knee before me, he pressed a kiss to the back of my hand. And standing again, he turned from me and walked slowly toward Lilt. I watched him walk away before I turned my back to him.

Henry walked toward me. "What did the stable boy want?"

I said softly, "He told me I would make a good queen."

"He's right." As Tristan led Lilt out toward me, Henry pushed one of my plaits back from my face. When I swatted Henry's hand away, a flicker of pain crossed his face before he gave a forced smile. Turning, he grabbed the reins from Tristan's hand and swung himself up to Lilt's saddle.

With a quick glance to Tristan, who wouldn't look at me, I called over to the group of men, "My lord king!" King William looked around to me and raised his hand to tell me he was listening. "Your brother has stolen my horse from me! How shall I ride south? Perhaps I should stay after all, as I am not one for hunting?"

"Oh!" the king called back to me. He coaxed his horse into a gentle trot and came closer. A few of the men trailed after him. "Mistress Matilda, I would love to share my saddle with you."

"You're a right wit, my lord king," Henry said, swinging himself down from Lilt's saddle. "It would be most ignoble of our lord king to share a saddle with a woman he has not wed."

King William glanced at Fitzhamon and then to Henry. Laughing, he said, "Oh alright, little brother. For that, you may share that little palfrey with Mistress Matilda, but she will have *my* marriage bed soon."

"A life of celibacy awaits," Henry muttered to me and frowned comically.

"I detest your touch and your words and everything about you," I said to him under my breath.

His eyes widened as he forced himself to smile again. "I am happy to see you still feel the same toward me as you once did." Without warning, Henry hoisted me up to Lilt's back. I could feel Tristan's gaze as though he were touching me.

Immediately, I slid down from Lilt's saddle and stumbled to my feet. "I will not ride with you," I announced, crossing my arms over my chest.

Everyone stared at me. Fitzhamon loudly cleared his throat. He was the only one who was amused. Everyone else was quiet. Tristan stared at me and when I met his gaze, he gave the smallest shake of his head.

King William anxiously bit his lip as he glanced over to his brother. "W-w-westminster is her favorite place, after all," he said. "She does not enjoy leaving here, except to exercise her horse."

Though he was clearly annoyed, Henry forced a laugh. "I pray you forgive me." He laid his hand over his heart and bowed lowly to me and straightened again. "I was simply doing as my lord king commands. Perhaps you should do the same?" I shook my head, ready to tell him what I thought of him, but he spoke again. "Boy," Henry called to Tristan. "Ready a horse for her. She may ride alone."

Tristan said, "There are no more horses at this stable, my lord. Forgive me, if I may be so bold to suggest — you ought to ride with Lord Henry, mistress. Our king commands it."

All the men, including the king, laughed.

"I—"

"I beg you forgiveness," Tristan looked down to my hands as they balled into fists.

Henry lifted me to Lilt's saddle again. Hoisting himself up behind me, he slid his arm around my waist. I didn't have any energy to fight anymore.

"I know it seemed as though I had forgotten you," Henry said into my ear. "But you need to know how wrong you are. Never a day went by where I didn't think of you. I pray you find it in your heart to forgive me for leaving you all these years."

Resting his forearm over my thighs, he rubbed his hand against my hip. I tried to pretend it was Tristan holding me there. As my tears slipped down my cheeks, Henry pulled me flat against his chest. With that, the hunting party left Thorney Island.

CHAPTER 22: WINDSOR CASTLE

We traveled slowly. At dusk, we arrived at Windsor Castle.

My bedchamber was draped in deep purple and was otherwise drab, gray and small. I was relieved it was a balmy evening because, while there wasn't glass, there weren't even canvases over the wide windows to keep the weather out.

After I dismissed the maid (who seemed uninterested in helping me anyway), I slipped my dress off and I crawled up into bed. As I lay my head on my pillow, a knock came at the door. I hoped it was the king there and not Henry. Before I answered or got up from bed, the door opened.

It was Henry, as I knew it would be. "May I come in?" he asked, half-smiling.

"No."

"Just for a moment, I promise."

"No. Goodnight, Henry." I pulled my blankets up to my shoulders.

"It's been seven long years." He shook his head as he slowly came to my side. "May I sit?"

"Of course not."

"Just for a moment. I want to talk to you." He sat down on the edge of the bed.

"Henry—"

"Yes, Matilda?" Reaching forward, he pulled the string tying the end of my plait. He watched as my plait came undone at the end.

Without deciding to, I sat up and smacked him hard across the face. "How many times do I need to tell you before you listen? Do not to touch me!"

He stood up from the edge of my bed and held his cheek. "You seem cold toward me," he said, laughing lightly.

"You shouldn't be in here." Steeling myself, I said, "I'm not one of your whores. I wasn't raised to act this way."

"What whores? I haven't any."

"What would you like to call them instead? Paramours? You count me as one amongst *how* many?"

"Don't let your aunt poison you. I'll never see you as anything other than pure and perfect."

"Leave. Now."

Looking into my eyes again, he seemed to study me. "I thought perhaps you were just playing at first, for dignity's sake like you did before. But you're serious aren't you? You truly are cold toward me."

I swallowed my tears. "It was a mistake, what we did that night together, years ago."

He shook his head. "You want me to wait even longer for you? It's been *years*."

"I was sure you'd forgotten me until today. I had no idea you were so eager to share my bed for all this time."

He was clearly deep in thought. "You're opposed only to living in sin, right?"

I didn't answer. I was opposed to *him*.

I slid down from my bed. Henry watched me as I walked past him. Sitting down on a wide stone window bench, I stared out the open window at the gently rolling hills of thistle and tall grass.

Henry followed and knelt before me. Grabbing both of my hands, he held them tightly in his own. "I still love you, you know. After all this time." He waited for me to say something but I stayed silent as I continued gazing out the window. "I need your goodness near me," he added.

He didn't sound sincere. Not like Tristan. I knew Henry was only trying to manipulate me. I just wasn't sure to what end. "Well, I suppose I would marry you but I've already told your *brother* I would marry him. You know, the *king*." Even if he'd had other women in the past, was it possible he truly did wait for me for these past seven years? Guilt panged my heart but I immediately pushed the feeling away.

"Right, of course. It's you. My virginal Scottish beauty. You are destined to be queen, as your mother and godmother were before you, and if you marry me, you believe you will not fulfill the Will of God."

"I'm not virginal," I said, biting my lip and looking down at my hands.

"A trifling. If you marry me, it will be just as though you never sinned with me. I know a good, trustworthy man who will marry us. You shall go tonight. He shall sail south with you and hide you in France. Once he receives word that all is safe, he shall come back for you and you shall confess your sins in preparation to marry. He will bring you back to me to Domfront and you shall re-cross the South Sea as my wife, and perhaps as the queen of England as well."

I stared at him. Slowly, as though it were a nightmare, I recalled that last night I'd seen him. Upon learning of the death of my parents and brother, I'd demanded that Henry kill King William.

"Who is the priest?" I asked quickly, though I didn't care what the answer was. Was he saying that his brother was soon to be dead? This meant that Henry would be king, as my godfather Robert was too far away in the Holy Land to take the throne first. And so Henry planned to murder King William? Or have someone else do it? What would he do? Poison him? Challenge him to a duel?

"His name is Anselm. He was the archbishop of Canterbury but dear King William banished him. The archbishop had travelled to Rome but he's since secreted himself into Normandy, and now to England for a time, to counsel with me. He's more trustworthy than even Bishop Osmund was, God rest his soul. He will hide you while I tell William you've run away."

"Why would a holy man take part in this?"

"Because William gets rid of bishops on purpose to take their money. I'm surprised you haven't heard gossip of this in court?" I reluctantly shook my head. Henry continued, "While the archbishop has been living in Rome, William has been taking the money from Archbishop Anselm's archdiocese and depositing it into his own personal treasury. This would be motive enough for any man, wouldn't you think?"

"I highly doubt a man so close to God would seek any such retribution. Seeking treason and lies to somehow balance theft?" I shook my head again. "But, all of this is no matter because I won't go with you. It is still my wish to marry King William."

Henry paused, "Cut with that. You love William as much as Satan loves Christ." He squinted at me as though he couldn't understand the language I spoke. "William wouldn't follow you into France. He simply cannot follow, nor would I let him."

"What will happen when William discovers you went against his command and married me?"

"Well, the marriage will need to remain a secret until it is safer for you to return to England, of course."

"Secret? And then what? You've done this before, haven't you? With other women? How many times have you been married?"

"Of course I have never done this," he said, making a face as though I were stupid for asking. "How could I have?"

I didn't care at all that I had offended him. "If the marriage is secret, what will your men believe my relationship with you to be? Is this the way you'd treat your wife? Have her slandered as a whore?"

"What does it matter what people think?"

"I suppose it's alright as long as *you* remain well-admired."

He stared at me. "In any case, you won't stay in Domfront for long. Perhaps only a few days. No one will ever have opportunity to believe you are my paramour. I have a plan, dear Matilda. I want you near me for it. I need you."

"But, what if you don't pull off whatever scheme you have concocted? Will your marriage to me become common knowledge even if your plan doesn't come to fruition? And what if I were to bear a child to you? What then?"

"It wouldn't be the first time a woman did that to me, but it won't—"

"A woman *did that* to you?" I scoffed. "Maybe if you had more self-control, *you* wouldn't do it to the poor women you call 'lovers.' Who is the latest? How many children did you father as you supposedly waited for me?"

Henry sighed. "They knew what they were doing. And because of me, they live comfortable lives, profiting off of their looks and their hold over me."

"Profiting? Am I to assume you still have relationships with these women who 'did this to you' even now?"

He paused as he gazed over my shoulder toward the hills. "Even if I seek comfort in the warmth of a woman's arms, it doesn't mean I have love for them in my heart. You are the only woman I've ever loved." He looked so aggravated, I was amazed he didn't raise his hand to me. I balled my hands into fists, ready to strike back if he did harm me.

"If you're going to hit me," he said softly, taking my hand in his hands, he gently released my thumb from my fist. "Do it like this." He laid my thumb along the outside of my knuckles.

"Gah!" I pulled my fist from his hold. "Anyway, what do you mean by comfortable lives?" I pressed. "What? So you give them houses and money and things?"

"Of course I do. I take care of my children, even if they're unwanted."

I gaped at him.

He said stiffly, "I may seem a brute but I am an honorable man."

"Yes, so honorable, my *lord*," I said. "Just as long as you don't mention your whores and heap of illegitimate children!" I punched my fist against his chest. "And how I found out about them! As your brother *laughed* at me for my love for you!"

"I beg you, forgive me. I just assumed you knew. I thought everyone knew," Henry said, forcefully taking my wrists in his hands and otherwise ignoring my assault on his chest. "I promised to come back to you. And I came back, didn't I?"

I stood up from my seat by the window as I yanked my wrists away from his hands. "Yes, *years* later! With hardly a word from you in all that time!"

Henry finally raised his voice louder than mine as he stood too. "You *know* I wrote to you, by the way! I didn't want to leave you! I beseech you, forgive me! I was just a bit busy taking over Normandy from your thieving, idiot godfather! You were safe with William. *Any* woman is safe with William!"

"Yes, though he did propose to me! And I have accepted him!"

"I knew he would," said Henry immediately, leaning closer to me. "It doesn't matter. You don't have feelings for him, do you? They're wasted if you do. Is that what the problem is? Your coldness toward me? Has William's pretty face confused you?"

"The king wanted me to have a whore of my own!" I sobbed, "Any man would do as long as I didn't marry you. Are you alright with that thought? That he proposed such a disgusting thing to me? You don't care at all. Though you say you have feelings for me, you left me with *him*, knowing he'd propose such a thing. I was a prisoner. I *still* am his prisoner."

"You're free, Matilda!" Henry threw his hands up, causing me to flinch. "Leave if you like. You don't have to stay with me, or William, or Abbess Mother Christina. Go make your own life. Go back to Scotland and leech off your brothers. Drive the axe down between Scotland and England and forever separate the lands. I won't stop you."

"Perhaps I will!" Without deciding to, I reached forward and grabbed Henry's forearms. "Henry, *you* left *me*. How could I ever forget the wrong you've done? You have the attention of God only knows how many women. You father scores of their children, and then what is left for *me*? Why didn't you take me with you back then? I *needed* you. I believed myself in love with you with all my heart, and now I hate you in equal measure! I have never hated anyone as I hate you!"

A knock came at the door and without a pause long enough for Henry or me to respond, the door opened. I dropped my hold on Henry's arms.

"Go away, William," Henry spat as the door opened.

King William stepped into the room but left his hand on the latch. As though Henry hadn't been rude, he asked in a curling voice, "Lovers' quarrel?"

"Yes, something you'd know nothing about," Henry shot back. "Leave us."

"If he hurts you, I'll have him beaten, Mistress Matilda," the king said in a grave voice. "Just say the word. Or I'll hang him if you like." He winked and pursed his lips.

"A beheading would be more fitting for a man of my station," Henry said flatly.

"Forgive me, a *beheading* then," William said, flourishing his hand as he bowed his head.

"It's alright. Henry was just leaving," I said, crossing my arms.

"Yes. You are fraternizing with my betrothed, little brother. You had better leave her unscathed."

"You're not betrothed yet," Henry said.

"Hm. Yes, not *yet*." William slowly backed away and pulled the door shut behind himself.

"I wonder if he was listening at the door the whole time," I said, thinking over everything we'd said.

Henry glanced back at the door and sat down in my seat by the window. "Knowing him, he probably wasn't. He's too lazy to be that nosy." He reached up and tugged my wrist but I yanked my arm away.

"Don't touch me."

"Relax. Will you sit down? I only wish to talk with you."

"Fine." I sat down. We sat next to each other in silence until he leaned back against the wall.

"You should be ashamed of yourself," I said. "How many children have you fathered? Do you even know?"

"I *am* ashamed. I have far too many," he said simply. "But you know, I do love you." He lifted his chin to the bed. "If my words won't convince you."

"Do not say such things." I stood up. "You don't want me to regret you any more than I already do. You're a ravenous wolf."

He laughed bitterly. "Just a bad joke, Matilda. Truly, you should sleep and we may talk more in the morning."

"Don't lie to me."

He reached forward and played with the ends of my hair which he'd pulled free of their plait. "You must be shocked to see me again. Maybe you had forgotten what I looked like."

"How did—"

"Because I had to fight to remember your face. And I can honestly say, my memory was not nearly as good as the real you. You have only become more beautiful with time. And you seem more... you seem to understand the ways of the world now."

"Th-thank you," I said, unsure if this was actually a compliment.

The corner of Henry's mouth turned up as though he were trying not to smile. "Actually, it's probably good that William heard us fighting. Now it'll be believable when I tell him you ran away."

"Your plan is deceitful. Why should I trust you? I hardly know you."

"But you do know me, *Edith*," he whispered, "And if you choose to be with William, you are against me now."

I stared at him.

"You will get everything you ever wished for," he whispered. "Trust me as you once did."

For the first and only time, I was frightened of Henry. "And what will you do if I don't go along with—"

"Avenging your parents?"

I shook my head. I wanted to say 'murder' but I couldn't force my lips to form the word.

"I beg you, do not go against me," he said. "You do not want me as an enemy, my love."

My path had been dotted with small, thatched houses and simple farms between the fields of brambles and thistle. About a mile away from the castle, I waited on a bridge that Henry had described. The night was clear, and I couldn't help but stare up at the stars and wish my heart would calm.

A man rode a dappled grey horse, and a second brown horse followed close behind. As the man came nearer, I knew he was a priest by his attire. He slowed and then halted his horse and the brown horse stopped too—I realized the second horse's reins were secured to the man's saddle on the first horse.

"Archbishop Anselm?" My voice had to fight the noisy creek rushing under us.

"Yes," he answered. "You are Matilda of Scotland? Lord Henry, Duke of Normandy, sent me to meet you." He had a slightly hooked nose, white-blonde hair and a full, white beard. I was surprised that he was handsome. I'd been expecting someone more like Constantine than an older version of King William.

"Yes, I am Matilda, my good archbishop."

"It is your wish to marry Lord Henry?"

I wasn't sure what answer the archbishop wanted. Was he purely Henry's man, or was he for the Church? If he was for the Church, he might feel some obligation to the king. He waited patiently for me to answer.

"I was going to say it is God's Will that I marry Henry, but, I do believe I should no longer presume to know the Will of God. I've been quite wrong in the past."

"Well, perhaps you should not have strayed so far from the veil, dear girl, that you be tempted to secretly marry your lover. Then you might know the Will of God more easily."

His words were meant to sting me, and so it was difficult to hide my sudden desire to laugh. He had so readily given me my answer! I bit my lip as I nodded. "Archbishop Anselm, truly you are a man of God."

"I am," he said simply.

"May I make a confession? I seek your counsel, my good archbishop. I worry over the harm it would bring to my love when our lord king discovers I have been stolen away." I started crying so easily, I shocked myself. By the kind look in his eyes, I knew Archbishop Anselm pitied me. "You are my only hope, my good, holy man. I must do what is right. I must return to Westminster and await my lord king. I must leave my love, Lord Henry."

He nodded as though I were answering his question. "Let us be off. I shall take you away from the duke of Normandy. For his sake, as you say."

"Alright," I whispered. Was it so simple? He was too ready to believe my lie. Was there was something I didn't foresee?

"Come along," he said. "You may even be back in time for Matins."

"Mm." I doubted we would make it back to Westminster in so little time but I didn't say so.

As I was so short and had no one to help me, I had to jump up to the saddle on the brown horse. I was relieved that the archbishop didn't care that I was riding like a man—I thought I would surely fall if I'd had to ride sidesaddle.

We began our journey with only the sounds of the horses' soft clomping on the pebbly path for company. The whole time as we travelled in silence, I felt as though none of it was actually happening. As though I'd wake up in the morning and be back in the Palace of Westminster and none of this would have ever happened. I would meet Tristan in the stables as I did every other morning.

Could it be true? Could I run away with Tristan as early as tomorrow?

I realized it after too long. "Archbishop," I said slowly, "Isn't... Forgive me, but isn't Westminster the other way?"

"Oh. Clearly."

"Perhaps, then, we ought to turn around?"

It was silent for too long. Was he Henry's man after all? Perhaps he would take me across the South Sea and hide me away in France after all?

But no. Somehow, I already knew what he was going to say before he said it. "I am taking you back to Romsey Abbey," he said in a careful tone. "Your aunt shall lead you to the right path. Truly, you never should have left in the first place."

I clenched my teeth. Should I have simply slid down from this saddle and went off on my own into the dark? I wasn't as naïve now as I had been seven years ago. No, I would play this man's game and wait until it was safer for me to escape again.

I didn't want to be afraid anymore. I didn't want to be afraid of King William possibly hurting or killing Tristan because of me. I didn't want to be afraid of Henry's plans. I didn't want to be afraid for my brothers in Scotland. I didn't want to be afraid that Tristan would marry Emmaline and leave me.

"So long as we do not fear death," I whispered. As the wind swept over me, my tendrils tangled over my face, and I knew I would never be free until I died.

CHAPTER 23: NEW FOREST

It was odd that I had left Wilton Abbey on the second day of Lammas, seven years prior, and now I was back at Romsey Abbey for the same feast day today. It was as though I'd made a futile little circle.

As he'd hoped, the archbishop left me at the front entrance of Romsey Abbey just as the nuns were beginning Matins. As the sun rose up over the eastern horizon, Aunt Christina followed me to the cloisters with a switch in her hand. Once back in my old cell, I pulled my expensive dress off which had once been my godmother's. Without a word, I braced myself against the wall.

Aunt Christina struck me with her switch twenty-one times and left without a word. There was no mistaking the blood which caused my chemise to stick to my back with the last eight or nine.

Long after my aunt left, I remained leaning against the wall as pain pulsed down my body. Truly, I welcomed the pain. I was relieved I hadn't urged her on by crying out. As a child, I had never managed to keep myself silent.

I pushed myself from the wall and slowly pulled my chemise off. I didn't want the wounds to dry with the material stuck in them.

Shivering, I moved to the window. I raked my hair forward over my shoulder, gingerly lifting all the stray hairs from the wounds on my back. As I gazed west toward the river and the forest beyond it, my eyes unfocused.

Would Henry believe I would wait another seven years for him, this time supposedly hidden somewhere in France? Longer? How long would it be until he realized I wasn't where he wanted me to be? How long before he learned the archbishop and I weren't truly in his pocket?

I felt myself smile though I felt like crying. I didn't care about what Henry thought. I only cared whether Tristan was still waiting for me.

For today, I would try to hide in this cell until Aunt Christina forced me to work. Tonight, I would secret away back to Thorney Island. Once I reunited with Tristan, we would journey north together. And somewhere along the way, we would find a priest to bless our marriage.

Would my bag still be waiting behind my headboard? Perhaps it wasn't worth the risk to enter the palace?

I stared at the rippling surface of the river as I forced my eyes to refocus. The branches of the trees along the bank nodded slowly in the breeze.

What if I was where God wanted me to be now? Did God care where I was or what I did? If there was such a thing as a calling, perhaps God had led me to where I was supposed to be, rather than burning a bush in front of me? But then, why wouldn't that mean I was called to be Tristan's wife? God had brought us together and let me fall in love with him for seven years.

As I lay, chest-down, on the straw bed in the corner on the floor, I remembered the day Tristan and I had gone ice skating together in the Moorfields this past winter. His crimson cheeks had glowed through his beard. We had laughed a lot that day — mostly at each other falling on the ice. And later as he kissed me, he had warmed my fingers by tucking them under his collar and pressing them against his skin.

If this was where God wanted me to be, then I welcomed death, and Hell thereafter. If I could not be with Tristan for the rest of my days, I was not afraid to die.

After a long afternoon of washing clothes, the sun began to set. I sat alone by the river where yarrow still grew. I had told the other nuns I wanted to get some fresh air before Vespers, but really, I was about leave. I refused to begin a futile circle back to here ever again.

As I thought about the journey I planned to take, a stranger on horseback rode hard from out of the woods, startling me. His horse splashed through a shallow part of the river downstream. Dismounting too quickly, he stumbled, pushed himself from the ground with his palms, and kept running. Without securing his horse to anything, he rushed into the abbey.

Slowly, I made my way to the mare. It was as though God had dropped the horse from the sky, just for me. I could ride now and get a lead before anyone could guess what had happened. I held the horse's reins and stroked her nose, trying to calm her.

However, it was clear this horse's rider was in need of help. In fact, he had seemed desperate.

Out of guilt, I decided that, if he didn't come back out by the time I counted to ten, I would take the horse and ride. And so, I waited where I was and counted.

By the time I counted to eight, Sister Agnes rushed outside with the man.

"Sister Edith!" the elderly nun called, "It's the king!" I was sure I couldn't have heard her right. The rider had looked nothing like King William. I stayed with the horse as the nun and the man ran toward me.

"What did you say, Sister Agnes?" I called.

"This man says," breathed the elderly nun, "King William was shot in the chest while hunting in New Forest. He asks for you as he bleeds. He may already be dead by the time you get back. Ride with this man. Go, now. I will explain it all to Abbess Mother."

"How did you know I was here?"

The rider said, "You seemed to have disappeared overnight by all accounts of the king's men, but then Bishop Ranulf knew of some reason that you might be here." The man took a deep, steadying breath. "May God strike me down if I'm lying about the king. Let us be off."

I glanced back at the abbey and then to the forest. "What do you expect me to do?"

"You would deny the king his last wishes?" Sister Agnes asked, crossing herself.

"Well, perhaps he might be helped." I grimaced and shook my head, turning to the man again.

"It's a short ride. Perhaps you'd be back by Nocturns," he offered.

"Yes, alright." I shook my head again. Why was I going? I didn't know. Perhaps I did still care about Heaven and Hell after all?

The rider helped me onto his horse's saddle. Together, we rode west into New Forest.

There was so much blood.

The king lay in the shade of a huge oak tree. Dusk was quickly falling. Not far from the king, a couple of men had set about making a small fire.

Upon finding the king lying on the forest floor, I knew immediately what had happened, and yet it seemed impossible.

Henry. Where was he? Why now? I demanded loudly, "What happened?!" Not one of the dozens of men answered who were gathered here in the forest clearing.

Though he was shining with sweat, Henry looked ghostly white as he pushed his way through the hunting party. "What are you doing here, Matilda?"

"What? What are you talking about? This man rode to Romsey Abbey and brought me here to help."

"Sir Walter Tyrrell," Henry said gazing at the man, "This is nothing for a woman to see."

Though he was breathless, the man who had brought me here explained in a rush, "I saw that the king was shot. I ran to him as he broke off the arrow and he said only, 'Matilda.' And this morning, Bishop Ranulf received news that Mistress Matilda of Scotland had just been delivered back to Romsey Abbey. I thought this was probably who the king wanted to see, and Romsey isn't far from here. I left at once, and—"

"She shouldn't be involved with this," Henry said quietly, glancing at me. He glanced over my homespun before he looked back down to his brother.

"But, perhaps I can help," I said quickly. Henry and I exchanged glances when I knelt before the king. What was I doing? I thought, perhaps I should let this man, this *murderer*, die? I should listen to Henry and simply leave. I could go back to Thorney Island *right now*. This was the man who, whether directly or indirectly, had meant the death of my brother and parents. He had thrown Scotland into a confused upheaval and forced my brothers from their homes, all while he'd held me prisoner until I agreed to bend to his will. And yet, I couldn't simply watch him die. I refused to stand by and watch *anyone* die.

As I knelt on the forest floor, Fitzhamon shook his head, whispering, "I dreamt of this. I dreamt of this," over and over, and so I gently pushed him aside. Meanwhile, Henry and the other men continued quietly arguing. King William's lips were bluish purple. Blood was smudged on his chin, as though he'd been drinking a goblet full of it. Leaning close to him, I smelled the blood on his jagged, shallow breaths.

"Why didn't you wait to ask — ?"

"I saw you, my lord, through the trees a short distance off." Tyrrell nodded once to Henry. "I knew you would understand what happened once you saw your brother, our lord king. Time was of the essence. If our king's wishes were to be honored, I didn't want to waste time asking for counsel. Forgive me, but it was clear what needed to be done."

"You were good to act," said Fitzhamon. "The girl is trained in medical sorts of things. Perhaps she truly might help — "

"But, Sir Walter Tyrrell, what happened?" Bishop Ranulf asked with an authoritative voice. "Did you shoot our lord king?"

"I don't know," Tyrrell said quietly, glancing toward Bishop Ranulf, "I saw an arrow fly into his chest. I watched as he broke off the end and he fell to the ground. I don't think it was mine. I had shot an arrow toward a passing animal only a moment before. But unless my arrow glanced at quite an angle off a tree, and I don't believe it did, I don't see how I could have hit him."

As Sir Walter Tyrrell spoke, I ran my hands over the king's chest, trying to find the broken-off arrow, but his tunic was made of thick leather and there was so much blood...

Finally I found it. "Oh, William," I whispered, leaning close to the wound so I could see it better in the low light of dusk. "Why did you break it off? The wound is so large now." I pressed the edges of the wound together but it still gaped open. "How it bleeds."

The king shook his head slowly in response as the men continued arguing over my head.

Tyrrell continued, "As you know, I'm—forgive me—I'm known to be an excellent shot, and I, well, it wouldn't be impossible, but it's been years since I've made such an error as to hit a tree or something which was not my intended target. Lord Henry, you were close by. Perhaps you saw better than I—"

"I didn't see. I only saw your white face afterward," Henry said. I looked up at him, momentarily distracted. His voice sounded strange to me, like someone else's.

Bishop Ranulf said to Sir Walter Tyrrell, "I believe it was your arrow, sir, but it certainly was an accident, to be sure."

"Hadn't anyone else shot an arrow?" Tyrrell asked. I glanced up at him with my mouth agape. This man would burn for Henry's sins. But there was no time to argue with them, and anyway, if I accused Henry, and then Henry became king, wouldn't he have to punish me too?

"I didn't mean to do it!" Tyrrell yelled, his voice quavering.

When no one said anything, I forced myself to look back down at King William again. He still had a pulse, but it was as weak.

"That will be hard to prove. You're the best archer among us, Tyrrell," Henry said somberly. "If I didn't know better, I would think you meant to hit him, as you're so good. Our lord king gave you the best arrows, after all."

"Ah, I was just going to say, check the arrow. Perhaps it was marked," said Roger de Clare.

"The head of the arrow is lodged high in his chest," I said, shaking my head. "If you pull it out to check, he will bleed to death."

Tyrrell's eyes widened in fear. To Henry, he said quietly, "My lord, I beg of you. Have mercy."

"Henry," I gasped, my voice catching from the hardened look in his eyes.

"Matilda, don't—"

"Do not allow this man to die for this. It was an accident, wasn't it?" I glanced down to William and back to Henry. "I beg of you. I couldn't abide the thought—"

Cutting me off, Henry said coldly, "Ride now, Tyrrell. Go abroad. You may still be spared."

"Right, right. You are virtuous and noble to spare me," Tyrrell said to Henry, tears falling from his wide eyes. "I beg you tell Adeliza I love her."

"Yes, we will," Bishop Ranulf said, glancing from Tyrrell to Henry.

Hastily, Tyrrell remounted his horse and rode away.

"The act of a guilty conscience," said Fitzhamon as they all, except for King William and me, watched Tyrrell ride away. "You are too good, Henry. I would have slayed the man, accident or not."

"What good would it do?" Henry asked in a hollow voice.

I was assessing the king as I normally would have as Brother Godric's apprentice in years past. High up under King William's right arm, the gaping wound of flowing blood was cooling and congealing around the edges. The wound was trying to close. Perhaps there was still hope?

"There's nothing you can do," Bishop Ranulf said. "He is going to die."

"Maybe not," I said quickly. "If it didn't hit both lungs, he might be able to survive. We need to bring him north to Wilton Abbey. Brother Godric may still be there. I heard he recently returned from the Holy Land. There may still be hope."

"Moving him would finish him, dear girl," Bishop Ranulf said, staring down at me. To my astonishment, he gave a small smirk.

"Not moving him will *also* finish him, my good bishop," I said. "It's only twenty miles. We would arrive there well before dawn." I was annoyed because I felt as though Brother Godric would have *tried* in this situation. Tried something. *Anything.*

Without asking, I took a dagger from the belt of one of the men nearby. He held his hands up to me, as if I were about to attack him. Instead, I knelt at the king's side again. And careful not to wound my patient, I cut his clothes so I could see the wound more clearly.

"The fire," I thought aloud as I tore at his thick leather tunic. "Perhaps if I burn the wound closed, the bleeding would be slow enough that we could bring him to Wilton Abbey." I looked up at the men surrounding the king. "Do any of you have a thicker blade than this little dagger?"

Henry's eyes went wide, but he stayed stock-still. No one said anything or moved at first. My skin itched with frustration.

"Henry!" I shouted sharply, "Help me!" My voice echoed into the dark forest around us.

After meeting my gaze for too long, Henry drew his sword from his belt and offered it to me, hilt first. King William mouthed something to me when I glanced down at his face, but he was not actually making any noise when he tried to speak.

I met King William's eyes. I was surprised he was still conscious, but he looked up at me, straight back into my eyes.

"Do not try to speak for now. I'm going to try to save you, William," I said, and quickly added, "my lord king."

Fitzhamon had begun to silently weep next to me. I tried not to look at him. I didn't want to be distracted from what I needed to do. I took Henry's sword and warmed the point in the heart of the fire nearby. "You there," I said, pointing to a man near me, "Get some more kindling and make this fire larger."

The man did as I said. The fire was soon larger. Once the tip of Henry's sword was glowing in the fire, I looked back over at Henry.

"I want you to pull the arrow from his chest. I will burn the wound shut."

Henry stared back at me. "Matilda—"

"There isn't anything else to be done," I said. "We may save your brother yet."

Finally, after a long moment, Henry bent down over his brother. With a quick huff of breath, he tried to grab hold of the broken piece of arrow which protruded from the king's chest. I was tempted to push Henry away and do it myself, but I wanted to be able to burn at the same time the arrow came free of William's chest. It took a few tries, but Henry finally got a grasp on the broken arrow, though it was slick with congealed blood.

"One, two…" I took a deep breath. "Three." Henry pulled the broken arrow from the king's chest as I pulled the hot sword from the fire.

As I burned the bleeding to a halt in the king's chest, some of the men around us groaned at the awful searing noise. Once I was sure I burned the wound bed closed, I dropped the sword to the forest floor and made the Sign of the Cross over the king.

Everyone there in the clearing stood immobile as they watched. My hands traveled from the king's chest, to his neck, to his face, assessing him, and feeling for a pulse.

The king's eyes were wide as they found mine again. "Breathe, William," I urged. But he couldn't breathe. He searched the features of my face for an answer, silently begging for help as his eyes grew more blood-shot and the rest of his face grew so blue it turned to a purple-grey. I could see doubt—doubt I was actually trying to help him, doubt he had any chance to survive.

He was suffocating to death.

To my dismay, Bishop Ranulf stepped forward and starting chanting in Latin: it was the king's Last Rites.

Somewhere in my mind, I knew if I didn't ask for his forgiveness, I would lose my chance forever. But the words never formed on my lips. I couldn't blink, let alone move my tongue to apologize for driving the last nail into King William's coffin.

In vain, I pushed my hands down over his wound, but there was no outward wound to stop with my hands. The wound was inside him. There was nothing that I could do.

"I dreamt of this," he mouthed to me—at least, that's what I thought he tried to say. He was trying to tell me something else but then he coughed without sound. As though from an overflowing well, blood flowed from his mouth, washing him in crimson.

"No." I choked on the rest of my words.

Finally, when the king's chest stopped heaving, my hands moved away from him. I was weak. Mechanically, I bent forward and laid my ear to William's chest. His heart wasn't beating. My shaking hands were completely coated in the king's blood and the side of my face was now warm with it too. I knew my face, homespun, everything, had been covered.

"King William is dead," I said finally, sitting back on my heels. Slowly, Henry leaned over his brother and shut William's eyes, breaking my trance.

Bishop Ranulf said in Latin, "In the name of the Father, and of the Son, and of the Holy Spirit."

My heart had stopped, too. What had just happened? Why hadn't that saved him? His lung surely had been punctured. Burning couldn't stop the flow of blood like with a limb, obviously. I wondered if I shouldn't have even tried to help. But I couldn't have stood by and done nothing. Either way, he would have surely died, unless we had travelled the twenty miles to Brother Godric. Perhaps Brother Godric… but what could he have done? Probably the same as I had done, right?

As though the hunting party all thought of these questions too, when I looked up at them, I found they were all openly staring at me.

"I truly thought that would help him. I intended to close the wound so he could be transported." I glanced from face to face, still on my knees by the king, my bloody palms held out to them in supplication. "Honestly. I would have done it for myself, or any of *you* if needed. You must believe me."

Silence answered back.

Then Bishop Ranulf said delicately, "Truly? Did you honestly want to save him? You may confess if you wanted to kill him, Mistress Matilda."

Henry shook his head. "Ranulf Flambard," he growled, "you—"

"No!" Fresh tears burned my eyes. "I didn't try to kill him. He was already dying. I, I was trying to save him—"

"It's alright, Matilda," Henry said, offering his hand, which was covered in blood, like mine. Henry looked tired. "No one here believes you tried to kill him." He helped me to my feet.

"Well, what now?" Roger de Clare asked, glancing around.

"Now," Bishop Ranulf said, "we ought to disperse so none here may be thought party to a murder, I do believe."

There were murmurs of agreement.

"You can't just leave his body here!" Horrified, I turned to Henry. "Henry, he's your brother!"

"He's dead now," Henry said softly. "No more harm may come to him. I must make haste to Winchester." He pressed a kiss to my cheek and then hastily wiped blood from his lips. "Don't take any vows, alright Matilda? I'm coming back for you. I beg you, do not be hasty."

I didn't respond.

After staring at me for a moment, Henry said, "Come on, Fitzhamon. I need you as witness."

Fitzhamon was still staring at King William's body. "No, but, we should take him back. I would very much prefer to bring him back, as Mistress Matilda says. I beg you, my lord, he is your brother. I humbly beseech you —"

"Now," Henry demanded. "I'll send men back for him once we reach Winchester. For all our sake. Sir Robert Curthose is on his way back from the Holy Land. He must not be allowed to win King William's throne."

Belatedly, Fitzhamon glanced around himself and meeting my eyes briefly, he tore his cloak from his shoulders and draped it over the king's body. He didn't cover his face though, and so it seemed, perhaps he was only trying to keep the dead king warm?

Then, he stumbled to his horse. A moment later, Henry was on Lilt's back and the two had disappeared into the black forest.

"Will one of you give me a ride back to the abbey at least?" I asked, glancing around. The other men were all mounting their horses. Bishop Ranulf was the last.

"Bishop Ranulf," I said, fresh tears mixing with the blood on my face. "I beg you, help me, my good bishop."

"I must journey with Lord Henry. God is with you, child. You'll find your way back, to be sure." I watched as he mounted his horse, and leading the king's horse behind him, he left.

I was alone with the king's body.

As I gazed down at William, I realized it was time to go. After seven years, it was finally time to leave him. I could go back to Tristan now and we would be free. It was so simple and perfect to be left behind.

And yet, my feet would not move.

Kneeling down before the king again, I wept. Gently, I lifted his cool hand in mine and held it to my chest.

"I had prayed you would die," I whispered to William's body. "Prayed to God for a sin on myself. And now that you are dead, oh how I pray you would breathe again. I beg you forgive me. I beg…" I drew in a deep breath as though I had been underwater.

It was my fault. Perhaps it was right that I stay here. I had killed him, hadn't I? I asked Henry to do this, though it had been years ago and in anger.

Perhaps it all truly had been an accident?

A twig snapped behind me. Leaving the fire burning nearby, I pushed myself to my feet, tripping over one of my skirts. I broke into a run away from the fire. Soon, it was pitch black in the forest.

I didn't stop running until I saw light flickering between the trees. Leaning back against a tree trunk, I pulled in gasping breaths as I tried to calm down. Finally, my heart and breath began to slow, and I blinked tears from my eyes.

"Lord God," I whispered, titling my chin to the sky and wiping sweat mixed with blood from my forehead. Glancing wildly around, I saw that I stood under the willow tree where Tristan and I had once shared a stolen apricot tarte. Forcing my feet to trudge just a bit further from the king and out from under the willow tree, I laughed. Of course I came back here.

I turned my back to Romsey Abbey and instead headed toward the river. Unhurriedly, I waded into the River Test and ducked down under the surface. I hastily scrubbed King William's blood from my face and hands. Pulling my hair out of my twisting plaits, I scrubbed my scalp as well. I wanted every last bit of blood off of my body. I was tempted to take my homespun off and leave it in the bottom of the river, but I had to come up for air. Breaking through the river's surface, I drew a deep pull of summer air, heavy and warm.

Someone far away was shouting for me. Were they coming for me because I'd killed the king? I decided to leave my homespun on for a little while longer.

I dragged myself from the river. Water dribbled from my hem into the grass. My waterlogged sandals squelched loudly with each step into the antechamber of the abbey. Aunt Christina met me at the doors, hurrying forward.

"Why didn't you answer me? Did he die?!" Aunt Christina's eyes were wide as she took in my appearance.

"Yes, he died," I said. "Our lord king is dead. I shouldn't have... I don't know what—"

"Where is he?" Aunt Christina asked. "Are they taking his body directly back to Winchester or Westminster? Oh, or perhaps the Tower?"

I fell down to my knees. Sister Agnes, who I hadn't noticed until then, came forward. As I began to weep like a child, my old nursemaid held me, patting my soaking wet back. "No," I whined, "God forgive us, we left him there. I left him there… Henry watched his brother die and then he left him. "

"*What?*" Aunt Christina yelled. "We need to get his body before animals… well… His body must remain unscathed for the Second Coming!" She crossed herself and then hurried away down a side-hallway.

"I killed him," I whispered, grabbing fistfuls of my sodden homespun. I watched as water squished out from the wool between my fingers.

"Of course you didn't," Sister Agnes whispered back. "It was a hunting accident."

"But, I tried to help him and I only made it worse."

"God is with you, Edith," said Sister Agnes, gently pushing my long, wet hair from my face with her rheumatic fingers. "We all have those times of questioning ourselves. But God sees what is in your heart. The king knows now too, for he is with God. You have nothing to fear."

I nodded dumbly, thinking it was equally likely William was burning in Hell, but I didn't want to point this out. I pushed myself from the floor. "I must go with Abbess Mother to help her find the body. She doesn't know where he is."

"I'll come with you," Sister Agnes said as I helped her to stand. "Go and change your clothes first. It may prove to be a long night." She patted my back again.

"Yes, thank you, Sister Agnes." We walked arm-in-arm back toward the cloisters. Once in my cell, Sister Agnes immediately went to the jug of watered ale by the window and poured some into a wooden cup while I changed.

"Drink this. You must be thirsty."

"Thank you." I gulped the watered ale down. With a couple of rushlights taken from our bedside tables, we hurried back to the front of the abbey. Then we joined Aunt Christina to search for the king's body in the dark.

Immediately, I led them to where the fire had been. But the king's body was no longer there. "Perhaps this means that one of the hunting party came back?" I said hopefully.

"Clearly a person would have had to put the fire out for it to have gone out so quickly," Sister Agnes said, nodding. "It was still burning when you left, right?"

"Yes," I said, staring down at the smoldering embers.

"Let's search the area. Perhaps, well," said Aunt Christina, "I want to be sure the body isn't still here. We three will stay close together. Let us not lose anyone else tonight."

CHAPTER 24: FROM THE ABBEY TO THE CATHEDRAL

After hours of fruitless searching, Aunt Christina allowed us to give up and go back to the abbey.

Even though I was exhausted, I could not sleep. Every time I closed my eyes, I saw the king staring back at me as he died. When I finally managed to nod off that night, I dreamt in red. William pointed his finger at me and blamed me for his death. When he began to strangle me, I woke and stared at the ceiling.

I heard the bell toll a while later, and so I heaved myself from my bed and went to Matins. I did not fall asleep afterward. Again I resolved to run away during Vespers. Did Tristan still wait for me? As soon as I allowed myself to wonder it, I was angry with myself for doubting him.

Before midday, a Godsend arrived at the front gate claiming to have been sent to assist Matilda of Scotland away to Westminster Abbey. As most of the nuns had no idea I had gone by that name, the man had nearly left without me. Sister Agnes alerted me just as he was about to leave.

As Aunt Christina ran after me and screamed for me to stay where I was, I ran out the front gate of Romsey Abbey. Tristan was not the man to come for me as I'd hoped, but it didn't matter. This man would take me to him. "Let us go! I am Mistress Matilda!"

When the man only stared at me, I untied the spare horse's reins from the man's saddle. When I jumped up to my borrowed horse's saddle, I startled her. I didn't mind when she bucked and then took off like an arrow.

I leaned forward on my saddle and snapped my reins, urging her faster. Finally, after years of Tristan's guidance and instruction, I realized I could ride on my own without trouble.

The man had trouble catching up to me, so after a while, I allowed my horse to slow. At least I had left my aunt behind.

The day was cloudy and humid. I was hot in my woolen clothing. Thankfully the man didn't force small talk on me and so, except for the clomping steps of our horses, it was quiet the whole way to Thorney Island. I never even learned my escort's name.

By the time we arrived at Westminster Palace, having changed horses at a travelling post, it was already supper time. Once through the open gate and into the stables, I held my breath as I glanced around for Tristan.

But he wasn't there. Yes, it was evening, but I, an invited guest, was obviously due to arrive. Surely he should have been waiting for me.

All the blood rushed from my face. As I looked around, I saw a boy I didn't recognize. I stared openly at him, disbelieving. The words of the boy and my escort washed over me without my ears hearing them.

Mechanically, I took the boy's hand when he offered it and I slid down from my saddle.

"She is a guest of the new king," my escort said proudly. "This way, Sister."

The boy smiled kindly as he began unsaddling my horse.

"I know the way," I said dully and walked away.

As I paced around the edge of the Great Hall in the shadows, I spied a few familiar faces, Rosamund amongst them. I couldn't stop myself from asking her. "Dear friend," I said softly, walking quickly to Rosamund and hugging her. She looked surprised but then recognized me.

"Oh, mistress," Rosamund said, hugging me and, when I released her, she bowed her head. "I am so happy to see you."

"As I am to see you," I said. "Pray, where is dear Emmaline? I will need her help. I am dressed so plainly for my reunion with Henry — Duke of Norm — "

"Yes, mistress." Rosamund betrayed me with a look of pity. "Surely the Crown Apparent shall be eager to see you." Rosamund bowed her head in a formal sort of way again. "Forgive me, my daughter is no longer in your service. She asked that I beg your forgiveness for leaving without being granted dismissal from you. I pray you will be satisfied with my help, or perhaps even a few of the ladies of the court might assist you, as surely you are soon to be queen, and it would be fitting to take on — "

But grabbing hard onto Rosamund's arm, I led her away from the others around us. "Where is she?"

Rosamund gave a tight smile. "My daughter has been married only yesterday. To your friend Tristan, as a matter of fact. The stableman. It was a most joyous ceremony! A beautiful day. Emma and her new husband shall work a lovely bit of land not far from here. They are two or three days' journey, I would think. Near Winchester. The Crown Apparent, our Lord King Henry, arranged for their tenancy there on a bit of land that had been his mother's, no less. We could not be more thankful. I pray you tell him how happy we are to have his magnificent intercession into our humble lives."

I looked down at my hands and then around the room. I didn't want to look at Rosamund anymore. "God bless their marriage. I shall be sure to thank, erm, King Henry when I see him next. I am so looking forward to reuniting with my love once again."

"Of course," Rosamund said.

Tristan's parting words—that he commended me to God… It sounded differently in my mind now.

Forcing a smile back to my face as tears clouded my vision, I whispered, "I will turn in early."

"Of course, mistress. The queen's chamber is readied for you. Perhaps I shall assist you?"

"No. Goodnight."

As I turned and walked away from Rosamund, I looked up at the high, arching ceiling and tried in vain to prevent my tears from falling. This huge room was far too full of people. Aimlessly, I wandered out into the hallway and down a side corridor. I only knew I didn't want to be in the Great Hall any longer. In fact, I didn't want to be anywhere any longer. "So long as we do not fear death," I whispered. I certainly did not fear death any longer. In fact, I whole-heartedly welcomed it. "I am truly free." As I ran my hand along the gray stone wall as I walked, I laughed bitterly to myself and let my tears fall where they may.

"Matilda?" Henry pulled me into a quick hug and released me just as quickly.

"My lord king." I laughed again.

"You didn't take vows, did you?" He glanced over my homespun.

"No." I didn't bother wiping my tears from my face.

"You're upset." He shook his head. "Forgive me. You are too good to come here so soon after William's death."

I closed my eyes, pressing the burning tears away from my lashes. Henry somehow knew about Tristan. That's how Tristan got his tenancy, after all. Henry had won everything and I had lost everything. "I was hasty in coming here."

"Hasty? This is the first time I've been able to bring you to me. It's the first time we may be together. I'm going to be king now."

Was he serious? I gazed up at him and I was surprised: his smile seemed a little unsure. He didn't seem to be proud or triumphant, as I had expected. "We can finally be married," he continued. "William, Normandy — no one may stand in our way any longer."

"But," I started, "what will happen when my godfather comes back from the Crusade in the Holy Land? You will have to fight again."

Henry looked over my shoulder at something which made his eyes widen in surprise. Distracted, I turned too. "King Henry!" a woman called from down the corridor. Neither Henry nor I said anything. Instead, we both stood still as the woman approached us. "Oh, pardon me, Sister. King Henry, my love—"

"Who are you?" I asked flatly. The woman was ash-blonde and much taller than me. I crossed my arms over my chest, hugging myself. After riding in the sun all day, I was cold.

"Oh," said the woman, eyeing me as though I was so rude I didn't deserve an answer to my question. The woman looked back to Henry. "Shall I meet you in your cham—?"

"Be quiet, woman," he said, his eyes hardening.

So Henry hadn't been faithful after all. It made me bitterly happy. I didn't need to feel guilty anymore. "My lord king,"

I said in a sing-song voice, "there is no need to hide your lover away from me." I turned to the woman. "What is your name so I may pray for you?"

"Thank you, Sister," the woman said and widened her eyes expectantly at Henry.

He looked like he was barely containing his anger, though I could clearly see that this woman had no idea. His paramour may have been beautiful but she was an idiot. I bit my lip to keep myself from laughing.

"Matilda, allow me to introduce Lady Sybilla Corbet of Alcester. Lady Sybilla, I introduce Mistress Matilda of Scotland, daughter of King Malcolm the Third of Scotland and the Queen Consort of Scotland, Margaret of Wessex. God rest their souls."

Sybilla's eyes widened further in surprise as she looked from Henry to me. "Oh, I see."

"Yes," he said, pressing his lips together as though he wanted to scold a child. "She and I are soon to be married."

She turned away without another word.

"I'll pray for you," I called to Sybilla's back as the woman strode quickly away down the corridor.

"I beg your forgiveness," Henry said immediately.

I patted Henry's arm, silencing him. "Didn't you say once that you didn't suffer fools? How did she manage to find her way into your bed? Did you have to draw her a map?"

"Don't be mean, Sister."

"Why shouldn't I be, *my love*? I could have been queen years ago to your brother if I had wanted. Why did I wait for you?"

"You are as bad a liar as me. You didn't wait for me."

I gasped but recovered quickly. "If you say you love me, how may you give your heart to another?"

"She doesn't have my heart. I bed her because she's beautiful and I am not good at being alone." He stared at me. I stared back and watched his face ebb from anger to unhappiness. "Let us never speak of her or any others like her again. It is *you* I love, Matilda. It is you I wish to marry and have at my side as my queen."

"And what if I want a husband who is faithful to me in our marriage?"

"I thought you were a woman of God?" he asked, raising an eyebrow. "Surely you wouldn't want to share my bed after we've had our children? Is that lustfulness I detect in your question?"

I bit my lip. He was too smart for my liking. "I cannot possibly answer you," I whispered, "other than to say I pray to marry a virtuous husband."

"Well, that's encouraging," he said, smirking.

"You're the last man I could possibly marry if my prayers are answered."

"Well, fortunately for me, God is not in the routine of answering prayers. And anyway, it would seem I am the only man you could possibly marry now, save Christ." He glanced back toward the corridor behind us. Was he expecting another of his paramours to pop up behind him?

Failing to fight my tears, I shook my head. "Fie, Henry, when did you become so cold-hearted?"

He turned his attention to me again. "Forgive me," he said softly, frowning. He wiped my tears from my cheek. "We've both had a troubling few days and tomorrow will be another hard one. I'll lead you to your chamber."

I took his arm when he offered it, mostly because my tears made it difficult to see the steps we climbed.

After he opened the queen's chamber door, he kissed my forehead. "I pray you find peace in your heart again."

"I thought God didn't answer prayers?"

He was quiet while he pushed my hair away from my face and behind my shoulder. Slowly, he bent and kissed a tear on my cheek. "Forgive me for leaving you so long," he said. "I love you, Matilda."

With that, he left.

After I finally fell asleep, I felt as though it was only a moment later when Rosamund tapped me awake. The sunbeams of dawn warmed the room in yellow rays.

"It's the king's crowning today. Time to dress, mistress," Rosamund said quietly.

"Fine." I didn't care. What was the difference whether I had slept?

She dressed me in a heavy white gown with golden accents—another of my godmother's, of course. Then, she adorned me in heavy lumps of jewels which I had never seen before. It took ages before she was satisfied with her work.

She gave me her arm to hold onto and led me down the stone stairs and along a wide passage. Exiting, we walked across the abbey garden and into the front entrance of Westminster Abbey.

A subdued gathering, dressed in their finest things, muttered quietly to one another as they waited. My gaze moved down the nave to the dais at the far end, past the transepts. The plush crimson and gold throne sat empty. Behind it, there was the old, familiar golden iconostasis which hid the altar.

All fell silent when the back double doors swung open. Two bishops, each holding one of Henry's hands, led Henry in as they slowly made their way to the crossing of the nave.

Out of the silence, the monk choir of the abbey began singing with a sweet, echoing timbre. When Henry and the bishops reached a large, ornate red rug in the crossing, Henry lay prostrate on the floor. The bishops did the same on either side of him.

I closed my eyes as I listened to the monks' voices. It sounded like a lament, though I knew they sang praise to God with the Latin words I knew so well.

The hymn was over and I opened my eyes. Henry was speaking in a low, commanding voice about promises to the people, and then the bishops took turns reciting some prayers, but I wasn't listening. The crowd said "amen" as one, like a crashing wave in my ears. I stared at Henry and wondered how my life had led me here again, to the precipice of marrying this man. After today, Henry would be king, the same Henry who had proposed to me under that yew tree, years ago.

My heart burned to see Tristan again. I wished he could be here to carry me through this new life with a new king. I wished I could talk to him and he could help me understand my jumbled thoughts. I wished he could just hold my hand one more time.

Why had I gone into the forest with that Tyrrell man? If I hadn't been such a coward, I could have come back to Tristan before it was too late. God had given me the opportunity and I had not taken it. If I'd taken Tyrrell's horse... but then Tyrrell probably would have been taken to Winchester and sentenced to death. Henry would have killed two men that night instead of one.

Henry did kill William. Didn't he?

Dust-moted light beamed down from the clerestory onto Henry as he faced the crowd of people. I watched the bishops anoint Henry with holy oil, until my eyes blurred. I stared up to the clerestory windows to keep my tears from falling.

Tristan left me. Though I felt rushed to return to Westminster, I finally allowed myself to realize: it wouldn't have mattered if I had gotten back before his wedding to Emmaline. Perhaps he had lain with me on that last day together only to ease his pain in parting from me, and not out of any promise to marry me? Or, worse, perhaps for all that time we spent together, I had only been a pretty convenience, and there had never been any love in his heart for me to begin with?

I shook my head. I wouldn't think those thoughts again. Of course he loved me. How could I doubt the love he had given me for nearly seven years?

The bishops chanted prayers in Latin and slid a ring on Henry's finger. They bowed as they held out a sword to him, which he sheathed on his belt, and they reached up and carefully crowned Henry. Finally, they handed him a sceptre and rod. As they stepped back from the crowned king, everyone suddenly shouted in unison, "God save King Henry!"

I joined in a beat late, but I said it too.

I had assumed this would be the end, but it wasn't. My feet were starting to ache from standing, which was unusual for me.

After a full Mass, there was an unnecessary amount of trumpeting which rang throughout the stony cathedral. And everyone shouted in unison: "God save King Henry! Long live King Henry! May the king live forever!"

The two bishops turned and started to walk back toward the entrance to the cathedral. Henry gestured to me to come to his side. I hadn't known I'd have to walk before everyone else—even Henry's sisters. If I had cared at all about anything anymore, I might have been nervous. I took his arm and he led me forward.

Together, Henry and I followed the bishops silently through the abbey garden. We passed the roses and other flowering bushes. Then, the procession curved around tall hedges, until the garden fell away. We stopped at the gate by the stables.

"Are you alright to ride on your own?" he asked.

I only nodded.

He helped me up to a cushioned saddle on a small white mare and then he swung himself up to the saddle of a larger black stallion. Soon, I coaxed my horse to follow his down the road.

Though the horses were to be kept at an ambling gait, if not faster, the journey would still take until dusk. A few other knights and ladies travelled on their horses with the new king but most of the people had remained behind at Westminster Palace.

At Winchester Cathedral, it seemed as though the whole city had gathered at the front steps. The crowd silently parted to let their new king and his entourage through.

Henry didn't drop my hand as we entered the nave. Directly in front of the altar, King William's body was laid out in an ornate silver coffin. Henry and I made our way forward and we both knelt before the dead king. I prayed until Henry pulled my upper arm so I would stand again. Holding my hand tightly in his, he led me off to the side a bit.

The funeral was short compared to the Coronation.

The next morning, Henry met me at my chamber door and we came in to the cathedral together, arm in arm. Everyone rose up in the cathedral when we entered. After a benediction from the bishop who lived here, we all processed outside.

Tall aspens surrounded us along the path to the cemetery. The leaves whispered to us. As the wind blew, I felt a hand on my hair. But when I reached up, nothing was there.

King William's gravesite was beneath the central tower of the Cathedral of Winchester. Other headstones of the royalty and clergy were also here. Someday, I thought, someone would have to cut down more of the talking aspens in order to make more room for the dead. Perhaps for my own grave.

As everyone gathered around, and the pallbearers carried the heavy silver coffin slowly closer down the path behind us, I leaned closer to Henry. "When I die," I whispered, "have them bury me at Westminster. I am happiest there."

He nodded once and met my gaze with his own. "When I die, have them bury me at Reading," he whispered back. "That is the place where I knew my father loved me, and it is where I knew you loved me, too." He turned his gaze back to the grave. "I wish we could go back there and live as commoners."

The pallbearers set the silver coffin heavily down at our feet.

After the bishop spoke about a place where there was no sorrow nor sighing, the pallbearers lowered the silver coffin into the grave using ropes. I heard the dull thud when the coffin reached the ground. Even kings couldn't be majestic in death, I supposed.

Henry picked up a handful of earth and threw it into the grave. I did the same.

As we turned and began walking away, Henry took my hand in his and interlocked our fingers together. I let him. "It went better than the last king's funeral," he said under his breath.

"Hm?" I wasn't sure if I was supposed to have heard him or not.

He glanced at me. "I just mean—his body didn't burst when they shut the coffin and I didn't have to pay off any hecklers. All in all, a good funeral."

"I see." I let out a dry laugh as I shook my head.

His crown shifted forward and covered his hairline completely as he kissed the back of my hand. "I am blessed to have you by my side."

"My lord king." I gazed toward the aspens ahead of us. As I became lost in my thoughts, I stopped walking. The others following us didn't know what to do when Henry also stopped with me, until Fitzhamon walked up behind us and came to my side.

"You look lovely today, mistress," he said, squeezing my shoulder as he gave a quick kiss to my cheek. Giving a small smile, I saw that his eyes were bloodshot and puffy. He continued down the tree-lined pathway ahead of us.

"Truly, I am fortunate to be here," I whispered as the others also passed by us, "after you left me alone."

"Matilda, come here," Henry said, and taking my hand in his, he led me over to stand under a many-trunked yew tree in the middle of dozens of headstones. "Tell me privately what troubles you," he said, gently guiding my face with his thumb so I would turn to him. "But do not act strangely like that again. From now on, you must always endeavor to act as your mother and your godmother did."

I gazed up into his eyes. "You left me alone. In the dark forest, you left me alone, save for your brother's body." I closed my eyes. "I couldn't carry him myself. By the time Aunt Christina and Sister Agnes and I—"

"I sent men to retrieve the body, but a few countrymen happened to travel through and find him," Henry explained in a gentle voice. "A charcoal burner named Purkis brought the body the twenty five miles in a two-wheeled wooden cart."

"A cart." I shook my head. "You must pray for forgiveness every day for the rest of your life, Henry."

"Mm. And you should pray for forgiveness as well, Matilda," he said. "Your desires are too hasty. You should be careful with your prayers."

"I shall," I whispered. As I tried not to openly weep, I lay my face against Henry's tunic as he hugged me.

CHAPTER 25: BETWEEN THE BOUGHS OF THE TREES

"Come back," Tristan says quietly. We are under our willow tree in the Moorfields. Sunlight beams brightly in between the boughs of the trees as though it is dawn, but it is actually dusk.

"I must be going. William waits in the garden for me —"

"My Edie, don't go." He wraps his arms around my waist, pulls me closer, and kisses me. He tastes like wine.

I whisper, pulling away from him, "Why did you leave me?"

He smiles as he holds my face in his hands. "Forgive me, my love."

"Let us stay here forever. Why did we ever leave before?"

I woke up crying. Sitting up in bed in the Tower of London, I hugged myself. It had been six weeks since I had lain with Tristan under our willow tree and now, every night, my dreams became more and more vivid. These dreams hurt worse than those red dreams of King William.

Six weeks.

I added the days again in my head: it had been two months since I'd last bled. I had never gone this long without bleeding. Brother Godric had taught me the signs and I had all of them so far. "No…" I whispered. "No, no, no, no, no…"

I was pregnant with Tristan's child.

I wanted to scream, but instead I calmly stood and walked to the window nearby. Slowly, I poured a glass of watered ale. I took a sip, and then another, and then a gulp.

How could I have forgotten about bleeding? Had Rosamund realized?

Was I truly pregnant? Perhaps I was dying of some sort of growth or disease instead? But my breasts were so heavy... This watered ale was making me nauseous even though I felt I would die of thirst. I hadn't bled in two months... I counted the days again. And again. I pinched myself. I wasn't dreaming. The bean stew we'd had for dinner had smelled utterly terrible. I'd barely eaten any of it. I had been surprised to realize that I could smell Henry from my seat next to him. His scent had smelled as strong as though I had my nose to his collar. He'd smelled good, like leather and wood smoke.

A few days after his brother's burial, Henry had read his "Charter of Liberties" aloud to all the scores of barons, knights, and lords who had been called to attend. Now that I was formally betrothed to Henry, he would not allow me to sit around and read manuscripts anymore. Rather, I had spent the last few weeks helping him compile a list of things to change from the way King William had done them in order to be in line with the Charter. The work had been a welcome distraction from myself.

I hadn't wanted to think about anything... I hadn't let myself realize it.

It was only a matter of time, Henry told me daily, before he and I were married.

As I clutched my goblet in my hand and gazed out my Tower window, I prayed he would find time to marry me before my illegitimate pregnancy started to show.

Even though I was wide awake, I crawled back into bed.

The door creaked open and Henry peeked into the room. "Hello," he said. "Did I wake you?"

I shook my head.

"Good." He clicked the door shut behind himself.

"I didn't say you could come in," I whispered.

"Forgive me. May I come in?"

"No."

He smiled at me. Slowly, he walked toward my bed and sat down on the edge of it. "We have to talk about something."

I watched as his smile fell from his face. "Alright."

"The Church does not think you should be taken away from your Bridegroom."

"I've never been married," I said flatly.

"You wore the veil," he said, raising an eyebrow. "Now that I've allowed Archbishop Anselm to come home from his banishment, he is already trying to convince everyone that you are a Bride of Christ."

"That meddler. Can't you just send him back to Rome?"

"My sentiments exactly," he laughed. "But no, he must stay. I need him to help keep the peace."

"I never took any vows. Anyone might put a veil on their head. It doesn't mean they are a nun."

"I know," he said, and leaned forward and kissed my forehead. "I'm glad you so fervently rebuke it. I'm going to leave for Old Sarum in the morning with the archbishop of York. We are going to speak to the archbishop of Canterbury on your behalf."

"That's not good. Archbishop Gerard doesn't like me either." I leaned back against my headboard.

Henry pulled my hand into his lap and held it tightly. "The archbishop of York thinks I should marry one of the women who bore children to me," Henry conceded. "He thinks you should be saved for someone who doesn't have children. That is, if it's proven you're not a nun. He doesn't know we've shared a bed already, or perhaps he'd consider changing his mind."

"Well, he's probably not wrong," I muttered.

Kicking his boots off, Henry slid back so he was next to me on the bed and leaned back against the headboard like I was. As he drew my hair away from my shoulder as though he were opening a curtain, he kissed my neck. I caught his scent again. Was I turning feral? Why did he smell so good to me? After all, he wasn't even the father of my child.

Child. I was dizzy.

"Henry," I said warningly. "I won't be one of your whores."

"But what if we're never married?" he said, lightly kissing my collarbone.

"You're the king. Change the rules."

He laughed. "That's a thought. 'All monks and nuns may hereby marry.'"

"I think," I started. As he pulled at the neck of my dress and kissed below my collarbone, I leaned away from him. "Let me talk to Archbishop Anselm instead. I might be able to convince him I'm not a nun."

"You'd do that?" He kissed my cheek.

"Of course. If I don't convince him, there may be no escaping the veil for me."

Henry nodded. His smile faltered a little and he kissed my cheek again.

"Henry." I lifted my hands to his cheeks and kissed his lips lightly, surprising him. "I am not the girl you knew seven years ago," I said, "but you are all I have in the world." My heart protested this thought, but I continued, "It would be fitting for us to get to know each other again."

"I want to know you again. I still love you," he said, "as I said before."

"But if I am to be your wife, and your queen, you need to treat me with the respect deserving of those offices, as you did these past weeks while we worked to enact the Charter."

He looked into my eyes and held my gaze. Could he tell I was hiding something from him? "I respected you these past weeks as you filled the duties I see fit for a queen. But as a husband and wife, surely we must treat each other differently than that of formal offices."

This made sense, and for a moment, I was derailed from my argument. "But…"

"I never want to be parted from you from this day forward," Henry said. "You are my wife, whether the Church blesses us or not."

"Thank you, my lord king," I muttered.

Henry smirked at my formality. "Don't call me that when we're alone."

"We need the blessing. A formal one from the Church. Otherwise I'm not queen. Nor am I your wife."

"Already we are blessed by God to be here together in this chamber. It is proof enough for me. We are here together against all odds. I fought so many battles. I should be dead and yet here I am."

"You were a good knight. That's why you're alive. God has nothing to do with battles."

"I love you, Matilda. I have loved you since we stood by the river and you called me a 'scullion.' I'll love you until I die."

My throat tightened. I stared down at his hands as he rubbed my palms against his, warming my cold fingers.

"Have I upset you?" His heavy eyebrows fell lower as he studied me. "You are trying to hide your unhappiness. I see it written in those jeweled eyes of yours."

I tried to bite my tongue but the words came anyway. "You *abandoned* me. I cannot forgive and forget as easily as you have. And… I fell in love with someone else while you were gone."

"I know," he said quickly, "I forgive you." He leaned down and touched his lips to my cheek again. "I pray you might forgive me for sending him away from you."

I was distracted by the faint hooting of an owl outside the glass-planed windows, and by the silence that otherwise pervaded the room.

He continued, "Likewise, I have sent my lover, Sybilla, away from myself. Could you have done the same?"

I shook my head. Gazing back into his eyes, I forced myself to say, "I beg you forgive me. I confess my heart still yearns for a married man. If you cannot forgive me this, I could never place any blame on you."

It was quiet again. Slowly, he ran his hand over my thigh, rucking up the material of my chemise as he did. "I forgive you."

"Henry."

"Don't be nervous."

"I know I probably don't deserve it, but I need you to promise me." I watched as my leg became more and more exposed.

"I am going to be your husband. I need to win your heart back from that lowly servant who stole it from me." He pulled the strings at my neck loose with his other hand. "We've already promised ourselves to each other before God with our betrothal. Is that not security enough for you? I cannot marry another while I am betrothed to you."

"I want you to promise me that you will not bed another woman again. If we are married, you must remain faithful to me."

He wrapped his arms low around my hips and pulled me so I was lying on my back. I held my breath as he nuzzled into my breasts. "Matilda, I'll give you anything you want."

My face flushed with heat. I couldn't fight the tears which fell down my cheeks. "Henry, promise me."

"I promise." He pulled me gently into a kiss. "Do you promise me the same?"

"Yes," I whispered. "I promise." What if I was unable to convince Archbishop Anselm I wasn't a nun? I needed Henry to think the child was his before it was too late. Though I logically knew this, my heart wanted to fight against his every touch. Instead, I closed my eyes.

CHAPTER 26: UNDER THE MONASTIC VEIL

When the king's assembly arrived at the little wooden cathedral in Old Sarum, a deacon told Archbishop Gerard and Henry to wait outside: I was granted an audience "alone" with the archbishop of Canterbury. So naturally, when I came in the small chamber off to the side of the vestibule, I was surprised to find my Aunt Christina waiting in the room with him.

Stepping forward, I kissed the archbishop's hand and then kissed my aunt's hand. The archbishop gestured to the floor and so I knelt before him on both knees. Sunlight shone in brightly through the dusty glass panes behind him, warming the room and forcing me to squint.

"God be with you, child. What have you to say?"

"Master, I am certain you clearly recall our journey together to Romsey Abbey. I had wished to hoodwink King William Rufus so I could secretly marry Henry — King Henry. Now that King William is dead, I am no longer running and I no longer need to be afraid of him harming his brother. I may finally unite with my love with the blessing of the Church. I beseech your forgiveness in leading you to believe I was called to the abbey."

"Abbess Mother Christina contends you wore the veil and you are a Bride of Christ," he said calmly, gesturing to Aunt Christina.

"And you should wear it still." Aunt Christina stepped forward. Lifting a black veil, she bent over and began to yank it down on my head.

The warm, small room was making me nauseous even though my stomach was empty. I had no more patience for anyone, let alone this woman. I tore the veil from my aunt's hands before it was fully wrapped under my chin. As my aunt stared, I threw the veil down to the floor and pushed myself to my feet, facing her.

The smack resounded in the small room and I stumbled back. Aunt Christina had raised the back of her hand to me and had struck me across the face.

Staring defiantly into my aunt's eyes, I stomped on the veil, ground my heel down, and stomped on it again. "I will *never*," I sneered, stomping once more, "wear that thing again. You aren't *saving* me from Henry, or any man. You are doing nothing more than making a farce of monasticism!"

"May God forgive you!" she shrieked.

"May God forgive *you* as well!"

"Thank you, Abbess Mother," said the archbishop, "I believe you've helped us enough." He remained seated in his chair with his hands folded in his lap. "You may go and serve God."

"Master." Turning to Archbishop Anselm, the anger fell from Aunt Christina's face as she knelt, took his right hand in both of hers and kissed it. "I beseech you, grant me your forgiveness for this unpleasant display."

"I forgive you as God forgives, Mother," he said.

She backed out of the room with her head bowed and quietly shut the door.

"Hand me that veil," he said, pointing at the cloth on the floor. My rage had turned my muscles into pudding. With a trembling hand, I handed it to him. He set it down on the arm of his chair. "Kneel again." I did. "Abbess Mother Christina said you are a woman of God. She said you would make an excellent abbess one day if you would follow your calling, take vows, and be tonsured."

"My calling is to serve the Lord our God," I said evenly, "but not under the veil of monasticism."

"You believe God calls you to lead the people of England as their queen and as King Henry's wife?"

I swallowed the bile that fizzled in the back of my throat. "Yes. God works through love. I love Henry and he is in love with me."

"The king has fathered children to three different women that are publicly known. Were you aware of this?"

"Yes," I whispered, though I hadn't known a number.

"You love an adulterer and a debaucher."

"'He that is without sin among you, let him first cast the stone.'"

He inclined his head to me and shut his eyes. "The real crux of the problem is, I cannot take Christ's Bride from Him for her to marry a mortal man."

I stared at the veil that hung on the arm of the archbishop's chair. "That hood I did indeed wear in my aunt's presence, chafing and fearful. But as soon as I was able to escape out of her sight, I tore it off and threw it in the dirt, and trampled on it. That was my only way of venting my rage and the hatred of it that boiled up in me. In that manner, and no other, as my conscience is witness, was I veiled." I took a stuttering breath. "Even if I had taken vows, let it be my sin if I turn away from my Bridegroom. Let me burn for all of eternity for it. You will be blameless for believing any falseness on my part."

"All I know of you before this is you lied to Henry who tried to lie to the king. And now I am confronted with what your aunt tells me. You must see my dilemma."

"If King William had found out that I loved his brother instead of him, I could not have lived with the consequences. What if Henry had been exiled or killed for it? You know what sort of man King William was, God rest his soul. It would have been my fault if any harm had come to Henry. It was far better for me to hide in a house of God than a house in France. I did it for my love."

"I cannot say whether it is God or Satan telling me this, but I feel that is the greatest lie of all," he said.

I stared and shook my head slightly, as though I didn't understand him. My heart sank. It was clear I would fail. I imagined giving birth to Tristan's child while wearing a homespun, and then my Aunt Christina walking away with the baby as it gasped its first cries.

I held my breath, waiting for him to speak.

"It does not seem as though you love him. Perhaps you only lust for power?" I shook my head again. He was far too close to the truth. He continued, "If you became queen, the people will know that you once wore the veil. England will not rejoice in the children you bear."

I swallowed hard and opening my eyes again, I forced myself to stare up at the archbishop's piercing scrutiny. "They will rejoice if the whole truth regarding the veil is known."

"It would take a lot of explaining."

"Pray, if I am queen, I will need an ear who listens closely to God's word. You saw clearly that I was astray before, when Henry tried to bog you down in our scheme. You led me toward a good, righteous path in returning me to Romsey Abbey. If I become Henry's wife, he and I would both need a good, righteous man as our spiritual father."

Raising both of his eyebrows, he loosely clasped his hands before his lips. "Whether or not you actually love Henry is not for me to judge. You need not love him to marry him. No, I am simply inclined to believe, after witnessing your aunt hit you for not wearing the veil, that she did in fact force you to wear it, as you say. We shall set it before a council of bishops, just for added reassurance, but for now I will tell you what I believe. Surely, you are no Bride of Christ. I will personally attest to such."

With such simple words, everything was decided. "God bless you, Master," I breathed.

"You may rise to your feet. Go and serve God."

CHAPTER 27: 11ᵀᴴ NOVEMBER, 1100

I was alone with Rosamund in my chamber in the Palace of Westminster. I was terrified. At any moment, surely Henry would burst in the room and proclaim the wedding was off and that he knew about the unborn child I carried. Perhaps my brothers would disown me. Perhaps Henry, my lord king, would have me hanged for lying to him.

Did Tristan know I was marrying Henry today? Rosamund would have asked Emmaline to come. Of course Tristan knew. Was he on these grounds right at this moment, as I vomited my breakfast into my chamber pot? Though my face was hot, I shivered as I wiped my mouth with a gold-threaded cloth.

My wedding dress was an antique. Just like the rest of my wardrobe, this dress had been my godmother's wedding dress, too. Henry had asked that I wear it, and so I did. I did anything Henry asked of me anymore.

The skirt and bodice were a rich, jewel-toned blue. The teardrop, floor-length sleeves were forest-green. There was a bit of a train, and there was fine golden embroidery in the shapes of crosses about the bodice, like an unmovable belt.

As Rosamund methodically pulled the antique clothes over the small swell of my lower abdomen, the sun shone brightly on the skirt: I saw white linen instead of blue silk. In shock, my trembling hands grasped at the white material over my belly, but it looked blue again. I would barely let myself realize it: in the sun, I had watched my hands pull a death shroud over the swell of my belly.

"I choose this," I whispered to myself. Whatever I just saw, I decided it meant nothing to me. I was saving myself from the veil and saving Tristan's child from orphanage by marrying Henry today. I would give Henry as many children as he wanted as long as he also kept Tristan's child safe and well.

My stomach churned with guilt which was wholly separate from my morning sickness.

"It's almost time, mistress," Rosamund said quietly.

"Alright."

And as clearly as though it was happening before me, I recalled Tristan under the blossoming willow tree at Romsey Abbey, with the flower crown of forget-me-nots on his head. I gasped as she tied the strings at my neck.

"Oh God, I beg…" I pressed my lips together as lay a hand lightly over my still-flat torso. "I'm going to be sick in my wedding gown, Rosa," I whispered.

"It'll pass, mistress," Rosamund said softly, wiping my tears away. "Take some deep breaths through your nose, if you will. Though it is uncomfortable, what a blessing it is for my future queen and my lord king."

"I don't know what you mean." I didn't move.

"Of course, mistress." Rosamund spent a little time tugging and smoothing the hem of my dress. As I ran my hands over the bodice and skirt, I took deep breaths through my nose just as my maid had instructed.

"Your veil," Rosamund said suddenly, glancing around.

"I thought I'd leave it off."

Rosamund paused. "No, of course not," she said. "What woman doesn't cover her head? Especially for such an occasion? You'd look strange without it. Anyway, it is clearly not a monastic veil."

She plucked the veil from where it rested at the end of my bed and began fussing with the veil and my hair.

"I wish Emmaline could come and do my hair," I said honestly and then immediately regretted saying Emmaline's name. Tears burned in my eyes again. "She is gentler than you."

"Forgive me, I am rushing," Rosamund said without attempting to be any gentler. "I feel it is time we be down already."

My wave of nausea passed as suddenly as it had come on. I suddenly felt hungry. "Do you think they'll have any pike at supper? I haven't had any good pike since I was a little girl in my father's court."

"I don't believe so. But there will be lampreys, as the king does enjoy them. I believe he also ordered some of your favorites as well."

"Oh. That was very thoughtful of my betrothed." I suddenly felt a wave of guilt so strong, I couldn't help but begin to cry again. I could not stop myself from saying earnestly, "God save my lord king."

Rosamund nodded emphatically and wiped my tears away. "You are lovely, mistress," she said, smiling at me. "It's as though this dress had been made just for you. It matches your eyes perfectly."

"Thank you, my long-suffering, steadfast maid."

Rosamund looked surprised. As she tried to hide her laughter, she walked to the front window and peered out toward the road, turning slightly so she could see the crowd below better. "It looks like it's about time," she said excitedly. "Are you ready?"

I was about to walk to the hanging tree. "Lord have mercy on me," I whispered.

"Oh, speaking of mercy," she whispered back, "I took care of the bedsheets—for later, mistress. Seeing as you won't bleed. It will be our secret."

"What? Henry won't expect—"

"Our lord king asked that I tell you I did so, mistress," she said, quickly, "In case you were worried over it."

"Oh." I was confused. "Why would I be worried?"

"Good." She nodded emphatically. "My mistress is such a strong, lovely woman. You make a most excellent queen."

"Thank you, maid."

She nodded again and offered her arm and led me down the hall. Soon, a procession of ladies joined us at the abbey garden. A little girl, one of Henry's sisters' daughters, happily tossed flower petals into the air as we walked.

We entered the abbey through the side door by the Pyx Chamber and walked slowly down the nave, away from the altar. The ladies left Rosamund and me in a side-room of the vestibule of Westminster Abbey.

Here, one of Henry's men hurried forward and spoke quickly and quietly to Rosamund.

I paced on the far side of the little room, fighting the feeling of claustrophobia. What was I about to do? Was I actually going to marry Henry and let him believe Tristan's child was his own? Becoming queen wasn't something to lust after, as Archbishop Anselm had insinuated. It was a burden. I had never believed it was the Will of God for me to wear the crown.

"I choose this," I whispered again. Though I had yet to feel Tristan's child move in my womb, I already wanted to protect this child more than my own life. After all, I couldn't stop loving him.

My neck was sore from trying not to shiver.

At the door, Rosamund finally said, "I'll tell her." She turned away and shut herself in this small room with me. "Henry and the archbishop await you on the front steps, as we expected, but there's been a slight change," she said.

"What is it?"

"The archbishop of Canterbury is giving a full account of his findings in regards to your wearing the monastic veil so there won't be any question over the validity of your marriage. Also, the archbishop is going to ask if anyone can argue that you are in fact a nun."

I looked up to the ceiling and gave silent praise to God that Aunt Christina had refused to come to the wedding.

"Just keep calm." Her eyes looked glassy in the low-lit little room. "Keep your eyes on the king. He loves you."

"Let's not wait in here any longer. I feel like I might be sick again." I stepped forward, but Rosamund stopped me with a hand on my arm.

"One more moment. Deep breaths." She stepped behind me and fixed my train. As a last touch, she pulled the veil over my face. "All ready." She grinned the same way my mother always did when I was little. "May God bless you."

"Mm." Sliding my hand under my veil, I pinched the bridge of my nose to keep from vomiting. "Thank you."

When Rosamund finally opened the door, I walked slowly into the vestibule at the entrance of the cathedral. The huge double doors to the outside had been swung shut by two old men, who seemed to be acting as guards. As I waited in the vestibule with my back to the altar, Rosamund fixed my train again. My heart was pounding so hard, I wondered if I shouldn't sit down for a moment.

I could just barely make out Archbishop Anselm's voice through the doors as his tone went up as if in a question. This was followed by a long, heavy silence.

The doors swung open and a choir began to sing a wedding song. A few lit candles led my way forward to the center of the steps in the morning sunlight. Slowly, I came close to Henry. He smiled at me as we stood together before a crowd of hundreds. The roads toward London were packed. And yet, except for the choir, all was quiet. Archbishop Anselm stood with his back to the huge mass of people as he glanced between Henry and me.

Just for a moment, as I looked at Henry, I thought of Tristan again. Was he happy in his marriage to Emmaline?

I wished I could forget Tristan. If I were going to survive, I needed to remember how to love this man who stood before me. If only I could make my heart understand my thoughts.

Henry wore a crimson tunic. His golden crown shone brilliantly in the sun. His shoulders were covered by a red cape with white ermine fur about his collar. Under this, but over his tunic, hung a heavy gold chain encrusted with diamonds, rubies and sapphires. Everything he wore looked lavish and, for perhaps the first time I could recall, he certainly looked like a king.

A group of men — many of which had been present at the burial and the Charter reading — stood behind Henry. Along with them, Constantine stood with his hands clasped behind his back, causing his large belly to protrude even further than normal.

Next to Constantine was Henry's only surviving brother, Robert Curthose, back from the Holy Land only a few weeks ago. I smiled politely at him and he gave a slight nod back to me.

I hadn't seen him in more than ten years until I spoke to him a few days prior to my wedding day. He had told me that because he was my godfather, he would set aside his differences with his brother for now and wish us happiness in our marriage.

The choir stopped singing. Except for a few chirping birds, all was quiet. The archbishop chanted prayers in Latin, and there was more music, and then more prayers again.

As the November wind blew my veil back against my face, I closed my eyes. Instead of Henry's sisters and random ladies behind me, I tried to imagine that my mother stood behind me. And my father and Edward. And my sister, who had written her regrets in not being granted dispensation from Wilton because of Aunt Christina's interference. In fact, none of my family, not even Alexander, who was too busy with Scotland's politics like my other brothers, had come to my wedding.

Archbishop Anselm said, "King Henry of England, wilt thou have this woman to be thy wedded wife? Wilt thou love her, and honor her, keep her and guard her, in health and in sickness, as a husband should a wife, and forsaking all others on account of her, keep thee only unto her, so long as ye both shall live?"

"I will."

The archbishop said, "Matilda of Scotland."

I met Henry's eyes and wondered if he truly would honor those vows. As he gazed back at me, I remembered the way he looked on the night he first left me in the Tower of London.

He did love me. I knew it in my bones.

Then, the archbishop stopped talking and I realized I was supposed to say something.

"I will," I said.

The archbishop took my right hand and Henry's right hand, and he tugged us closer together as he said a prayer. Constantine stepped forward and handed Henry two gold bands.

"Matilda, repeat after me," the archbishop said.

Henry and I exchanged rings as we said our vows, and Archbishop Anselm spoke again and read a passage from the Bible in Latin.

He pronounced us, "husband and wife."

After lifting my veil and pushing it back, Henry softly kissed me. I felt my face flush with heat as the crowd of people cheered in the streets.

When Henry took my hand and we both faced the crowd, the archbishop stepped aside and shouted, "God save King Henry and Queen Matilda!"

The crowd shouted back three times, "God save King Henry and Queen Matilda!" And turning our backs to the crowd, Henry led me back inside of Westminster Cathedral.

All of our favorite foods—honeyed almonds, goose liver pâté, stewed roasted lampreys—amongst many other dishes, were served at a lengthy dinner in the Great Hall of the Palace of Westminster. With every bite I took, my morning sickness abated a little bit more. I ate until I felt as though my dress would tear at the seams.

Once I finished my food and wine, Henry took my hand in his. "Come on, love, it's time we go." He stood from his seat at the center of the head table.

As I stood with him, many others stood too and the dull rumble of conversation died down.

A man shouted, "God save the king and queen!" and so the crowd shouted three times in response, "God save the king and queen!" before they all then bowed to us.

We started down the stone steps off of the dais. Down the center of the room, an aisle cleared for us. That was when I saw Tristan. As though he knew I had found him, he raised his head and met my gaze with his own.

He stood toward the back of the room by the doorway. Emmaline was linked arm-in-arm with her mother. Rosamund smiled at me, meeting my glance before bowing her head again.

How could Emmaline be so oblivious to her husband's feelings? I was perhaps fifty feet away from Tristan and yet I could feel him as though he were under my fingertips.

Tristan stared at me the way he often had when we were alone under the willow tree. I tried to look back at him but it was like looking directly into the midday sun. My blood seized in my veins. I wanted to run to him, but instead, I kept holding onto Henry's arm and walking slowly forward.

At the door, I walked within a half a foot of Tristan; my skirt brushed up against his hand as I passed by. I couldn't hold his gaze this close. Not while touching Henry.

But looking down was worse: I saw Tristan's hand, slack at his side, and I saw his hand turn and touch the skirt as I passed him. A hundred memories of that hand's touch flooded my mind. I could barely breathe.

Once we left the hall, everyone lifted their heads from their bows. With wolf-whistles and shouts of well-wishes, Henry led me to the corridor and up the stairs at the end. To my utter confusion, a few bishops and a fair number of knights and lords were following us. Meanwhile, some women, including Emmaline and Rosamund, followed too and sang a wedding song.

As we walked upstairs to William's old bedchamber, everyone was still following us.

I glanced nervously over at Henry. "Why are they still following us?"

"I can't hear you over the singing," he said, shaking his head. He kissed my cheek.

At the door of his chamber, Henry picked me up and carried me over the threshold to the bed. A few of the lords and bishops laughed.

And from my seat on the bed (the bedclothes had already been pulled neatly back), I saw that probably twelve or so knights and bishops had followed Henry into the king's bedchamber. They stood at the end of the bed and formed a small crowd.

Rosamund stepped forward and took my shoes and crown off of me and guided my legs up into bed. Henry sat down on the other side and also took off his shoes and crown and swung his legs up. Two of the bishops stepped forward and literally pulled our blankets up over our legs.

I was shocked. "Henry," I whispered in his ear, "are they all going to stay in here?" One of the men at the end of the bed chuckled quietly. I forced myself not to glance at him.

"Yes, love," he said softly back. "Didn't you know?"

"How would I know this unless someone told me?"

"It's customary. If there is ever question of the legitimacy of our first child as heir, these men would testify for us. It's for our sake that they are here." As I kept staring at him, he leaned toward me, watching my reaction all the while. "I beg your forgiveness, my love." Laying his hand gently on my cheek, he pressed a kiss to my lips and then leaned away again, checking my reaction.

I swallowed hard. Though I wanted to scream, I stayed silent.

Taking my hands in his, he twined our fingers together. "We're alone," he whispered, his lips tickling my ear. "We're in our marriage bed and I'm in love with you." Turning so he was on top of me, he said softly, "Wrap your arms around me so you may only see my face."

Taking a stuttering breath, I did as he said.

"Close your eyes, my love, and forget. Forget everything," he whispered in my ear. "It'll be alright. I love you more than you'll ever know, my beautiful wife. I love you without end."

Shutting my eyes as tightly as I could, I failed to fight my tears.

CHAPTER 28: THIS SIDE OF THE CHILDBED

The pub in Winchester rumbled with conversation and laughter. In the corner of the room, a young man played a vielle and an old man played a drum. After Henry and I were each served a wooden cup of ale, we stood in the corner near the musicians and drank, watching the happy group of people dance in the center of it all. After I finished my ale, Henry took my cup and set it down before he dragged me out and we joined in a quadrille.

As we came together as we danced, I said, "You should be thankful I'm starting to be able to handle my ale again or I probably would have gotten sick on you by now."

"I am thankful for all I do not have thrust upon me, my queen. Does the baby like the dancing?"

"It makes him sleep, I think."

But the music stopped and someone shouted, "God save the king and queen!" And everyone else repeated the words in a chorus.

Henry looked around as though he had forgotten where he was and then he smiled as he let go of me.

"Sing a song for us, my good queen!" called the barmaid, smiling widely.

I glanced to Henry and gave a slight shake of my head.

He stepped forward. "The queen is tired from dancing, but perhaps you will be content with a song from your king?!"

The men and women around him shouted, "Hurrah!"

He took the vielle from the man who'd been playing it and sat down in his vacated seat. "Let us watch a few dancers as I play," he said to the quieted crowd.

Except for a few sets of young couples, the floor cleared as Henry began to turn the crank. As he played, with his eyes down on the instrument in his lap, he sang a song that was often sung around harvest time at Wilton Abbey. The words were from Song of Solomon. For a moment, I was lost in Henry's voice.

I couldn't help thinking how Tristan would never sit in front of a crowded pub and sing. I clenched my teeth and pushed my guilty thoughts of Tristan away, just as I did every day.

Glancing over to the small glassless front window of the pub, I thought I saw a ghost — Tristan was walking down the road. His head was down, fighting the damp, early spring air.

Discreetly, I wove my way through to the back of the crowd. When I thought no one was looking at me, I tucked an arm protectively under my baby belly. Rosamund rested a hand on my arm, trying to gently stop me. I quickly shrugged her off and hurried after him.

Soon, Tristan turned down an alley between two of the stalls up the hill. Hurrying to catch up to him, I reached out and grabbed his arm. On one side, a busy blacksmith kept his fire blazing despite the cold. On the other, a merchant sold bolts of wool.

"Edie," Tristan gasped and hastily added, "My queen." He bent to his knee, immediately dampening his leggings with muddy, melting snow. I pulled him up again.

"Tristan." I hadn't thought this through. My dreams of the willow tree came so often, it was as though no time had passed since I'd seen him last, but surely it felt differently for him to see me now. Hastily, I pulled him into a hug, pressing my cheek to his. The baby in my womb kicked at my ribs slowly, gently asking me why my heart was beating so fast. I whispered, "I pray you forgive me."

"No, it's alright." I let go of him and stepped back as he stared down at my baby belly.

"It's yours," I whispered, answering the question written in his eyes. I watched my words cut him, and tears glassed over his eyes. It hurt me to see him this way, as much as the day he left me. He was leaving me all over again.

"Edie…"

"Henry believes it is his. I am nearly two months further along than he thinks I am." Quickly glancing around, I grabbed Tristan's wrist and pressed his hand to my belly. His child kicked under his touch. "The baby awoke."

"Edie," he said again, his face blotching with pink under his beard as he stared at his hand. "I…"

"Come see the child once he's born. I beg you. Even if you won't see me again," I pleaded. "I shall be here at Winchester for some months for my confinement, perhaps longer. No one will question your presence — so many men visit the king and his men. If you do come, find Fitzhamon amongst the men. I promise he will help you."

Tristan gazed down at my belly again, and tears rolled down his face and into his beard. "What… what might… I beg you forgive me for what I've done, my, um, my queen."

I shook my head. "It's alright," I whispered. I knew I should leave, but my cold, damp feet were unwilling to move away from his. I longed to warm my cheek on his again... "I cherish this baby because he is yours. Forgive me for telling you. I will love it until my last breath."

I rushed to search the features of his face. Under his eyes, he had new purple half-moons, as though he had not slept for weeks. His pleasant, sky blue eyes still seemed older than the rest of him. His beard was less kept. His hair still shone like golden silk threads in the sun. His lips no longer played with a smile as I gazed at him.

Tucking my hand under the curve of my baby bump, I hurried back to the pub.

No one other than Rosamund seemed to have noticed my absence. When Henry finished his song, everyone clapped. The dancers bowed to him. When he found me in the crowd, he gave me a faint smile. Had he noticed my absence? I forced myself to smile back.

As we left the pub, Rosamund stared at me. I stared back for a moment before she looked pointedly away.

"It's Godric and Godiva!" called one of our knights as he followed us out the pub door. His fellow knights of the consort tried to shush him, but too loudly. Clearly they'd all had too much ale.

"Godric and Godiva?" Henry repeated, glancing over his shoulder. He laughed and said to the knight, "I recommend to you, and to *all* my men—find an English woman for a wife. They are smarter and they taste better."

The knights all laughed wildly at this. I bit the inside of my cheek to keep from yelling at Henry. "I'm half Scottish, lest you forget," I said, forcing a smile.

"But which half?" he laughed. "I could never forget it, my feisty wife." He offered his arm and I took it. While the knights and their ladies continued to laugh and talk, we made our way closer and closer to Winchester Castle. Our entourage kept their distance from us — I assumed it was so we couldn't hear their drunken conversation.

"Fie, it's cold," I said, wrapping my shawl closer around myself.

"Don't say 'fie.' It is unbecoming of a queen."

"I beg your forgiveness, my lord king."

That spring, I gave birth to a darling baby girl. She had Tristan's golden hair and my eyes. Henry named her Euphemia.

Tristan did not come to visit her, but I didn't mind. In any case, this baby was more than I could have ever asked for from him. I fed her myself and she took her naps tucked next to me in my bed. She gave her first smiles to me and I gave her all my smiles in return.

For the next half of a year, though I was married to a man that I could not quite remember how to love, I had peace.

Seven months after Effie was born, just after New Year's Day, I woke in the morning with a painful fullness because of all the breastmilk the baby hadn't drunk overnight. She was gone from her normal spot next to me in my bed... As I hurried to her bassinet, I swallowed a scream. My infant daughter wasn't there either.

As my second child kicked inside my womb, silently asking me what was wrong, I quickly calmed myself. Rosamund must be bathing or changing Effie, or getting her some air in the garden. Surely all was fine. I had woken this way once before, after all. Except for the breastmilk part. But then, babies do start sleeping through the night at some point or another. Perhaps, I thought as I pressed my arms against my breasts, I should have taken Henry's advice and hired a wet nurse after all? The milk was quickly soaking my chemise.

Soon, Rosamund creaked the door open and paced toward me. Her face was red and blotchy. Was she was ill?

Henry followed the chambermaid into the room a moment later.

My chemise was now soaked from my neck to my waist with breastmilk. Wrapping one arm over my belly, and one across my breasts, I shivered. "What is that look on your faces?" I glanced between the two. "Henry? Why do you look so — ?"

He took my hand away from my belly, led me to the edge of my bed, and we sat down. Rosamund wrapped a heavy blanket around my shoulders.

"It is my duty to tell you..." But he stopped talking and swallowed hard. He stared down at our hands. "Euphemia has fallen asleep in the Lord this past night."

"No." I squeezed Henry's hand. "No, it cannot be. She was so healthy. Only yesterday — "

"These things happen, my queen," Rosamund said softly. "The baby died in her sleep. There is nothing to be done."

"Rosa?" I tore my hand from Henry's and stood. I screamed, "This is your fault! You damned, useless maid! How else could this happen?!"

She glanced to Henry. "My queen, I beg you — "

"You are laughing at me, aren't you?! You are glad this has happened! You have never been on my side, never once! You knew Tr — " I gasped, stopping myself from saying anything else.

"My queen," Rosamund whispered, shaking her head. She began to quietly cry, but I didn't care.

"Matilda." Henry stood.

"Leave my sight and never come back again," I whispered to my chambermaid. Pulling the blanket tighter about myself, I covered my leaking breasts. "This is your curse on me, you damned witch! Isn't it? Leave before I burn you alive!" And cupping my arm under my pregnant-again belly, I fell down to the floor as I wept. "Go! Get away from my sight!"

Rosamund shook her head. "Forgive me." She turned and hurried from the room. I never saw her again.

Henry knelt down on the floor and pulled me into his arms.

Archbishop Anselm thought, as I was so close to my confinement for the birth of my second child, it would be best to have a closed casket for my Euphemia. And so, as he was my spiritual father, I was not allowed to see Tristan's daughter again.

Henry had her buried there at Winchester Cathedral next to his brother, William. She was buried within hundreds of yards of where she'd been born and had never seen any more of the world.

Had I truly been pregnant with Tristan's child and given birth to his beautiful baby girl? As I stood heavy with my second child at my first child's grave, I remembered how my wedding dress had shown me a death shroud. It had been hers. God was punishing me for lying with Tristan under the willow tree. Euphemia's death was only what I deserved.

After the funeral, Henry left for Oxford and then for London. He said it was to assure that the barons still stood behind him as there were rumors that Robert wanted to take England. However, I knew it was truly to get away from my grief.

I had seen stillborn births too many times while assisting Brother Godric in Old Sarum. It was entirely different to view death from this side of the childbed. Each one of those soft, cold babies had suddenly become my child all at once. Why hadn't I been kinder to the mothers I was supposed to have helped? I was mortified when I recalled any time I had said, "You might have another someday."

I wanted my beautiful Euphemia back. She was the only person in the world I had ever fallen in love with at the moment I saw them. No other child would ever coo just the way she did. Would smile in her sleep exactly the way her father had smiled. Was perfectly beautiful the way she was...

And anyway, how could any woman willingly risk doubling this Hell I found myself in?

Even so, in the matter of weeks after the burial of Tristan's daughter, I was confined and gave birth to Henry's daughter. She had my hair and Henry's calculating look in her eyes from the day she was born.

For months after giving birth, I did not sleep more than an hour at a time because I checked and re-checked her to make sure she was alive and breathing. There was no question that I would absolutely feed her myself, as I had done with Euphemia. No one was allowed to touch her except me. And, once he finally came back to me after months of travel, I allowed Henry to hold her as well.

When Henry met our genuine first child together, he said, "She'll be Matilda. Like you and my mother. You see that thoughtful look on her face? She is a fighter, just like you."

After Maude's baptism, Fitzhamon took me to visit Effie's grave again because her headstone had just been set. Both dates on her headstone were wrong. She'd been born May 11th, and was taken from me on January 4th.

"July 1, 1101 to January 5, 1102," Fitzhamon read and then glanced over to me. "My queen, I don't know how —"

"It is strange," I said, shaking my head slowly, "but I do not want her grave to be disturbed by replacing the headstone." I stared at it a moment longer. "Oh yes, didn't you know? Those dates are correct."

"I see," was all he said. Then he slowly paced a few feet over to the foot of King William's grave. I slowly followed. After Fitzhamon crossed himself, he came back to my side and said quietly, "The stableman's wife died in childbirth only a few weeks after Euphemia fell asleep in the Lord. Their child passed as well, as it was born too young to breathe."

"Oh." Once again, I envied Emmaline. Why had I not died as she had? It would have been far more peaceful than my ever-wakeful nightmare I was living. Keeping my second daughter alive was a cold and grueling existence while I never stopped mourning my first. I panicked any moment where baby Maude was sleeping or simply quiet.

A few days later back at Westminster, I received a letter from Lady Sybilla Corbet. In her letter to me, she happily proclaimed the birth of her third healthy child with Henry. I didn't cry or become angry. I thought perhaps I'd never cry again. I finally allowed myself to face it: Henry had always been who I knew he was.

A month later, Henry returned from his trip to Normandy. After he held Maude and she finally smiled at him, I took our baby away and calmly handed him Sybilla's letter instead. He read it by the window in the light of the evening sun, and turning to the fire in the hearth, he didn't say a word as he burned it.

Later, as he kissed my neck, he swore his relationship with Sybilla was nothing to him. Meaningless. If he were honest with me, perhaps I was the more sinful? "The stableman had never been meaningless to you, after all."

In any case, I became pregnant that night for the third time. Nine months later, I gave birth to our son, William Adelin.

More and more, I stopped caring so much about my own sadness. Instead, I focused my attention and prayers on my Maude, and my Adelin, and Henry's plans, and my works as queen. And always, I prayed for Tristan.

By forcing a smile on my face and ordering good works be performed with my extravagant allowance, I eventually found a tenuous sort of peace. I helped anyone who asked for my help. Paupers, lepers, the elderly, the infirm...

My fourth child failed to take her first breath. In my dreams, she was just as beautiful and plump and perfect as Effie had been before death. I wasn't allowed to see this child in her coffin either. And because she hadn't been baptized, she had to be buried without the normal funeral rites.

As Henry and I walked away from our baby's unconsecrated grave in Reading, I told him, "Her name is Elizabeth." She hadn't formally been named, as she hadn't been baptized. But I knew he would understand me.

"That is a name worthy of a queen's daughter," he answered. As I held onto the crook of his elbow, he lay his hand gently on mine.

"I will not lay with you ever again," I said, staring straight ahead to our horses. "I cannot do this again."

"Did the physician tell you?"

"Hm?"

"You cannot have another. It seems the trauma from Elizabeth's quick birth will prevent you from conceiving."

"Oh," I said softly. "No. No one told me."

Glancing over to me, he gave a sad smile before he pecked a kiss to my temple. "My good queen, you've given me my heir and a spare. How could I ask for anything more from you?"

I nodded. "Thank you, Henry."

After Elizabeth was buried, I pulled myself from sleep every morning and remembered what my life was. Each day, I chose to live my life only for the good of England. Nothing else was needed now.

CHAPTER 29: WINCHESTER REVISITED

It rained for forty days. Then, on October 7th, 1107, the central tower of Winchester Cathedral collapsed. Since Henry was away in Normandy, I was acting as Regent. And so, it was my duty to meet with the bishop of Winchester and survey the damage.

Adelin and Maude stayed behind at Westminster. I hoped to make this a quick trip, so I brought along only a few of Henry's most trusted men.

When we arrived, I was not surprised workmen were shifting the rubble away already. I was, however, not expecting the rubble to have fallen directly on top of King William Rufus's grave. And the fallen stone was not only on William's grave, but it was also spread all around it.

My Effie's small headstone was completely covered.

The twenty-foot tall pile of broken stone weighed on my knees as I trudged my way into the small cemetery.

"It serves them right for burying such a profane man in a sacred place, king or not," said one of Henry's men.

"Hold your tongue, sir," I whispered sharply. I was satisfied that the man at least looked abashed. "You will scurry ahead and inform the master mason that the queen has arrived. Hurry now, you small man." The knight stared at me for a moment and so I stared back. Finally, he turned and jogged over to the pile of rubble. Then, I told the rest of my group to continue over to the fallen tower without me. As always, they did as I commanded them.

As a cool breeze carried the scent of dying leaves over me, I stood still. My tendrils danced with the wind and tickled my neck. Closing my eyes, I stood amongst the old, towering aspens as they whispered to me.

The day of William's burial, Henry had called it a "good funeral." At the time, I had thought it was a strange thing to say, but now I knew what he meant. After all, Euphemia's funeral had not been peaceful. What I did remember of that day was only of pain. Pain in my breasts from the breastmilk that wouldn't go away, pain in my head from no sleep, pain behind my eyes from weeping...

With my Elizabeth, there had been only the indignity of judgement. I wasn't supposed to grieve for her because I wasn't allowed to fully recognize her as mine. And then there was no mention or remembrance of her thereafter by anyone other than me.

Opening my eyes again, I gazed up at the whispering trees. They creaked and swayed with the wind. Along this path toward the graveyard, they were alone here, and untouched. Though their leaves had turned a different color for now, after all, they were still the same trees they always had been.

A man paced toward me from the pile of debris. My escorts were all a far way off surveying the damage — too far away to properly guard me. I was quite alone. And yet, even from this far away, there was something so familiar in the way this man held his shoulders as he walked.

"My queen," he said as he neared me.

"Tristan," I whispered.

When he reached me, he bent to his knee and kissed the back of my hand. "Forgive me. Your men said you wished to speak to me."

I stared down at his blonde hair, shining like gold threads in the autumn sun. Was I dreaming? "They did? Oh! Rise up!" I flinched. "Are you a mason now?"

He rose to his feet again but didn't meet my eyes. "I help where help is needed. So I am heading the clearing here until the master mason arrives from Oxford next week. We've had some volunteers, seeing as King William's... and well, it's a proper cathedral..."

I announced loudly, "I commend your wife and child to God." I had accidentally used the voice I normally reserved for court.

Tristan finally met my gaze and gave a small smile before he gazed down to the grass at his feet again. His eyes were puffy. From lack of sleep? Surely it wasn't for the same reasons I was also fighting tears? I said in a softer tone, "I should have written to you years ago when... when our daughter fell asleep in the Lord. However, I had trouble finding the right words. Forgive me."

"Thank you, my queen."

"I pray daily for you."

"I pray for you, too." He lifted his face to me again and gazed back at me. I watched as he stared at my eyes, and then my eyebrows, my hair, my ears, my neck "And for our daughter," he said softly. "I visit her every day. It is why I am heading the clearing now."

We were both silent. He tilted his head and watched tears fall from my eyes. Then his gaze fell to my lips and then to my collar.

I turned back to the pile of ruin. Looking at him still hurt as much as it had on my wedding day. "It is a Godsend that you live close to here. I am grateful you may visit her so often."

"Aye—"

"Oh, forgive me." I shook my head. "Perhaps I am keeping you from your work?"

"I beg you, my queen, allow me to walk with you about the grounds for a bit. It is a gift to see you again." He crossed his arms over his chest.

He thought it was possible I would say 'no' to him? After not seeing him for seven years, I was ashamed I could still read his face so easily.

Suddenly, he glanced around. "I shall tell your men what we are doing, alright?"

"Yes, alright," I whispered. I watched him walk away, speak with the bishop and one of Henry's men, and then he jogged back to me.

He offered his arm to me. After hesitating, I took it and forced a smile onto my face. I hoped he didn't notice how cold my hand was. As expected, his hand was warm when he rested it over my hand on his arm.

I had forgotten what it was like to feel nervous.

He glanced down to me and smiled wryly. "I'll be honest. I'm not sure what to say to you now. If I do something to offend the queen, I beg you forgive me."

My breath was caught in my throat. Why did he still have to be so beautiful? "Ah. I see. This is fine." Truly, it wasn't normal to be escorted by a common man this way, but I would never tell him so.

"You look just the same," he said.

I thought he looked just the same too, but I didn't think I should say so. "You're too kind. My many offices, however, leave little time for sleep."

He laughed. "Yes, isn't that always the way of it?"

I half-smiled and nodded. "However, I have much for which to be grateful. I have born healthy children enough to perpetuate the crown. And as of late, the king leaves me for large swathes of time wherein I may rule the country as I see fit. I am free to elevate my causes with abandon. It's quite a lovely life, all told. I am truly blessed."

Tristan met my gaze as the corner of his mouth twitched. "I am happy to hear that."

He saw through my rote speech as though I hadn't spoken. I was only relieved. "You are?" He caught me looking up at him again. I could see that same look I knew so well but had almost forgotten. I knew he wasn't afraid of me. Even Henry seemed nervous around me anymore.

He looked down at my hand where it rested on his arm. Absently, he rubbed my knuckles with his free hand, warming them as we walked. "Yes. I behold my beloved queen, righteous and virtuous. You have become that which God had always intended for you to be. My Edie is gone now."

I prayed my heart would slow down. "Your Edie," I whispered, as though I were talking to myself, "Nothing more of me is needed in life now. Nothing except the Will of God."

"That has always been true," he whispered back.

We had made it around to the opposite side of the cathedral. Now that I could not see the fallen debris, I took a deep breath. "Whether I am queen by the Will of God or the will of Satan, I am now Queen Matilda, forevermore."

Tristan stopped walking and faced me. A sad smile found its way to his face as he looked down at me. "It was the Will of God. Never doubt it."

As I held his gaze, I had to stop myself from reaching up to his cheek to comfort him. He was smiling, but still, I could feel it—his heart ached just as mine did. Would I always be able to see him this way?

Or, perhaps it was only my imagination? Was I only seeing and feeling what I hoped to see and feel? Was he simply trying to be polite?

I couldn't hold back any longer. As I began to cry, Tristan held me tightly against his chest and I held him weakly back. Gently, slowly, he ran his hand over my hair. His scent did more to calm me than even his touch. As I lay my head on his chest, I felt him lightly kiss the top of my head. I wanted him to hold me forever.

Instead, I forced myself to calm down. And though my heart desperately protested, I pulled away from Tristan's embrace. *He chose to leave me,* I reminded myself. Surely, he didn't want to touch me. This thought was enough to take a small step back from him.

"Rosamund fell asleep in the Lord," Tristan said evenly. "Two summers ago. Did you know?"

"God forgive me, no. I didn't know," I whispered.

"She told me you'd heard of Emmaline's confinement, and that you sent her to help on our farm and with the baby. Rosamund lived with me until her death." Tristan stared over at the stone wall of the cathedral. "I should have sent word to you when she passed away."

"Thank you for providing a dear friend some comfort in her last years. I fear—she lied for my sake so many times. I never deserved her kindnesses…" Huffing a deep breath out, I started slowly walking away from him. I did not want to cry anymore, but the tears came anyway.

He followed closely behind me and soon, he gently grabbed my arm. "I beg you, wait a moment, my queen. The men will think I mistreated you if they see your face now."

"Would they be wrong?" He was silent as I wiped the tears from my face once more. "Forgive me."

Tristan stepped so he stood in front of me again and wiped more tears from my face. "You must know. It wounds my heart to see you. But it is pain I gladly bear just to stand near you again. Forgive me, I never stopped loving you."

"Forgive you?" I couldn't help it when I gave a short laugh. I glanced over at the cathedral and then around to the trees on our other side. It was difficult to look at his face, but at least we were standing somewhere green and restful.

"I'm happy my foolishness still amuses you." His light blue eyes still held an unending gentleness, even now.

I could hear the golden aspens whispering again, far away from us. "Do you forgive me the same?"

"What did you say?"

"I love you, Tristan. I love you as much as the day you promised to run away with me. I never stopped. Forgive me." I stared ahead at the collar of his tunic. It was gray and dusty.

Cupping my cheek, he guided me to look at his face again. "If you want forgiveness, I grant it to you. If you want my love, my life, anything—I will do anything to give it to you."

I reached up and touched the hand he rested on my cheek. "I… I can hardly believe you…" I grimaced as I tried not to weep.

He pulled me into his arms and held me. "I thought I was loving you by letting you go all those seven years ago. I regret it. I regretted it every moment since parting with you on that day."

"Tristan…" I wished I could stop crying. Again, I pulled myself from his arms. But once I did, I immediately stumbled back to him again.

And my gasp never escaped me as he pressed his lips to mine.

Without a thought, I returned his kiss. It was as though I had never married Henry, and Tristan had never left me. For that moment, time rewound and we were seven years younger.

Too soon, he broke away. Steadying me with his hands on my upper arms, I could see he was contemplating something. I waited impatiently for him to speak, or else, dare I hope he would kiss me again?

Finally he said, "I beg you forgive me. I shouldn't have done that."

"I forgive you," I said quickly. My mind was blank. I worried that I might pass out until I remembered again to breathe. I ran my hand down his chest — yes, he was truly standing before me.

"Fie, it still feels the same to kiss you."

"Let me visit your farm," I said without thinking. "I want to see it."

"It's a humble place, not fit for a queen."

"One day," I said quickly, "after my children begin their own lives away from me, we shall hide away together. Perhaps in Scotland? I will work as a midwife and you may work the land. We shall be together until the end of our days."

"That sounds like Heaven." As I caressed his bearded cheek, he wiped the tears from my face again.

I whispered, "If you love me, you will do this with me one day."

"I will go anywhere with you, as long as you are safe."

"Safe from what? From Henry?" I bit my lip as I wondered how to voice my thoughts. I said finally, "I have not lain with him in years and I never will again. As I cannot have children any longer, he and I have agreed to a relationship of the formal offices of king and queen only."

Tristan clenched his teeth as he took my hands in his. "I beg your forgiveness, but I cannot pretend to be unhappy to hear this."

"I am happy for it too, honestly," I said, glancing away toward the cathedral.

He pulled me into his arms again and hugged me. "When might you visit my tenancy? Tomorrow?"

"I am allowed?" I laughed. "I can't come tomorrow. I'm acting Regent for now."

"He's out of the country?" Tristan leaned away a bit and so I lifted my chin. Like he always used to, he pecked a kiss to my lips when I did this.

I smiled at his smile. "Yes. Truly, I don't think Henry would care if I had you near me now, as long as we are secretive. After all, I have befriended Lady Sybilla Corbet of Alcester — now that he has discarded her. In fact, I arranged the marriage of my favorite brother, King Alexander of Scotland, to their most beautiful, virtuous daughter, who is also named Sybilla. The two were married only a few months ago."

Tristan scrunched his face and shook his head. "That is strange, to say the least."

I laughed easily and shook my head in turn. "Visit me at the castle. Come at dusk."

"At dusk? Shall I sleep there?" He smiled and touched his nose to mine.

I smacked his chest. "Tristan —"

"You blush the same as you did when you were a girl." And threading his hands into my hair, he kissed me again.

As the bishop of Winchester chattered on about the cost of rebuilding, I did not listen. Nearby the debris over my daughter's grave, a mourning dove perched on a wind-swept yew and sang. But when it met my eye, it hastily took flight.

CHAPTER 30: EPILOGUE: MAY DAY, 1118

In the middle of the night on Easter Sunday of 1118, a woman came to one of my hospitals for the poor. The strangest thing about her was not her rare, incurable illness. Rather, as long as she had her eyes closed, she looked like my twin.

Two weeks and two days later, by the change in her breathing, I knew the woman was going to die in the matter of hours. My son, William Adelin, helped me secret her to my queen's chamber at Westminster.

It was time for me to leave. I had lived this life as queen for long enough, and Tristan wanted to fulfill his promise to me.

"The people will be sad without their May Day celebrations in the morning," I lamented. I wore a plain blue linen dress and good leather boots. My hair was plaited as though I were much younger.

Adelin and I stood at the side of the queen's bed as we gazed down at the strange, dying woman there. Though he didn't know her, my son bent down and held her hand. We watched as she slowly rasped another breath.

"They'll be sadder to believe you are dead, my good queen mother," he whispered, holding her hand tightly in his. "You have made England a better place forever through your good works."

"I pray you're right."

"I am. And you have endured father for long enough. He will still have me here to help him and to take over for him someday."

"Yes." I nodded. "You've written—"

"To Maude. Yes. She says she understands and she loves you dearly and she promises she burned my letter."

"Oh, my dear boy." I shook my head. "I hate to leave you." He was beautiful, like King William had been, but with Henry's smile and my eyes. "My dearest son."

"I'm your *only* son." We both smiled as he hugged me. I breathed in his scent from his tunic because I could no longer reach his hair. "Oh, I can't leave you here alone with him." Pulling him down to me, I kissed his cheek.

"You can, and you shall. Mother, your children are grown. I will be married in a few short years."

I smiled. "You shall make a better king than even your father."

"Thank you, Queen Mother," Adelin whispered as he hugged me.

"Yes. Send word to me if ever you are in need of my counsel. Or, come by Henry's fastest ship and visit me. I shall welcome you with open arms to my humble farm."

"I will. I promise."

I nodded as I took one more long look at my son's face. "I love you."

"I love you. Farewell, Queen Mother. I commend you to God."

"Thank you, my beloved Adelin. I commend you to God." With one last kiss to his cheek, I let go of my son.

Hurrying down to the stables, I found Tristan waiting with a readied horse. Snuggling in the saddle as though we were young again, we started the long journey north together.

In my heart, I said goodbye to Henry as I left him behind.

As the May Day bells rang in London, Adelin informed Henry that I had died in the night. I had been "sick" for some time, after all. The bells were ceased at once and all of England mourned Good Queen Matilda.

As we rode, I held Tristan close to my chest, and I mourned her too.

We ate and drank in the occasional pub. At night, we stopped to sleep under the stars. Once in Scotland, we bought a small farm not far from Dunfermline.

And Tristan and I lived together for the rest of our days. We cherished each other, and we were happy.

The End.

AUTHOR'S NOTE

The English language in which this is written has had about a thousand years of evolution from the English language that Edith/Matilda would have thought or spoke in. I have chosen to use contractions and other informal types of speech throughout this novel instead of sticking to the stereotypical Shakespearean sort of language you might expect (anyway, Shakespeare was about half a millennia after this story takes place).

That said, I have made every attempt to keep to the linguistic intentions they would have used. For example, Edith/Matilda is never called 'princess' because, in this time period, feudal titles were earned (or were bestowed upon the wives of those who held titles) and not inherited. They didn't quite yet have the concept of a title through the sake of birth alone. Because she was unmarried, Edith/Matilda is also not called 'lady' or 'milady' or any of those other titles we would expect today. However, she was still recognized as part of the nobility through the sake of her birth. Without getting too much into etymology, it seems she would have been called some form of 'mademoiselle' until she married someone with a title.

So why is Henry not called 'your grace' when he is a duke and 'your majesty' or 'his royal highness' when king? In short, they didn't do that yet. Also, it seems that Henry's famous nickname, 'Beauclerc', was only bestowed upon him posthumously (in about the 14th century)—a small fact I was unhappy to discover, because I do love this nickname, and I think he would have liked it too.

Those of you who know the history of these once-living characters will recognize a few direct quotes from when they were alive. For example, King William's real-life quote about Westminster Hall: "The hall is not big enough by half, and is but a bedchamber in comparison to that which I mean to make."

Also, many of the major events of this story are true to life. I don't know what color Edith/Matilda's eyes were — maybe they really were forget-me-not blue? However, King's William's eyes truly were supposed to have been two different colors.

Also, while Wilton Abbey was known for its excellent education, I know of no monk-hospitallers who had a workroom there, nor of any who might have trained Edith in medicine during her time there. However, she did like to get her hands dirty when it came to the sick and poor, and she even built a few hospitals. So, making her a hospitaller-in-training was really no stretch.

Sir Robert Achard probably didn't lose his foot. I found no record of it, in any case. He really was Henry's instructor on battle sorts of things though, and Henry really did say that thing about an ass wearing a crown.

Edith/Matilda was truly very short. She did wear clothes that were considered old and out of fashion. She was expected to be a nun, at least by her Aunt Christina. King Malcolm did throw a fit at Wilton and tear a veil from her head. And she did say that she stomped on a monastic veil and had worn it. "That hood I did indeed wear ... was I veiled," is another direct quote.

The "Two True, One False" game was a blatant tactic to wedge a bit more history into the story. Henry's were factual (except for, possibly, his thoughts of serving God and country); Matilda's were fictional.

We don't actually know where Edith/Matilda was for those seven years after she ran away from Wilton Abbey.

Also, it's not impossible that she was already a few weeks along with her first pregnancy when she married Henry, though I doubt Euphemia was another man's child.

The blood bubbling up in the abbey garden, while perhaps the most fantastical aspect of the book, also supposedly happened.

The elephant in the novel is perhaps the eleven year age disparity between Henry and Edith/Matilda. To contemporary readers, a fourteen-year-old (who, born June of 1079, had been thirteen only two months prior to August, 1093) and a twenty-four-year-old (who, born September of 1068, would be twenty-five in a month) falling in love is mildly outrageous at best. I can only say that once you "became a woman" back then, you were seen as such. After all, in that time, you were lucky to live to sixty, if you were first lucky enough to live through infancy. Henry is remembered as having "always been taken" with Edith/Matilda. From this popular quote of his, it is highly likely they had a long-running affection for one another.

I hope you may now remember something else about King Henry I other than the fact that he died from a "surfeit of lampreys." (A detail I didn't include because, well, who cares about *that* when he was so complex and misunderstood?)

In any case, this is foremost a love story and not an educational text. I hope you were able to enjoy this story for the work of fiction that it is. I beg your forgiveness for my liberties.

Thank you for reading.